Myths, Gods & Immortals
Anansi
New & Ancient African Tales

This is a FLAME TREE Book

Publisher & Creative Director: Nick Wells
Editorial Director: Catherine Taylor
Editorial Board: Gillian Whitaker, Catherine Taylor, Jocelyn Pontes, Simran Aulakh, Jemma North and
Beatrix Ambery

FLAME TREE PUBLISHING
6 Melbray Mews, Fulham,
London SW6 3NS, United Kingdom
www.flametreepublishing.com

First published 2025

Copyright in each story is held by the individual authors
Introduction and Volume copyright © 2025 Flame Tree Publishing Ltd

The narrative sections in the introductory essay ('Ancient & Modern: Introducing Anansi') are retold
by the author in her own words. The extract from Martin Owusu's *The Story Ananse Told* (1971) on
page 11 is printed with permission from the author. The extract from Andrew Salkey's 'Anancy' (from
Time for Poetry, 1988, edited by Nahdjla Carasco Bailey) on page 37 is printed with permission ©
The Andrew Salkey Estate. The Akan ditty on page 73, quoted by J.B. Danquah in *The Akan Doctrine
of God* (1968), is used with permission of Taylor & Frances Informa UK Ltd - Books, permission
conveyed through Copyright Clearance Center, Inc.

25 27 29 30 28 26
1 3 5 7 9 10 8 6 4 2

ISBN: 978-1-80417-934-5

All rights reserved. No part of this publication may be reproduced, stored in a retrieval system,
or transmitted in any form or by any means, electronic, mechanical, photocopying, recording or
otherwise, without the prior written permission of the publisher.

Publisher's Note: The stories within this book are works of fiction. Names, characters, places, and
incidents are a product of the authors' imaginations. Locales and public names are sometimes
used for atmospheric purposes. Any resemblance to actual people, living or dead, or to businesses,
companies, events, institutions, or locales is completely coincidental.

Content Note: The stories in this book may contain descriptions of, or references to, difficult subjects
such as violence, death and rape, but always contextualized within the setting of mythic narrative,
archetype and metaphor. Similarly, language can sometimes be strong but is at the artistic discretion
of the authors.

Cover art by Flame Tree Studio based on elements from Shutterstock.com: Bay Media, Sanit
Fuangnakhon, tajimpranto, Tiny Art, Vibrands Studio, WinWin artlab

A copy of the CIP data for this book is available from the British Library.

Printed and bound in China

Contents

FOREWORD

Professor Emily Zobel Marshall 6

ANCIENT & MODERN: INTRODUCING ANANSI

by Ivana Akotowaa Ofori 10

1. Foundations and Origins 11

2. Character and Conventions 37

3. Representations and Interpretations 73

4. Reincarnations and Complications 106

MODERN SHORT STORIES OF ANANSI

How the Orb-weaver Learned to Carry Stories

Ian Ableson 147

The Secrets of JamestownLighthouse

Benjamin Cyril Arthur 160

Ananse City Dawn

Bernice Arthur 177

Ananse and the Infernal Tale

Emmanuel Blavo 189

Kwaku's Squad: Daughter of Leopard

Bryoni Campbell 204

CONTENTS

Anansi and the Hot-Lanta Flow

Sara Chisolm..218

The Rainmaker

Yazeed Dele-Azeez...232

Anansi and the Christmas Dinner

A.L. Dawn French..247

A Night in New Orleans

Yeayi Kobina...256

Anansi and Păcală

Alina Mereşescu 269

Descendance

Ella N'Diaye..284

Pepe Gets Married

Florence Onyango 297

Six to the Rescue

Frances Pauli...308

Anansi's Journey Around the World

Shruti Ramesh 319

Taxi Brousse

Peter K. Rothe 332

Sacrifice

Chisom Umeh 348

BIOGRAPHIES..**362**

MYTHS, GODS & IMMORTALS...................................**367**

FLAME TREE FICTION...**368**

❈ 5 ❈

Foreword
Emily Zobel Marshall

he spider, with its ability to capture pray larger than itself, its strong web of gossamer threads made from its own substance, its unending patience and its clever disguises, is a creature which has fascinated and enthralled cultures throughout history. Spiders and their webs have played a key role in global folklore and myth.

Anansi, the anarchic trickster spider of West African origin, has woven an intricate web of tales across the African Diaspora. Continually adapted to the needs of the society that tells his tales, Anansi has become symbolic of the traumas of enslavement and the resilience of the enslaved, the cultural fusions of the postcolonial Caribbean and the migrations of its people.

From the seventeenth century to the early twentieth century, Anansi was tightly bound to the political, religious and social life of the Asante people of Ghana. Anansi did not hold a divine or god-like status amongst the Asante, but his role was that of the mediator: in disputes between men and women and, on a wider scale, between humankind and Nyame, the Asante supreme deity.

Among the Asante, Anansi was a folk hero who often tested the boundaries of acceptable behaviour. He was a crossroads figure, existing between two worlds in his role as mediator or messenger between humankind and Nyame. However, in Asante Anansi stories, at every opportunity Anansi wreaked havoc in the human world and undermined the omnipotent Nyame. Anansi's actions were often anti-social and destructive and he could invert all biological and social rules: he could disconnect his own body parts, change his sex, abuse his guests and even eat his own children.

Anansi was a breaker of the rules and Anansi tales were used by the Asante to air problems and frustrations. A great king or corrupt headman could be criticized through the medium of an Anansi story, and criticism of these powerful figures would be unacceptable under any other circumstance. Anansi was a part of a culture in a continual state of flux where binary oppositions were tested to strengthen the social structure. Just as there exists both a male and female god in traditional Asante religion, each with a share of divine power, Pelton tells us that 'all Asante beliefs and institutions embody doubleness so that everyday life reveals an ultimate order'.

Anansi stories were vehicles through which the Asante could explain, scrutinize and question the world around them. They were also celebrations of the intricacies and beauty of language and the Asante delight in Anansi's use of tricky wordplay and double-entendres to get the better of his adversaries.

ANANSI IN JAMAICA

From the sixteenth century onward, Anansi tales travelled with enslaved Asante men, women and children across the Atlantic Ocean and into the Caribbean. In Jamaica, Anansi came down to earth; in his physical form he adopted human characteristics as he became more man and less spider and pitted his wits against Tiger rather than the Asante god Nyame. It is in the plantation context of captivity and conflict that Anansi took on renewed roles and functions. Instead of functioning as a tester of the chains, Anansi helped to break them. He shifted from being assimilated into the sacred world of the Asante to become representative of the Jamaican slaves' human condition.

The tales moved from the world of make-believe to inspiring everyday strategies of resistance and survival on the Jamaican plantations. In my book *Anansi's Journey: A Story of Jamaican Cultural Resistance* (2012), I show how Anansi not only reflected and inspired models of behaviour for physical resistance, but played a multi-functional role in slaves' lives, establishing a sense of continuity with an African past and offering them the means to transform and assert their identity within the boundaries of captivity.

Today Anansi can be found in story books across the globe. Some of these stories have been sanitized and Anansi has lost much of his anarchic trickster energy. Anansi's anarchic liminality lies in his existence in betwixt and between places and spaces. Thanks to his web he is nether fixed to the earth or sky, but is free to walk on the ground, burrow into the soil or float through the air, if he so chooses; he can live in and between all realms, wild and domestic. Anansi's web in the Jamaican Anansi tales is his getaway vehicle, and so familiar are Jamaicans with Anansi that the term 'Anancy rope' denotes spiderwebs of all types. There are multitudinous significances in Anansi's web, which not only offers him camouflage and a safe hiding place but it is also a lethal weapon and trap, ensnaring those who dare to cross it.

FOREWORD

High up in the rafters or trees, Anansi has a clear view of the world from his web – a sense of perspective and a far-reaching gaze. He can observe, unobserved, what is going on below him. Like the 'house slaves' and servants of the Great Houses, he can listen and compile information that can be used against his adversaries.

The English language is full of metaphors, similes and allegories which use the image of the spider and the web. Spinning and weaving a web signify a creative and life-giving process linked to storytelling, construction, fabrication, complicating and tangling, eluding and escaping. Anansi weaves his way through binaries and spins fresh formations in new environments. The web represents not only creation but an intricate interconnection of networks and cross-roads which can entangle and ensnare or bridge gaps, creating new pathways linking separate spaces and peoples.

Each spider's web is different – the design can never be replicated. Like every element of the cultures of the African Diaspora, each new web Anansi builds must be modified to fit new spaces and environments. This process of continual adaptation, so central to survival, enabled enslaved people to maintain a culture which, through its ability to embrace ambiguity and adaptation, both survived and resisted the confines of brutal enslavement. As we see from the contemporary stories in this collection, Anansi continues to adapt to inspire new creative practices and modern mythologies – he is present in our contemporary moment. Perhaps as you read this an Anansi, a liminal creature of the wild, is watching you from the corner of the room, just biding his time.

Professor Emily Zobel Marshall

Ancient & Modern: Introducing Anansi

by Ivana Akotowaa Ofori

1.

Foundations and Origins

All stories – myths and legends – belong to me:
Those about the Elephant, the hunter and the bee.
Yes I bought Anansesem with my wisdom
From Nana Nyankopon now in his kingdom.
– Martin Owusu, from *The Story Ananse Told* (1971)

A MULTI-FACETED CHARACTER

frica, the Caribbean, the United States and South America. There are some things about this character that most of these communities agree upon: that he is a trickster, that his roots are West African and that he has a connection to spiders. Yet there is rarely consensus on how to spell his name. Ananse, Anansi and Annancy are only a few of the many documented variations, which will soon be explored. Throughout this text, the spelling 'Ananse' will be used primarily when referring to him specifically in the Akan, Ghanaian or West African contexts, and 'Anansi' in nearly every other context. A section or paragraph may therefore switch back and forth between the two.

This exploration of Anansi emphasizes representations of Anansi from Ghana and Jamaica. While these are far from the only countries in which Anansi plays a significant cultural role, they are the ones most often associated with him in the English-speaking world, due to particularly high concentrations of Akan people and/or particularly strong Akan cultural influences. The reader will nevertheless encounter many mentions of Anansi from other countries and cultures.

Peppered throughout the expository texts are a few Anansi stories which have appeared in various documents between the nineteenth and twentieth centuries from the Gold Coast and the Caribbean. Most of these stories are recorded by several authors in different contexts, with subtle differences in their versions. The tales included in this text are all rewritten, generally as composites of tales in collections compiled by R.S. Rattray, Martha Beckwith, Harold Courlander, Pamela Colman-Smith, Mary Milne-Home and W.H. Barker.

While the information in this text is drawn from multiple sources, significant portions, particularly those concerning Anansi's legacy in Jamaica, are sourced from and recorded in Professor Emily Zobel Marshall's 2012 book, *Anansi's Journey: A Story of Jamaican Cultural Resistance* (hereafter referred to as *Anansi's Journey*).

While far from exhaustive, these sections expose many sides of Anansi. Some are possibly surprising and many are contradictory. Even more suggest that there are aspects of this character that are likely impossible to kill, regardless of who tries – the forces of slavery, colonialism, modernization or Death himself.

ANANSI'S NAME

One major reason why there is so little consensus on how Anansi's name is spelled is the fact that the stories about him all began as oral traditions. Translations of these stories into written form left the spelling of Anansi's name at the mercy of several European writers' attempts to use Latin alphabet systems for the African, Akan word 'ananse' and the popularity of their chosen spellings in the decades and centuries after the first Anansi stories were published.

Spelling Ananse in West Africa

In Ghana, the character in question is generally known as Kwaku Ananse. In the Twi language, the word 'ananse' literally means 'spider'. It is typically a common noun and not a given name. Twi is indigenous to the Akan people of West Africa who have a concentrated population in Ghana, although there are major clusters in Côte d'Ivoire and Togo as well. Twi has several dialects, including Asante Twi, which is spoken by the Asante people – the largest sub-division of Akan people in Ghana. Nor is Twi the only Akan language. Another is Fante, spoken by the Fante people – a sub-division of the Akan found generally along some parts of Ghana's coast. While Kwaku Ananse is understood to have originated specifically with the Asante people, other Akan groups within Ghana seem to know him just as intimately.

In Akan culture, the name Kwaku is traditionally given to male children born on a Wednesday. 'Kwaku' would be the typical Asante Twi spelling, with 'Kweku' more popular in Fante and a French-influenced spelling, 'Kacou', favoured in Côte d'Ivoire. An understated yet fundamental characteristic of Kwaku Ananse in West Africa, therefore, is the fact that he was born on a Wednesday.

The regions in which Ananse stories were collected in West Africa had a strong influence on how authors chose to spell his name. The 1930 collection *Akan-Ashanti Folktales*, compiled by the British anthropologist R.S. Rattray, refers to the character as 'Kwaku Ananse' because his stories were collected primarily in Asante territory in the Gold Coast, now Ghana. However, American missionary W.H. Barker's *West African Folk-Tales*, also collected in the Gold Coast and published in 1917, calls the same character 'Kweku Anansi', and describes him as hailing from 'Fanti-land', as the informants were sourced in the coastal region of Accra. Ivorian author Bernard Dadié's collection, published in 1955, calls the same character 'Kacou Ananzè'.

Spelling Anansi in the Diaspora

Ananse, along with the oral storytelling traditions that carried him, travelled with enslaved Akan-speaking people during the transatlantic slave trade, so that he is now known by many variations of the same name. In some cases, he found his way back to Africa. For example, he now features in folktales from West African countries such as Sierra Leone and Liberia, which do not have high concentrations of indigenous Akan people. Nevertheless, these are countries where several descendants of enslaved people who may have had Akan roots were repatriated or deported between the eighteenth and nineteenth centuries.

Some of these formerly enslaved people were from Jamaica, heavily influenced by Akan presence.

More popular spellings in Jamaica and other parts of the Caribbean are 'Anansi' and 'Anancy'. In *Anansi's Journey*, Zobel Marshall references the 2002 *Dictionary of Jamaican English* by Cassidy and Le Page, which identifies several variations in diverse texts, including Ananzi, Anansay, Annancey, Nancy, Annancy, Nance, Anawnsy and Anancy.

For the most part, his Akan first name, 'Kwaku' has been dropped outside of southern West Africa and replaced with prefixes such as 'Brother', 'Brer', 'Bra', 'Ba', 'Compère', 'Compè' and 'Kompa' – and these are only the masculine prefixes. Feminine variations of the character's name include 'Aunt Nancy', 'Ann Nancy', 'Sis' Nancy', 'Miss Nancy' and 'Little Miss Nancy'. Anansi, as we will explore later, is quite the shapeshifter, the shift in gender being just one aspect of his vast capacity for transformation.

Pronouncing Anansi

Along with the spelling changes – and all the factors that hindered the retention of indigenous African languages in the 'New World' – came pronunciation changes. Ghanaians will typically pronounce 'Ananse' with the lowest tone in the middle syllable ('nan'), and the 'e' at the end sounds closer to the vowel sound in the English word 'sin' when pronounced in a standard British accent. However, in the Caribbean and elsewhere the middle syllable is given the highest tone, and the final syllable is pronounced just like the English word 'see'.

NON-AKAN ORIGINS IN THE MIX?

Kwaku Ananse may be an Akan character, but the Akan people by no means have a monopoly on the spider as a prominent figure within African folklore. As Zobel Marshall notes in *Anansi's Journey*, there is the character Turé, who features in the lore of the Zande people in North and central Africa. Other ethnic groups whose folktales include spiders are the Hausa people of West Africa and the Kaka people of Cameroon.

The names of these other spiders may not be as popular as Ananse's. Yet folklore is so fluid that the possibility that the Akan Ananse may have interacted with other African spiders must not be swiftly discounted. British anthropologist R.S. Rattray even called into question whether many Ananse stories really were indigenous to the Akan people. In the Preface to his *Akan-Ashanti Folk-Tales* collection, he remarked upon how similar some of the stories were to the folklore not only of other African ethnic groups, but also to some folktales outside of Africa. Robert D. Pelton, author of the 1989 nonfiction book *The Trickster in West Africa*, noticed 'striking similarities' between a certain Asante folktale and a myth from the Ofayé people, who are indigenous to Brazil. Rattray's hypothesis was that the similar stories found within lands far apart from one another have common origins; they may therefore have travelled within or across continents through forms of slavery which pre-dated the Europeans' chattel model.

A prime example of an Ananse story, which may either have influenced or been influenced by a non-Akan culture, is the story about a magic bowl and whip. About 20 years before Rattray compiled his *Akan-Ashanti* collection, he had published a collection called *Hausa Folk-Lore* in 1913. The Hausa people comprise another powerful ethnic group indigenous to West Africa, the largest concentration of which resides in present-day Nigeria. *Hausa Folk-Lore* contains a story about a man who had two wives. One of his wives finds a spoon in the bush during a famine, which produces food when activated by a specific dialogue exchange. The spoon is later taken out of this family's possession. The wife who first discovered it eventually finds a whip in the bush; this delivers a merciless flogging whenever it is activated by a nearly identical dialogue exchange. By the end of the story, the spoon and the whip have been introduced to society for the first time, where they have remained since. *Akan-Ashanti Folk-Tales* includes a popular Kwaku Ananse story quite similar to the following, although specific details vary according to culture and author.

'Ananse and the Beautiful Dish'

A huge famine came upon the land in which Kwaku Ananse lived with his wife, Asɔ, and their four sons, Ntikuma, Tikelenkele, Afudohwedohwe and Nankonwheaa. Each day Ananse would go out to the bush to forage for wild yams, which he brought back for Asɔ to cook and feed the family.

One day, while Ananse was out in the bush, he came across an earthenware pot lying upon the ground. He exclaimed, "This dish is beautiful!"

The dish responded, "My name is not beautiful."

"What is your name?" asked Ananse.

"I am called Fill-up-some-and-eat."

"Then fill up some for me to see," Ananse dared to order. The dish filled up with the most delicious palm nut soup and Ananse ate it all.

Satisfied, he asked the dish, "What is your taboo?" For every magical object had at least one – something with which it was forbidden to come into contact, lest its magic be neutralized. The dish told him that its taboos were a gun wad and a little gourd cup. Ananse noted this and then took the dish home. He hid it up on the ceiling and went back to the bush to forage for wild yams for the rest of his family.

Later, Asɔ finished cooking the yams which Ananse had brought. She invited all her family to come and eat.

With all the airs of a benevolent patriarch, Kwaku Ananse declared that he would not dare to partake in the meal. Let the woman and children eat; what need had he, an old man, for food? If his wife and children were satisfied, that was all Ananse needed to be happy in this world. He watched them all eat without him.

Afterwards, he went up to the ceiling and said, "This dish is beautiful!" The dish responded that its name was not "beautiful". The exchange ensued just as it had earlier in the bush, culminating in a magical meal which Ananse promptly consumed.

Day after day, Ananse excluded himself from his family's dinners while he gorged himself on the magic dish's soup in privacy.

After a while, Ananse's firstborn son, Ntikuma, grew suspicious. He did not understand how his father, who never ate, never seemed to get any thinner.

Ntikuma got his opportunity to investigate one day while Ananse was away foraging. Ananse's son went up to the ceiling and discovered the dish. "This dish is beautiful!" he couldn't help but remark.

The dish replied, "My name is not beautiful."

Just as Ananse had done, Ntikuma discovered the process that made the dish fill up with soup. He quickly called his mother and brothers to come and share in the food.

After they had all eaten, Ntikuma asked the dish to disclose its taboo and the dish obliged. Ntikuma then sent his brother, Afudohwedohwe, to procure the forbidden items – the gun wad and the little gourd cup – which Ntikuma touched briefly against the dish, before setting all the objects aside.

Done with the day's foraging, Kwaku Ananse returned home. As usual, he declined Asɔ's invitation to eat with the family. But when he went up to the ceiling and called the dish beautiful, there was no response. At first he thought that his inelegant clothes were the problem. He changed into a much finer tartan cloth, but still the dish would not respond. Finally, looking around his room, up on the ceiling, he discovered the taboo objects and knew at once that Ntikuma was behind whatever had happened. Angrily, he smashed the dish, changed into his regular attire and returned to the bush.

While he was out, Ananse discovered yet another magnificent object: a long, slender branch. "This whip is beautiful!" he gasped.

The whip declared, "My name is not beautiful."

"What, then, is your name?"

"Abridiabrada," said the whip. *Swish-and-raise-weals*.

Ananse requested, "Swish a little for me to see."

Thereupon the whip flogged Ananse mercilessly. It would not stop, no matter what Ananse did. After a while, a benevolent bird nearby took pity on Ananse and told him, "You must say to the whip, 'Adwoberεε' – *cool down*."

The moment Ananse said, "Adwoberεε", the whip went completely still.

Ananse had gotten an idea.

He brought the whip home and put it in the same place where he had previously put the dish. At dinnertime, when Asɔ finished cooking and invited Ananse to eat, his refusal was heated. "How many times do I have to tell you before you understand? The food I bring home is for you and the children!" He then pretended to go away, just as he had been doing when he still had the dish. After enough time had passed, he hid himself away so that the others would think he had left the house.

Ntikuma, excited, concluded that his father must have found some other wonderful object. He called all his family to go with him to the ceiling, where he pronounced, "This whip is beautiful!"

"My name is not beautiful," replied the whip.

Ntikuma asked its name and the whip replied, "Abridiabrada."

"Swish a little for us to see," said Ntikuma eagerly.

At once, the whip began to flog Ntikuma, his brothers and his mother.

At this point, Ananse emerged from his hiding place and laughed at them all, encouraging the whip to continue and to flog Ntikuma especially hard. When Ananse himself was satisfied, he said the secret word, "Adwoberεε", and the whip went still.

Ananse then cut the whip into tiny pieces and scattered them everywhere. He is the one who introduced the whip to society. This is also the reason why parents now whip their disobedient children.

The Implications of Ananse Stories' Murky Origins

It is not clear whether the Hausa tale about the spoon and the whip influenced the Akan one or vice versa – or if they may have somehow developed independently of one another. However, the similarities do lend credence to the idea that some Kwaku Ananse stories may not be wholly indigenous to the Akan. One might ask whether this makes the task of exploring Ananse's supposedly Akan roots a waste of time. The answer Rattray would give is: certainly not – because whenever folklore is transmitted it is adapted, either on a small scale or a large one. During his story collection process, Rattray listened many times to the same stories, in Akan villages far apart from one another and from the mouths of local storytellers from different sub-ethnic groups. The 'same' story was never once the same.

Different cultures or environments affect the adaptations as well. For instance, the Hausa tale about the spoon and whip reflects a different setting than the Akan one, which contained dishes such as palm nut soup and groundnut soup — staples of Akan cuisine. Ananse's motivations and pretexts are different from those of the characters in the Hausa tale.

Any folktale that features Kwaku Ananse speaks volumes about what kind of person the Akan consider Kwaku Ananse to be and what he would and wouldn't do, regardless of the plot's origins.

Understanding Kwaku Ananse as an Akan character is therefore a window into the Akan psyche; it allows us to trace continuities and divergences through his incarnations across the world.

ANANSE ACROSS THE ATLANTIC

The motif of Kwaku Ananse chopping things up and scattering them about, thereby introducing them to the rest of the world, is a staple of Akan folklore. However, the unfortunate reality of how people of African heritage were forcibly dispersed throughout the world in such large numbers will always be incomparably darker than a folktale. We cannot speak of Ananse's migration without speaking of the transatlantic slave trade.

Ananse's Most Popular Destinations

Today, outside of Ghana, the name Anansi is most likely to be associated with Jamaica. The strong, lasting influence of Akan culture – and, by extension, Anansi stories – on the Caribbean island is often attributed to Akan dominance during the slavery and plantation eras.

Some of the Africans forcibly transported to the island refused to remain enslaved and formed their own independent settlements: the Maroons. Maroon existence pre-dated the British takeover of Jamaica, but a good portion of Maroon leadership during British occupation was said to consist of people of Akan heritage, or people who had at least left Africa from the Gold Coast, now known as Ghana. Various collectors of Anansi stories comment on the fact that Maroons tend to remember more

Anansi stories than Jamaicans from other parts of the island, and that the stories told by Maroons are often closer to their African versions – likely due to the Maroons' relative separation from colonial influence.

In *Anansi's Journey*, Zobel Marshall notes how some contemporary researchers, for example Silvia Kouwenberg, believe that Akan influence in Jamaican culture has been overemphasized. However, Zobel Marshall argues that data shows that the largest single group of enslaved people brought to Jamaica between 1665 and 1700 – which Kouwenberg cites as Jamaica's formative period – came from the Akan and Ga-Adangbe groups of the Gold Coast. Many of these individuals had first been taken to eastern Caribbean islands such as Barbados; they were then transferred to Jamaica once the British acquired the island from the Spanish.

Zobel Marshall also references Orlando Patterson, who posits in his 1973 book, *The Sociology of Slavery*, that the enslaved people of the Gold Coast were in a good position to impose their customs and language onto the nascent Jamaican creole society. He argued this was in part because these people were already more accustomed to their new Caribbean environments, and also because they came from ethnic groups with social and political dominance in West Africa. Their cultural influence – and, by extension, the influence of Ananse – may therefore have transcended their relatively lower numbers in the overall statistics of Jamaicans' ethnic origins.

Stephanie Smallwood, in *Saltwater Slavery* (2007) explains that before Jamaica became the top destination of slave ships from the Gold Coast, that destination was Barbados. At some point in the seventeenth century, Barbados claimed one out of every two ships from the Gold Coast. Unsurprisingly, Anansi remains a dominant folktale character there, too. Later, between 1721 and 1725, when it had become typical for one third of the ships departing from the Gold Coast to land in Jamaica, the next most popular destinations were Suriname and Berbice in South America. These were followed by Barbados and other parts of the Dutch Caribbean, for example Curaçao. In many of these places, Anansi survived throughout the subsequent demographic shifts.

Ananse's Least Popular Destinations

Whichever destinations had large groups of enslaved people from the Gold Coast became the most likely to retain versions of Ananse's Twi name and some of his oldest Akan stories. But where people from the Gold Coast were too greatly overwhelmed by Africans from other regions, Ananse, though marginally present, struggled to make his way into the spotlight. One of these places is the United States.

In the USA, Anansi – in the form of Aunt Nancy – is best known in coastal southern states such as North Carolina, Georgia and Virginia, in close proximity to the ports where slave ships were most likely to dock. However, as Smallwood explains, during the seventeenth century most new African arrivals to Virginia and low country Carolina came from the Senegambia and Bight of Biafra regions, not the Gold Coast. Ships from the Gold Coast often reached destinations like Virginia only after the British and Dutch Caribbean colonial powers had already made their selections from the human cargo.

Besides demographic composition, historian Lawrence Levine considered in his 1977 book *Black Culture and Black Consciousness* that another reason for Anansi's obscurity in the US might have been the ecology. He argued that spiders may just have been less relevant and ubiquitous in the new US environment than they were in West Africa.

In the USA very few Anansi stories were recorded before the twentieth century, but there were some. In an 1898 volume of the *Journal of American Folklore*, a folktale from North Carolina features a main character called Ann Nancy. Ann Nancy's victim in this story is Buzzard, whose secret store of food Ann Nancy discovers. Buzzard, in turn, discovers Ann Nancy in the act of thieving, but she sweet-talks her way into being released. However, the ungrateful character repays this benevolence with evil, eventually causing Buzzard to go bald by scalding him with hot water.

In the US Anansi became more popular in the twentieth century, no doubt linked to an influx of West Indians into the country. According to Nancy Foner in the introduction to *Islands in the City* (2001), this began around 1900 and peaked in the 1920s. A majority of these immigrants settled in New York. Non-coincidentally, a number of folktales collected by Arthur Fauset and published in 1928 include the character Nancy (with male pronouns this time); the informants of each Nancy tale had been born in Jamaica. These tales were collected in Philadelphia, a state that shares a border with New York.

Diasporan (Dis)continuities

There are clear continuities in the story about Ann Nancy and Buzzard. A popular Akan tale ends with Kwaku Ananse going bald after an attempt to hide scalding-hot beans in his hat, and several Jamaican folktale characters meet their end by having boiling water poured over them.

The most glaring *dis*continuity might be Anansi's gender. Perhaps in the social setting of the US the phonetic similarities between Anansi's name and popular female names of European origin were too difficult to overlook. In the Caribbean, Anansi's name has been only selectively feminized – for example in the use of riddles, which might begin with the placeholder phrase of 'Little Miss Nancy'.

Furthermore, in the New World, as Levine's book details, many of Anansi's adventures survived, while his character and form did not. For example, of the animal tricksters who survived in the US, it was the rabbit, not the spider, who gained the most fame. This is partially due to Joel Chandler Harris's *Uncle Remus* story collections, the star of which is Brer Rabbit. The trickster rabbit is more central in East African, Angolan and some Nigerian folklore, while a hare known as Leuk is well known in Senegalese folklore. The large influx of enslaved West Africans from Senegambia and the Bight of Benin to the USA could very well have been responsible for the Rabbit's eclipse of Anansi there.

Something similar may have happened in Haiti. Some adventures which in other countries are attributed to Anansi are in Haiti experienced by two characters: Uncle Bouki and Ti

Malice. Bouki means 'hyena' in the Wolof and Fulani languages spoken in the Senegambia region. Ti Malice may be related to Leuk, the Senegalese hare.

The most popular tale which cuts across Anansi's canon, and those of the characters linked to him, might just be the Tar Baby story. Versions of the Akan iteration of this tale appear in Rattray's *Akan-Ashanti Folktales*, Barker's *West African Folk-Tales* and Courlander's *The Hat-Shaking Dance*. They generally go as follows.

'Why Spiders Are Found in Dark Corners'

A time of famine once came upon the land where Kwaku Ananse and his family lived, but they were well off. This was because Ananse was a skilled farmer and had reaped a large harvest, against all odds. Even though there was more than enough food for his family, Ananse was greedy and sought a way to keep it all to himself.

Ananse went up to his wife, Asɔ. He told her that he had not been feeling well and wanted to consult a medicine man. Returning from his 'consultation', Ananse regretfully informed his wife and son, Ntikuma, that he had been told he had only eight days left to live. The medicine man, he said, had given the following instructions: that Ananse was to be buried nowhere else but in a grave dug next to the yam patch of the family farm, and that they were to bury Ananse with all the necessary cooking and eating utensils so that he could take care of himself in the afterlife.

Asɔ and Ntikuma dutifully dug the grave and filled it with the requisite materials. After eight days Ananse pretended to die and was soon buried.

By day, Ananse remained hidden in his well-stocked grave. By night, he crept out to steal his family's produce and returned to his grave to cook and eat it all by himself.

After some time, the family noticed that their crops were continuously disappearing. Asɔ tried praying to the spirit of Ananse to protect the farm, but the crops continued to disappear. Following the neighbours' advice, Ntikuma came up with a different plan to catch the thief. He built a life-sized human figure out of sticky gum from a rubber tree and placed it in the middle of the farm.

That night Ananse rose again to steal some more food. This time he encountered this lone, silent figure in the dark.

"Hey!" Ananse said. "What do you think you are doing here, on my farm?"

The figure did not respond. Ananse, incensed at the person's rudeness, threatened to strike him if he did not answer or leave immediately. The rubber figure did neither, and so Ananse struck it with his right hand – but the hand then refused to come loose.

"If you don't release me at once, I will strike you with my left hand, which is even stronger than my right!" Ananse threatened.

Still the figure gave no response. Ananse carried out his threat. Again his hand stuck fast to the figure. Ananse tried again, uttering threat after threat and striking blow after blow, until his two hands, his two feet, his head and his belly were all stuck to the figure. No matter how violently he struggled, he could not get free.

When morning came, Asɔ and Ntikuma came to find none other than the supposedly dead Kwaku Ananse as the captured thief. They paraded him through the village, where all the neighbours laughed and jeered at his ridiculous state. Once they pried him off the sticky figure, Ananse, unable to deal with the shame, turned himself into a spider. He ran into the nearest house and hid up on the darkest corner of the ceiling.

This is why spiders tend to be found in dark corners even today.

Anansi and Other Animal Tricksters

In Harris's *Uncle Remus* collection, it is Brer Rabbit who is caught with a figure of tar and turpentine constructed by Brer Fox and placed in the middle of the road. There is no mention of a famine or food and Rabbit is no thief. Although Brer Fox laughs mockingly at Brer Rabbit once the latter is caught, there is no moral or explanatory conclusion to the tale. Nor are the characters' motivations as detailed as they are in the Kwaku Ananse stories.

Anansi does appear in more recognizable form in the Uncle Remus tale titled 'Brother Rabbit Doesn't Go to See Aunt Nancy'. In this story, Aunt Nancy is an old witch who has the power to summon all the animals once a year to 'make peace' with her. One year Rabbit decides not to make the annual pilgrimage, neither respecting nor fearing Aunt Nancy as the other animals do. Brer Rabbit tells the others that when they go, they must ask Aunt Nancy to shake hands with them. The other animals do so when they make their pilgrimage. Aunt Nancy deflects and tries to tighten her cloak, but it slips. The animals thus catch glimpses of her extra arms, exposing the fact that she is half-woman, half-spider. Even her house, which once looked like it was cloaked in fog, is merely a spider's web. The animals run off and report back to a rather smug Brer Rabbit.

The rabbit appears in the peripheries of some Akan Ananse stories, but not quite as a trickster.

Given that enslaved people of various origins were forced together in the New World, it should be no surprise that their indigenous tricksters interacted in some stories. Besides the spider and the hare, another trickster figure popular in Africa is the tortoise, particularly in the region of present-day Nigeria. A couple of Anansi stories recorded by Melville and Frances Herskovits in Suriname involve Rabbit and Anansi outsmarting Tiger in the same tale. In another, Anansi tricks Tortoise in the first part of the tale, only to be outsmarted by Tortoise in the second half, where the latter uses Anansi's own tactics better than Anansi himself.

ANANSI'S FAMILY

Kwaku Ananse's family has gone through nearly as many transformations as the character himself. The only one who seems to have retained a semblance of his original Akan name is his firstborn son, who Ghanaians know primarily as Ntikuma.

Anansi's Firstborn Son

Ntikuma is the name and spelling that Rattray uses in his *Akan-Ashanti Folk-Tales* collection for Ananse's eldest son, and it is the one that is most widely accepted in Ghana today. W.H. Barker's collection calls the same character Kweku Tsin, and

Harold Courlander's collection – which gleans from preceding collections such as Barker's and Rattray's – includes stories where two sons of Ananse appear together, one named Intikuma and the other Kweku Tsin. Each of these collections was recorded in the twentieth-century Gold Coast. The spelling of Kweku Tsin follows a standardized Fante language writing system. Some modern Fante speakers speculate that it could be an anagram of Ntsi, a Fante-sounding version of 'Nti', which happens to be the first syllable of the Twi canon's Ntikuma.

The name Ntikuma has survived remarkably well in the Caribbean islands, even if his relationship to Anansi has become more ambiguous. Variant spellings and pronunciations include Tacoma, Tukoma, Terrycooma and Tookerman. Some Caribbean tales refer to this character as Anansi's son, others merely as his friend, neighbour or unrelated secondary character. But often, as in the West African tales, their relationship involves rivalry. In some regions, for instance in Suriname, Anansi's son seems often to go unnamed, although he performs the same role as his counterparts in the African and British Caribbean stories.

Perhaps Fante storytellers bestowed the same day-name, Kweku, upon Ananse's firstborn because he takes the most after his father. Ntikuma is portrayed as more heroic than his father is. In one Barker tale, Kweku Tsin saves an entire population from the clutches of a dragon. He does not seem to share Ananse's most negative traits, such as greed and gluttony, but he is extremely clever and even more cunning than his father. In one Jamaican story recorded by Beckwith, Anansi's firstborn is not called a variation of Ntikuma at all, but 'Cunnie-more-than-father'. Cunnie-more-than-father outsmarts Anansi by discovering the name of a type of yam which Anansi tries to conceal from his family. He also cleverly sidesteps all the traps that Anansi and Tiger have laid in an attempt to kill him.

Anansi's Other Sons

Across the world, the number of Anansi's sons varies. In Ghana he often has three, besides Ntikuma. Their names are Afudohwedohwe, Nankonwheaa and Tikelenkele (or Tikonokono), and they are well known because of the comic relief they bring to Ananse stories. The Twi onomatopoeia of their names reflects their roles as caricatures. Afudohwedohwe loosely translates into English as 'belly nearly big enough to burst'. Nankonwheaa translates loosely as 'thin, spindly legs' and Tikelenkele loosely as 'huge head'. Their names describe their appearances, which occasionally drive the plot of the story, but are otherwise superfluously ridiculous. In one Rattray story Kwaku Ananse sends these three sons to search for figs for him to eat. Upon reaching the fig tree, Tikelenkele tries to climb, but when he looks down, the weight of his head causes him to fall to the ground and crash. Afudohwedohwe laughs at him so forcefully that his huge belly explodes. Nankonhweaa tries to run and tell Father Ananse what has happened, but his spindly legs snap and detach from his body, staying on one side of a fence while the rest of his body flies over it.

Rare instances do occur when Ananse's sons bear none of the aforementioned names. A story from Courlander's collection describes his sons being born with their names already known to them: Akakai ('Able-to-see-trouble'), Twa Akwan ('Road-builder'), Hwe Nsuo ('Able-to-dry-up-rivers'), Adwafo ('Skinner-of-game'), Toto Abuo ('Stone-thrower') and Da Yi Ya ('Lie-on-the-ground-like-a-cushion'). These are relevant to the story's plot, in which each child rescues Ananse from danger according to the power for which he is named. The names are never repeated in other stories.

Anansi's Wife

Early twentieth-century collections from the Gold Coast often refer to Ananse's wife as Asɔ (sometimes Asɔw, or anglicized as Aso), particularly Rattray's. The word 'asɔ' is Twi for 'hoe', a fitting name for a character created by a largely agrarian society. A Rattray tale even credits Ananse for indirectly introducing the hoe to African society. The literal meaning of Asɔ's name never seems particularly relevant to the stories, although the irony is obvious to a Twi speaker when Asɔ refuses, in a Rattray tale, to help Ananse build a farm, claiming that it is not the type of work she, as a woman, should do.

In modern-day Ghana, Ananse's wife is generally known as Ɔkɔnɔre Yaa (anglicized as Okonore Yaa). It is not clear how this change in name occurred. Yaa is an Akan name for girls born on Thursday, as Kwaku is for boys born on Wednesday. Ɔkɔnɔre is more like a term of endearment than a proper name, loosely translating to 'sweet' or 'lovely'. Whatever the cause for the name change, it seems to paint Ananse's wife as beautiful and innocent, maybe even serving to elicit sympathy at the idea that someone so good should be saddled with such an incorrigible trickster for a husband.

However, Rattray's stories indicate that Ananse's wife was not always so sweet. She is occasionally the mastermind behind Ananse's trickery – for example, the one who explains to her husband how to trick a python and a swarm of hornets into captivity. Again, in stories from the Caribbean and Suriname, Anansi's wife is sometimes his accomplice. She helps him to lure a string of animals to their deaths by inviting them to mourn for someone who isn't really dead, for instance. In a story recorded in St. Vincent, it is Anansi who pretends to play dead, while his wife enacts her grief with melodramatic singing and wailing. In a few Surinamese tales, Anansi's wife is even the one who outsmarts *him*.

Neither the name Asɔ nor the name Okonore Yaa seems to have survived across the Atlantic. In some cases, the fame of Ntikuma's name has cast a shadow over Anansi's wife. In Milne-Home's 1890 collection, *Mama's Black Nurse Stories*, collected in Jamaica, Anansi's wife is called A-toukama, whose phonetic similarity to 'Ntikuma' is difficult to miss. In Colman Smith's 1899 *Annancy Stories*, also collected in Jamaica, Anansi's wife is called Crookie. In *Anansi's Journey*, Zobel Marshall references the scholar Jean Purchas-Tulloch, who explains that this name is derived from 'Cookie', a term that refers to a literal cook.

In the Surinamese tales recorded by Melville and Frances Herskovits, Anansi's wife is consistently called Sa Akuba. This sounds as though it might be derived from the Akan names of Akuba or Akuaba, which often appear in Rattray's Akan tales. The first half of the name, 'Akua', is the feminine counterpart of Kwaku – that is, given to girls born on Wednesdays. In Akan culture the name Akuaba refers mostly to a special type of fertility doll in the image of a woman with pointed breasts. The Akan storytellers who served as Rattray's sources seem to have used it to refer to any kind of humanoid statue, including equivalents of the 'tar baby' figure. There is one instance in Herskovits's Surinamese collection where Anansi's wife is called as Affi – another name directly traceable to West Africa. In Asante culture the name Afia – or, in Ewe culture, Afi – is given to girls born on Friday.

Anansi's Daughter

If there are any Anansi stories from Ghana in which Anansi has a daughter, they must be difficult to find. Even in the Caribbean they are rare, but she does appear. Often unnamed, she tends to feature in one type of story, involving Anansi and Death. There are many variants, but the core narrative involves Anansi discovering that Death has a wealth of food. Anansi seeks to gain favour by giving Death his daughter in marriage. Before Anansi makes his offer, Death seems mute and harmless. After he is given Anansi's daughter, however, things change. Anansi returns to check on her, only to discover that Death has eaten her up – and has also mysteriously found his tongue. Anansi's daughter, it seems, lives in the tales only to die at Death's hands. In the Surinamese version of this tale, recorded by Melville and Frances Herskovits, this daughter's name, like her mother's, is Akuba.

Anansi's Mother

Anansi's mother is yet another peripheral female figure with little agency. In a Gold Coast tale from Rattray, Kwaku Ananse gives

Nyame – the Akan God – his own mother, in addition to the objects Nyame has requested of him as part of a challenge. On Ananse's part, the presentation of his mother is a gesture which indicates that he thinks nothing of exceeding impossible expectations. In this tale, she verbally consents to being handed over to God.

Anansi does not always treat his mother so flippantly as a transactional object. A Jamaican story in which Anansi teaches his mother to call him by a new name in order to save her life clearly shows that Anansi can be protective of her.

In Akan stories Anansi's mother had a name: Nsia, which translates from Twi into the number six. It is common for Akans to name some children by number, according to the order of their births. Some confusion arises from the fact that Nsia was also sometimes the name of the Akan God Nyame's mother instead. There is at least one Rattray story in which Anansi refers to Nsia as both his own mother and Nyame's, and another in which Ananse marries the daughter of Nsia, thereby becoming Nyame's brother-in-law and Nsia's son-in-law. Traces of Nsia's significance remain in the Caribbean. There is a popular Anansi story trope in Jamaica in which it is taboo for characters to pronounce a certain number. Sometimes this number is six. One Jamaican informant told folktale collector Martha Beckwith, whose *Jamaica Anansi Stories* was published in 1924, that 'six' was taboo to say because it was the name of Anansi's mother.

2.
Character and Conventions

Anancy is a spider;
Anancy is a man;
Anancy's West Indian
And West African.
– Andrew Salkey, from 'Anancy' in *Time for Poetry* (1988), edited by Nahdjla Carasco Bailey

ANANSESƐM: THE SPIDER'S AUTHORITY OVER STORIES

The story in which Anansi gets the right to have all stories named after him is one of the most popular ones worldwide. In most versions, some other folktale character initially owns all stories. In Ghana, the previous owner of all tales is Nyame or Nyankopɔn, the supreme God of Akan cosmology. In Jamaican versions, such as the one recorded by P.M. Sherlock in his 1954 collection *Anansi the Spider Man*, the previous owner is the Tiger. In each version of the tale, Anansi's success hinges on the capture of dangerous and powerful creatures with the use of his wit. This story is closely related to the tradition of calling all folktales, fables and fairy tales 'Anansi stories' – even those in which Anansi does not appear. The term sometimes even applies to riddles and games. It is not clear whether the folktale came first or if it was created to explain this practice.

In Twi, the word for all folktales is 'Anansesɛm'. This is a compound word comprised of two parts: 'ananse' – the Twi word for spider – and 'asɛm'. The latter can be translated not only as 'issue', but also in many contexts as 'story'. If a Twi speaker were to say they wanted to relate a story, using only the word 'asɛm', their audience would likely expect an anecdote from the speaker's real life. On the other hand, if a narrator announced that they were going to relate 'Anansesɛm', their audience would expect pure fiction – or at least something that masquerades as such; they would not be surprised if Kwaku Ananse never featured in the tale. Rattray's 1930 collection of *Akan-Ashanti Folk-Tales* includes 75 stories. Kwaku Ananse appears only in 26 of them, and sometimes only tangentially. Each story is nevertheless referred to as 'anansesɛm' at the end.

The phenomenon exists outside Ghana as well. Matthew Lewis (1775–1818), owner of a Jamaican plantation, kept journals during his time on the island. He wrote that the Black folk of Jamaica were 'very fond of what they call Nancy stories', and immediately proceeded to narrate a story in which Anansi did not appear at all. As Zobel Marshall notes, not a single one of the 'Nancy stories' Lewis recorded included even a mention of a spider figure. Martha Beckwith's 1924 collection of Jamaican songs, stories and riddles was simply titled *Jamaica Anansi Stories*. The 1899 collection by Pamela Colman Smith, which includes a number of folktales clearly derived from European traditions and in which Anansi makes no appearance, is similarly titled *Annancy Stories*.

It is important to note that in the Akan context not every story which a European might classify as 'folklore' is Anansesɛm. Some stories with fantastical elements are considered historical and accepted as cultural truths. A classic example is the story of how the Golden Stool, the ultimate symbol of Asante power, came into this world. The tale includes dramatic elements such as a priest calling forth a stool from the sky; it descended from a black cloud amidst rumblings of thunder. The stool was determined to hold the soul of the Asante nation. To this day it remains an important symbol among the Asante people. Kwaku Ananse, on the other hand, as important a symbol as he might appear, is the embodiment of falsity. Fiction is the only domain under which the spider holds authority…usually.

'How All Stories Came to be Known as Spider Stories'

There was a time when all stories belonged to Nyankopɔn, the Sky God, also known as Nyame. All stories were thus called Nyankonsɛm. But Kwaku Ananse wanted all stories to belong to him instead.

Ananse was not the first person to desire this. Many more powerful people had tried and failed to buy Nyame's stories. This was why, when the lowly Ananse approached Nyame and made his request, Nyame sized him up and asked him if he was sure he could do it.

Kwaku Ananse had never been one to back down from a challenge. "How much would it cost to buy your stories?" he asked.

"Nothing in this world can purchase them," Nyame said, "unless you are able to bring me the creatures Onini, Ɔsebo, Mmoatia and Mmɔborɔ." (Python, Tiger, Dwarves and Hornets.)

"Is that all?" Ananse scoffed. "I'll bring you all of these creatures and even add my own mother, Nsia, as a bonus!"

Thus challenged, Ananse left to try and capture some of the world's most dangerous beings to present to Nyame in exchange for his stories. But he found himself at a loss on how to go about it. Luckily his wife Aso was able to set him on the right path.

Following her advice, he cut a branch off a palm tree and acquired some creeping vines. He took them to the stream where Onini the Python lay. As he was walking, he pretended to be two different people having an argument: himself and also, in a much higher pitch, his wife.

"It's longer than him!" he said in his high-pitched voice.

"No, it's not," he replied in his regular tone.

"Yes it is! It's longer than him."

"You're a liar, I said it's not!"

"Ah-ha, there's the creature himself, lying over there."

The make-believe conversation was loud enough for Onini to hear every word. As Ananse approached, the python lifted its head and asked, "What's all this commotion about?"

Ananse answered, "My wife Aso, can you believe her! She thinks that this palm branch is longer than you are, and I'm trying to tell her that nothing could possibly be as long as the great and mighty Python!"

Onini puffed up with pride and invited Kwaku Ananse to come and measure him, to prove once and for all that he was the longer. He stretched himself out to his full length beside the branch, whereupon Kwaku Ananse was able to tie him up with the creepers, leaving the snake entirely unable to escape. Victorious, Ananse took the first of the required creatures to Nyame.

Again, following his wife's instructions, Ananse performed another elaborate ruse to trap the Mmɔbɔrɔ. He filled a gourd with water and then, when he approached a swarm of hornets, poured some of the water over them and the rest over himself. He then covered his own head with a plantain leaf to provide a makeshift umbrella.

"It's raining!" said Ananse to the hornets. "See how I've had to cover my own head with this leaf? Why don't you all come under my gourd, where it's dry, until the rain stops?"

The Mmɔbɔrɔ thanked Ananse profusely and accepted his offer. No sooner were they within the gourd than Ananse covered it up, and, gloating, carried the hornets off to Nyame, another arm of his quest completed.

Once more returning to his wife for advice, he devised a plan to ensnare Ɔsebɔ, the Leopard. He dug a hole close to a spot where Ɔsebɔ's footprints indicated that he had passed, then covered the hole up. He went home to sleep and returned to the hole at daybreak. Ɔsebɔ lay helpless at the bottom of the deep pit.

"Drunk *again*, Ɔsebɔ?" Kwaku Ananse taunted. "If you hadn't been intoxicated, maybe you wouldn't have fallen into this pit! I might help you, but if I do, you'll forget all about it and repay my kindness by pouncing on me or my children whenever you see us about."

"I wouldn't do that," the Leopard promised. "Just help me out of this hole and I will leave you and all your kin alone."

So Ananse cut two sticks, placed them in the hole and got Ɔsebɔ to grab hold of them with his paws. The Leopard started to climb. As soon as his head was within reach, Ananse smacked it with his knife, knocking Ɔsebɔ out so that he fell right back to the bottom of the pit. Ananse retrieved his body with a ladder and, gloating once again, handed the Leopard over to Nyame.

He still had to capture the Mmoatia – clever and wicked forest-dwelling, humanoid creatures, about three feet in height and with feet that pointed backwards. To trap one of these, Kwaku Ananse carved an Akuaba doll – a humanoid female figure made of wood. He covered the doll with some sticky latex which he had tapped from a tree. Then he cooked some εtɔ - a meal of mashed yams – and put some in the Akuaba doll's hand, leaving the rest in a dish. He tied a string around the doll's waist, that he might manipulate it like a puppet, and placed it at the foot of the odum tree where the Mmoatia liked to come and play. Soon enough, two Mmoatia showed up. When they saw the Akuaba doll with the tasty-looking εtɔ, one of them asked, "Sister Akua, may I have some of your food?" Far out of sight, Ananse tugged the Akuaba doll's string so that it appeared to nod its consent.

The Mmoatia ate and when she was finished, tried to thank the Akuaba doll. The doll, of course, did not reply. The creature said to her sibling, "She's not acknowledging my thanks!" The second told the first, "Slap her for her rudeness!" And so the first slapped the Akuaba doll. Her palm met the sticky latex and got stuck fast. Her sibling advised, "Slap her with your other hand!" She did, then cried out in dismay, "Now *both* of my hands are stuck!" The second gave a final piece of advice: "Hit her with your belly!" As soon as the Mmoatia did so, with her belly now stuck to the doll, Ananse emerged and tied the creature up. He carried her off to give to Nyame. He passed by his house to get his mother and took her along to be handed over to Nyame.

Nyame, upon receiving these last on the list, called everyone from every village, every royal and official title-holder in every region of the kingdom, all the leaders of the army, and he said before them all, "All the powerful kings who came before Ananse couldn't buy Nyankonsɛm from me. Kwaku Ananse has done what all of you could not. He's brought me Onini, Ɔsebɔ, Mmɔborɔ and Mmoatia, and even his mother Nsia! Praise Ananse!"

All the people praised him.

"Kwaku Ananse," declared Nyame, "Today and forever more, Nyankonsɛm will no longer be known as Nyankonsɛm, but as Anansesɛm."

This is how all stories came to be known as spider stories.

ANANSI'S DEBATED DIVINITY

Of all the figures who could hold authority over stories, why the spider? The tale preceding this section is derived from the version Rattray collected in twentieth-century Asante territory. Versions from outside Ghana typically do not involve a religious figure at all, but the Akan version does. Perhaps this is one of the reasons why many have reached into Akan religious traditions to explain the choice of Ananse as such an important figure.

Ananse as a Primordial Being

Zobel Marshall, in *Anansi's Journey* mentions A.B. Ellis, author of *The Tshi-Speaking People of the Gold Coast of West Africa* (1877), who hypothesized that the Akans might have had an early chief nicknamed 'the Spider'. Ellis had heard of an indigenous belief that the forefather of all men was an ancient hero who was sometimes a man and sometimes a spider. If there are any folktales which explain how Ananse created mankind, they do not seem to appear in the best-known written sources. Nevertheless, Zobel Marshall continues, the idea that the spider created mankind survived the transition to the Caribbean, to the extent that Isabel Maclean, a white Christian who lived in Jamaica, worried that children surely could not grow into good adults after learning that humankind's creator was a spider.

The many titles for the God of the Akans include Odomankoma and Ananse Kokoroko (sometimes spelled Kokuroko or Kokroko), the latter of which translates as 'Great Spider'. Zobel Marshall also quotes the Kenyan philosopher John S. Mbiti and Ghanaian politician and scholar J.B. Danquah, who is celebrated as one of Ghana's founding fathers. The former wrote that because Ananse symbolizes wisdom for the Akans, God is given the title Ananse Kokoroko to emphasize his wisdom. The latter insisted that the link between the folktale character and God was a mere confusion of names, implying that neither one was responsible for the other.

Other than sharing a name with God, there is no evidence that Ananse plays a role in any Akan religious ceremonies, even though creatures like the Leopard do.

We cannot discount the possibility that Ananse's primordial existence is a great lie concocted by the character himself. A Gold Coast folktale in Courlander's collection suggests just that. In that story, Ananse is called upon as a judge because the quarrelling animals cannot decide whom among themselves is the oldest. The Guinea Fowl claims to be so old that he stamped out a great fire with his feet because there was no one else to do it, explaining why his feet are red. The parrot claims to have beaten the iron of the first blacksmith's hammer into shape with his beak, explaining why his beak is bent. Other animals give similar arguments until Ananse, the judge, declares the argument pointless because *he* is the eldest; when he was born, there was no ground to stand upon, nor within which to bury anyone; when his father died, Ananse had to bury him in his own head. To this the other animals can offer no argument, so they acknowledge that he is the world's oldest being.

Ananse and God

It cannot be denied that Ananse and Nyame have extensive encounters with one another in Akan folklore. Not only does Ananse bear an authority once reserved for Nyame as the owner of stories, but also the two are sometimes depicted as relatives – if not by marriage, then by a storyteller's implication that Nyame and Ananse share a mother.

But the Nyame of Anansesɛm is not the same as the Nyame of Akan religion. The latter is sacred and must be treated with respect at all times. The folktale version of him is more like a king – proud, fallible, covetous and the ultimate holder of authority in a material society. Most importantly he can be tricked, a significant indicator of his lack of omniscience.

Furthermore, there seem to be no folktales which indicate that Ananse has the divine powers of a Creator: someone who can form something out of nothing, such as a God. Instead Ananse is often an originator, in the sense that he brings into society things that already existed elsewhere – hidden inside the bowels of a drum, or in the bush, or on the fringes of society. If Ananse creates anything, it is from existing materials, as he does by accident in a Jamaican story which credits him with the creation of sorrel. This classic Jamaican hibiscus drink is based on the West African sobolo, as it's sometimes known in Ghana, or zobo, as it's also called in Nigeria.

In the Akan stories, Ananse's relationship to Nyame is rarely one of rivalry. Nyame is not particularly antagonistic towards Ananse, but he is a proud monarch, and demands the best in the kingdom, as a king will. Sometimes this looks rather like bullying. For instance, there is a Rattray story in which Nyame claims all of Kwaku Ananse's wives for himself. However, this is only because Ananse promised to bring him a beautiful woman in exchange for Nyame's sacred sheep, then defaulted on the promise by marrying all the women himself. Nyame cannot tolerate his messenger saying that Ananse has made a fool of him.

Nyame is thus not a powerful bully whom Ananse must overthrow, but rather a royal figure to whom Ananse is subordinate. He does not receive Nyame's stories by outsmarting Nyame nor by stealing them, but by outsmarting all the other creatures whom Nyame requests. Nyame's role is often to set challenges for Ananse that are meant to be impossible – if not capturing dangerous creatures, then reading his mind, or weeding an impossibly itchy plantation without scratching himself. Ananse consistently rises to the challenge, leaving Nyame responsible for rewarding or punishing Ananse as he sees fit. Even when Ananse manages to escape Nyame's punishment, the king is not left humiliated, nor is the hierarchy between them overturned.

Conspicuously, God as a prominent folktale character all but disappears in the diaspora, with very few exceptions. Beckwith's *Jamaica Anansi Stories* include a tale in which a crab asks God for a head, and in which a character called Massa Jesus is cuckolded in his own home by a man called Sammy de Comferee. Most of the roles Nyame occupies in Akan stories – setting challenges or providing reward or punishment – are assumed in Caribbean stories by the king. In other circumstances, for example in the story about Anansi's acquired rights to all stories, his place is taken by the Tiger.

It is possible that, in environments where Christianity was strongly imposed upon the enslaved, God was deemed too sacred a character to debase through folktale. Even so, many Christian elements have crept into Anansi stories, in spite of God's absence. Some Jamaican Anansi stories involve Anansi pretending to perform christening ceremonies; they may feature supporting characters who are parsons or reverends, or include church weddings. Some Surinamese tales involve Anansi disguising himself as an angel in all-white to deceive a priest or to trick his mother.

ANANSI'S PHYSICAL FORM

Kwaku Ananse's Twi name leaves him with a permanent nominal connection to spiders, but his physical appearance is a matter of great ambiguity and debate, even in his native land.

Spider/Man

The illustrator's note in Rattray's collection describes intense debates between the 12 local illustrators chosen to make art to accompany the stories. The intention behind selecting artists indigenous to the Gold Coast was that no-one could depict the idiosyncratic creatures of Akan mythology, such as the Mmoatia, better than those most familiar with the culture. And yet it was not the depiction of such creatures that caused the most contention among the illustrators, but that of Kwaku Ananse himself. They had strong but differing opinions on whether Ananse was a spider, a man or both. Their eventual compromise was to draw him sometimes as a man and sometimes as a spider. Modern Ghanaians still seem unable to decide whether Ananse is a spider, a man, a half-spider-half-man or a creature who can alternate between spider and human form. He is, and has always been, fluid.

If Anansi is a spider, his species remains undecided, although he never seems to be the venomous type. There is a tale that explains how the character became a 'Daddy Long Legs' and others that explain why he lives on the ceiling. Many stories explain why Anansi is the type to be found under rocks, while a few depict him running underwater. Pamela Milne-Home, in the introduction to her 1890 collection, mentioned that Jamaicans called a large house spider with hairy legs and yellowish stripes 'Anansi' in real life, and that they believed killing this type of spider brought bad luck. Storytellers cannot even seem to agree on how many legs Anansi has. One Jamaican reported to Zobel Marshall, author of *Anansi's Journey*, that Anansi had 10 legs, five on each side, and that he could both shake them all out into visibility or keep them tucked in.

Anansi's family members are not exempt from the mystery surrounding their form. Although Asɔ's name translates to 'hoe', she and her sons are often described as nothing but humanoid, even if caricatured. Some Jamaicans explained to Milne-Home that Tecuma is another name for Anansi; others said that Tecuma was a type of spider, different from Anansi's type. In some stories all of Anansi's family members are described as spiders and in others none – not even Anansi himself.

Master of Disguises

In Jamaica, there seems to be a much greater degree of consensus about what Anansi's human form looks like. According to Pamela Milne-Home and Walter Jekyll, he is an undersized, extremely ugly and hairy old man with long nails. However, Pascale de Souza noted in her 2003 article 'Creolizing Anancy' that he is depicted as an old lady in St. Martin, a young woman in the Carolinas and a young boy in the Bahamas. An earlier section explored how Anansi's gender shift in the USA is likely a consequence of phonetics. Yet his gender-shifting is not without its precedents. In a Rattray story, Kwaku Ananse declares to his uncomprehending wife that he is saving up some food to eat for when his monthly period arrives – although Ananse at this moment is likely just being annoying.

Anansi has always been a master of disguises, bestowed with the ability to shift form. In some instances, his transformation is not entirely voluntary. Some stories explain that it is shame that causes Anansi to transform into a spider and hide. Stories published by A.B. Ellis in 1895 reveal how Ananse and Ntikuma can transform themselves between human and spider forms, a superpower integral to their abilities to outwit the chief and populace of a certain village. There are a few versions of a Caribbean folktale in which Anansi transforms himself into a baby in order to discover other characters' secret names. A version of this tale involves Anansi transforming *himself* into the mother, while transforming a different young man into a baby. A tale in Beckwith's *Jamaica Anansi Stories* includes the name 'Nancy' as part of a song which causes a man to transform back into his true form – a bull – raising the possibility that Anansi's transformative powers lie within his name. Zobel Marshall reminds us not to forget the 'Little Miss Nancy' riddle format, popular in Jamaica. Little Miss Nancy could be anything at all in a riddle, stretching Anansi's shapeshifting powers far beyond the constraints of a typical folktale.

Man to Beast and Back

As recently as the twentieth century, anthropologists such as Edward Burnett Tylor have insinuated that 'primitive' people, including Africans, anthropomorphize animal characters because they are incapable of distinguishing themselves from animals. He could not have been more wrong. If Anansi and his supporting cast are animals whose actions, thoughts and desires are indistinguishable from those of humans, it is because something cleverer than anthropomorphism has taken place: theriomorphism.

If anthropomorphism is the bestowal of human characteristics onto animals, then theriomorphism is its opposite: the bestowal of animal characteristics onto humans. Rattray suggests that stories that were once about humans – perhaps from real life, perhaps from other tales absorbed into the Akan repertoire – became filled with animal characters instead. The reasons for this include the anonymity of real personalities and immunity for storytellers. For the Akan people, Anansesεm was an avenue for people to speak of others – neighbours or chiefs, for example – concerning things that would be improper to relate publicly in any other form. By changing characters' names, and even their physical forms, they created useful folktale archetypes. Real-life personalities thus obscured, the storyteller would not be liable for any accusations of libel, especially from members of society much more powerful than them. And so if, in any Anansi stories, characters with animal names seem like humans, this might be because the stories are in fact describing real people under false names.

Appropriate Form for a Trickster

Rattray insisted that deliberate thought went into the matching of human personalities to animal forms, based on shared characteristics. One might imagine how a human tattletale could be depicted as a rat, given the modern connotations, or how a strong, fast and aggressive person could be depicted as a leopard. What kind of thought therefore went into the choice of a spider's form for a trickster archetype?

The most important pattern of animal trickster tales might be that of the smaller, weaker animals triumphing over the larger, stronger ones through the use of wit. If the animals were physically dominant, they might not need to rely on wit and would therefore not be tricksters. The Rabbit is soft, the Tortoise is slow and the Spider is smaller than both. But a trickster must also have advantages. The Rabbit has its speed and the Tortoise has its shell. Yet the spider is able to construct a web that traps prey – what better metaphor for a trickster's entrapment of his victims?

The spider's invisibility is both a blessing and a curse. It can hide undetected in dark corners, on the ceiling, underwater, even within grass. Anansi, ever desirous of the spotlight despite his size, is often forced into invisibility only when he is defeated or shamed.

A trickster is frequently an ambiguous character. Neither conclusively hero nor villain, he is someone whose victories over bullies might be celebrated, but whose failures do not move an audience to despondency. He is neither here nor there. Pascale de Souza's 'Creolizing Anancy' sheds light on how the spider's form makes him a perfect candidate for liminality, ambiguity and indeterminacy. The spider is both within and apart from society: living in the home yet tucked up in nooks and rafters, somehow both part of, and apart from, the household. Its web also gives a spider the illusion of flight, leaving it suspended between the sky and the ground, a trick of the eye.

There is indeed intelligence, it appears, behind the choice of a spider for a trickster.

ANANSI AND CULTURAL VALUES

If we accept that folktales – even the ones that are not indigenous – tell us something fundamental about the cultures in which the stories are told, it follows that Anansi stories reflect some important cultural values. This could be quite alarming to anyone who knows the fundamental features of Anansi's character. He is a selfish glutton who cheats and lies to get more than his share of anything, frequently displays little regard for the people he calls friends and family and is often a gratuitous killer of other characters – usually so that he can eat them.

There is a widely held notion that the African Ananse is consistently punished for his immoral behaviour while the Caribbean Anansi is not. This supposed shift has been explained by the enslaved population's need for a folk hero who could be praised for his ability to defy the powerful. But in truth, many Akan tales – at least those that have not been adulterated for the sake of young readers or to reflect authors' religious influences – show that Kwaku Ananse gets away with his behaviour just as often as his New World counterparts. He suffers no consequences for cutting off the Elephant's behind to eat it, nor for blackmailing his wife into keeping the secret of how he won her hand, nor for refusing to pay his incurred debts. One thing this tells us is that the impartation of conventional moral values may never have been the primary reason for Anansi's existence.

Anansi and Morality

It is true that some Anansesεm seem specifically designed to teach morals, even including those that feature Kwaku Ananse, especially when he is punished. At the same time a distinction can be made between the primary purposes of animal trickster tales and general moralistic fables, both in Africa and in the diaspora.

American historian Lawrence Levine explained that the lessons embedded within animal trickster tales often contradicted the morals in other tales. While typical folktales might uphold the values of friendship, asking for help and kindness, animal trickster tales might show that friendship is fragile, that it might occasionally serve a character to bypass asking for help and to resort immediately to trickery, and that altruism might be rewarded by suffering. Levine emphasized that trickster story morals did not supplant typical ones; they only assumed a temporary precedence, neutralizing ordinary morals for specific contexts rather than creating new counter-moralities. Indeed, for an enslaved population, knowing how to manoeuvre cleverly within obviously cruel and irrational systems would be as critical as learning how to become a good person in different contexts.

But what role would the counter-morals of Anansesεm have played before transatlantic slavery? Some of the Akan cultural values implicit within Anansesεm include the impoliteness of pointing out the origins of a foreigner, the dangers of leaving a child with a woman who loves them less than their biological mother, the impropriety of laughing at another's misfortune and the importance of obeying wise and powerful elders, even if their instructions do not seem to make sense. Many stories with these morals do not feature Kwaku Ananse. But one recurring lesson in Akan Anansesɛm is of particular importance to understanding Ananse's role: that dismissing the member of society who is easiest to dismiss – the youngest, or weakest, or intellectually challenged – is a big mistake. The spider's small form puts him physically in the position of such an underdog. But we know from experience that not all underdogs are pure of heart. Kwaku Ananse diversifies the canon, and thereby expands the archetype's role.

FUNDAMENTALS OF ANANSI'S CHARACTER

Clearly Ananse has always represented something more complex than a cautionary figure to teach moral uprightness. To understand his varied purposes, we must first establish some fundamental aspects of his character.

Selfish Glutton

Several Anansi stories involve him finding a source of food in the midst of scarcity – a farm, a magic pot, a tree, something else – and trying to keep it all to himself. Pascale de Souza has speculated that famine played such a central role in these tales because of the chronic food shortages Akans faced in their earliest days of migration southward in West Africa.

In the African stories, it is often when Kwaku Ananse indulges his selfish gluttony that he faces consequences. The 'tar baby' trap is arguably the most famous of them. Within this gluttony trope, Ghanaian philosopher Kwame Gyekye identified a clear moral message. In *African Cultural Values* (1996), he explained that in Akan society, what is 'good' is defined according to what benefits the entire community and 'evil' according to what is detrimental to collective wellbeing. Kwaku Ananse desire to hog food at the expense of his family, his community or even the characters who helped him to find it is one of the clearest representations of moral violation. It makes sense that Ananse would be consistently punished for this.

The context changes in the Caribbean, where enslaved people may have suffered hunger not because of their environments, but because of their masters' stinginess. In these circumstances, a character who could manoeuvre his way into food might well be celebrated – especially if that food came from the master's storehouse. Anansi often steals corn, gungo-peas, mangoes or sheep from someone else's farm, then gets away with framing a different character for it.

In the Caribbean, Anansi doesn't just find mysterious sources of food like he does in Africa; he also orchestrates situations by which he might eat his fellow characters. African precedents do exist – for example in an Akan story, in which Anansi tricks his way into eating the meat of an elephant's behind – but the trope is much more violent in the Caribbean, where Anansi's victims do not survive. His strategies are brutal. He boils characters in hot water, has them impaled on stakes and takes advantage of magical spells which cause animals spontaneously to drop dead if they defy certain laws. And yet, even in these cases, Anansi regularly tastes his own medicine. Monkey eats Anansi after getting him impaled on his own stake; Duck eats Anansi after getting him to trigger the consequences of a magical spell and drop dead.

Ultracompetitive

One of Anansi's most consistent characteristics, which often takes centre stage when his selfish gluttony does not, is his competitiveness. He simply cannot resist a challenge, whether it's to buy stories off the world's most powerful figure, to get the unattainable girl in marriage, to make a mute person talk or to discover the names of characters that nobody else knows. If there is anything at all that no other creature has been able to achieve, Anansi is determined to establish himself as a legend by accomplishing it. We will soon see that this forms one of the bases for considering Anansi as a cultural hero. His means, of course, are trickery and immorality. Selfless heroism, in the folktales, is often reserved for human main characters, such as the Caribbeans' famous ol' witch boy, or African characters such as the Hunter and last-born child. Even those sometimes resort to trickery, although their motives are often pure.

World's Greatest Liar

Almost as legendary as Anansi's selfishness is his dishonesty. In the Caribbean, this often plays out in tandem with his schemes to eat other characters – for example, when he tells them that he will let them out of a pot of boiling water if they utter an agreed word, with no intentions of following through on this promise. In the African canon, however, Ananse seems to love lying for the sake of being more outrageous than anyone else, fuelled by his competitive nature. Kwaku Ananse and his son Ntikuma conspire to lie so excessively that Kyiriakyinnyeɛ – the character who tells the tallest tales – is forced into fatal humility. An earlier section mentioned a story about Ananse lying his way into being confirmed as the oldest creature in the world.

So great a liar is Anansi that he is capable of crafting the perfect Catch-22. In a Courlander story, Ananse's desire to eat a fly, a moth and a mosquito causes him to propose a contest of lies. If Ananse were to say that he does not believe their stories, they may eat him; if they were to say that they don't believe his, then he gets to eat them. Ananse does not comment on their ridiculous, chronologically impossible tales. In turn, however, he speaks of how the fly, the moth and the mosquito once escaped from within some coconuts that he had planned to eat, but that now, at last, he has found them. The three insects cannot call this story true, because they would be acknowledging that they are indeed Ananse's escaped food. However, they cannot call Ananse a liar either, because the contest rules would therefore allow Ananse to eat them. In the end they settle for simply flying away.

Master Musician

It is unclear how the association between Anansi and masterful music ties in with the other aspects of his character. Yet, along with trickery and fibbing, music might be Anansi's greatest talent.

Earlier we referred to an Akan story about how Ananse tricked the Elephant into giving up his large behind for meat. In that story, the tricked Elephant sends child after child to Ananse to demand their father's stolen flesh. Each time Ananse makes the Elephant children dance so much that they return home without it, too ashamed to admit that they were thoroughly distracted by the irresistible music. When Father Elephant himself comes to demand what he is owed, he experiences Ananse's mastery for himself, then decides that dance is payment enough for the stolen meat. Even Nyame is persuaded to send for Ananse when he hears that the latter is playing music on earth which is only fit for a king.

The story of Ananse and the dancing Elephant survives in the Caribbean, but another layer is added to his mastery of music: his skill with the fiddle (or, in St. Vincent, the violin) becomes essential to his ability to woo eligible women, triumphing over rival suitors like Tiger. Anansi ruthlessly eliminates any character who threatens to be better than he is at winning over women, even when they do not rival his musical prowess.

SETTING AND AUDIENCE

Prior to the colonial period, there is very little recorded and accessible material about local storytelling culture among the Akan. We are left to extrapolate from documentation from the eighteenth, nineteenth and twentieth centuries about how Ananse stories were traditionally told. This documentation was largely compiled by British and American individuals, who were rarely present to witness how the stories were told among Africans and African-descended people outside the influence of colonialism or the impact of slavery. In most cases these writers were second-hand collectors rather than first-hand witnesses.

The social and geographical divide between the races had much to do with this. In the New World, a strict hierarchy defined the racial divide. In Jamaica, for example, enslaved field workers lived in separate quarters from the white planters' Great Houses, encouraged to be self-sufficient to save the colonists money. Yet it was not unusual in plantation Jamaica, nor in the era following, for Anansi stories to be told to white people. Two of the earliest records of Anansi stories from Jamaica come from the diaries of plantation overseer Thomas Thistlewood, written between 1748 and 1786, and the *Journal of a West India Proprietor*, written by plantation owner M.G. Lewis between 1815 and 1817, both of whom are referenced in *Anansi's Journey*. Neither of these colonists crossed the social borders themselves to collect the stories. They heard the stories when enslaved people came into *their* spaces. Milne-Home recorded in her 1890 collection that Black nannies in Jamaica could relate Anansi stories to their white masters and mistresses, their white children and house servants.

In the Gold Coast, collectors such as W.H. Barker collected Ananse stories from colonially educated Africans in English and then made his own edits. The most notable exception to the trend of white collectors not being personally present for storytelling sessions is R.S. Rattray. He took the care to be a live witness, attending storytelling sessions in remote Akan villages where the tentacles of twentieth-century colonialism were likely to be weaker than in major cities. Rattray recorded and published tales from storytellers directly in Twi. The available documents show that several features of Anansesɛm sessions were consistent across Akan villages far apart from one another; many of them were carried forward into the Americas.

Communality

The telling of Anansi stories is traditionally a communal affair, conducted in public and attracting a crowd. Barker and Rattray's writings indicate that among the Akans, in dry weather, villagers would typically gather in the village street, all seated in a circle around that evening's storyteller. In rainy weather the session might take place within the relative shelter of a compound house verandah, still as publicly as possible, with the audience kept partly dry by the eaves jutting over the verandah roof.

Today in Ghana, there seems to be an impression that Kwaku Ananse stories are exclusively for children. However, there are many indications that the storytelling experiences were suited to audiences of all ages. Barker asked his readers to picture evening at sunset in the Gold Coast, in the moments between the day's hustle and the beginning of nocturnal noise; women pounding fufu, men lounging and loitering by the walls, children playing games. Sunset transitions into deep darkness with an impressive quickness, slowing down activity and conversation and inducing drowsiness. A lantern becomes the centre of attention. Someone calls out to the people to come and listen to a story and the men, women and children draw closer to listen to familiar folktales.

Similarly, a Maroon named Captain Smith from More Town, Jamaica, interviewed by Zobel Marshall in 2005, recalled of his childhood that Anansi stories were told after people had cooked and eaten in the evening. During the dry seasons a family would sit outside on the veranda and listen to stories, often told by a grandparent. While the grandparent relayed the stories, children from other homes would come around to listen and stay late into the night.

Reserved for the Night-Time...Mostly

The idyllic scene painted by Barker is evidence enough that Ananse stories in the Gold Coast were related after dark. Many have remarked upon the fact that Ananse is largely divorced from Akan politics, religion and social architectures. The mere fact that he is such a ubiquitous character in the regular nightly activities of the Akan and yet so glaringly absent everywhere else indicates a certain sanctity. It is almost as though he ceases to exist among the Akan once the sun is up. Given all that we will soon see the character represents, this is quite significant. Nevertheless, Rattray noted that there were some occasions that allowed for Ananse stories to be told in the daytime, the most important of which was the funeral of a well-known storyteller.

In the Caribbean, prohibitions against telling Anansi stories in the daytime could be severe. *Anansi's Journey* mentions a 1900 article in the *Daily Gleaner*, a leading newspaper in Jamaica, which stated that a 'true Nana' would never tell an Anansi story in the daytime. Such a woman was meant to warn children that if she were to do so their mother would turn into a broomstick, or some other catastrophe would occur. Melville and Frances Herskovits recorded that in Suriname it was a widespread superstition that whoever told Anansi stories in the daylight would have their soul taken away by the spirits of the dead.

It is possible that the nighttime-only convention was a tool for maximizing daytime productivity in Africa and the Caribbean. In *Anansi's Journey*, Zobel Marshall wrote of Jamaican Maroon men telling Anansi stories in the daytime during agricultural seasons when the women were busy with work and the men were free from their ordinary duties.

Anansi at Funerals

Ananse's role in Akan funerals seems to be limited to the commemoration of storytellers. This is far from the case in the Caribbean. In fact, Melville and Frances Herskovits stated that Anansi stories in Suriname were most important for their role in complex rites for the dead; this was indeed the reason for the daytime prohibition taboo.

In the Caribbean, a strong association between Anansi, ghosts, witchcraft and the dead cannot be denied. Plantation owner M.G. Lewis, in the early nineteenth century, wrote in his diary that the prerequisite features of an Anansi story were that they contained a witch or a 'duppy' (generally a ghost or spirit) or some other fantastical personality. Death himself, or a character very similar to him, features in many Anansi stories under names like Brother Dead, Dry-Bone and Dry-Head.

A funerary tradition usually known as 'Nine-Night' is practised in many Caribbean countries, including Jamaica, Suriname,

Trinidad and St. Vincent. Its African origins are partly reflected in the Kwaku Ananse stories from Rattray's collection in which funeral rites are only completed after eight days. In parts of the Caribbean, for instance Suriname, Anansi stories are told to or around the dead before they are buried. Often it is on the final night, when community members gather for a final wake in a dead person's home, that there is lively drumming, dancing, games and telling of Anansi stories. In keeping with African practices, funerals in the Caribbean can be as festive as weddings.

Some say that Anansi stories are used during Nine-Nights to entertain the duppy of the deceased. Others say that they are meant to fend the duppies off or to help the deceased to transition to the other side, rather than to linger and pester the living. Some say that Anansi stories are really told for the entertainment of the mourners, to lift their spirits and fill the space with laughter.

FEATURES AND FORMULAS

Various cultures developed sets of features that were common to most, if not all, Anansi stories, from conventions around who usually told them to exactly how they began and ended.

Anansi Storytellers

In the Akan context, Rattray wrote that storytellers were usually elderly members of society. Milne-Home indicated that in Jamaica they were often old women, although men might also gain some renown as great Anansi storytellers. Melville and Frances Herskovits spoke of informants who came from families of well-known storytellers in Suriname.

Barker emphasized that African storytellers, while exceptionally skilled as raconteurs, were not the inventors of the folktales they told, although they were often responsible for altering stories at each telling to suit the circumstances or the environment. This is evidently true in the diaspora as well. Anansi stories from Ghana might feature foods like palm nut soup, while their Jamaican equivalents might feature ackee and saltfish. Details such as the names of currencies and places easily change as well, across the diaspora. According to de Souza, an Anansi storyteller in the diaspora might even draw upon their natural surroundings as props.

The personality of a storyteller also makes a difference: which stories they choose to emphasize or repeat, the order in which they tell the same familiar tales, which details they embellish or omit. Even their faults add flavour. Rattray's transcriptions included multiple slips where storytellers who had forgotten to mention some relevant details earlier suddenly amended their errors.

In a 1985 article the American folklorist Roger Abrahams described some of the storytellers who told Anansi stories in St. Vincent with characters who were themselves similar to Anansi, with respect to their social position and speech patterns. Anansi's social indeterminacy and selfishness are fundamental features, and his mangled speech, in the Caribbean, is a defining characteristic. Anansi storytellers were socially marginalized; they often lived alone and were considered selfish. They might be ordinarily bashful and speak with stutters, yet they could perform stories boldly and fluidly.

Anansi storytellers across the world had to be skilled enough to maintain their lively audience's attention, assuaging any listlessness with techniques like starting songs, heightening suspense with well-timed delays and skilful impersonation and acting.

Melville and Frances Herskovits wrote of how older Surinamese women would encourage children to repeat the Anansi stories they had heard to one another, with all the required features, paving the way for future generations of storytellers.

Audience Participation

Not only were Anansi stories deeply communal, but they were also highly interactive. In Suriname, for instance, interruptions to the narrative were woven into the very fabric of the tradition: audience interruptions were called 'kot' tori' (cutting the story) and musical interruptions were called 'kot' singi'. A storyteller might be interrupted just a few sentences into their story by a member of the audience who claimed to have been there when the events of the story were unfolding. The storyteller might ask them what they saw, and then the interrupter would begin a song, and the rest of the audience would join in. Such traditions are rooted in Akan culture. Ghanaian scholars such as Efua T. Sutherland wrote of the many songs – 'mboguo' in Twi – and audience interjections that featured in Ananse story performances.

Anansi Songs

Songs and music have traditionally been integral parts of Anansi stories from the beginning, as the existence of mboguo indicates. Many stories have specific songs attached to the narratives, directly relevant to the story's plot. At other times the songs interspersed throughout the narrative seem to have no immediate relevance. Not only is this true in the Caribbean – where many of the songs' original lyrics may have been lost or their meanings forgotten, along with indigenous African languages – but also in Africa. Furthermore, many Anansi story collections include entire sections dedicated only to songs.

The power of music is often evidenced by Anansi himself, whether to condemn him or save his life. An Akan story in Rattray's collection goes like this: During a famine, Kwaku Ananse, while searching for food, comes across some spirits at the stream, catching fish with their skulls, which they have detached from their bodies. When Ananse asks to join them, they detach his skull for him and teach him the song they sing while splashing for fish. When they leave, they warn Ananse not to sing the song in their absence. However, when Ananse hears their song from afar, he starts to sing it too. Immediately his skull falls off. The spirits return at his behest to help him fasten it back on – a one-time only offer, they warn – but Ananse repeats his mistake the next time he hears their song. His skull falls off again, and this time the spirits do not return to help. Ananse thus has no choice but to fasten his detached skull on to his backside. This story explains why the backside of the spider is so large while its head is so small.

Anansi himself is often depicted as a skilled musician who plays an instrument so well that other characters might exonerate him for his crimes – or even drop dead from dancing.

Beginning Anansi Stories

Among the Akan, as in Rattray's collection, there were certain formulas by which many stories opened and closed. Sometimes, the opening refrain was, 'Yɛ' nse sɛ, 'nse sɛ o', which Rattray translated as 'We do not really mean; we do not really mean (that what we are going to say is true)'. In the Caribbean, formulas for opening stories appear irregularly and vary widely. Stories might open with rhymes, likely of European origin, such as this one from the Bahamas: 'Once upon a time, a very good time/ Monkey chew tobacco and spit white lime'.

Opening formulas could be used by storytellers to get an audience's attention before beginning the tale itself. In St. Vincent, amidst the rambunctious activity of a wake, a storyteller would call out 'Crick-crack!', to which the appropriate response would be 'Rockland come'; the call and response would then be repeated until the storyteller was satisfied. In Suriname a storyteller might call 'Kri, kra, all men on their kra-kra!' or 'Hark tori!' or 'Er, tin, tin!', to which the response would be 'Tin, tin, tin'. At other times the story would begin with a proverb or an invocation, giving the audience a clue as to the content of the particular story they were going to hear.

Despite Colman Smith's Jamaican *Annancy Stories* consistently beginning with a variant of 'Once in a long before time', the temporal settings of Anansi stories have traditionally been ambiguous. In Rattray's collection Akan storytellers began stories by introducing one or more characters as simply being 'there'. For instance, one begins, 'Yɛse Kwaku Ananse na ɔwɔ hɔ...' ('They say that Kwaku Ananse, who was there...'). There is no equivalent to 'once upon a time' because each story almost seems to begin the timeline of the universe all over again. There is no need to wonder if Kwaku Ananse married Asɔ before or after he married Nyame's daughter, or how he could be alive in a new story after one has just heard a tale that concluded with his death.

The ambiguous temporal setting thus ensures that characters can recur. It's also useful because many Anansi stories are set in pasts that are either anachronistic or which could never have existed; the story which explains how spiders became bald, for example, implies a bygone era in which spiders had full heads of hair. Pascale de Souza has emphasized the fact that both African and Afro-American folktales provided the sense of an ongoing present. Roger Abrahams also explored how the oral performances of these stories focused on the here and now, addressing the daily practicalities and problems of a given community. This is why Anansi can see a doctor or go to church. He is not a relic of a distant past. He is timeless.

Concluding Anansi Stories

One of the oldest Anansi story traditions involves ending the tale with some kind of explanation or lesson – not necessarily a moral, although those do occur. The explanations offered might concern natural phenomena – the appearance of certain animals, their habits and habitats, characteristics of plants or celestial bodies, and so on. The explanations could also be social, concerning relationships such as those between parent and child, spouses, the origins of social taboos, inheritance customs and more. As often as not, the explanations tacked onto the ends of stories have little to do with the plot itself, but are included for tradition's sake.

Sometimes after the explanatory statement comes a concluding tag, which also varies from culture to culture. In Rattray's Akan stories, one of two formulaic phrases nearly always occurs. The first is 'M'ananses m a metooe yi, s y d o, s nny d o, momfa bi k na momfa bi mmer me'. Rattray's translation of this is: 'This, my story, which I have related; if it be sweet, (or) if it be not sweet, take some elsewhere, and let some come back to me'. The second goes 'M'ananses m a metooe yi, s y d o, s nny d o, monnye bi nni, na momfa bi mpene me'. Rattray's translation of this is: "This is my story, which I have related; if it be sweet, (or) if it be not sweet, some you may take as true and the rest you may praise me (for the telling of it)." These tags indicate an expectation that the storyteller's skill must be appreciated as much as the narrative itself. They also contain explicit invitations for others to modify the stories and eventually to repeat them, acknowledging the fluidity of the art form.

By the early twentieth century, it had become traditional in Jamaica to end stories with a variation of "Jack Mandora, me no choose none!" The origin and purpose of this statement

ANCIENT & MODERN: INTRODUCING ANANSI

has mystified many. Explanations, many of which are explored by Zobel Marshall in *Anansi's Journey*, include the belief that Jack Mandora is the name of a storyteller; that Jack Mandora is 'the doorman at heaven's door' to whom the storyteller is explaining that they would not behave as the wicked Anansi does and be denied entry to heaven; that Jack Mandora is a fictional person to whom the story is addressed – a disclaimer to absolve the storyteller from accusations of libel towards particular people; that the phrase only appeared as a concluding tag to Anansi stories with tragic endings; that it comes from an old English nursery rhyme or radio broadcast that went as follows: 'Jackanory, I'll tell you a story, and this is how it's begun, I'll tell you another of Jack and his brother and now my story is done.'

Many tales in Colman Smith's 1899 *Annancy Stories* ended with proverbs such as 'Cotton tree eber so big, but little axe cut him!'. Surinamese Anansi stories recorded by Melville and Frances Herskovits also ended with proverbs sometimes. However, there were also more straightforward concluding tags, like 'A kaba', which translates to 'It is finished', or 'Na tori kom kaba', which translates to 'The story is at an end'. A popular concluding tag in the Antillean islands is some variation of the rhyme 'The wire bend/ The story end'. Sometimes 'wire' is replaced by 'bow', 'tin' or 'pin'.

Another concluding tradition is for the storyteller, or sometimes a member of the audience, to insist that they were witnesses to how the characters finally turned out, or to explain how the conclusion of the story brought them to their present moment. A storyteller in St. Vincent, for example, claimed to have eaten some of the meat from a bull who was killed at the end of a story he had just told. The narrator in of one of Colman Smith's stories claims to have seen some characters buying yams at the market after the story's end. Even in the USA, the fictional Uncle Remus makes similar claims. It is a vicarious idea that anyone at all from this world can be an active participant in Anansi's world.

3.
Representations and Interpretations

> *"Who gave word to Hearing,*
> *For Hearing to have told Ananse,*
> *For Ananse to have told Odomankoma,*
> *For Odomankoma*
> *To have made the Thing?"*
> – An Akan ditty, quoted by J.B. Danquah in *The Akan Doctrine of God* (1968)

ANANSI AND THE POWER OF LANGUAGE

The power of language is a central theme in Anansi stories. Several plots hinge on verbal traps. Specific dialogue formulas are essential to activating magical objects such as the pot and the whip and, in a Jamaican Anansi story, the mysterious 'Fling-a-mile', which lives in the bottom of a pit. The wrong words in Anansi stories – and sometimes even the right ones – could have consequences ranging from mild humiliation to gruesome death. These are a few of the popular language tropes in Anansi stories.

Starting Something You Can't Stop

A recurring trope involves a character knowing the words to activate or open something, then not knowing the words to deactivate or reverse the process. Anansi and his family suffer when they do not know how to make the magic whip stop flogging them. In an Akan story, the creation of spear grass is a direct result of Kwaku Ananse's ignorance of the right words to make a magic blade stop cutting; Ananse himself is beheaded as a consequence. A popular pattern in the Caribbean involves Anansi knowing how to open the door to a secret storehouse of food but not knowing – or forgetting – the words that enable him to get out.

Uttering Forbidden Words

There is also the trope, which frequently appears in Beckwith's 1924 Jamaican story collection, of characters uttering words which cause them spontaneously to drop dead. Sometimes this word is a number which, for whatever reason, no character must ever speak. On other occasions it is the verbal mockery of another character that is forbidden. In each case Anansi is the victor, hatching schemes by which other characters are tricked into uttering the forbidden words so that Anansi may eat them. Yet he also ends up a victim himself at the end of most tales, getting killed and eaten by smarter characters who cause him to fall into his own traps. In 'Creolizing Anancy' Pascale de Souza stressed that, even though Anansi's ability to extricate himself from tough situations lies in his gift with words, it is important for Anansi to fall into his own verbal traps occasionally. If he never did, Anansi would cease to be a trickster, becoming rather the undisputed god of language.

The Incriminating Song

Another popular tool of Anansi's in Caribbean folktales is the incriminating song. After performing some terrible action, Anansi teaches some scapegoats to sing verses which make it sound as if they, rather than Anansi, performed the action. In Jekyll's version of a well-known Jamaican story, Anansi eats Tiger's entrails while Tiger is busy washing in the stream. Anansi then teaches some monkeys to sing 'Yeshterday this time me a nyam Tiger fat'. Tiger thus concludes that the monkeys are responsible for his trouble. (Tiger then tries to take revenge on them, but the Monkeys confess that Anansi taught them the song, and the story ends with both Tiger and Monkey getting flogged by soldiers from Big Monkey Town.)

The Power of Names

The power of names is an extremely important Anansi story trope. Sometimes Anansi will cleverly change his name to serve his schemes. In an Akan tale, he tells Akwasi-the-Jealous-One to call him Sɔre-kɔ-di-Asɔ. This means that each time Akwasi invokes Ananse's false name, he is giving the latter permission to have sex with his wife, Asɔ. A Jamaican story in Beckwith's collection tells of a woman whose husband told her that all of her money was to be saved up for a rainy day. Anansi persuades her to give him all of the money by telling her that his name is Mr Rainy Day.

In some stories, names are closely guarded secrets – often because the utterance of a name could cause its bearer spontaneously to drop dead. Anansi is often scheming to discover people's hidden names and is often successful.

Not knowing someone's name can be equally perilous. A Jamaican story tells of Anansi, Tiger and Parrot changing their names to nonsensical, near-musical phonetic arrangements, then agreeing that whichever mothers call them by their old names will be killed and eaten. Anansi saves his own mother by sneaking away from the group in advance to teach his mother his new name.

There may be temptation to ascribe the hidden name pattern to European staple tales such as Rumpelstiltskin. Indeed, Rumpelstiltskin and other European classics have been adapted into Caribbean folklore. However, the pattern may have Akan precedents too. In a Rattray tale from the Akan, for example, an old witch refuses to give a hungry girl any food until she can discover the old witch's name. The old witch eventually curses the character who reveals her secret name to the girl.

'HOW JEALOUSY CAME INTO SOCIETY'

There was a man so jealous that he was called Akwasi Niŋkuŋfoɔ – Akwasi-the-Jealous-One. He had a wife called Asɔ, but was insecure because of his inability to get her pregnant. Akwasi thus took her away to live with him in a small settlement where no-one ever visited, out of reach of any other man who might take her away from him.

Nyame, the Sky God, became displeased that Asɔ had spent so long married and yet had never conceived. Nyame therefore set a challenge to all the young men: whoever was able to impregnate Asɔ could claim her as his wife. All the men rose up to Nyame's challenge. Kwaku Ananse watched them all try and fail. Finally,

Ananse himself went up to Nyame and told him that he could complete the challenge, if only Nyame would give him some gunpowder and bullets. Nyame obliged and Ananse set to work.

He made his way through several different settlements, where he distributed the gunpowder and bullets. He told them all that he came in the name of Nyame, for whom he was the soul-washer, and that the people were all required to use these materials to kill as much meat for him as he could carry. While the villagers were off hunting, Ananse wove together the largest palm-leaf basket ever seen, within which he eventually collected all the meat that the villagers brought.

Ananse carried the basket on his head and, with great effort, trekked all the way to the remote village where Akwasi-the-Jealous-One and Asɔ lived. When he got to the stream at the mouth of their settlement, he dumped a piece of meat into it and carried on through the entrance.

Asɔ was first to see the mysterious visitor approach and called her husband to come quick. Ananse declared to them both that he was Nyame's servant and would be spending the night. Akwasi was quick to agree; who would want to risk Nyame's wrath by refusing to oblige his servant?

Asɔ drew Kwaku Ananse's attention. "Agya barima, some of your meat seems to have fallen into the stream."

Ananse scoffed. "That's nothing. I have so much meat that you can feed the portion that fell to a hungry dog."

Asɔ gave the meat to her husband, both of them convinced that a wealthier or more important man had never before graced their steps.

Once invited inside, Ananse requested some food. Asɔ offered to cook. Ananse demanded that she bring a pot large enough to fit 40 hindquarters of meat. Loading the meat into the pot, Ananse boasted that this was but a small portion to cook with; if only Asɔ had a larger pot, he would have provided so much meat that her teeth would have fallen out from all the chewing.

When the food was ready, Asɔ took out her portion and went to sit by the fire, leaving the men to share the food from the dish on the table. As Akwasi and Ananse ate, the latter complained that there was no salt in the fufu. Akwasi tried to ask Asɔ to fetch some, but Ananse rebuked him. "You don't disturb a lady when she's eating!" he protested. "Go and fetch the salt yourself."

Akwasi left to find some salt, and Ananse seized the opportunity to pour some purgative powder into the soup that they shared. "Never mind!" he called, having poured it all. "I brought some salt of my own!" Akwasi returned to the table and continued his meal, suspecting nothing. Ananse announced that he had eaten his fill and Akwasi alone enjoyed what remained.

Soon all had eaten and were satisfied. That was when Akwasi realized that he had never asked his visitor's name.

"My name," said Ananse when asked, "is Sɔre-kɔ-di-Asɔ."

"Rise-up-and-make-love-to-Asɔ," Akwasi-the-Jealous-One repeated. "Asɔ! Have you heard the name of our visitor?"

"Yes, Agya, I've heard," said his wife.

It got dark, and the hosts prepared a spare bedroom for their visitor. But when they tried to show him to it, Ananse became indignant. "I am the soul-washer to Nyame. From the day I was born, I have never slept in a closed bedroom and I won't start now. I sleep only in Nyame's open veranda. Naturally, I cannot sleep in *your* open veranda, for that would make you equal to Nyame. My only option, then, is to sleep outside the door to your closed bedroom."

Again, who were they to risk the wrath of Nyame?

A portion of the night passed uneventfully, but after some time the purgative began to work within Akwasi-the-Jealous-One's belly. He desperately needed to use the outdoor latrine, but his bedroom door had been locked by the visitor from the outside. Akwasi tried to call out and wake him, "Agya barima!" But his cries of the respectful "Father man!" were met with nothing but the chirping of cicadas. Writhing and uncomfortable, Akwasi had no choice but to call out the visitor's name: "Sɔre-kɔ-di-Asɔ!"

Immediately Kwaku Ananse responded, opening the locked door. Akwasi hurried outside and Ananse went into the bedroom.

"I believe you heard your husband when he called out to me to Rise-and-make-love-to-Asɔ," Ananse said to Asɔ.

"I heard," said Asɔ. Ananse made love to her and returned to his post outside the door before Akwasi returned from easing himself.

Eight more times during the night, Akwasi-the-Jealous-One called out to "Sɔre-kɔ-di-Asɔ" and eight more times, Kwaku Ananse rose and made love to Asɔ in Akwasi's absence. When morning came, Kwaku Ananse packed up and left.

It was two more months before Asɔ realized that she was pregnant. At first Akwasi feared that her swelling belly was a symptom of illness. But she reminded him that some time ago, he had commanded a visitor nine times to rise up and make love to her. Akwasi-the-Jealous-One was furious. "If he's the one who impregnated you, you are his matter now, not mine. Come and let's hand you over."

The two began the journey to Nyame's village, and on the way Asɔ gave birth. When they got to Nyame's village, Nyame asked Asɔ to point to the father of her child, as all his subjects were clearly visible on that day, roofing the huts. Asɔ identified Kwaku Ananse sitting on a ridge-pole and pointed to him. Kwaku Ananse scurried away and perched in the middle of the roof. When Asɔ identified him with a pointed finger once more, Ananse fell to the ground.

Ananse was incensed that he, sacred soul-washer to Nyame, had been dirtied with red earth on a Friday, and so Akwasi-the-Jealous-One was forced to sacrifice a sheep in atonement. Nyame then gave permission for Akwasi-the-Jealous-One to hand over his wife to Kwaku Ananse. However, the child of the adulterous union was killed and cut up into pieces, and scattered all among all people. This is how jealousy came into civilization.

ANANSI AND THE RELIEF OF REPRESSION

Many of the older Akan Ananse stories are remarkably vulgar. However, available documents suggest that even these were likely told in the presence of children. This is a matter of particular intrigue, considering that the Asante people have been considered pillars of propriety and order even by colonial standards. Why, then, would members of such proper society paint images such as Kwaku Ananse having adulterous sex with a woman while her husband is in the throes of diarrhoea, or Ananse wiping his buttocks with yams during a famine, or Ananse plucking okro with his penis – and then receive delighted laughter, rather than disgust, from their audience? One possible reason is because their society would not permit them to speak of or laugh at such things in any other context. A member of the audience during a storytelling session once told Rattray that it was 'good' for the Akan people to be able to laugh at people and things that they ordinarily could not, even if they wanted to.

The opening statement that is included in most of Rattray's Ananse stories, "Yɛ" nse sɛ, "nse sɛ o", could be translated as something close to, "We don't say, don't say, o". The salacious connotation here is that the disclaimer primes a reader not only for fiction, but also for a taboo which has been temporarily permitted. In the night, around a bonfire, with the name of Ananse as a shield, members of Akan society could release enough steam to cope with the repressions imposed by the stringency of their culture during daylight hours.

Lord of Nonsense

The relationship between Anansi stories and the rare opportunity to be vulgar in an otherwise prim society was not lost in transmission across the Atlantic Ocean. While many authors admit to altering parts of the Caribbean folktales for children's sake, the work of researchers such as Roger D. Abrahams exposed the prevailing relationships between Anansi and rudeness. Anansi's role in St. Vincent provides a good case study.

Abrahams' 1982 research paper on wake amusements focused on Richland Park, a Vincentian society that operates according to well-defined social codes. These include the understanding that the domestic space – the 'yard' – is a place where order, respectability and the discipline of children is of the utmost importance. In contrast to the yard is the domain of the crossroads, public spaces epitomized by the market in Kingstown, the island's capital. The crossroads are the domain of everything a Vincentian might refer to as 'nonsense': loud, boisterous, rude, argumentative and boastful behaviour. So closely linked is Anansi with the concept of nonsense and vulgarity that a 'Nansi story' is just as easily or often referred to as a 'nonsen' 'tory' ('nonsense story') or 'nas'y 'tory' ('nasty story'). The phonetic similarities are both clever and appropriate, and there are few places where Anansi thrives more in his nonsensical glory than during a Vincentian Nine-Night ceremony. While other public crossroads events such as Carnival and various Christmas activities also encourage nonsense-making in the crossroads spaces, it is the Nine-Night that transcends social barriers by bringing nonsense behaviour out of the crossroads and into the yard, via Anansi.

Yet vulgarity also exists within the Vincentian Anansi tales. Abrahams records one Anansi story in which the storyteller claimed to have been on the scene at the end of his story, to have taken one of the animal character's testicles and eaten it over the course of a week. Another story describes Anansi trying to suppress his uncontrollable farting while he is meant to be playing dead.

Even the games played during wakes – which all fall under the category of Nansi stories on the island – are opportunities for sanctioned rudeness. Abrahams describes one game, Contrady Partner, in which the leader of the game is allowed to pair up unlikely couples, then make deprecating comments to one half of the couple about their pretend partner, within earshot of the person being disparaged.

According to Abrahams, Anansi himself is considered an embodiment of rudeness in St. Vincent; he is the 'lord of nonsense' who breaks every possible code of acceptable behaviour. Anansi's is the name under which 'rude activities carried out rudely' might take place.

Anansi's Unrefined Tongue

Given the rudeness that Anansi embodies, it only follows that he would not be the most elegant of speakers, even if the manipulation of language is the greatest tool in his trickster arsenal. In the Akan context this would often manifest as verbal rudeness – insults lacing his words as he addresses other characters, culturally specific obscenities like "Your mother! Your father!" In the Caribbean his unrefined tongue is transformed by the requirement to speak in the language imposed upon the enslaved population. In English, Anansi's speech becomes mangled into a form known in Jamaica as 'Bungo talk'. The connotations are generally negative – that Anansi is too African or primitive to have an adequate grasp of English, or even mastery of any standard creolization.

When performing Anansi's lines, a storyteller might give Anansi a nasal, nearly unintelligible way of speaking, with exaggerated fumbling and foolishness. Some Jamaican collectors have written that this is because Anansi spends so much time interacting with beasts that he has started to sound like them. Some of his pronunciation errors are directly related to the Akan language. In Jekyll's collection, the Jamaican Anansi has trouble pronouncing words such as 'ready', 'foolish' and 'little'. This can be traced back to Ghana where, until today, Akan people's difficulty with pronouncing the letters 'r' and 'l' is a characteristic for which native speakers are often teased.

Anansi's mangled speech is, first, a source of entertainment, eliciting much delighted laughter from an audience. However, his speech style has also been attributed by some writers to the idea that Anansi, especially in post-plantation Jamaica, came to embody the internalized racism which the New World setting had imposed on Black people's self-perception. Anansi may have symbolized, for some descendants of slavery, the basest and most shameful version of a Black man, unequivocally deserving of ridicule.

AKAN CULTURAL HERO

Scholars have often debated whether the term 'hero' accurately describes a folktale character who exhibits such amoral behaviour as Ananse does, especially when examinations of Akan culture reveal that most of his traits are typically considered deplorable. Nevertheless, the Akan stories set Ananse up to deserve the title of hero by ascribing to him the following roles.

The Introduction of Character Traits, Social Norms and Other Phenomena into Society

There seems to be no end to the phenomena that Ananse introduces into society, perhaps the most famous of which is wisdom. Others in the Akan canon include jealousy, contradiction, birds, toothache, diseases, snakes and dangerous beasts, the whip (and the practice of whipping disobedient children) and the tradition of keeping issues between spouses confidential.

Generally Ananse introduces things by chopping something up and scattering the pieces everywhere. This sets his stories apart from other Akan folktales, which end with incidental or accidental origination events. The act of chopping and scattering depicts Ananse as someone who introduces things with levels of agency and deliberation afforded to few other Akan folktale characters.

With the notable exception of wisdom, the things that Ananse introduces tend towards the undesirable. This could be interpreted as a key distinction between Ananse and the Creator. Even though there is a rare freedom of vulgarity with which Akans may speak of Nyame within folktales, there still seems to be a reluctance to attribute the origin of unfavourable things to a sacred deity. Ananse therefore plays an extremely important role by filling this gap. As the embodiment of undesirable traits, he becomes a hero in a counterintuitive way by stepping into roles which are not appropriate for the Creator to play.

Even the stories that cite Ananse as an originator do not credit him with invention – another distinction between him and the Creator. For instance, Ananse had to meet a jealous person and a contradictory person before he could disperse jealousy and contradiction throughout the world. The whip, the birds, diseases and snakes all existed somewhere before Ananse made them popular. His role is to take what is on the fringes and bring it into the centre. While society may ultimately suffer for Ananse's actions, he himself emerges victorious in nearly all of his origination stories – except, ironically, the one about wisdom. If the Akan people are disinclined to attribute the introduction of negative phenomena to Nyame, they are equally reluctant to present Ananse as anything other than heroic for bringing those things into society.

Succeeding Where No-One Else Has Before

Another pattern which establishes Ananse as a hero is the fact that he consistently accomplishes tasks where everyone before him has failed. Before Ananse, people tried and failed to buy the rights to Nyame's stories, to impregnate Asɔ, to get away with contradicting the famous contradictor, to weed Nyame's plantation without scratching themselves and more. So established is this pattern that, in at least one story, Ananse's boast is taken at face value before he even has a chance to prove it. In one Rattray story, Ananse claims to know the thoughts in Nyame's head and flees immediately. Nyame at once concludes that Ananse's claim was true because, purely by coincidence, the thoughts in Nyame's had to do with the very place where Ananse had impulsively announced he was going.

Other Anansesɛm include tricksters other than the spider: the Antelope, the Crow, the Hare and a few humans. These characters' victories are often isolated, however, rather than presented against a backdrop of other characters' previous failures. Ananse's reputation as a trickster is elevated above all the others; it is more impressive because, in addition to being victorious, he is also exceptional.

Punishing the Antisocial

Harold Courlander wrote that, in Ananse stories, there was no need to be explicit about which characters were or were not behaving badly because Akan cultural values were already so deeply ingrained into the people who heard these stories. This is why it might be more obvious to an insider why Ananse is heroic for defeating characters such as Kyiriakyinnyeɛ (or Hate-to-be-Contradicted) and Akwasi-the-Jealous-One in Rattray's collection.

Asante culture forms the backdrop to these tales. For such a communal society, the act of isolating oneself – of living apart from society, as these two characters do – is abhorrent and unacceptable. It is Ananse's responsibility to bring those on the fringes back into the centre of society, by violent means if necessary. Ananse's trickery causes Kyiriakyinnyeɛ to return to society first by visiting Ananse (ostensibly to watch him cut okro with his penis) and then by being cut up and scattered among society. Ananse's cuckolding of Akwasi causes him to come all the way to God's village – the governing seat of all society.

In being brought back, however, the antisocial must also be punished for their violations of Akan sensibilities. Kyiriakyinnyeɛ does more than enough to justify his death, having killed all the other animals for contradicting him before Ananse came around. In a case such as Akwasi's, more cultural context is needed to explain why his problem – that of infertility – is considered punishable. In Asante society sterility has historically been treated like a crime. Malcolm D. McLeod, in his 1981 book *The Asante*, records that sterile men and women were not even buried in the same way as fertile members of society. Instead, they were buried near the village refuse heap in shallow graves. Their corpses were physically mutilated and verbally abused, and their spirits warned not to return to life still sterile. Fertility, on the other hand, is highly celebrated by the Asante. This is why, as Pelton notes in *The Trickster in West Africa* (1989), it is not adultery which is glorified in Ananse's actions against Akwasi-the-Jelaous-One, but rather fertility. It is difficult to view Ananse as anything but a hero when he exhibits a trait so important to the society which made him. Besides, God is the one who set the challenge to impregnate a sterile man's wife in the first place – which alone speaks volumes about cultural priorities.

In a different Rattray story, Ananse punishes his own wife, Asɔ, for her antisocial behaviour. Asɔ refuses to help Ananse clear land for a farm, plant crops and tend to them, and yet is eager to benefit from the harvest. In this twist on the tar baby story, Ananse pretends to die; he buries himself with all the harvest so that Asɔ cannot enjoy what she did not work for. The moral of the story is that when a member of one's community asks for help, you must assist.

Ananse is a hero for refusing to allow the antisocial to thrive, for taking people (and things) which have been on the fringes of society and reintegrating them. He upholds the social pillars of Akan society by punishing those who violate them, and by doing what is necessary to mend society when a character creates a rip in the cultural fabric.

AKAN VILLAGE IDIOT

A popular sentiment is that there are more morals to be gleaned when Kwaku Ananse fails than when he succeeds. And yet, even in the tales where he is shamed, any implied morals seem secondary to the goal of merely ridiculing Ananse for being a fool. The context for this is likely also the relief of repression.

The Leopard and Nyame are good candidates for storytellers who wish to portray powerful or sacred members of society in their stories with cloaked identities. Ananse serves as a placeholder for any commoner whom a storyteller dislikes, however, especially a person they consider greedy, deceitful, full of himself and far less wise than he thinks he is. In Rattray's bluntly titled tale 'Ananse, the spider, said he was going in search of a fool, while all the time he himself was a fool', the Crow, Osansa, cheats Ananse out of all the money he worked for through reverse psychology. Until the very end of the tale, when the villagers flog Ananse for insulting their intelligence, Ananse believes he is deftly avoiding all the traps that the Crow had set to cheat him.

Sometimes Ananse embarrasses himself without anyone else's help. In the story of how his hind parts become larger than his head, for instance, this happens because he cannot follow the simple instruction not to sing the song of the lesser gods in their absence. There are also several variations of a story where Ananse leaves behind his hard-won trophy, a captured elephant, to go chasing after a bird; he loses both. His own attempts at cleverness often backfire on him: he causes himself to go bald, brings about his own death by a spear which he steals from a witch and gets caught in the tar-baby trap while trying to steal food. It is possible that the multitude of adventures attributed to Ananse only strengthen the shield of anonymity which he affords.

One of the most telling signs of Ananse's role as a placeholder used for ridicule in the Akan context is his relationship with his firstborn son.

Disgraced by Ntikuma

In many Akan stories Ananse's disgrace is brought about by his own firstborn son, Ntikuma. It is in fact a rare occasion when Ananse has the last word against Ntikuma, as he does in the story about the pot and the whip. Ntikuma is also notably absent from many of the tales in which Ananse emerges victorious.

The story about the pot of wisdom establishes their relationship well. Ananse, who believes that he has gathered all the wisdom in the world, is angered and shamed by the fact that Ntikuma has wisdom that Ananse does not. In other stories recorded by Barker, Kweku Tsin (aka Ntikuma) tricks Ananse into relinquishing meat which the latter stole from the former. When Ananse tries to frame Kweku Tsin for a murder which he himself committed, Kweku Tsin tricks his father into proudly confessing his crime.

The fact that Ntikuma is Ananse's son is important in a culture where age and wisdom are considered largely intertwined and shame is to be avoided at nearly all costs. To be shamed by anyone is bad enough, but to be shamed by one's own son is such a reversal of the social order that an Asante audience would likely understand the extent of Ananse's mortification immediately. There are things in traditional Akan society that younger members of society may never say to their elders, along with grievances they may never share in the hope of getting justice and ways in which they have exposed their elders' folly but may never receive praise for, due to cultural expectations. For such people to release their repressions, it might be necessary for Ntikuma consistently to expose his father, Ananse, as a fool.

THE ANANSI PARADOX

As we can see, Anansi himself is a wealth of contradictions. He is at once cultural hero and village idiot: a figure whose ways must both be emulated for survival in a harsh world and eschewed for social cohesion. He is at once rebellious against and subservient to higher authority. Also, both smart and a fool...

Pelton described him in *The Trickster in West Africa* (1989) as the embodiment of Asante doubleness, a paradox. Christopher Vecsey, in the 1981 article 'The Exception Who Proves the Rules: Ananse the Akan Trickster', also considered Ananse's duality to be integral to Akan society and cosmology. Yet there is also a sense of stability within his permanent liminality. As Pelton points out, no matter how rogue Ananse's actions, they never lead to Promethean chaos. Various stories, even those included in this text, show how Ananse's actions tend to restore society rather than dismantle it. Vecsey described Ananse as 'the exception who proves the rules', a character through whom Asante life is reaffirmed and given meaning. Through him the Asante people may freely question fundamentals of their collective beliefs, such as the extent of Nyame's authority, and be comforted by Anansesem's paradoxical reaffirmation of that authority. Vecsey believed that the Asante people were able to strengthen their faith in their deities and societies by incorporating doubt, through Ananse, right into that faith.

In other cultures, however, these roles may be too many for a single character to fulfil. Take Haiti, for instance, where Anansi's counterparts have been identified as Ti Malice and Bouki. The tension between Anansi's contradictions is partially resolved by splitting diverging aspects of personality between two characters. Ti Malice is the cunning, clever character; Bouki is foolish and greedy. The burden is thus lifted off a single Anansi character, seeking to be both the culture's wisest creature and its biggest fool.

'ANANSE AND THE POT OF WISDOM'

The selfish Kwaku Ananse gathered all of the wisdom in the world in a single pot. He wanted to be the only person with access to wisdom, and so decided to hide the pot of wisdom at the top of the tallest tree he could find. He took the pot of wisdom and tied it to the front of his body with some string, and then began to climb. Or at least he tried. He never got very far until he inevitably slid back down, unable to manoeuvre himself with the pot strapped to his belly.

By and by his son, Ntikuma, came around to find out what his father was up to. Having observed Ananse for a while, Ntikuma volunteered, "Father, would it not be better if you were to strap the pot to your back instead of your front? Then you would be able to climb easily."

"Oh, get away from there!" Ananse growled at his son. "You are a small boy with nothing in your head." And Kwaku Ananse went on as he had before.

After several more failures, however, he stopped to think. Nothing was working. He had to give his son's advice a chance. As soon as he strapped the pot to his back, he found that he was able to climb the tree with remarkable ease.

Annoyed and ashamed, he cried out, "I thought I had collected all the wisdom in the world, but here is this child who might as well have been born yesterday, full of wisdom that I didn't even have!"

From the top of the tree, Kwaku Ananse threw down the pot in his anger. It smashed into several pieces, its contents dispersing everywhere. So it is that wisdom came into society. Everyone who went to gather some wisdom from where the pot fell is now wise. If anyone is foolish, it is because they did not show up to collect some of the wisdom before it all ran out.

THE WISDOM OF ANANSI

The spider, in Akan culture, is a symbol which represents wisdom. This is why one of the appellations given to the Akan God is Ananse Kokoroko, the Great Spider.

More evidence is found in the canon of Adinkra symbols – a set of pictorial representations of Akan social and spiritual values, each of which represents a different set of ideas. One such symbol is *Ananse Ntentan* (also spelled *Ntontan*), which translates as 'Spider's Web'. It represents 'wisdom, craftiness, creativity and the complexities of life', according to Willis's *The Adinkra Dictionary* (1998). The spider was likely chosen because, small though it is, it feeds and protect itself with the web that it weaves. The *Adinkra Dictionary* explains that the spider demonstrates how individuals who may be considered insignificant can nevertheless make the best of their ingenuity and the resources at their disposal. The folktale character demonstrates the same thing.

In traditional Akan culture, one of the most royal roles is that of the ɔkyeame – often translated as 'linguist' – whose responsibilities include acting as a spokesperson for a chief or king, relaying the ruler's words to his interlocutors and vice versa, even – and especially – when the ruler himself is present. An integral part of an ɔkyeame's paraphernalia is an ɔkyeamepoma or 'linguist staff', which would typically have a design at the top to illustrate some relevant Asante proverb.

One such staff, dated sometime between the nineteenth and early twentieth centuries, is held in the Metropolitan Museum of Modern Art in New York, USA. The design is a visual representation of the saying that "no one goes to the house of the spider to teach it wisdom". While it may not be clear whether the primary inspiration here is the folkloric character or the deity called Ananse Kokoroko, the spider's association with power, authority and wisdom remains clear.

The folktale about Ananse and the pot of wisdom is perhaps the least ambiguous association between wisdom and Ananse in the folktale canon. Ironically, it is one of the tales which depicts him in his most foolish version. Still, the fact that he considers wisdom something worth hoarding is an acknowledgement of its immense cultural value. The selfish Ananse never covets something unless he is thoroughly convinced of its value and ability to serve him.

Often, when people call Anansi wise, it is due to a conflation of wisdom with cunning. Cunning is a prerequisite for trickery, and so central to the trickster plot that even when the animal trickster is defeated, as Levine points out, it is rarely due to brute strength, but by trickery or wisdom even greater than theirs. At the same time, another definition of wisdom is embedded in Anansi stories. Wisdom is the quality that prevents a person from being taken in by a trickster's cunning ways. This is why characters in Barker's collection are described as wise for keeping some information from Ananse or for not believing his stories.

Anansi teaches the value of wisdom whether he is victorious or humiliated. When he is victorious, it is because he has used his cunning and wisdom to his advantage. When he fails, it is because he was not wise enough to avoid being trapped, even by traps he himself initially set.

ANANSI AND AUTHORITY FIGURES

Ananse's role in the relief of repression, in the Akan context, stretched as far as the provision of storytellers with a space within which they could speak irreverently of sacred, powerful and ordinary people such as chiefs, priests or neighbours under the guise of popular character archetypes. This practice had many cultural precedents. For centuries the Apo ceremony, as well as the rites involved in enstooling new chiefs in Wirempe and Kwawu, involved brief windows of time during which anyone could verbally assault the chief-designate or other members of the royal family. There was also a custom known by the Twi verb phrase of 'bɔ akutia'. This allowed an offended person to air their grievances towards someone higher up in the social hierarchy than themselves. In the presence of the real offender, the offended person would address their uninvolved friend as though the friend were the offender, thereby getting their grievances off their chest without liability. In Africa as well as in the Caribbean, Anansi stories performed similar functions, as the relationships between Anansi and various authority figures in the folklore canons show.

NYAME AND THE LEOPARD

The most frequently recurring authority figures in the Akan Ananse stories are Ɔsebɔ (the Leopard) and Nyame (the Sky God). The choice of Nyame, a deity at the top of the power hierarchy in Akan cosmology, is a self-explanatory choice. As previous sections have already established, Ananse's relationship to Nyame isn't particularly antagonistic. Ananse outwits Nyame, but never completely undermines his power or authoritative role.

As for the Leopard, the Asante people have historically considered it to be the ruler of the forest. It symbolizes strength, ruthlessness and power. In a folktale, the Leopard might be a tyrant who utilizes brute force but is not particularly quick-witted. The tales which embarrass the Leopard the most tend to be those which explain how he got his spots.

Tiger

Popular as the Leopard is, he does not seem to appear in the same stories as Kwaku Ananse as often as one might expect. This changes in the Caribbean, where Tiger often becomes the victim of Anansi's witty schemes. Tiger is clearly powerful; in Jamaica it is he, rather than God, who first owns all the stories in the world. Tiger is also frequently depicted as a slow-witted bully, although he does play several tricks of his own across Caribbean Anansi lore. Anansi's triumphs over Tiger epitomize the predominant trope of animal trickster tales: the small and weak triumphing over the powerful and strong through their cleverness.

Massa, Buckra and the Huge Unknown

Since 'Massa' or 'Buckra' is often inserted into Caribbean Anansi stories as a human authority figure, it is not clear that Tiger is necessarily meant to symbolize white authority in the Caribbean tales. A less ambiguous link might be drawn between the Elephant and Massa. The Akan word for elephant, 'Ɛsono' (or 'Ɔsono') carried over into Jamaica in the form of 'Assono'. The physical image of the elephant did not survive nearly as effectively, possibly due to the absence of elephants in Caribbean landscapes. As Zobel Marshall points out, in some stories Assono is described as a 'huge unknown' and a reward is put out to discover exactly what he is. In a Jamaican tale by P.M. Sherlock, Anansi consistently refers to Assono as 'Massa'. In this story Assono is the authority figure whom Anansi eventually conquers by making him dance until he dies.

Dry-bone

A different bully, perhaps as famous as Tiger in Caribbean Anansi stories, is Dry-bone. Also known as Dry-head, Dry-skull or Go-long-Go, he is sometimes conflated with Brother Death and sometimes ascribed the powers of an obeahman, a practitioner of the magic arts. Dry-bone is a frightening, powerful and sinister figure, much more dangerous than Tiger. He is able to attach himself to people's backs so thoroughly that he cannot be displaced. To those cursed to carry him, he becomes incrementally heavier upon their backs. Dry-bone, too, has Akan precedents. In Barker's 1919 collection of tales, a king enchants a box that contains the dead body of a dwarf whom Ananse killed. As punishment, Ananse is obliged to carry the box forever, for it can never be laid on the ground. Of course, he gets out of his sentence by persuading some ants to carry the burden instead. In a different story Ananse tries to steal a magic grinding-stone, which becomes impossible to set down from his head.

Zobel Marshall wrote in *Anansi's Journey* that Dry-bone is suggestive of the influence, power and cruelty that a master inflicted upon workers in the plantation era. This interpretation is supported by the consistent portrayal of Dry-bone as neither a fellow trickster nor as dim-witted as Tiger, but rather as a bully, getting what he wants through pain and fear.

ANCIENT & MODERN: INTRODUCING ANANSI

'MY FATHER'S OLD RIDING HORSE'

Anansi and Tiger were courting the same girl. When Anansi saw that the girl had started to favour Tiger more than him, he decided to do something about it.

"I don't know what you see in that Tiger," Anansi said to her. "Between you and me, that poor fellow is nothing more than my father's old riding horse."

The next day, when Tiger went to visit the lady, she told him that she no longer fancied him, as she had discovered that he was nothing but an old riding horse. Tiger was appalled. "Who told you such a great big lie?" he roared. The minute he discovered that Anansi was responsible, he marched straight to Anansi's home.

Anansi, from his window, saw Tiger approaching. He quickly tucked himself in bed, pretending to be dangerously ill.

Tiger stalked into Anansi's home and demanded that Anansi go at once with him to inform the lady that what he had said about Tiger was not true. Anansi wailed that he could not possibly go anywhere in his condition. He was doped up on the doctor's medication and far too ill. Tiger, adamant, declared, "You will go to her home *today* to clear my name, even if I have to carry you myself!" Reluctantly Anansi conceded.

Before Tiger could put Anansi on his back, Anansi requested a saddle, so that he would not be jostled around too much upon Tiger's back and so aggravate his headache. He also asked for a bridle and reins to pull Tiger back if the latter began to go much faster than Anansi's weak body could handle. Finally

Anansi requested a whip, so that he might fend off any flies and mosquitoes that bothered them on their journey.

As the two approached the lady's house, Anansi on Tiger's back, Anansi sat up much straighter in his saddle, all traces of sickness vanished. He pulled at the reins and cracked his whip until Tiger had no choice but to accelerate into a gallop. Anansi, now operating in his full strength, took off his hat and waved it about with enthusiasm.

This was the image the lady saw as Tiger involuntarily galloped right past her front yard. Anansi, upon Tiger's back, yelled to her, "You see! I told you that Tiger was nothing but my father's old riding horse!"

Tiger was so ashamed that he ran off into the bush and was never again seen among civil society.

WHAT ANANSI MEANT TO THE ENSLAVED

Anansi rarely seems to come up in conversations about slave rebellions in the Caribbean, but several authors and academics are convinced of the part that he played. They believe that Anansi stories did not inspire resistance in themselves, but that the morals and strategies contained within Anansi tales may have influenced the methods of enslaved people's rebellions on both a small and large scale.

Anansi and Organized Rebellion

In *Testing the Chains: Resistance to Slavery in the British West Indies* (1982) the historian Michael Craton wrote that, to

ANCIENT & MODERN: INTRODUCING ANANSI

Jamaican slaves, Anansi was as much a hero of resistance and a symbol of freedom as human leaders such as Cudjoe, Nanny and Tacky. The Windward Jamaican Maroons whom Zobel Marshall encountered in the early 2000s expressed similar sentiments, as she notes in *Anansi's Journey*. Interestingly, all three of these human leaders were of Akan or Gold Coast origin and the many of the details in the following paragraphs are described more extensively in Zobel Marshall's book.

Cudjoe, who lived between the mid-seventeenth to the mid-eighteenth century, was a Maroon leader. He contributed significantly to the formation of autocratic systems for the Leeward Maroons. Tacky was a religious leader believed to have magical powers. He led of one of the most famous – and most violent – rebellions in Jamaica between 1760 and 1761, comprised overwhelmingly of people of Gold Coast origin. Soon after Tacky's Rebellion a legislative committee is said to have proposed a ban on slaves from the Gold Coast, which was rejected. Nanny, a leader from the nineteenth century, was also said to be an obeahwoman with magical powers. A war tactician, she has been described as having worn bracelets and anklets made out of the teeth of the white soldiers she killed. She is also said to have worn a girdle full of knives dipped in human flesh and blood, and to have been able to catch bullets and cannonballs in her vagina, buttocks or petticoats, then eject them back to her enemies and annihilate them.

Zobel Marshall noted that, much like stories about Anansi, stories about Nanny vary based on who is telling or listening to them. While there is little textual evidence of Nanny's existence, she is still celebrated as one of Jamaica's seven national heroes and a memorial has been erected for her in Moore Town. It is worth noting that Anansi was also occasionally ascribed obeah powers.

These rebel leaders may have been like Anansi in terms of ethnic and geographical origin and the powers ascribed to them. However, there were many more ways in which tactics spoken of in Anansi stories featured in organized slave rebellions.

One of these is the theme of the sham funeral. Besides the prominent role Anansi stories played in Caribbean funerals, there was also the fact that the character often used fake funerals to catch animals for food. The funerals which enslaved people attended were quite real, but, like Anansi's, they served a less obvious purpose. Details of the Hanover Plot of 1776, for example, were fleshed out when enslaved people gathered on Sundays during time off from work and during large gatherings such as funerals. Enslaved people who were most trusted by their masters as messengers used the opportunities to recruit more people. One might draw parallels to the image of Anansi as a watchman on Buckra's farm, as many Jamaican folktales depict him: hired to catch the thief when all the while he *is* the thief himself.

There was also the Sam Sharpe Rebellion of 1831. The context here was that the enslaved Jamaican population had caught wind of the successful slave rebellion in Saint Domingue (renamed Haiti). They also believed that the king of England had outlawed slavery and that the white population of Jamaica was keeping this knowledge from the enslaved population. 'Elite' slaves, with more access to Buckra than others, were able to glean information from overheard conversations and disseminate information back to the members of their race.

One might draw parallels to the recurring Anansi story theme in the Caribbean, in which a character either overhears, observes, eavesdrops or 'studies' other characters in order to outwit them. Monkey does so to avoid Anansi's sham funeral scheme in one story; Cunnie-more-than-father does so in order to escape Anansi's plots to kill him in another. The leader of this particular rebellion, Sam Sharpe, was a Baptist preacher; an educated man, he spread the incentivizing news of slave liberation through his sermons and used prayer meetings to organize rebellions. This is not dissimilar to Anansi's tactics in the tales in which he fashions himself as a minister to carry out 'christenings', always with an ulterior motive.

Anansi and Individual Rebellion

Zobel Marshall coined the term 'Anansi tactics' to describe the techniques by which individual enslaved people undermined the plantation structure. She describes in her book that these were small, covert acts of resistance which helped them preserve their pride and humanity, yet were less risky than participating in organized slave revolts. Such strategies could be encapsulated by the Jamaican proverbial expression 'play fool fe catch wise'. These tactics involved a performance of 'Quashie syndrome'. Besides being a name of Akan origin, one of the definitions of 'Quashie' in Cassidy and Le Page's *Dictionary of Jamaican English, quoted in Anansi's Journey,* is 'a backward person who refuses improvement'. In essence, enslaved people rebelled by pretending to be more foolish than they really were.

As *Anansi's Journey* details, records of Anansi tactics abound in the nineteenth-century journal entries of Matthew Lewis, who inherited the Cornwall plantation in Jamaica from his father. The enslaved people of Cornwall spread the rumour that Lewis would liberate them all. When the man himself came to Jamaica they wasted several nights and days in revelry, instead of carrying on with work. One of the slaves even 'accidentally' let the cattle out to trample all over the best cane on the plantation; although the other enslaved people were clearly aware of the damage, no-one made a move to stop them. Lewis recorded how plantation workers would re-open their old wounds, then rub dirt into them to get out of work. The image comes to mind of Anansi pretending to be sicker than he is so that Tiger will carry him.

Some would also chat to any passers-by to avoid doing work. A reader of Rattray's collection might recall Anansi's decision to work on Nyame's plantation only on Fridays when people go to market, so that he might talk to them while he weeds. A version of this story exists in Jamaica as well, in which Nyame's plantation is represented by a 'cowitch property' (cowitch is *Mucuna pruriens*, a Jamaican stinging nettle plant).

Enslaved people whom Lewis described as the most adroit and intelligent relentlessly performed Quashie syndrome. One of them, Cubina (whose name is of Akan origin), was tasked with shutting all the windows to keep out cats. He performed the duty religiously, even though he had known each time that the cats would simply return five minutes later through a broken window pane. He said nothing about the broken pane to his master until pressed. He also routinely let all the pigeons out of the coop and escaped his daily tasks with a performed commitment to waiting patiently inside the coop for their return. Nicholas, a carpenter, tasked with creating a box for sweetmeats, first made it so small that only a single jar could fit inside it. Receiving feedback, he constructed a new box far too large. And even when he finally built a normal-sized box, he nailed it shut so securely that an attempt to open it caused it to shatter completely.

Lewis's description of the enslaved as 'persevering tricksters' indicates that he was the type of victim who knew that the trickster was up to something, yet fell into their traps anyway, as Zobel Marshall observes. This archetype exists within a few Anansi stories, especially the Akan ones. Reading between the lines, Kyiriakyinnyeɛ, or Hate-to-be-Contradicted, knew that Kwaku Ananse was telling him tall tales; he went to Anansi's farm ostensibly to watch him pluck okro with his penis, likely knowing that he would witness no such thing. Similarly, Akwasi-the-Jealous-One laughed to his wife Asɔ when Anansi declared his name to be 'Rise-up-and-make-love-to-Asɔ' – yet he desperately tried to avoid saying it when he needed to be let out to the bathroom. Like Lewis, both characters fell into Ananse's traps anyway because the spider's web had been too elaborately laid to afford them escape.

4.
Reincarnations and Complications

> "When you kill Ananse, the tribe will come to ruin!
> When you pardon Ananse, the tribe will shake
> with voices!"
> They said, "Listen, listen!" And again, the horn sounded:
> "When you kill Ananse, the tribe will come to ruin!"
> R.S. Rattray, from *Akan-Ashanti Folk-Tales* (1930)

ANANSI'S EVOLUTION

he Anansi who became known in the Caribbean and the Western world has evolved dramatically from the Ananse who first populated West African stories. But the character has not remained stagnant in any of his iterations, neither on the African continent nor in the diaspora. This section explores some of the main catalysts for his transformation in the modern world, the various mediums through which he has been continuously re-created and some of the complications associated with his evolution.

From Oral to Literary Tradition

For the first few centuries and decades after Ananse was forced with enslaved Africans into the New World, he remained primarily part of an oral tradition. Some of the most profound changes began to take place when his tales were committed into writing, not least of which were the language and style with which they were documented. This, in turn, affected the content of the stories, with a few exceptions.

In the Gold Coast, among the Akan, white nineteenth-century collectors such as W.H. Barker and A.B. Ellis published Anansi stories in standard English, rather than the Akan languages in which they must have initially been told. In the twentieth century Rattray would complain of how several local idiomatic expressions were wholly omitted in the process of translation. He explained that, prior to him, white collectors sourced Akan folktales by assigning English-educated Gold Coast locals to collect the stories on their own, then submit them to the white collectors in English for editing. However, because the commissioned Gold Coast locals had been educated in English by colonial, missionary institutions, they may have felt compelled to edit out the uncouth, vulgar elements so characteristic of Ananse stories.

White twentieth-century collectors in Jamaica, such as Walter Jekyll, also admitted to making similar amendments for the sake of children who might be exposed to the Anansi stories he had collected from Black Jamaicans. Yet shielding children from Anansesɛm's vulgarity did not seem to have been a great concern in the traditional Akan setting, likely due to a culture that drew strict distinctions between the daylight world of propriety and the nighttime sessions during which the forbidden was temporarily permissible.

Anansi's New Authors

Written documentation of Anansi stories used to be primarily the domain of white collectors. Since at least the 1960s more people of African descent have committed Anansi stories to writing, a development catalysed largely by political shifts. For instance, the Gold Coast achieved independence from British rule in 1957 and became Ghana. Jamaica gained their independence from the British in 1962. Leaders of both countries actively encouraged the reclamation and appreciation of indigenous folklore as part of initiatives that coincided with, and were influenced by, movements from other Black communities across the world, including the USA's Black Power Movement. No longer merely a source of entertainment and relief of repression as he had been in the Gold Coast, nor primarily a symbol of rebellion and autonomy in the slavery or plantation era as he had been in the Caribbean, Anansi now became a tool through which newly independent Black nations could counteract the colonial narratives about Black inferiority. He became a source of national and cultural pride.

The racial identities of Anansi's authors continue to be diverse. In Ghana, to this day, the most well-known and beloved author of Ananse stories might be the late Peggy Appiah (née Cripps), the white, British-born wife of the late Joe Appiah, a Ghanaian lawyer and politician. Her earliest collection titles were *Ananse the Spider: Tales from an Ashanti Village* (1966) and *Children of Ananse* (1968). In Jamaica Andrew Salkey has authored some of the best-known Anansi collections for adults and for children, including *Anancy's Score* (1973), *Anancy, Traveller* (1992) and *Brother Anancy and Other Stories* (1993).

Anansi's Wider Audience

Zobel Marshall wrote in *Anansi's Journey* that the modern Anansi of written tradition is virtually unrecognizable as the Anansi of the plantations. This is not only due to the political shifts, but also to the fact that Anansi has since turned into a cultural commodity in a commercial world. If Anansi's role in older days was to spread a message among Black folk – such as the covert airing of grievances or survivalist lessons – Anansi seems now to have become a character who needs to be made appealing to various audiences, so that the products associated with him will sell successfully.

Anansi's new audiences are not only wider, but, as Zobel Marshall put it, whiter. Anansi has made his way into British schools, mainstream channels of Western TV and film, and into popular literature consumed largely within the UK and USA. The intended audience has not only affected Anansi's moral inclinations and speech style, but also, in some cases, his face and race. A prime example, which Zobel Marshall points out, is the cover of David Brailsford's 2004 book, *Confessions of Anansi*. The author himself is white and British-born, though married to a Jamaican woman. The book's cover was illustrated by John Stilgoe, a white British artist. It features Anansi with a pink face and straight nose, while the rest of his body is hairy, brown and arachnoid.

Anansi and Socio-Political Commentary

Jamaican storyteller Louise Bennett started to compile Anansi stories and poetry written in 'dialect' – also known as patois, or Creole – about two decades before Jamaica gained independence.

She reclaimed Anansi as a tool for anti-colonial resistance and, through her work, pushed back against some of colonialism's more insidious tools such as internalized racism. For example, Zobel Marshall describes how, in her story 'Anancy and Yella Snake', a dark-skinned Anansi is in competition with a light-skinned – or 'yella' – suitor for a woman's affection. The woman assumes that marrying a fairer-skinned man can elevate her social status. However, following an extremely popular trope in African folklore, the suitor she chooses over Anansi turns out to be a disguised monster: in this case a snake. In Bennett's story Anansi rescues the woman from Yella Snake using tactics that involve stroking the snake's ego – a familiar trope that dates back to the earliest Akan tales about how Kwaku Ananse got all stories named after him.

As Zobel Marshall observes, Andrew Salkey's *Anancy's Score* (1973) is a daring collection which portrays Anansi as a politicized figure: a freedom fighter, a symbol of resistance and hope, a religious leader. She points out that through Anansi, Salkey couches commentary about many issues – nuclear power, the war in Vietnam, the wealth divide and the apathy of politicians in Jamaica, the role of the 'third world' in relation to the US and UK – within Anansi's adventures. The collection was illustrated by Jamaican artist Errol Lloyd. Zobel Marshall wrote that both author and illustrator were influenced by anti-colonial thinkers such as C.L.R. James and John La Rose, which no doubt affected how they perceived and portrayed Anansi.

The Jamaican pantomimes that featured Anansi from 1949 to 1998 also challenged powerful figures in Jamaican society, including rich businesspeople and corrupt politicians.

ANANSI IN MODERN NOVELS

Perhaps because the oral traditions of Anansi stories are easier to translate directly into short stories than novels, Anansi features less frequently in the latter; even when he appears, it is as a secondary character. It is difficult to argue that the most commercially successful novels that feature Anansi have been those written by Neil Gaiman, a white British author. Anansi has also been reincarnated in novels by Caribbean authors Nalo Hopkinson – of Jamaican and Guyanese heritage – and Barbadian author Karen Lord.

Gaiman's Anansi

A version of Anansi appears in Neil Gaiman's *American Gods* (2001) and *Anansi Boys* (2005). In both novels Anansi is described as a Black man with a pencil moustache who typically wears a green fedora and lemon-yellow gloves. At various points he is also seen as a small, elderly Black man with silvering hair; as a jewelled spider with emerald eyes; as a tall man with the complexion of teak, six arms, a face painted with red stripes, a headdress of ostrich feathers, riding a lion; as a young Black boy dressed in rags with a diseased left foot; and, finally, as a tiny brown spider.

References to some of the most popular Anansi tales abound, including the tales in which Anansi tricks Tiger into performing as his father's old riding horse, Anansi steals Tiger's testicles and blames the monkeys for it and the tale about how he got the right to have all stories named after him. In the novels Tiger remains Anansi's deepest and most dangerous rival.

Gaiman's Anansi loves storytelling and karaoke. Singing is how he exercises his supernatural powers to 'make things happen'. He smokes cheroots, is a convincing liar, is sexually promiscuous and continuously unfaithful to his wife. He spends his afternoons fishing off bridges and his evenings in bars. Circumstances surrounding Anansi can easily be simultaneously grave, comedic and vulgar. For instance, in *Anansi Boys*, Anansi dies of a heart attack during a karaoke performance. As he collapses, he grabs at a nearby woman's chest, tearing off her blouse in the process, and leaving her breast exposed to the public. Even in death, he is self-aggrandizing, describing himself as so clever, handsome, charming and cunning that it would take several days to detail these qualities properly.

Although in reality Anansi belongs almost exclusively to the worlds of African and Caribbean folklore and not to religion, Gaiman's Anansi has a history of being worshipped and sacrificed to as a god. Curiously, whenever a recognized African deity is mentioned in relation to Anansi in the novels, it is Mawu – one of the Supreme Beings of the Ewe pantheon – rather than the Nyame or Nyankopɔn of the Akan people.

In *Anansi Boys*, Anansi has two children, Fat Charlie and Spider. Originally the two were one, but they were split apart by force in early childhood, whereupon their characteristics were cleanly divided. The 'tricksiness', 'wickedness' and 'devilry' went to Spider, while Fat Charlie was left with no magic, a propensity for embarrassment and generally bad luck – not dissimilar to the splitting of Anansi's characteristics in Haitian folklore between Ti Malice and Bouki. In *Anansi Boys* all members of Anansi's family are US Americans by birth or residence but of West Indian descent, including Anansi himself.

Lord's Anansi

Barbadian author Karen Lord's incarnation of Anansi appears in her 2010 novel, *Redemption in Indigo*. The secondary character is never called by Anansi's name, but referred to simply as 'the Trickster' or the 'spider of Ahani', Ahani being 'the place where con men hold their conventions'. Described as 'the godfather of the troublemakers', Anansi's ability to shift between man, spider and half-spider-half-man, are central to his role in the narrative.

The ambiguity of the spider's ethics are also highlighted in this novel. The narrator describes the spider as having once been happy to trick and exploit humans for his own amusement until, somewhere along the line, he grew fond of humans and decided to use his wiles to help rather than harm them. However, the narrator continues to caution the reader against assuming whose side the spider is on until the entire tale has unfolded; even in his apparent benevolence, he remains untrustworthy and heavily layered. The narrator holds the spider up as a mirror to the readers: 'Look to the Trickster to see your eccentricities, your talent for mercy deep-hidden underneath a fearsome exterior.'

Hopkinson's Anansi

Nalo Hopkinson's science-fiction novel *Midnight Robber*, published in 2000, is saturated with Caribbean folklore; it includes numerous references to Anansi, even though he never appears as a fully formed character. The novel's narrator refers to him as a trickster and a liar, but in the novel's universe he is as much a fictional creature as he is in reality – a folkloric figure about whom entertaining stories are told. At one point the novel's main character, Tan-Tan, watches a cartoon featuring Brer Anansi as a source of relief when she is troubled.

Midnight Robber is full of 'anansi stories' – a term which, in the novel as well as in several Black cultures, refers to all fictional tales and is even once as a synonym for a lie. When used as part of this term, Anansi's name is written as a common noun. In this novel also, the term 'anansi story' includes duppy stories – scary tales about dead spirits and mythical Caribbean monsters such as jumbies and the rolling calf. Just as in reality, the scarier anansi stories in the novel are told during ceremonial settings such as Nine-Night and Jonkanoo festivals. Several complete anansi stories are included in the novel as interludes that break the main narrative. Instead of Anansi, their main character is Tan-Tan, and each tale is a highly exaggerated, fairytale version of things she has really been through. In this way the novel gives unusual insight into the likely processes by which traditional Anansi stories may first have been formed.

Reference to Anansi's traditional canon abound. For instance, Tan-Tan mercilessly whips a mother who has just ruthlessly whipped her son – calling to mind the story of Anansi and the magic whip. Included also is an anansi story interlude titled 'Tan-Tan and Dry Bone'. This story echoes a popular Caribbean tale, at least one version of which is recorded in Walter Jekyll's *Jamaican Song and Story* collection. In the Jekyll tale Anansi gets tricked into carrying 'Dry-bone' home, but wriggles his way out of the burden by making a deal with Fowl-hawk to come and carry Dry-bone away. It is, of course, Tan-Tan and not Anansi who gets saddled with Dry Bone in the novel's version, and it is the buzzard, Johncrow, who comes to her rescue. But Johncrow's plan cannot be executed without Tan-Tan's Anansi-like cunning. She strokes Dry Bone's ego in much the same way that Anansi strokes the Python's ego in the story where he gets all stories named after him.

Anansi's name in the novel is used frequently in reference to the book's highly advanced, science-fiction version of the internet. It is often conflated with Nanny, the name of the Jamaican Maroon heroine. The technological structure that connects and governs society in this novel is known by many names: the Grande Nanotech Sentient Interface (from which the acronym NANSI can be formed); the Grande Anansi Nanotech Interface; Granny Nansi's Web; the Anansi Web. When personified, it is referred to simply as 'Granny Nanny'.

Popular opening and closing tags of Anansi stories feature lightly in this novel as well. The narrator uses the expression 'crick-crack Anansi back' as an interjection, and a solitary 'crick-crack' to open a story. The 'Tan-Tan and Dry Bone' interlude concludes with 'Wire bend/ Story end', and the very last words of the novel are 'Call that George, the story done/ Jack Mandora, me nah choose none!'

ANANSI AND THE STAGE

Zobel Marshall records that Anansi occupied a prominent place on Jamaican stages, beginning around the 1950s and thanks to organizations such as the Jamaica National Pantomime and the

Little Theatre Movement, and storytellers such as Louise Bennett (also known as 'Miss Lou'), Ranny Williams and Barbara Gloudon.

In Ghana, by the 1960s and 1970s, the art of Anansesɛm performances had evolved through new traditions such as Concert Parties – travelling music and theatre troupes which stopped to put on shows in various villages and cities, incorporating aspects of Anansesɛm. The Ghanaian playwright and cultural activist Efua T. Sutherland spent time during those decades conducting research on the emergent 'specialist groups' who now performed Anansesɛm professionally. This led her to develop and classify a style of theatre called Anansegoro. Other Ghanaian playwrights, such as Martin Owusu and Yaw Asare, contributed to the canon of Ghanaian plays about Kwaku Ananse.

Anansi and the Jamaican Pantomime

Zobel Marshall also records that the Little Theatre Movement put on 10 Anansi pantomimes between 1949 and 1998. Barbara Gloudon was the author of two of them: *Moonshine Anancy* (1969) and *Anansi Come Back* (1993). Louise Bennett and Ranny Williams often teamed up to perform Anansi stories on TV, on stage and on the radio.

Zobel Marshall's book also details that Jamaica's Anansi pantomimes served several purposes, from the personal to the social, and moved beyond mere entertainment. Researcher Ruth Minott Egglestone wrote that Anansi, on stage, taught audiences a 'philosophy of resistance', allowing them to combat hardship with humour rather than succumbing to bitterness. The use of patois within the pantomimes, championed especially by

Bennett, alongside culturally specific jokes provided an avenue for Jamaican patois speakers to bond and even to enjoy the pantomimes in ways that may have excluded non-patois speaking audiences. Gloudon attributed Anansi's success within the art of pantomime, a form in which good must triumph over evil in the end, to the fact that Anansi was a lovable villain in whom members of the audience could see themselves.

Anansegoro: Ananse in Ghanaian Theatre

Efua Sutherland classified Anansegoro as a style of traditional theatre with established conventions, best showcased in her seminal 1975 play *The Marriage of Anansewa*. The play's main character, George Kweku Ananse, digs a hole for himself when he leads four local chiefs from various Ghanaian ethnic groups to believe that they are each exclusively petitioning Ananse for the hand of Anansewa, his only daughter, in marriage. The deception works superbly for Ananse as the chiefs shower Ananse with gifts and money during the courting period, according to Akan traditional customs. However, when each chief decides almost simultaneously to perform the final ritual that would bind Anansewa as his wife, Kweku Ananse, knowing that his daughter cannot be wife to four different men, comes up with a clever scheme to extricate himself and marry Anansewa off to the suitor she prefers – while losing none of the wealth he has gained from his deception. In fact, he even gains more. His strategy is a popular one in the traditional folkloric canon: a faked death – in this case Anansewa's. This play takes the trope a little further with an equally faked miraculous resurrection.

Anansegoro's unique features include the role of Storyteller and mboguo. *The Marriage of Anansewa* draws heavily upon both.

The Storyteller in Anansegoro is an actor who plays the role that a traditional Anansesɛm storyteller would have played in the village: the omniscient and sole narrator of the story, who nevertheless is fully permitted to participate in the events of the play and is responsible for making the audience feel like participants as well. His main prop would be a staff, the likes of which an Akan ɔkyeame – the linguist or official spokesperson for an Akan chief – would hold. In *The Marriage of Anansewa* the Storyteller is an independent character. However, in Ghanaian playwright Martin Owusu's 1971 play *The Story Ananse Told*, Ananse is both narrator and character. This allows him to toot his own horn in the first act, but in the second, another character, the king, asks Ananse why he is participating in the narrative when he is supposed to be the narrator. Ananse's candid response is that he does not want to be forgotten by the audience. His ego thus allows Ananse to play remarkably well into an Anansegoro convention.

Mboguo is an Akan word for the musical performances within Anansesɛm and Anansegoro. They would always be performed in the context of the performance and narrative, usually led by the Storyteller but sometimes contributed by a member of the audience, who was permitted to halt the performance to start the song. Mboguo could involve hand-clapping, drumming, castanets and a gong to mark the rhythm; they could be accompanied by comic miming performed by the theatre troupe members. A series of mboguo would typically begin the Anansegoro performance, and a troupe's signing-off song would close it. In addition to opening and closing performances, the mboguo could break the Storyteller's flow for a multitude of reasons: to reflect the mood of the play's events at a given moment, to contribute to the pace or characterization of the story, to inspire the audience or to indicate shifts in the story's setting. Mboguo could even be started just because of someone's desire to show off.

Anansi's Defiance of the Theatre's Divide

Sutherland declared that her biggest challenge in adapting Anansesɛm into Anansegoro came from the attempt to evoke the same sense of community participation that the older tradition held. Her way of addressing this in *The Marriage of Anansewa* was to cast a group of Players to act the role that an audience might have played, had there been no separation between performers and audience created by the stage.

Zobel Marshall records that in the Jamaican pantomime tradition, Gloudon also found beauty in the fact that Anansi was not confined by the proscenium arch – a barrier between the audience and actors which she felt aligned more with European storytelling traditions than those that evolved from Africa. In fact, Gloudon wrote Anansi's defiance of borders into her pantomimes. At the beginning of *Moonshine Anancy*, the character is crouched at the side of the stage; when he finally emerges into the centre, he boasts about how nobody noticed him in his hiding place, even though he was there for so long. As Gloudon said, he could even go down and speak to the audience if he wanted. Whether in West Africa or the Caribbean, Anansi had a penchant for defying the boundaries created by the stage.

Transition into Twenty-first-Century Theatre

In the 1990s a new class of professional storytellers in Jamaica started to perform Anansi stories on stage for a fee. Zobel Marshall noted that this made it unaffordable for most Jamaicans outside of the elite and middle class. Yet Anansi still continued to serve as a symbol of shared history and remembrance, continuously linked back to his origins. Zobel Marshall attended a storytelling event in Jamaica in 2005, in which Eintou Springer had Anansi taking a rope across the Atlantic Ocean to link Caribbeans back to the African continent.

In Ghana, since the turn of the century, one of the most notable reincarnations of Ananse on the stage is from Yaw Asare's 2006 play, *Ananse in the Land of Idiots*. In this play Kwaku Ananse's character speaks of Efua Sutherland as though he knew her personally. He thanks her for seeing him not as a villain, but as he really was, and for accurately documenting the story of his daughter's marriage. In this play Ananse speaks directly to the audience, getting them to participate in the play with common Ghanaian call-and-response phrases. Asare's Ananse is not as benign as Sutherland's, however. He is a remorselessly lascivious, cheating liar who thinks nothing of hoodwinking an important chief's betrothed daughter into becoming his wife, causing the deaths of her fiancé and the chief's guard in the process. No matter how many crimes he commits, Ananse escapes without consequence. He never sees himself as amoral, but continuously justifies his actions. At one point Ananse entreats the audience to consider his perspective. "Now tell me; what is wrong with a man employing his God-given latent talents to cope with the challenges of a hostile world?"

ANANSI ON TV

Since the late twentieth century, Anansi has made a few appearances on TV in Africa, the Caribbean and the Western world. This section explores a handful of notable programmes.

Ring Ding

From 1969 to 1980, a variety show called *Ring Ding* aired on Saturdays in Jamaica. Its host was Louise Bennett, also known as Miss Lou. It was recorded in front of an audience of children and featured a cast of children who helped her perform poetry, Jamaican folk songs and many Anansi stories. She was often helped by fellow Jamaican storyteller Ranny Williams. The TV programme was a thorough celebration of Jamaican culture and heritage. Miss Lou was particular about using patois – which she referred to specifically as 'dialect' – as a legitimate and artful language in which to create art.

By the Fireside

Very similar to Jamaica's *Ring Ding* was the 1990s Ghanaian TV show *By the Fireside* – a storytelling programme headlined and scripted by venerated Ghanaian actress Grace Omaboe, also known as Maame Dokono. This show also aired on Saturdays on GTV, Ghana's national public broadcaster.

Maame Dokono was also joined by an audience of children gathered around her. They often doubled as actors, playing out scenes from the various Ananse stories which she narrated. Storyteller and audience would often dress in African traditional attire or patterned cloths. The show was lively and interactive, with the children often beginning, interrupting and ending stories with mboguo, including traditional drumming, dancing, the singing of local folk songs and clapping.

The storytelling and acting took place both in English and local languages. While Kwaku Ananse often appeared in his Akan iteration, there were episodes that drew from different Ghanaian cultures as well. For example, an episode included a dramatized story whose main character was Ayiyi, which means 'spider' in the Ewe language. Kwaku Ananse's Ewe counterpart was easily recognizable, thanks in part to the potbelly that Ghanaians often portray Ananse with, as well as to the large spider web prop before which Ayiyi delivered his lines.

In December 2019 the e-Ananse library in Accra put on an event called 'By the Fireside @ Osu', during which Maame Dokono and some of her original cast members were invited to give a stage performance of *By the Fireside*. This event continued into 2020 as a monthly occurrence.

Gargoyles

In February 1996 an episode of Disney's *Gargoyles* animated series featured Anansi as the main antagonist. The 34th episode of season 2 was titled 'Mark of the Panther' and incorporated a mosaic of West African folklore and culture. Besides Anansi there was 'the Panther Queen' – likely a reference to the legend of Sarraounia Mangou from Niger; the episode's events also seemed to take place in Nigeria. Anansi's character was voiced by American actor LeVar Burton, of Star Trek fame.

Anansi in this episode is a large spider whose primary goal is to manipulate as many humans as possible into feeding his gluttonous desires. He has the supernatural power to change humans into panthers (and back again) and wields this power manipulatively, with abundant promises and shameless duplicity. At some point Anansi bargains with the Panther Queen to build a giant, spider web-shaped city in his honour; its inhabitants are to be responsible for keeping him well fed. Interestingly, the city is animated from aerial view as a minimalist web shape with seven sections, just like the Akan Adinkra symbol *Ananse Ntentan*.

At the end of the episode the main characters are able to use Anansi's gluttony to defeat him. They cut him down from the webbing that elevates him because he has grown too fat to fight without the added support. In the midst of defeat, Anansi begs for mercy with more promises: "I will spin you wishes, give you treasures beyond counting", to which one character truthfully replies, "Your gifts always come with a price, trickster".

American Gods

Between 2017 and 2021 the American premium cable network Starz aired three seasons of *American Gods*, a TV show adaptation of the Neil Gaiman novel of the same name.

Gaiman is credited as an Executive Producer and co-writer on a few episodes.

This show features what is likely the most-watched portrayal of Anansi on screen worldwide. The character is played by the African American actor Orlando Jones, and in most appearances he wears suits and ties with bright colours and patterns. Most of the time Anansi speaks with a southern US accent, although it occasionally slips in and out of West African and West Indian inflections.

Anansi's grand and dramatic introduction comes in the second episode of season 1, in an emotionally charged scene set in 1697, aboard a slave ship. In an odd mosaic of Black cultural representations, an enslaved Igbo-speaking man prays to the Akan figure of Anansi; he addresses him not as a folkloric character but as a god, using the French-Caribbean title of 'Compé'. When Anansi appears, he has little compassion and several harsh truths about the fate of Black people in America, delivered in an angry monologue, sometimes with a sardonic smile. He incites a rebellion, persuading the enslaved people to kill all the white people aboard the ship and set fire to the vessel, at the expense of their own lives. While Anansi is mostly human during in this scene, he is shown for a few seconds at a time in his spider form: a colourful, fluorescent, hairy tarantula. Later in the series another scene shows him as a bare-chested man with dreadlocks and multiple little black eyes upon his forehead, in addition to the two on his face.

Throughout the series, the angry monologue is a staple of Anansi's character. His speeches are almost invariably about racial injustice in America and his aim seems to be to incite the characters – especially those of African descent, whether god or human – to war. This iteration of Anansi is a storyteller and his vocation – loaded with the clever suggestion of spider imagery – is tailoring.

Anansi appears in only two of the show's three seasons, and the reason for this is a subject of mild controversy. Orlando Jones, the actor who portrayed Anansi, put out a video on Twitter in 2019 in which he suggested that Anansi was written out of the show because the new season 3 showrunner thought the character's anger and urgency to get things done sent "the wrong message for Black America". Various representatives from the network, the production company and the TV show's communications platforms put out statements declaring that Anansi's absence was simply due to the character not being central to the storyline they were pursuing in season 3.

ANANSI IN FILM

Anansi has also featured in various films since the twentieth century, some of the most notable of which are *Anansi the Spider* (1969), *The Magic of Anansi* (2001) and *Kwaku Ananse* (2013).

Anansi the Spider

Anansi the Spider is a nine-minute animated short film produced and directed by Gerald McDermott, an American filmmaker and creator of children's picture books. The animation is characterized by pattern-filled animation, bold strokes, angular shapes and bright colours. It is narrated by Athmani Magoma.

Anansi the Spider begins in the style of a documentary, providing historical context about Akan Asante people and culture. The main narrative is a story about a time when Anansi fell into trouble and was rescued by his six sons. After this dramatic ordeal, he discovered the moon and determined to give it to one of his sons as a reward. Unable to decide which of them deserved it the most, he surrendered the moon to Nyame, the Akan God, who placed it in the sky so that it would benefit everyone. A written version of the folktale on which this film is based appears in Harold Courlander's 1957 collection, *The Hat-Shaking Dance and other Tales from the Gold Coast*, co-authored by the Ghanaian Albert Kofi Prempeh.

The Magic of Anansi

The Magic of Anansi is a seven-minute animated short film created for the National Film Board of Canada and directed by Jamie Mason. Subtitled 'A Traditional West Indian Tale', it was written by Sugith Varughese, a Canadian actor of Indian birth and heritage, and narrated by Winston Sutton, who colours the script's standard English with his subtle West Indian inflections.

Anansi is depicted as a small, purple creature with eight limbs. His webs, in the beginning, are boxy and ineffective at catching bugs. Nobody respects him, least of all Tiger, who challenges Anansi to bring him Snake in order to gain his respect. Anansi does so, playing in the usual way on the Snake's egotistical desire to prove that he is longer than a stick. However, when Anansi presents the captured Snake, the latter is ridiculed so thoroughly that he bursts into tears. Even though Tiger declares that Anansi has at last earned his respect, Anansi rejects it because it has come at the expense of Snake's feelings. As a reward, Nature grants Anansi the ability to spin beautiful sticky webs that are much more effective at catching bugs.

The screenplay was adapted from Mary Withers' 1993 work, *The Magic of Anansi*. This book itself seems to derive from Jamaican author P.M. Sherlock's 1954 version of the tale that explains how all stories came to be named after Anansi. This film's emphasis on empathy and morality clearly showcases some of the ways in which Anansi has been modified, especially in the Western world, to suit his newer audiences and serve new purposes.

Kwaku Ananse

Ghanaian-American filmmaker Akosua Adoma Owusu's 2013 live-action short film, *Kwaku Ananse*, follows the story of Nyan Koronhwea (as it is spelled in the credits). She is the daughter of Kwaku Ananse who has come back to Ghana from abroad to attend her father's funeral. Owusu, who co-wrote the screenplay, took several creative liberties with Ananse's Ghanaian canon. Nankonwheaa, known to Ghanaians as the one of Ananse's caricature-like sons, characterized by comically long and spindly legs, is portrayed as female. In this film Ntikuma is no longer the first of Anansi's children, but appears instead to be Nyan Koronhwea's younger brother. The narrator tells a version of the story about Ananse and the gourd of wisdom in which it is Nyan Koronhwea, not Ntikuma, who advises Ananse to strap the gourd to his back instead of his stomach.

The film's cast is studded with Ghanaian celebrities, including singer-songwriter Jojo Abot as Nyan Koronwhea and Grace Omaboe, aka Maame Dokono of *By the Fireside* fame, as Ananse's bereaved wife (called Asɔ Yaa in the credits, but referred to as Okonore in the film). Koo Nimo, one of Ghana's most prominent highlife and folk musicians, plays the eponymous Kwaku Ananse and contributes two major songs to the soundtrack, one of which includes vocals by Jojo Abot. Another contributor to the soundtrack is the Ghanaian highlife and Afrobeat musician Ebo Taylor, headliner of the Apagya Showband, with the song 'Kwaku Ananse'.

In this film, Ananse's funeral takes place according to traditional Asante customs, although his coffin is spider-shaped – likely a tribute to the art of 'fantasy coffins' which, in Ghana, is more closely associated with the Ga ethnic group. Fantasy coffins are typically designed to depict the vocation or aspirations of the deceased.

Elements of magic and folklore are woven into Owusu's semi-autobiographical narrative. Overwhelmed by Ananse's funeral, Nyan Koronwhea later seeks an audience with her father in the spirit world, demanding answers for why he decided to hide all the world's wisdom in the gourd that doubles as his musical instrument and for why he lied to her—presumably about having a secret second family in Ghana. Ananse responds that he wished for people to come directly to him if they wanted wisdom and offers to share some of it with her. Ananse hands his gourd to Nyan Koronwhea. She places it into a river, where it seems to multiply into several gourds that are dispersed by the river's current. After this, she is reconciled to her deceased father and the family he left behind in Ghana.

The narrator concludes the story with the Twi equivalent of the statement, "This is how wisdom came into the world", followed by a Twi delivery of the traditional Asante concluding formula included in many of Rattray's stories: "This is my story; whether it is sweet or not, take some away and bring some back".

Ananse in Modern Ghanaian Music

In post-colonial Ghana, Kwaku Ananse has found his way beyond the mboguo of traditional Anansesɛm performances and into studio recorded music. Some of the most notable songs that feature him are 'Kwaku Ananse' (1977) by the Apagya Showband; Koo Nimo's 'Anansi Song Story'; Pure Akan's two-part 'Asɛm A Esii Kɔyɔbɛda' (2021); and Amerado's 'Kwaku Ananse' (2023). Notably each of these songs is performed in Akan language – either Twi or Fante.

They span a range of genres. Koo Nimo and the Apagya Showband take on more traditional folk music forms, translated into the highlife genre and telling Ananse stories in song form. For instance, the Apagya Showband's song has its lead singer, Ebo Taylor, crooning a Fante-language version of the 'tar baby' story, in which Ananse pretends to die and be buried with cooking utensils; he then robs his family's farm every night to feast alone until his son, Kweku Tsin, traps him with a sticky, rubber-covered, wooden doll.

Amerado's song is a typical Ghanaian Afro-pop song. The Twi lyrics are largely personal and only reference Ananse for comparison's sake. The singer explains that, like the folkloric character, no matter what he does – speak, remain silent or even sleep – people always seem to find a story to tell about him.

Contemporary Ghanaian musician Pure Akan's two-track song 'Asɛm A Esii Kɔyɔbɛda' is particularly noteworthy because of how closely it adheres to the conventions of Anansesɛm and Anansegoro. The song employs aspects of audio theatre to replicate the atmosphere of a village storytelling session. Like all of Pure Akan's songs, it is delivered entirely in Twi. The singer plays the role of a storyteller named Kwa Appiah – derived from Pure Akan's legal name – and what sounds like a cast of children plays the role of his fireside audience. The song begins with a traditional call and response between storyteller and audience, amid local drums and percussion instruments. Throughout Kwa Appiah's storytelling, the children offer the classic interjections, commentary and mboguo. Pure Akan himself delivers an Ananse story over an Afro hip-hop beat in rhythmic rap, except in the transitions between parts one and two, perhaps to increase suspense, and, at the very end, to conclude and deliver the moral.

The tale itself concerns Kwaku Ananse's struggles to reap the benefits of his own hunting traps and attain justice when it turns out that the Leopard, Ɔsebɔ, has been stealing his meat all along. The village elders are unable to help him without a witness and the Leopard himself denies all accusations. Ananse therefore resorts to his cunning ways to trap the Leopard in a hole and shame him before the entire village. In this story, he succeeds. The concluding moral delivered to the children in Twi comes down to the following: *If something is not yours and you go ahead and take it, it won't end well for you. You will be shamed the same way the Leopard was shamed by Kwaku Ananse.*

Pure Akan features in Ghanaian filmmaker Eric Gyamfi's 2023 film, *Certain Winds from the South*, delivering a performance of the same story in a quiet village at night, without instruments or audience, speaking directly to the camera.

Ananse's Wealth: The Spider in Politics

In the foreword to Efua T. Sutherland's 1975 play *The Marriage of Anansewa*, the author emphasizes one of the common interjections that audiences shout out during Anansesɛm performances: 'Ananse's wealth!' She explains that the expression refers to successes and triumphs which are unlikely to last. Another likely connotation of 'Ananse's wealth' is wealth acquired through immoral means, in keeping with Ananse's character. Two of the most notable political personalities who have been associated with the character's name in this way are John Ackah Blay-Miezah and Edward Seaga.

Anansi's Gold

Ghanaian-British author Yepoka Yeebo's 2023 non-fiction book, *Anansi's Gold: The Man Who Looted the West, Outfoxed Washington, and Swindled the World*, is a deep dive into the life of John Ackah Blay-Miezah, a twentieth-century Ghanaian con artist. The portrait Yeebo paints of Blay-Miezah is remarkably similar to Ananse's – a series of very slight name changes with titles acquired and dropped along the way; a presence established across various countries and continents; real or reported associations with some of the most powerful members of society; the manipulation of numerous authority figures; the acquisition of obscene amounts of sometimes fleeting wealth; a strategy that made him too slippery to pin down or prosecute for long; a tongue smooth enough and a personality charming enough to get him out of most types of trouble; and the type of ambiguous personality that made as many people willing to entrust him with vast amounts of their wealth as to push for him to be put permanently behind bars. The primary con that Blay-Miezah ran for most of his life was a version of the following story: that Kwame Nkrumah, Ghana's first president, had hidden millions of dollars in cash and gold in Switzerland, and that if people would only invest through Blay-Miezah, they would reap incredible returns. This grand lie financed Blay-Miezah's lifestyle in one way or another until his death.

Yeebo described Anansi as a person who wielded the power of stories so well that they changed the world, altering people's perceptions of reality until they aligned with his own. She summarizes the link between Blay-Miezah and Anansi thus: "John Ackah Blay-Miezah was Anansi. His story of Nkrumah's secret fortune rewrote Ghana's history and made him fabulously rich. Then it destroyed him. But the story outlived Blay-Miezah. Decades after his death, people are still telling his story and are still hunting for Nkrumah's gold."

The Anansi Politician

Zobel Marshall wrote that author and researcher Laurie Gunst painted Edward Seaga, the fifth Prime Minister of Jamaica, as "the Anansi politician, stopping at nothing to achieve his aims". In 2003 Seaga gave an address in Oxford on the impact of folk culture on Jamaican identity, explaining how people at the bottom of the social chain in Jamaica were the ones who needed to resort to 'Anansi tactics' in order to 'carve a space for themselves'. Zobel Marshall explains that, interestingly, Gunst used the same expression against Seaga, stating that 'he came home to Jamaica to carve a place for himself'. She accused Seaga of abusing his position as Minister of Welfare and Development, with which the Jamaicans who nicknamed him the 'Minister of Warfare and Devilment' probably agreed. Gunst and other parties within the media publicly held him responsible for so much political turmoil and controversy that Seaga sued for libel. However, in 2003 an out-of-court settlement worth several million dollars was ruled in Seaga's favour (Zobel Marshall, 2012).

ANANSI IN EDUCATION

Between Africa, the Caribbean and the Western world, Anansi has been incorporated into educational systems since the twentieth century. This has not come without its complications and controversies, especially in Jamaica, some of which will be explored in this section.

Integrating Anansi

In the Caribbean the decisions to incorporate Anansi into the educational system were coloured by the desire to maintain British standards in the classroom, especially pre-independence. Zobel Marshall explains that this involved making several adjustments to Anansi's character and stories. For one thing, the content had to be made suitable for a younger audience, so that it was no longer as vulgar or violent as the folk canon. For another, the stories for use in schools were all written in standard English, as the colonial government aspired to eradicate the use of Caribbean Creole dialects in the classroom. Anansi's main functions in this era were the promotion of children's literacy and of Christian moral values. No longer could he be a crass, incorrigible rogue. He became a rascal who repented, changed his ways and was duly punished for his crimes. For example, Trinidadian writer Al Ramsawack published a version of the bowl and whip story for educational purposes, recounted by Zobel Marshall in *Anansi's Journey*, in which Anansi stops the whip before it can cause serious damage to his family members, then promises to change. This is in stark contrast to Rattray's Akan version of the tale, in which Ananse gleefully eggs the whip on to flog his family until the story ends.

Zobel Marshall also writes that Anansi was also used as an educational tool in Britain. Newman and Sherlock's 1936 collection, *Annancy Stories*, was incorporated into the Beacon Library primary school education programme. Besides being written in Standard English so that British children could understand it, the book was also illustrated by Rhoda Jackson, whose depiction of Anansi quite resembled the infamous golliwog doll.

Anansi has been incorporated into West African educational systems as well, especially following the waves of independence around the 1960s. In Ghana Peggy Appiah, author of several Anansi stories, published a series of Asante-inspired folktales specifically designed to help Ghanaian children learn English. Many of her works were assigned in primary and secondary schools in various West African countries. Efua T. Sutherland's 1975 play, *The Marriage of Anansewa*, has been a seminal text for years. So has Yaw Asare's 2006 play, *Ananse in the Land of Idiots*, at some point been made a mandatory text in Core Literature by the West African Examinations Council.

Anansi's Journey tells of how, in the 1970s, Rastafarian author Dennis Forsythe developed a sociology course for the University of the West Indies' Mona Campus in Kingston, Jamaica. The course centred on his largely negative concept of Anancyism. For Forsythe, Anancyism was the social phenomenon that had turned Jamaicans into immoral hustlers and capitalists. However, Forsythe's course was dropped and his contract terminated following strong challenges from his faculty colleagues.

Anansi's Impact as a Pedagogical Tool

While Anansi might be as effective a character as any to promote literacy, the attempts to sanitize his character and stories through educational texts seem to be largely ineffective. Zobel Marshall wrote that even through textbooks, "children could still identify with [Anansi's] anti-authoritarian energy, humour and scampish behaviour". She also documented how, between 1930 and 1931, Jamaican newspapers advertised a nationwide story writing competition. Responses to this advertisement eventually led to a collection of 5,000 Anansi stories written by Jamaican schoolchildren aged 7 to 14, compiled by Reverend Joseph Williams. The stories, some original and others retold, were far from the 'textbook-suitable' versions. They included murder, violence, innocent people coming to ruin, thievery, disrespect for familial authority figures and the stealing of 'Buckra's' property. Furthermore, most of them were written not in standard English but in Jamaican patois.

A 2009 psychology thesis by past University of Ghana Masters student Jonathan Kuma Gavi involved a study of children's comprehension of the moral themes in Kwaku Ananse stories with respect to cheating behaviour. Gavi's conclusion was that teaching children moral behaviour by telling them what society abhors is not feasible. Children, he explained, process moral stories differently from adults. Their interpretations of the text are based on their prior knowledge, and the nature of their lived experience – societal corruption, broken promises from their own parents and so on – feed into their perceptions of the text. Gavi's thesis suggested that Ghanaian children were likely seeing Kwaku Ananse act as they had seen real adults act. They did not therefore have enough reason to think of him as an antisocial character who should not be emulated, despite the shame he sometimes faced as a consequence for his actions.

Calls to Ban Anansi

Zobel Marshall notes that by the turn of the twenty-first century Jamaica had spent decades locked in political turmoil. An intense rivalry, mainly between the Jamaica Labour Party and the People's National Party, involved corruption, gun violence, illegal drug trades and gang activity. *Anansi's Journey* describes in detail the contention surrounding Anansi's perceived role in the formative parts of young Jamaicans' lives. Many people felt that Anansi served as inspiration for Jamaican gangsters and criminals, among them Laurie Gunst, who considered gangsters to be the most sinister expressions of Anansi. There were some who felt that such behaviour was indirectly encouraged from an early age. The term 'Anansi syndrome' was used to refer to trickery and unethical behaviour, especially if exhibited by children. It seemed that even teachers were not convinced that the attempts to alter Anansi for the classroom could eclipse the ideas that he represented: 'ginnalship' or cheating, and the arts of outsmarting people. For reasons such as these, the Jamaican educator Pauline Bain called for a ban on Anansi as a folk hero during a Jamaica Teachers Association conference in March 2001.

Zobel Marshall explains how the call to ban Anansi sparked a raging debate, partially documented in various degrees within Jamaica's national newspaper, *The Gleaner*. Several readers opined that Anansi represented a decline in education and societal values. The psychiatrist E. Anthony Allen even argued that Anansi was being manipulated, to the extent that he no longer taught lessons such as the weak's triumph over the strong, but was now used to show how individuals might acquire for themselves what they desired, at any cost. Others agreed that regardless of the purposes Anansi served in the past, he had now been thoroughly transformed into a character who represented only fraud, lies, selfishness and materialism. Dr Ralph Thompson, a contributor to *The Gleaner*, suggested replacing him with characters such as Pinocchio (Zobel Marshall, 2012).

Other citizens argued vehemently against the calls to ban Anansi, with at least one reader of the *Gleaner* threatening to mount the 'mother of all demonstrations' if people did not leave Anansi alone. In 2003 Edward Seaga, the former Jamaican Prime Minister, explained that the people looking to ban Anansi were part of the privileged classes and not the lower classes, who generally did not have access to formal education.

Zobel Marshall concludes by stating that Anansi stories in Jamaica are no longer used in literacy programmes. However, teachers are free to tell them to students if they wish. Students also continue to use Anansi as part of poetry, music and drama performances, and continue to submit Anansi stories to annual competitions organized by the Jamaica Cultural Development Commission.

Copyright in Ghana: Who Owns Ananse?

Since 1985 in Ghana, Ananse has been removed from the public domain. He, along with every other aspect of Ghanaian folklore, is protected under copyright laws – a matter of concern and contention for many.

Ananse and Ghanaian folklore were first brought under copyright protection in a 1985 Act, later replaced by a similar Act in 2005. One feature they both had in common was that they protected folklore in perpetuity, rather than for a limited period of time. In 2018, an article titled 'Who owns Ananse? The tangled web of folklore and copyright in Ghana' was published in the *Journal of African Cultural Studies*. Its author, Stephen Collins, writes that these laws made Ghana the only country in West Africa to codify the prohibition of its own citizens' use of folklore – even if adapted or in derivative forms – for commercial purposes, unless they had explicit permission and made requisite payment. However, Ghana is not totally anomalous; in other countries where folklore is protected by copyright, those laws also extend into perpetuity. As it stands, the Ghana National Folklore Board requires anyone who intends to use folklore for commercial purposes to register intent and to pay to them "a fee that the Board may determine".

Stephen Collins also states that the newer Act 'has far more potential to prevent Ghanaian artists from engaging with their folklore' than its predecessor. For one thing, while the older Act protected 'works of folklore', the newer one protects 'expressions of folklore', whether 'literary', 'artistic' or 'scientific'. While the older Act protected against the sale of Ghanaian folklore-based works made outside of Ghana and imported into the country, the newer one applies to works made both inside and outside Ghana. The older law declared Ghanaian folklore to belong to the Republic of Ghana, while the newer one ascribes the rights to the President of Ghana on behalf of the Republic. Furthermore, while the older Act used the past tense – 'were created' – suggesting reference only to folkloric works considered part of antiquity, the new Act uses the present tense – 'are created' – suggesting that the law applies to works that are still being created and those that will be created in the future, as long as the law remains effective. Collins speculates that Ghanaian artists, if discouraged from drawing on their own folklore by the financial barrier of this Act, would resort to drawing inspiration from elsewhere. The fact that the fee is undisclosed by the Board poses another hurdle, making it difficult to prepare for adequately.

Collins expressed an understanding that the Ghanaian government would want to protect against the unregulated exploitation of folklore, especially in the digital age when exploitation would be easier than ever. Nevertheless, he insisted that whichever measures are put in place ought not to stifle Ghana's potential to develop its folklore by expanding traditions such as Anansegoro.

Gertrude Torkornoo, the 15th Chief Justice of Ghana, had an article published in 2012 in the *Annual Survey of International & Comparative Law* entitled 'Creating Capital from Culture – Rethinking the Provisions on Expressions of Folklore in Ghana's Copyright Law'. In this article she uses the words 'unacceptable' and 'imbalance' to describe the situation that prohibits Ghanaian citizens from using Ananse in the same ways as he is being used in numerous works of art created and distributed outside Ghana. Her perspective lines up with Stephen Collins' words about how the Act implies that "the only people in the world who are not permitted to write about Ananse without permission are Ghanaians writing for a Ghanaian audience".

Although no artists have yet been prosecuted under this act, the fact that it exists continues to leave the possibility open.

Torkornoo insists that, "If the current law is to act as a tool for development, it is important that it is reviewed and amended, because as is, the law disincentives [*sic*] development."

ANANSI AS A SYMBOL

Anansi and his stories represent so many things to so many people based on their background, generation, culture, religion and more. Naturally, such an ambiguous character would engender starkly polarizing and complex opinions. This section explores a few of them.

Some Caribbean Perspectives

Zobel Marshall documented what Anansi means to different people in *Anansi's Journey* from Caribbean perspectives. Included here are some of them.

For Barbadian poet and academic Kamau Brathwaite, the Anansi story is a nearly perfect example of the type of improvisation that jazz music relies on. The structure of the stories, in his opinion, with their thematic repetitions and rhythms, creates the literary equivalent of a melody.

Guyanese writer Wilson Harris interpreted Anansi as a figure who represents a link between the old and new worlds of Black culture, from Africa to the nations across the Atlantic. For him Anansi does not represent a total recall of the past, but is used in a way that symbolizes renewal and rebirth. Similarly the Jamaican professor and composer Barry Chevannes positioned Anansi at a cultural crossroads, a liminal space. He echoed Robert D. Pelton in his interpretation of Anansi as a character who, through disorder, creates order. Chevannes also spoke of Anansi as someone who represents such ambiguity that it causes significant tension when people try to categorize him.

Dr Joyce Jonas, former lecturer at the University of Guyana, understood Anansi as the antithesis of the plantation owners' Great Houses, the representation of everything the colonial establishment rejects as 'folk'.

Some older Jamaicans, within the last 20 years, have said that Anansi now represents the negative characteristics exhibited by younger generations, including individualism, greed and lack of respect for others. Like them, Dennis Forsythe, the Jamaican author of *Rastafari: Healing of the Nation*, understood Anansi as a wholly negative figure. For him the concept of Jamaica as Babylon is represented by Anansi, the 'Babylonian spider', pitted against the righteous Lion of Judah. Forsythe referred to the CIA in Jamaica as 'the leading Anancy' (Zobel Marshall, 2012).

Jamaican writer Barbara Gloudon saw Anansi through religious imagery as symbolic of the human condition – the simultaneous state of having fallen from grace as well as the continuous redemption from that state. Reverend Daley from Webster Memorial Church in Kingston also used religious terminology to interpret Anansi as the "errant child who is forgiven" and whose stories carry themes of sin and redemption. Chevannes, however, cautioned against viewing Anansi according to a Christian framework on the basis that most Jamaicans do not view Anansi as sinful; instead they generally believe that whoever Anansi takes advantage of deserves it. In a slightly similar vein, the Jamaican author P.M. Sherlock insisted that to focus on Anansi's morality was to miss the point of his stories. He was, in Sherlock's opinion, meant to be used as a satirical weapon through which the storyteller took revenge on those who had wronged them, not necessarily for the sake of moral instruction (Zobel Marshall, 2012).

Zobel Marshall explains that Jamaican storytellers Velma Pollard and Louise Bennett shared the opinions that the value of Anansi was to teach his audience how to avoid being tricked, to show how people could be hurt if they allowed themselves to be vulnerable and to illustrate how they could come to ruin if they were greedy, thoughtless or stupid. Marshall paraphrased this idea as follows: "The message is: use your intelligence like Anansi, because if you are stupid, an Anansi will expose your weaknesses."

Some Ghanaian Perspectives

Ghanaian playwright Efua T. Sutherland wrote of the character, "Ananse appears to represent a kind of Everyman, artistically exaggerated and distorted to serve society as a medium for self-examination." She also described Ananse as an artistic tool by which society could criticize itself, as indicated by the popular expression 'Exterminate Ananse, and society will be ruined'. A version of this appeared in one of R.S. Rattray's *Akan-Ashanti Folk-Tales* stories.

In 2022 the National Museum of Ghana was re-opened after being closed for renovation for a number of years. The new design is based on the theme of 'Unity in Diversity', to which effect the entire ceiling of the small museum is taken up by a three-dimensional spider web; in the middle of this is a huge, black, 3-D model of a spider. Hanging from the large spider is a much smaller model of the same figure. The plaque near the entrance to the museum exhibition suggests that Ananse, a creature of wisdom and wit, symbolizes the diversity of the various cultures that have come together to form the Ghanaian people. It further suggests a parallel relationship between Anansesɛm and "the common story that is Ghana". Beyond this, however, there are no other artefacts, installations or further references to Ananse, his history or his significance. Nor does there seem to be any critical engagement with the paradox of how Ananse – a predominantly Akan character – represents the diverse collection of ethnic groups that make up Ghana's citizenry, many of whom are not Akan.

At the same time Ananse's ubiquity across Ghanaian ethnic groups today is difficult to dispute. Even in Accra, Ghana's capital city and the historical capital of the Ga ethnic group, Ananse reigns over Ghanaian folklore. Nana-Ama Danquah, a Ghanaian author and the editor of *Accra Noir*, an anthology published in 2020, wrote in the book's introduction: "There is one name that every child in Accra who is able to walk and talk definitely knows – Kwaku Ananse. He is the closest thing we have to a mascot or a superhero".

KEEPING ANANSI ALIVE

A widely held sentiment is that Anansi stories, especially among the twenty-first-century youth, are no longer as popular as they were in the past. And yet, others argue, even if the old stories are not regularly retold, young people carry on his legacy in other aspects of ever-evolving Black culture. For example, as Zobel Marshall notes, Anansi-inspired proverbs continue to be widely used in Jamaica, including patois forms of the expressions 'Play the fool to catch the wise', 'Cunning is better than strength' and 'If there's trouble in the bush, Anansi will bring it into the house'. Zobel Marshall references Jamaican writer Velma Pollard, who pointed out that, even if younger Jamaicans no longer tell Anansi stories in their entirety, they quote from them in the DJ booth between popular dancehall tunes.

The more recent contributions of artists such as Pure Akan and Amerado in music, Akosua Adoma Owusu and Eric Gyamfi in film and Anansi's popularity in the *American Gods* TV show, not to mention the books that continue to spread the character's tales, suggest that Anansi, in his many iterations, will continue to infiltrate newer art forms in creative ways through the changing tides of culture within and outside the African continent.

Modern Short Stories of Anansi

How the Orb-weaver Learned to Carry Stories

Ian Ableson

When Trickster Anansi first won ownership of all the world's stories from Nyame the Sky-God, the world was small, and the task was manageable. Stories were then a sacred thing; each told with reverence, each passed down from one generation to the next in song and speech by well-practiced tongues. New stories emerged constantly, tweaked and refined by successive tellers, and when this happened Anansi would go and collect the story, as was his duty. And it was an important task, for a tale that was not collected by him was just a series of words without a soul, and it would soon lose its vitality, peter into nothingness, and be forgotten by the world at large. But Anansi was diligent in his duty, and he could easily handle new stories at the pace at which they emerged. So it was that all the stories in the world were called Spider Stories, and Anansi knew them as well as he knew his own eight legs.

But time went on, and the human world grew large and varied, and the ways of storytelling changed. No longer was it only the realm of oral storytellers, experienced faces illuminated by the soft glow that came from mixing the burning warmth of campfires with the cold light of the stars. Now stories were written on vellum parchment and papyrus made from sedges and paper made from hemp. Anansi adapted to this easily. Sure, there were more stories now, but those who could write were few, and the process of penning a story with ink made from ground lampblack was laborious. Anansi had no trouble keeping up with written stories, and sometimes he marveled that humans bothered to write at all. Then humans developed new technologies for writing, and suddenly stories came quickly. Anansi adapted to this as well, but it still surprised him. Then such technology became widely accessible; in a few short years many people owned a machine capable of writing a story, and then Anansi began to worry. And just when he'd gotten used to mechanical writing, stories changed again. They were developed and filmed by entire teams of people working together, preserved on screens and shown to millions, visuals solidified in a way that had never been done before, and this was the first time Anansi stumbled. When he'd first taken ownership of the stories from Nyame Sky-God, they'd been told differently every time. The speaker, the listeners, the season, the time of day, the thousands of possible interruptions and variabilities that came with life in the world – all of these made for a story that changed thousands of times. To have a story preserved in a single format, told the same way, at the same pace, with the same people doing the telling and very little left to the imagination of the listener – this was difficult for Anansi to accept. But once more he adapted, and he thought that surely, surely this was the final way that stories could change.

Anansi had been wrong other times in his many centuries of life, but when he thought back later, he acknowledged that he may never have been quite as wrong as that.

HOW THE ORB-WEAVER LEARNED TO CARRY STORIES

Comic books. Manga. Video games. Wrestling – wrestling! A *sport*! Web videos, tabletop roleplaying games, web comics, tabloids, podcasts… Fanfiction alone nearly sent Anansi into a nervous breakdown. The modern world burst at the seams with stories, and Anansi had come to his wits' end.

Now, Anansi was proud of his ownership over the Spider Stories, and for many years he stubbornly toiled on, powering through the exhaustion that dragged at his limbs like anchors dragging through a reef. But one day, mind blurred by years of fatigue, he reached a level of desperation that led him to approach Nyame Sky-God.

"Nyame," said Anansi with a congenial smile, "long ago I bought the world's stories from you. You set before me four tasks that you thought to be impossible – for it has been a long time now, and I hope we can speak of these things with candor – and said I may take ownership of the world's stories should I complete them. Well, I brought you vain Onini, the python, and captured the gullible Mboro Hornets, and I trapped Osebo the leopard, and I tricked Mmotia the Fairy. You were true to your word, Nyame, and for that I am forever thankful, and I was able to afford the stories. However, I have been giving it much thought in recent years, and I believe that I have not been fair. The modern world is rich in tales and songs; it would be the epitome of selfishness for me to claim them all for myself. I would like to offer you the opportunity to buy some of the stories back from me, so that we might enjoy the thrill of ownership together. I can assure you that my asking price will not be as hefty as yours."

Nyame Sky-God may not have been as clever as Anansi, but he was no fool. He could see the tiredness sunken into Anansi's eight eyes, and the strain dragging at his eight legs, and he laughed. "You come to me bearing a plate of thorns disguised as honey and cream. I think the burden of ownership has become too much for you to bear. I will offer you a different deal, clever Anansi – you may give the world's stories back to me, their rightful owner in the first place, and they will be Sky Stories rather than Spider Stories, and you may slink home and occupy yourself with the rest of the world."

This made Anansi furious, and he stormed off without another word. To surrender all the world's stories back to Nyame would be a harsh blow to his pride. It was not his way to give up so easily, and he began to think about how he might trick Nyame into taking back some – some, but most certainly not all – of the stories. So focused was he on his schemes that he did not notice the little orb-weaver spider that trailed behind him.

"Clever Anansi!" she called, and although the little orb-weaver had to call him several times, so engrossed was he in his plan-making, eventually he heard her and stopped. "I overheard your conversation with Nyame Sky-God. Please, do not give the stories back to him. All the world's arachnids are proud that you are the owner of the world's tales. Let us help you ease your burden! Show me how to collect stories, and I will teach my cousins, and they may remain Spider Stories."

"Oh?" scoffed Anansi. "And how would you propose to do such a thing, little one? Do you understand what it is, to own the world's stories? Only when I have collected a tale, only when

I have taken it apart and balanced its pieces on my body, can it become a true story, and from there another vehicle by which the living come to understand the universe. Without proper care, it will fall apart, fade into the cracks and be devoured by time's uncaring maw, and then become nothing but words. Each one of my eight legs play a vital role in the collection process.

"On my first leg ride the characters. Many of them are human – people, it seems, love telling stories about themselves – but I have carried animals and aliens, all manner of beings magical and mundane, even fellow gods. Even myself. They are the drivers of the story, and rightfully take the first spot.

My second leg is reserved for the setting. Soot-swept alleys, glistening biotech skyscrapers of metal and glass, alien obsidian deserts, towering forests that smell of pine tar and crisp winter air – every time, every place, forever. All these and more have my second leg carried.

My third leg is the place for the 'happenings'. Have you carried a reunion of star-crossed lovers on one leg, little orb-weaver? No? What about the hypocritical declaration of a world-weary king? A mysterious kidnapping? A passionless genocide? My third leg is a place where the deepest love and the darkest recesses of human hearts sit peaceably together.

On my fourth leg I take the word choice. Does the storyteller weave together music and rhythm, in the manner of griots and bards? Are their words plucked from the deep knowledge of their people, each one carefully selected and slotted into place? Or are they blunt, forceful, passionate, accessible? Without the fourth leg, there is no way to know.

My fifth leg carries the dialogue. Declarations of love in tongues long dead, curses spat with rage and longing alike, promises kept only to be broken at a later time. Do you know how many languages have ever existed, little orb-weaver? I do.

On my sixth leg, I hold the silences. The space between words, the breath before a plunge, the pauses that allow time for comprehension. The burden is light on my sixth leg, but it is no less important. Often the absence of words is just as essential in the telling of a tale.

On my seventh leg, I hold the 'purpose'. There are many of these – stories entertain, yes, but they can also inform, or serve as warning, or offer a new perspective. They can make sense of the nonsensical and realign the universe in the hearts of the listeners. Every story has a purpose, even if the storyteller themselves might struggle to tell you what it is."

But before Anansi could give the little orb-weaver instructions about the eighth and final leg, he hesitated. This wasn't right, he thought. For so many years I alone have known the secret of owning stories – apart from Nyame the Sky-God – and here I am, relinquishing my secrets to the first spider who asked. Perhaps I should hold something back, Anansi thought. Perhaps some secrets are meant to be kept. And so, Anansi lied.

"On the eighth leg I must carry the final piece of the story – the words 'The End'. This is crucial, for otherwise the story won't know when to stop, and it will leak out into the world. It may even leak into other stories, infecting them with its own purpose. Forgetting this last leg is disastrous, for otherwise how will the stories remain separate from each other? After loading all of these onto my body, I lash the story together with my webbing and carry it home, where it may be catalogued. Only then is the story owned. Only then is it truly *alive*."

Upon hearing Anasi's passion, the little orb-weaver acquiesced, and she agreed that she would make no attempt to help. But she was more like Anansi than she seemed, and once she thought she was out of range of his hearing she quietly said to herself, "I have eight legs, just as you do, Anansi, and now you've told me how to carry a tale. I will help you whether you wish it or not."

But Anansi was clever, and he had known many beings like her in his long years, and he did not need to hear the little orb-weaver say these words to know that she would try. With a sigh, he left her alone, and went to see Aso, his wife. If he was to trick Nyame into taking on the burden of owning some of the world's stories, he would need her advice.

* * *

After giving it some thought, the little orb-weaver decided that a child's story would be best for her first attempt. While it would be thrilling to impress Anansi by collecting some culturally significant tale masterfully woven together by an expert storyteller, the little orb-weaver acknowledged that she should start small.

It did not take her long to find a suitable child, for children are always telling stories. This one had written his on lined paper, with nothing but a well-loved pencil and simple and occasionally misspelled words. It was perfect for practice and the little orb-weaver eagerly approached the paper when the boy was called by his mother for lunch.

Remembering Anansi's words, with her first leg she gathered the characters. There were not many of them – a black cat, an orange cat, and a cream-colored dog. She examined each one of them in turn, flipping them this way and that, making sure to gather all of their beings onto her first leg. When she was satisfied that they were all balanced and resting comfortably, she turned her attention to her second leg.

The setting of the story was just as simple as the characters. A small clearing within a forest, very close to the young boy's house, where he sometimes played with his friends. Carefully the orb-weaver collected dappled sunlight, a quiet creek weaving through banks thick with riparian vegetation, and several flat stumps, scars of historical logging. She gathered all of this, even though the boy had called it only 'The Woods', and arranged it upon her second leg. Now the orb-weaver was gaining some confidence – this was easy! Far easier than Anansi had made it seem. She would gather this story, and she would take it to Anansi, and he would see that she could be trusted to help him.

Next came the 'happenings' within the story. Here, for the first time, the little orb-weaver hesitated. The story, written on a single piece of lined paper, did not have much in the way of 'happenings'. The two cats and one dog were in the clearing in the woods, and they meowed and barked in the manner of their species, but they did not appear to do much else. After some time spent hemming and hawing, the little orb-weaver picked up the very first sentence in the story, about how they'd all met in the woods, and also the black cat jumping onto a stump and the dog chasing its tail. Her third leg felt much lighter than the other two, but she supposed there was nothing for it.

Fourth was word choice. Another blessedly simple task, as the child's words were short and unsophisticated. The orb-weaver awkwardly balanced shaky handwriting and one-or two-syllable words on her fourth leg, and that was that.

After word choice came dialogue. Here, the orb-weaver found to her relief that the choice was clear, as the child had placed quotation marks around the words "meow" and "bark" several times. She balanced all five of these instances on her fifth leg. She was beginning to feel the weight of the story now, but she was confident in her ability to finish the task at hand.

Then came the silences. Because the story was simple, the silences were placed more for comprehension than for any deeper purpose, and the orb-weaver had no problem gathering the little things onto her sixth leg.

The 'purpose' – this was difficult. The little orb-weaver squinted at the story this way and that, but try as she might she could not determine its purpose. She was getting antsy, skittering back and forth across the lined paper, worried that the boy would soon return from lunch. In the end, she decided that the purpose of the story was to explore the inner lives of animals, perhaps even ones that the little boy knew personally. The 'purpose' balanced awkwardly on her seventh leg, and it seemed almost right, but perhaps not quite. She moved along, a little less sure of herself.

The boy had written the words "The End" at the bottom of the page, and the orb-weaver retrieved them with her eighth leg, careful not to let any of the other pieces of the story fall in the process. For a moment, she thought she had done it, and she nearly celebrated. But something was wrong. She knew that what she had was not a story. It was the pieces of a story, yes, but it was not right. It did not feel like the stories that Anansi owned, brimming with vitality; it was as though she'd tried to construct a body from its parts, and had nothing to show for it but a stitched-together mess. Quietly, the orb-weaver despaired.

* * *

Meanwhile, Anansi had not found the kind of advice he had hoped for.

When Anansi finished telling her about the events of the day, his wife, long-suffering Aso, scolded him for his treatment of the orb-weaver. "Anansi, you say the burden of stories has come to be too much for you. And yet, when help is offered, you would rather rely on your tricks than accept it? You may have eight eyes, my husband, but sometimes you cannot see the answer dancing before them. I will not help you deceive Nyame Sky-God, not until you reconsider the orb-weaver's offer."

And Anansi grumbled, but he was reprimanded, and when he thought for a while, he understood his wife's reasoning. With some reluctance, he left his home to track down the orb-weaver.

And so it was unknown to the little spider that Anansi had found her, and he had watched her efforts from the shadows. He watched the orb-weaver shake and struggle to lash together the words on her back with her webbing, pieces of the story shifting out of place. He saw the care with which she had gathered the pieces of the story, and Anansi felt a deep shame at his deception. He emerged from the shadows.

The orb-weaver cried out in remorse, both at her inability to carry the story properly and at the way she had gone behind Anansi's back. "Clever Anansi! I am sorry to have doubted you. You are right – even this simple child's story has proven too much for me. I have been arrogant. Collecting stories is a task reserved for those much greater than I."

Anansi sighed. "You call me Clever Anansi, little orb-weaver, and it is true that is how I am named. But I am also Old Anansi now, and perhaps sometimes I am Anansi Who Is Reluctant to Change with the World. But I will fix that now. What I told you about the eighth leg was only partially true. First the part that was true – stories do leak into the world. But there is nothing that you, or I, or anyone, can do about it. The webs we weave are nothing compared to those the world has woven. Stories twine together like the strings that comprise a rope, and when they separate again they take pieces of each other with them. So it is, and so it has always been, that every tale is influenced by those that come before it, and it will influence many that come after. Second, the part that was a lie – you don't need to carry the words 'The End' on your eighth leg. A story knows when to end; it can manage this without any help from us.

"On your eighth leg, you must carry the soul of the story. Every story has a soul, carved out of the heart of the teller, then twisted and unmade and remolded by the emotions of the listener.

Without its soul, a story is just a collection of words. Come, little orb-weaver. Let us carry your story properly."

Then Anansi reached forward over the little boy's paper, and with the clawed foot at the end of his eighth leg he carefully extracted the story's soul. It was a bright, shimmering thing of silver and blue, fresh and young, innocent in its view of the world. Gingerly, Anansi placed the story's soul on the orb-weaver's eighth leg. The effect was immediate; the soul bound together all the other pieces of the story, solidifying them on the orb-weaver's back. And with its soul in place, the orb-weaver stood by in wonder as the 'purpose' on her seventh leg realigned. For this was not just a story about understanding the world – it was a story written by a little boy who desperately wished to have pets, and who thought that maybe if he could write a story about animals getting along and having fun, his parents might let him keep one of his cousin's newborn kittens.

And Anansi smiled at her. "You are no longer just a little orb-weaver. You are now a carrier of stories, and my messenger." And even as the orb-weaver rapturously thanked Anansi, the trickster was glad, for the ability to share his burden lifted a weight off all eight of his shoulders. He thought for a moment. "Tell me, Messenger of Anansi... How many cousins do you have?"

* * *

And that is why the webs of orb-weavers are among the most beautiful and delicate, for each one is woven by a spider inspired by one of the world's tales. They are common in yards, in

HOW THE ORB-WEAVER LEARNED TO CARRY STORIES

parks, in gardens, anywhere that humans may gather. If you see orb-weavers out in these spaces, leave them be, for they are messengers of Anansi, and they are collecting Spider Stories. And remember, dear reader, and remember well, that the Trickster Anansi has now relieved much of his burden, and he has time to turn his attention to other matters, and he is always curious about the ways of humanity...

THE END
(Though it is unnecessary to say so.)

The Secrets of Jamestown Lighthouse

Benjamin Cyril Arthur

Once upon a time, when the earth was still a mere empty space, Nyame, the supreme being, created a son. He shaped his son's destiny with his mastery and made him highly intelligent. He infused his son with his divine essence, giving him a mind of his own that would eventually water its greed for more than he was given. This son, a new creation, would bridge the gap between God and humans through his divinatory and oracular wisdom.

In some years to come when the first human was created, the human would worship him and call him Agya Ananse (Father Ananse).

* * *

The beam from the old lighthouse cut through the inky night like a knife, casting an eerie glow over the sea. Standing at the base of the towering structure, Selorm squinted down at the tattered map clutched in his hands. He was a sixteen-year-old boy, with curious brown eyes, and an unquenching thirst for adventure. He turned the map upside down and stared at it quietly.

"We're here," he announced. "We've finally found Kwaku Ananse's lair."

"A-are you sure about this?" Akosua's voice wavered beside him. "The festival is about to begin for crying out loud. Grandma needs our help at the shrine."

Gunshots and loud cheers suddenly filled the night sky. The Homowo festivities had begun. The ban on loud noise had just been lifted. Grandma was going to be pissed when they returned home.

Selorm exchanged a look with his boyfriend Kwame, who was peering intently over his shoulder at the map. A steely glint shining in his eyes. He turned to his cousin Akosua. "You want to return after everything we've been through to find this place? Not a chance!"

"Selorm, this is the one place grandma had warned us to never visit. Remember when she told us the story of her twin sister who went into the lighthouse and never came out."

"Yes," Selorm replied. "But have you thought that maybe she lied to us to get us to stay put and not wander around?"

Akosua sighed. She knew how stubborn her cousin Selorm was, but this was dangerous. She could feel it. She turned to Kwame but Kwame looked away, silently agreeing with Selorm.

They had found the tattered brown map in their grandmother's belongings, with the words 'Kwaku Ananse' written in bold red letters. They had followed the ancient map's clues for months, through dense forests, old forts, even crocodile-infested rivers. They had to be close.

"Something just doesn't feel right," Akosua continued.

MYTHS, GODS & IMMORTALS: ANANSI

"Or you're just scared," Selorm replied.

"You can go home if you want to," Kwame added and Akosua chuckled. "If I go home, who's going to make sure you don't kill yourselves?" She took the map from Selorm and stared at it. "And you're sure this is the exact location?"

"Yes," Selorm replied.

Akosua pulled her blue sweater tighter as she eyed the ominous darkness pooling in the doorway. "I don't like this. What if he tries to trap us or worse, steal our wisdom?" Her voice had become barely more than a whisper.

"What wisdom?" Kwame asked. He poked Akosua's head and sighed. "There's nothing in there."

"Idiot!" Akosua yelled angrily.

Squaring his shoulders, Selorm mustered his bravest face. "We've come way too far to turn back now. Who knows if we'll ever get another chance?" He gestured to the map with its delicate lines and faded Adinkra symbols.

"This thing is our only hope of meeting the real Ananse. Are you willing to miss that? Imagine if we actually find him."

"Aren't you a bit afraid?" Akosua asked

"Afraid is not a word I have in my dictionary."

Akosua turned to Kwame. "This is how it starts and before you know it, you're having dates in cemeteries, surrounded by ghosts."

Kwame and Selorm laughed. Akosua's shoulders slumped, and she shuffled her feet in the damp sand. After a moment, she gave a resigned sigh and a hesitant nod.

Selorm flashed her a reassuring grin. "That's my cous! Don't worry, I'll protect you." He puffed out his chest.

THE SECRETS OF JAMESTOWN LIGHTHOUSE

"Protect me with what?" Akosua asked. "Your skinny arms or your big mouth?" Kwame burst into laughter and Selorm tackled him playfully.

Akosua walked past them towards the door.

"Flashlights?" she asked.

"Yes," Kwame replied. "Two, in the bag."

"And what else, did you follow the list?"

"Yes mam, there's a bottle of water, biscuits and a pocket knife."

"Okay" she replied, leading the way as they walked closer to the lighthouse. Once they reached the doorway, they pushed open the heavy wooden door, and its rusted hinges groaned in protest. A musty, damp odour wafted out, carrying hints of mould, decaying wood, and the salty ocean air. They stepped over the threshold, their flickering flashlight revealing a cramped entryway with peeling wallpaper and scattered debris.

"Beautiful!" Selorm exclaimed.

"More like dead," Akosua retorted. She shuddered, her heart pounding in her ears. "This place feels... wrong."

"It's... it's not that bad," Kwame replied. He led them into a derelict sitting room. Shredded curtains fluttered around shattered windows. Piles of old furniture were scattered everywhere, some pieces smashed and riddled with termites.

A narrow hallway opened to their left, the floor thick with grime and cobwebs. Kwame swept the beam towards a stairwell at the far end, the steps ascending up into utter blackness.

"The path... must be up there," he murmured, his voice barely audible over the groan of rusted metal and crashing waves.

163

"Hello?" Selorm's voice echoed down the corridor. "A-Ananse? You here, spider dude?"

A loud bang made Akosua jump from fright. She turned around and found Kwame and Selorm laughing.

"It's not funny, guys."

"It is, from–" A deafening boom suddenly rang through the building. Akosua jumped from fright again.

"Seriously!" she yelled, throwing an old book at them.

"That's not us," Selorm said.

Another loud boom rang through the lighthouse, followed by lightning and thunder that rattled the rickety foundations. What followed was a sudden heavy rainfall that began pelting the sides of the lighthouse.

"Upstairs," Akosua said and they began climbing the stairs.

Their footsteps echoed hollowly as they climbed the spiral staircase. Up above, the lighthouse beacon continued its endless sweep across the shoreline, searching... watching... waiting.

When they reached the last floor, they stopped by the glass window. Not far from where the window was, on the wall, written in red ink, were the lines:

Faako a esum kata asase so,
Na apon bue ma sunsum nyinaa guan no
ɛhɔ na ɔdaadaafo no de ne ho sie hann
Na ɔnwene nsɛmmɔne

"What does it mean?" Kwame asked. Selorm and Akosua chuckled.

THE SECRETS OF JAMESTOWN LIGHTHOUSE

"What! I'm a Fante and this is Twi," Kwame said to her.

"Fante and Twi are basically the same," Akosua replied.

"It's not!"

"It is!"

"Quiet you two," Selorm exclaimed. "Look." He pointed to the wall. The words had slowly begun to translate into English.

> *"Where darkness doth sweep upon the earth,*
> *And doors fade as shadows flee,*
> *The trickster hides from the light,*
> *To spin tales of doom."*

Kwame read it out loud, his voice barely audible over the raging storm. "The freaking wall just translated itself. We should go, this place is creepy as–" Another rumble of thunder hit the lighthouse, shaking the old building.

Kwame scrambled back towards the wall, and Selorm looked at Akosua. Even he had to admit, this scary rain-lashed lighthouse was worlds away from the Ananse tales they'd grown up with. Whatever waited for them at the top, they would face it together – or not at all.

A piercing screech from the sea drowned out the thunder. A sound so ghastly and unnatural it stole their breath away. It wasn't the sea waves crashing, or whales. It was something infinitely more ancient. And very much alive.

The beam from the lighthouse swept across the black sea, its twin pillars of light cutting through the nighttime veil like searchlights scanning for unseen threats. Frozen in stunned silence, the three friends stared intently into the swirling darkness, ears straining for any sound amid the relentless crash of waves.

Kwame's lips parted, about to vocalize the dread settling in his gut, when movement flickered at the very edge of the light's reach. Something massive skittered across the ocean's surface with unnatural speed.

The beams swung uselessly, always a hair too late, as the creature wove an evasive path through the shadows. It seemed to almost sense the light's path and instinctively recoil, dodging away with preternatural agility. A shudder passed through Akosua as she glimpsed a fleeting silhouette. Selorm opened his mouth, possibly to cry out, but the jagged shape abruptly ran directly towards the lighthouse. That snapped the three friends from their horrified trance.

"RUN!" Kwame's voice shattered the night as he bolted down the stairs, sneakers skidding over the floorboards. Akosua and Selorm fled blindly down the spiral stairs behind him, the skittering sounds of that ungodly thing's onrushing approach echoing all around them.

Kwame's heart thundered against his ribcage so hard he thought it might burst through his chest. What ungodly creature could make such an unholy screech? He didn't want to find out. Selorm was behind, his trembling hands feeling out each step to keep from plunging headlong into the shadows. At last, a dim rectangle of grey light appeared below – the entrance! Kwame flung himself against the door and they tumbled outside, falling in a tangle of limbs onto the... grass?

THE SECRETS OF JAMESTOWN LIGHTHOUSE

* * *

Kwame blinked, sucking in gulps of air as his eyes readjusted to his dark surroundings. They weren't on the beach. Somehow, impossibly, they were now in the middle of a dark forest.

Towering trunks with smooth amber bark soared high, their leaves filtering the dark clouds. The earth, dry and barren.

"Where are we?" Akosua asked. She sat up slowly, looking around with a mixture of wonder and bewilderment. The sea was now a faint murmur. None of them had an answer. One second they were scrambling out of that lighthouse in a blind panic, the next, here. Kwame looked up, and noticed the sky had neither moon nor stars.

Selorm climbed to his feet, brushing dirt off his t-shirt as he tentatively explored the clearing. "I've never seen trees like these before." He touched one of the trees. Rather than rough bark, the surface was smooth, almost rubbery to the touch. And it looked like it had a face. He touched what looked like a nose and drew his hand back.

"This is what happens when you don't listen to me!" Akosua yelled.

A strangled yelp came from Kwame. "Uh, guys?!" He pointed a shaking finger upwards.

Selorm slowly lifted his gaze to follow his stare, and his breath caught in his throat. Sitting in one of the trees were webs, woven together into an unimaginably enormous nest and there in the middle of the web, something gargantuan, furry and plump moved. A rasping chuckle reverberated all around them, shaking the trees.

"Well, well..." rumbled an ancient, gravelly voice from everywhere and nowhere. "As the elders say, it is the stubbornness of the child that has made the mother know all the elders in the village."

Akosua and Kwame shrank against Selorm, their faces draining of colour. Kwame's heart thudded rapidly as he managed to spit out the words.

"A-Ananse...?"

Another low chuckle shook the floor before the reply came.

"Who else, little ones? I've been waiting for you..."

He swung down from the tree and as his feet touched earth, he transformed into a man. He was black as the earth, human from his legs to his neck. His head however was inhumanly big, eyes protruding. Akosua held onto the torchlight with all her might. She should have said no when the boys convinced her to come. She looked back at the door they had entered from. It had slowly begun to lose colour, as if fading away.

"We mean you no harm," she finally uttered.

"Oh I know," Kwaku Ananse replied. "What can you three do to Kwaku Ananse?"

Selorm held onto Kwame's hands. "We just wanted–"

"To know if I was real. Now you know. Are you going to kill me, like your ancestors did?"

"We don't–" Kwame began.

"I have been here, alone for centuries. It gets boring when your companions are trees. It would be easy if trees were good audiences for a storyteller like me but alas, they are not. Why don't we have a little story time?"

"There's no need for a story, we will be on our way—" Akosua began.

"Silly," Kwaku Ananse cut in. "I think it is time for another Anansesem. Sit!" he commanded and suddenly Akosua, Kwame and Selorm found themselves seated on the floor in front of Kwaku Ananse.

"Once upon a time," he began, "it was during a terrible drought season. People were dying of hunger so the community came together to start a farm. A farm that would feed everyone for a long time. Everyone was forced to work. But I didn't join them. Kwaku Ananse does not work. So I slept and enjoyed myself while the villagers worked because that's the right thing to do. And then when it was time for harvest, the villagers refused to give some.

So I devised one of my clever schemes. I pretended to be deathly ill, convincing my wife that when I died, I wanted to be buried on the farm with cooking supplies so I could make food in the afterlife. The foolish woman fell for it and soon I was 'buried' on the farm with all my needs.

As soon as night fell, I came out and feasted on the juicy yams, plantains, and other vegetables growing abundantly around my grave. I would stuff myself full, then return to my tomb before dawn. Ananse the clever spider was well fed and happy as he should be.

But my gluttony didn't go unnoticed. After spotting the dwindling crops, my infuriating villagers set a trap. Sure enough, that night when I emerged to hunt for food, I was startled by this strange man. I tried to get a response from him, calling him but the man said nothing. You know how us spiders can get when angered – I just kept hitting it until I was completely stuck fast by the gum, immobilized from legs to head!

By morning, the entire village found me in such a pitiful state, trapped to the gum figure I had mistaken for a real man. I'll never forget their faces when they realized the truth. They unleashed their fury upon me with scathing words and hearty blows. They punished me for being smart and then they imprisoned me here."

The three children sat in silence as Ananse finished weaving his story. His eyes glittering with mischief.

"And that, little ones, is how this mighty creature fell from grace," Kwaku Ananse continued, his voice resonating all around them. "Of course, I've taken a few… creative liberties over the millennia. A good story is nothing without a little spice. After all, no one wants to know that I was killing children too." He got up from the floor. "That day, when they were burying me, I cried, calling Nyame. I begged him to save me, but he ignored me. The humans, his latest creation, were better than me. You are better than me. Impossible!"

Kwame, Akosua and Selorm exchanged looks of terror. They were thoroughly creeped out by Kwaku Ananse's looming presence and the fact that he just told them he had been killing children.

"Nyame trapped me here. He made sure I could never leave. He, however, said nothing about children entering." He looked at the faces of the terrified children and smiled. "You did not find the map. I found you, just like I found your predecessors."

He pointed to the trees around. "My collection." He turned to Kwame who had began walking backwards, slowly. "What's the matter?" He asked Kwame, "You look like you've just been caught in someohe else's web!" He threw his head back and laughed at his own joke, his body jiggling grotesquely.

Kwame looked up at him. "Please let us—"

That's as far as he got before Kwaku Ananse struck him with stunning speed. A thick streamer of silk lashed out from Kwaku Ananse, pinning his arms to his sides in one fluid motion.

"Kwame!" Selorm and Akosua shrieked but were choked off as another jet of webbing caught Akosua in the face, plastering her mouth. She fell backwards, hands scrabbling at the suffocating strands as Ananse cackled with sadistic delight.

A gout of webbing narrowly missed Selorm as he dove behind a thick root. Kwaku Ananse reared up further on his back legs, mandibles clicking wildly as more webbing sprayed out of him. "I honestly cannot wait to tell your tales to the next unlucky fools who venture in here."

Sticky strands lashed Kwame's legs as he twisted away from Ananse's relentless assault. More webbing splattered across his back, weighing him down. Kwame twisted in desperation, frantically brushing away the webs. "Help!"

The trees suddenly began moving. Thick gnarled vines snaked up from the earth to ensnare the trapped children. Akosua screamed as rough woody vines wrapped themselves around her ankles, dragging her towards Kwaku Ananse.

Selorm thrashed against the vines, panic glazing his eyes as he met Kwame's terrified gaze.

Akosua's fingernails pulled desperately against the compacting webbing, trying to tear it off. Twisting onto her back, she grabbed the only thing she could find, her flashlight, and turned it on directly in Kwaku Ananse's face, ready to throw it at him.

The brilliant light pierced the dappled shadows in a sweeping arc. Kwaku Ananse recoiled with a shrill screech of agony, his gangly legs scrambling backwards, repulsed by the intense light. His face burned as if they had poured hot oil on him.

Akosua seized the moment to yank futilely at the webbing plastering her limbs. After freeing herself, she ran towards Kwame and pulled him loose.

"What happened?" Kwame asked

"Light," she replied. "He doesn't like light. It burns him."

"The trickster hides from the light," Selorm said.

Kwame turned to him. "Huh."

"The poem in the lighthouse, it said he hides from the light to trap. In his story, he came out during the night to steal the food or kill the children. He only hunts in the dark."

Kwaku Ananse screeched again and the three kids began to panic.

"Hurry!" Selorm shouted as he began to pull at the vines and leaves around him.

They pulled him free and sprinted back towards the door. Vines and branches whipped around in a frenzied attempt to stop them but they kept running. By the time they reached the door, only the handle was visible.

Kwame pulled at it but it wouldn't budge.

THE SECRETS OF JAMESTOWN LIGHTHOUSE

"Shit! Shit! Shit!" Selorm yelled. He joined Kwame and pulled and pulled but it still wouldn't budge. They could hear Ananse approaching. Akosua pushed the boys from the way and flung herself at the door with all her strength. The veil broke and she fell through, Kwame and Selorm following.

They fell out of the door onto the beach, gasping for air as the lighthouse creaked above them. Kwame's chest heaved as he gulped down the salty ocean air in ragged gasps. "Is... is everyone okay?" he managed between breaths, looking at Selorm and Akosua with wild eyes.

Selorm nodded, rubbing a bump on his head but otherwise unharmed. Akosua had burn marks on her hand. They helped her up and rushed home. They ran through the traffic, through the loud jubilations and drums straight to Akosua and Selorm's grandma's house. Grandma was seated by the shrine pouring libations. She looked up as the kids ran into the compound and walked up to them.

"Where have you been and why are you running?" she asked.

"Nowhere, we were just by the beach," Selorm replied.

"How many times have I told you not to swim at night?"

"We weren't swimming, Nana," Selorm replied.

"Where were you, Akosua?" she asked firmly.

"We were at the beach, Grandma," Akosua replied. She sat beside the charcoal pot pretending to warm herself but the moment Grandma turned to face Selorm, she threw the crumpled map into the fire. No one was ever going to find the map again. She got up but Kwame pulled her back, pointing at the fire. The map was in there but it wasn't burning. The brown paper lay amidst the flames, untouched. Suddenly the electricity went off in the whole town.

"Lights off!" Kwame said jokingly but as he lifted his eyes to the moon and stars disappearing from the sky, he began to panic. "That door was a seal," he began. "To keep him from our world... and we broke it."

They all turned to the lighthouse. The light beams had gone off; colossal webs had begun to spread all around it. And then that screech, the sound they knew all too well, began to ring in the night sky. Somehow they knew their otherworldly tribulations were far from over. Kwaku Ananse was coming for them.

"Selorm!" Kwame yelled, panic gripping him, "say something!"

Selorm's eyes fluttered open, instantly filling with terror as he lifted a trembling finger to point behind them. "L-look…"

Dread flooded Kwame and Akosua as they turned to follow his stare. There, hanging by the lighthouse, crouched Kwaku Ananse. The three kids scrambled backwards in sheer horror as Kwaku Ananse ran towards them. Akosua's shoulders began to shake with sobs of fright.

Just then, Grandma pushed them to her side.

"What have you unleashed unto this world, children?" she queried.

"G-grandmother!" Akosua cried.

"I told you not to go to that lighthouse," she shouted to the kids.

She turned to Kwaku Ananse. "So, the legendary Ananse walks this world once more." Her voice took on a hard edge. "I should

THE SECRETS OF JAMESTOWN LIGHTHOUSE

have known my grandchildren would be the pawns to set your webs of mischief loose again."

Ananse reared back, his bulbous abdomen pulsing menacingly.

"Your twin sister sends her regards," Kwaku Ananse said to Grandma and Grandma tore off her scarf, revealing an intricately carved wooden spider figurine affixed to a necklace.

"It's been exactly eighty years since you took her from me, Agya Ananse. I have been waiting for you. You may have immense power in your realm of stories and riddles," Grandma intoned. "But here, you are bound by the rules and respects of Nyame and my ancestors." She began chanting in an ancient Ghanaian dialect. The figurine grew searing hot in her palms as Ananse suddenly recoiled, twisting around in pain. Grandmother stood tall, chest heaving slightly from the exertion of subduing the legendary trickster with her ancestral powers.

Suddenly, the ancient lighthouse flared back to life. The rotating lamps burned with an intensity that seemed to crackle with mystical energy. Kwaku Ananse's spider form immediately recoiled against the searing beams of light. He screamed in pain as his skin began to burn.

Sure enough, the light became an irresistible vortex, pulling Kwaku Ananse back towards the lighthouse. Kwaku Ananse's spindly legs skittered frantically as he fought against the powerful force but it was no use. With a hair-raising screech of fury and agony, Kwaku Ananse's body burst into flames and he ran back towards the doorway, propelled by the blazing energy until he fell through the door and it closed shut with a bang.

As abruptly as the lighthouse had flared to life, the lamps dimmed. The children stared in stunned silence before turning to Akosua's grandmother with a mixture of awe and fear in their eyes.

The old woman simply gave a grim nod, tucking the spider talisman safely back beneath her shawl.

Straightening up, she fixed each child with a stare that bore straight into their souls.

"I am disappointed in you three. For lying to me, you're going to weed the farm, no phones, no television and no library. And that goes for you too, Kwame. Every morning, report to my house."

"Yes, Nana," Kwame replied. The other two nodded soberly in vow. They had peered beyond the veil of make-believe into the ancient, primordial power. And they silently promised to honour the wisdom that had saved them. As the pale moon peeked over the cliffs, Akosua, Selorm and Kwame exchanged a look of relief. The trickster spider had been put back in his place – at least for now.

Ananse City Dawn

Bernice Arthur

Right after the heavens had stopped their drumming and the sun started sneaking through the tired clouds, Ananse finally woke up from what seemed like a century-long nap. Stretching out in his age-old web, a real work of art that had hugged him tight through the storm, he felt the dew-sparkled threads stick to him like old friends. Shaking off the sleep, Ananse tried to get a hold of himself, but it wasn't easy. His many eyes squinted, adjusting to the brightness, and what he saw nearly made his heart drop to his belly.

The place was buzzing all right, but nothing looked familiar! It was as if someone had played a fast trick on him while he slept. Where he expected soft soil and the comforting rustle of leaves, there was now unending chaos, with humans – well, at least they looked kind of human – rushing about like they had ants in their pants. They were diving into metal beasts and popping back out like toast from a toaster!

"Ei, are all these people for real?" Ananse whispered to himself, lost in the madness around him. "And what's with these metal boxes they keep jumping in and out of?" Tiptoeing with all the grace a spider could muster, Ananse moved through the crowd. Not a familiar face, not one nod or smile his way – it was like he had turned into a ghost in his own land. He wondered, "Where's the big baobab tree that used to stand tall at the crossroads? What happened to the cozy huts that dotted the land like mushrooms after the rain?" All swallowed up by a sea of concrete and glass – no sign of the old world he remembered.

"Chale, I've really been away too long, haven't I?" he muttered, feeling the weight of years hit him. The realization was as heavy as the concrete around him. The world had no chill now, buzzing non-stop, all light and noise, leaving no space for a storytelling spider like him. "Ah, this world has changed, paa," Ananse sighed, a mix of wonder and a pinch of sadness seasoning his voice. "Looks like I've got some catching up to do. What kind of world be dis sef?" Ananse sighed, feeling like he had a whole millennium on his shoulders.

There he was, smack in the middle of Madina, the heart of Accra's never-sleeping hustle. Just as he was getting his bearings, a *trotro* – those minibuses that zip through Accra like they own the place – nearly took him out! "Aseyyyy, look straight!" the mate shouted at him. The mate's voice cut through the chaos, sharp as the machete used at the coconut stalls. This mate was dancing through traffic and people with a skill that reminded Ananse of his web-weaving days – except this was no delicate thread; it was pure survival.

Dodging the *trotro* like a pro, Ananse's many eyes popped wide open at the whole spectacle of Madina market. Market women in dazzling prints called out over heaps of fresh yams and ripe mangoes, *trotro* mates chanted stops like town criers of old, and traders hawked everything from phone cases to fried fish, claiming every inch of pavement they could. The air was a thick soup of smells – plantains kissing hot oil, mixed with the tang of *trotro* exhaust. It was chaotic, yes, but it smelled like life, loud and vibrant. Ananse, our legendary spider trickster who'd last roamed these lands in 1750 when Saltpond was just a chill spot by the sea and everyone was easy to trick, was now wide-eyed and bushy-tailed in twenty-first-century Accra. After pulling off a stunt so cheeky it nearly caused a riot, he'd dipped into a deep sleep that took him through centuries in what felt like a blink.

Dodging *trotros* and sidestepping market stalls here in Madina, Ananse was a spider out of time. Each step he took was a step into a world that buzzed with more energy than the electrified lines above the *trotro* routes. "Ei, the world rush paa these days," Ananse mused, his eight legs barely keeping up with the pace. As he navigated through the market, absorbing the sights and sounds of a city pulsing with life, Ananse's old trickster spirit sparked within him. "Maybe I no fit play the old tricks," he thought, "but this new world… it dey ripe for some new schemes."

Now, waking up in 2024, Ananse found himself slap-bang in the middle of a world he could barely recognize. They call it the Gen Z era, a time when everything moves so fast that even the youth seem to be playing catch up! Madina was bubbling with energy, everybody out there hustling, with pickpockets so smooth they'd have your wallet, smiling, before you even noticed, and street vendors pitching soap like it was the latest iPhone model. Ananse, who was once the chief of tricksters, the Asante Kotoko of cunning, now felt like just another guy lost in the shuffle. His legendary schemes seemed like child's play in this fast-paced world where every Tom, Dick, and Harriet was a mini con artist.

Wandering through the throng at Madina market, he watched a woman move through the chaos with a grace that made it look like she was dancing through a quiet room. She had a balanced basin on her head, and her posture was an elegant masterclass. Curious and lost, Ananse called out to her, hoping to catch a bit of familiar ground. "Akatasia, this place be where?"

The woman stopped, her eyes softly landing on the tiny, confused spider before her. A smile spread across her face as she replied, "This is Madina, my friend."

"But e be like Saltpond, no?" Ananse's voice was hopeful, clinging to a thread of familiarity in this dizzy world.

Her laughter, bright and clear, cut through the market noise. "Oh no, we dey Accra. This is Madina market. Saltpond dey far for Central Region," she explained, amusement twinkling in her eyes.

Ananse's mind spun. So far from home, yet right in the thick of life's hustle! As the lady moved on, her basin still steady, Ananse's thoughts raced.

At that moment, as the market buzzed around him, Ananse felt the weight of his new reality. A whole cocktail of feelings stirred in Ananse. He was wowed by Madina's loud spirit and color, yet there was a little tug in his heart for the slow, sweet rhythm of Saltpond. But there was also that tickle of adventure creeping up on him. If he had once been the star of Saltpond with his tricks and tales, what magic could he spin here among Madina's lively crowds? Fired up with this new zest, Ananse watched as Akatasia blended back into the sea of people, her basket still steady atop her head like she was born to carry it. Just then, under the sharp glare of the noon sun, Ananse found himself at the heaving Madina bus stop. The place was a circus! *Trotros* zooming in and out, sellers shouting over each other, and the never-ending dance of commuters. In the middle of this chaos, a *trotro*, painted in the loudest colors you could imagine, screeched to a stop right before him. The door banged open, and the mate – a lean fellow with quick eyes and an even quicker voice – leaned out. "Where you dey go?" he snapped.

"Jamestown," Ananse shot back, picking up on a name he'd just heard tossed around by a group nearby. It seemed as good a destination as any in this sprawling maze.

"Hop in," barked the mate, waving Ananse toward an empty seat with an impatient flick. With a mix of hesitation and a dash of curiosity, Ananse clambered into the *trotro*, still a stranger to the ways of this buzzing city commute. The minibus was alive with its own world – passengers chatting, a baby crying for attention, and highlife music setting a lively backdrop. The journey took on its own rhythm with the mate zigzagging through the narrow aisle, his hands outstretched for fares, as smooth and slick as an okra soup. Ananse, lost in the scenes flashing by outside – street hawkers, colorful billboards, *trotros* packed like kelewele in a frying pan – was rudely snapped back to reality when the mate's sharp voice pierced his bubble. "Sssssh, my guy, give me money!"

Ananse blinked, startled. "What money?" he asked, a genuine note of confusion in his voice. The mate's face twisted like he'd just bitten into a raw chili. "Don't vex me, oh! You no know sey you for pay? You think sey *trotro* dey run on thank yous? Abeg, make you pay before you make me boil," he snapped, his patience wearing thin. A low grumble rolled through the other passengers, some tossing sharp glances and others mumbling under their breath about Ananse's apparent cluelessness or sly act. Just as the mate was about to signal the driver to toss this freeloading spider onto the street, a calm voice floated forward from behind. "I go pay for am. Just take am go where he dey go." Ananse craned his neck to see his unexpected hero – a middle-aged man with a calm aura and a smile who seemed to understand Ananse wasn't entirely up to speed with this new world. With a quiet "thank you," barely louder than a sigh, Ananse acknowledged the kindness.

As the *trotro* picked up speed again, a single tear rolled down Ananse's cheek. It wasn't just the random act of kindness that touched him but the realization that this fast, loud world still had room for the old spirit of community and generosity. This simple gesture rekindled a warmth in Ananse, reminding him of the communal bonds that were central to his tales back in the day. As Ananse looked outside the window of the *trotro*, the Jamestown lighthouse caught his gaze like a shiny new calabash in the sun. With its bold red and white stripes slicing through the dimming skyline, it stood like a king in its court, commanding the bustling street with an air of unwavering authority.

"Massa, I go drop here!" Ananse shouted with an urgency that even surprised him. He was mesmerized, his spider heart beating a wild rhythm of awe and excitement. The *trotro* mate clapped the vehicle's roof twice, signaling the driver, and with a screech that could wake ancestors, the minibus halted. Leaping out, Ananse couldn't help but marvel aloud. "Eish, see how big it be! I dey see the lighthouse with my own eyes o! E be too fine!" His words tumbled in a cascade of wonder, bouncing off the ancient walls that had seen many a storm and sunshine.

Compelled by a force he couldn't resist, Ananse made ritualistic rounds around the lighthouse. Each loop drew him deeper into a trance of admiration, his spirit syncing with the pulse of this grand guardian of the coast. After his seventh lap, as if on cue, the heavens started to grumble, and the clouds thickened, ready to spill their secrets.

As the day's light faded, Ananse lifted his eyes to the lighthouse's beacon, a solitary sentinel poised against the encroaching night. "Just like me," Ananse mused, a soft chuckle escaping him. As twilight took its full hold and the first raindrops began their gentle descent, Ananse sought refuge under the nearest shelter – a small, somewhat cozy nook by the lighthouse. Just as he was about to stretch out and maybe catch a few winks, a booming voice shattered the peace.

"Masa, masa, what do you think you are coming to do here?" It was deep and loaded with suspicion. Ananse turned, only to meet the stern glare of a towering man, muscles bulging, beard thick, and head as shiny as the lighthouse itself. "Chale, shift from here! You wan thief my fishing nets again? I no go gree today, o!"

"I no be thief o," Ananse protested, his voice thin as a strand of spider silk, barely audible over the rising wind.

"Don't let me lay my hands on you, eh," the man growled, stepping closer, a frown carving deep lines into his face.

Again, Ananse pleaded, "Seriously, I no be thief!"

That's when the man, known to the local folk as Nii, paused and looked at Ananse. Noticing the genuine fear and the involuntary shivers that wracked the skinny spider, Nii's features softened. Perhaps he had been too quick to judge. "Alright, come with me then," Nii grumbled, a mix of resignation and compassion in his voice. "You go fit sleep for my side since you dey shake like a leaf."

Surprised by the sudden change in tone, Ananse's eyes widened. Gratitude washed over him as he followed Nii, navigating through Jamestown's rain-slicked streets, a small figure trailing behind the large man like a shadow at twilight. In this unexpected turn of events, there was the gritty kindness that Ananse had come to recognize as the true spirit of this vibrant, unpredictable place.

Nii's place was tucked in a corner of a teeming slum, a small shack that could easily be missed if you weren't looking hard enough. It was nothing fancy, just a few wooden planks and pieces of corrugated iron thrown together, but it was bustling with life and laughter. Inside, it was like stepping into a whole new world. The space was tight, and the lighting was dim, but the room was alive with the energy of Nii's family. Five kids of different sizes buzzed around like bees around honey, their laughter and squeals filling every nook and cranny. Nii's girlfriend, with her warm smile and sparkling eyes, greeted Ananse like he was an old friend dropping by for a visit. As Ananse stepped in, he was struck by how a small space could hold so much life. Every corner of the room had a purpose: mats rolled out on the floor for sleeping, pots, basins, and pans hanging on the walls, and even a small TV perched on a makeshift shelf. Despite the simplicity and the squeeze, the place was rich with warmth you wouldn't find in many big houses. It was a stark contrast to the cold, soggy world outside.

Nii introduced Ananse to everyone, making it clear he was their guest for the night. The children were all eyes on Ananse, probably wondering about the tales this strange visitor might share. Ananse felt a wave of gratitude wash over him. Here he was, a stranger, yet welcomed like family. That night, as Ananse curled up on a small mat Nii had laid out for him, the room was filled with the soft, steady breathing of a family at rest. Lying there, Ananse's mind wandered back through the years. Back in the day, he'd have been plotting some clever trick or spinning a wild tale, but here in this humble home, he found something much deeper – simple acts of kindness and a place where he truly belonged.

It dawned on him that even an old trickster like him could still learn a thing or two – lessons about humility, generosity, and the strength of community ties. These were the natural treasures, far more valuable than any scheme or story he'd ever concocted. As the rain played a gentle rhythm on the tin roof, a soothing lullaby for the night, Ananse felt a peace like never before. The day's unexpected journey had brought him to a safe haven, not just in a physical sense but deep within, in the heart of Jamestown. Here, nestled among new friends who felt like family, Ananse found a home away from home. In this place, even a wandering spirit could find rest and maybe, just maybe, a new beginning.

The morning in Jamestown didn't just tiptoe in; it came through, bringing with it the familiar city symphony mixed with the distant lullabies of the sea. As dawn's gentle light sieved through the makeshift patchwork of Nii's home, Ananse stirred from a sleep cradled by warmth and laughter. The kids, buzzing with barely contained excitement, were like little breezes swirling around the room, their whispers tickling Ananse awake with promises of new adventures.

Around the humble wooden table, the aroma of millet porridge cooked up a storm of homeliness. With the ease of many mornings, Nii ladled out hearty helpings, each sweetened with a swirl of honey – a golden touch he'd hustled for at the market. The kids, eyes wide and sparkling with awe and mischief, kept sneaking peeks at Ananse. They were still enchanted by the web of tales he'd spun the night before.

Kojo, the eldest and unofficial leader of the pack, gulped down his breakfast with the urgency of a commander readying for a mission. With a mischievous grin, he tugged at Ananse's sleeve. "Mr. Ananse, we get something dope to show you today," his voice bubbling with a cocktail of respect and youthful zest. The rest of the crew wolfed down their porridge, not wanting to miss out on whatever caper Kojo had cooked up. Out in the streets, Jamestown was waking up loud and lively. Their path was a living alleyway lined with market stalls splashed with color, old colonial relics whispering secrets of the old days, and laundry lines resembling festival banners crisscrossing above. The air was thick with the smells of freshly baked bread and the sea's briny kiss, painting a vivid sensory picture that could make your head spin. They arrived at a quaint little internet café hidden behind the animated chaos of the market square. It was a cozy nook of technology sandwiched between the town's rustic charm. Inside, the walls were plastered with posters of far-off places and yesteryear's tech wonders, each workstation a portal to another world.

Naa, the café's queen bee, greeted them from behind the counter. Her presence was both regal and comforting, a familiar face to the neighborhood kids who'd grown up chasing digital dragons under her watchful eyes. "The kiddies wan show you the new kind games dem dey play. E no be like the olden days' stories, but still, stories be stories," she chuckled, her voice warm and welcoming. She pointed them towards a corner where an old computer hummed, its screen aglow with anticipation. The space around it was a collage of colorful stickers and doodles, each a tiny testament to the joy and escapades experienced right there.

Kojo and his siblings dove into action, their fingers blurting over the keyboard and mouse. They fired up a game the local gang loved – a fantasy quest teeming with mythical beasts and sprawling kingdoms. As the game booted, their chatter filled the air, piecing together the lore and rules for Ananse, who was caught up in the whirlwind of their enthusiasm.

Ananse watched, utterly transfixed as a universe unfolded on the screen. In this world, legends lived and breathed with clicks and keystrokes. There were tales not unlike his own, woven with modern threads of pixels and digital dreams.

As he dove headfirst into this novel realm of storytelling, guided by the eager voices of the children, Ananse felt a profound connection between the ancient art of his fables and this vibrant new medium. It was a revelatory moment, affirming the timeless essence of storytelling – its power to morph and adapt yet remain profoundly tethered to the human spirit. This encounter wasn't just an introduction to new-age lore; it was a bridge linking eras, a blend of past wisdom with future wonders, all coming together in the heart of Jamestown, under the watchful eyes of Naa and the spirited guidance of the children. For Ananse, this was more than a lesson; it was a revelation, an exhilarating adventure into the evolving narrative of life itself. But now, where does he go from here?

Ananse and the Infernal Tale
Emmanuel Blavo

The web weaver spun
And a new tale was formed

With painstaking precision, he wove together this new tale from his mind's depths, carefully navigating through memories and controlling every thought with fierce determination. For any hint of a plot hole (oh, how he hated those!) would rattle his confidence and shake the foundation of the story. The mere thought of doubt creeping in would poison his creativity and fill him with anxiety, causing him to second-guess every action taken. And if enough plot holes were to seep into the narrative, the entire world within would twist and writhe until it crumbled to nothingness. His grip on the story was crucial, for it held the power to create or destroy an entire universe.

And the weaver was too greedy and vain to let that happen.

Ananse sat on his throne, tapping his fingers as he spun another tale. The throne, designed like a spider's web with silver and gold threads, had a seat of fine spider silk. Gemstone spiders adorned the arms, symbolizing his cunning. The backrest showed his legendary exploits, and the legs resembled branches with insects in webs. A glowing spider-shaped jewel at the center symbolized his watchful presence.

He let out a heavy sigh. How peculiar it felt to have a headache – a sensation typically reserved for mortals. His eight eyes stared vacantly at the other unoccupied thrones, and his mind briefly pictured the former deities sitting on their stations. For a brief moment, self-doubt crept into his mind. Had he made a mistake in crafting this elaborate tale to maintain his divine power? Doubt gnawed at him as he pondered the consequences of his boldness.

He never would have dared to think this in the beginning, when he won his final game against Onyankopon to become the supreme deity in their little corner of heaven. He still remembered the horrified look on Onyankopon's ancient bearded face as he walked in triumphantly, with a smile wider than the heavens plastered on his face as he returned from a daring mission that no one expected him to survive.

He smiled as he claimed his reward, ignoring the angry glares from the other deities. Asaase Yaa, the earth spirit, radiated power and stability.

Owuo, the deity of death, stood beside her. His imposing figure and gruesome trophies exuded fear.

Ta Kora, tall and muscular with electrified hair, held an air of confidence as Onyankopon's son.

As Ananse basked in the attention, he couldn't help but notice the tension between Ta Kora and Owuo. The two deities had a long-standing rivalry that was currently on pause – for now.

In his typical arrogance, Ananse had invited his entire family to witness his victory over Asaase Yaa. His wife Okonore Yaa stood dutifully by his side, while his sons Ntikuma, Tikelenkelen, Nankonhwea, and Afudohwedohwe fidgeted nervously behind him. He especially hoped that Ntikuma would see this display of intelligence as a way to one-up the boy after their previous altercation involving the pot of wisdom.

Despite his outward bravado, Ananse couldn't shake off the twinge of jealousy he felt towards Ntikuma – perhaps seeing a better version of himself reflected in his son's intelligence reminded him of his own shortcomings.

He snapped himself out of this train of thought to focus on the other deities and his next step. With a newfound sense of power and control, Ananse plotted his next move. His ambition knew no bounds as he set his sights on reshaping reality itself to glorify himself and himself alone. As he looked out at the other deities who had once looked down on him, his eyes gleaming with malicious intent, he saw nothing but obstacles to be eliminated. A twisted grin spread across his face as he reveled in the thought of reshaping reality itself into one grand tale that glorified him and him alone.

With a wave of his hand, he stripped the deities of their divine status, making them mere mortals. Their shrines and temples now bore his name. He reveled in the idea that cities, festivals, and myths would honor him now.

Ananse changed his form, calling upon Onyankopon's power. He felt the energy filling him with strength and authority, but his ambitions twisted him into a grotesque mix of human and spider. His body contorted, hands became spindly limbs, and eyes multiplied on his face. Patterns emerged on his torso, a warped reflection of his twisted divinity.

But it wasn't enough for Ananse. He turned to his family, the source of his frustrations. With a cruel glint in his eye, he rewrote their histories to ensure they suffered. Memories of happiness and success became ones of misery and defeat. He felt no remorse, only satisfaction, as he watched his grand tale unfold.

He had similar designs for the deities present, equally cruel and wanton:

Onyankopon now lived a mortal life, doing mundane tasks. He was married to a demanding woman whose constant requests for fufu caused him frustration. He often injured himself while pounding cassava, and the fufu was frequently inedible. He wondered what sins he had committed to deserve this fate.

Asaase Yaa now lived as a feeble old woman with little to her name. Her farmland yielded no crops, and her only possession was a treacherous walking stick. Ananse, who she had outwitted many times, cursed her with a life of struggle.

Owuo and Ta Kora were turned into bickering neighbors, constantly at odds over trivial matters. Ananse kept them occupied with each other to prevent them from turning their animosity elsewhere.

His family was condemned to a bleak, barren village. The sun scorched the earth, and winds whipped dust into spider-shaped devils. People lived in mud huts, wore ragged clothes, and

ANANSE AND THE INFERNAL TALE

survived on meager crops. Their reverence for Ananse sustained them more than food. They offered tribute and punished dissent, knowing only Ananse.

Ntikuma's new life was pitiful. If Ananse had fully controlled his mind like the others in the village, he might have found joy in worshiping their spider deity. Once bright-eyed and resourceful, Ntikuma was now frustrated and worn out, living in a backward village with his mother and siblings. His days were filled with menial, meaningless tasks. His mother, sweet but forgetful, spent her days singing praises to Ananse. She could switch moods suddenly, especially when her other children were a nuisance. She also wouldn't tolerate any criticism towards their beloved spider. Ntikuma didn't remember his father, suffering headaches whenever he tried.

The only tangible reminder left of their beloved patriarch was an ornately decorated calabash pot that hung from the ceiling in their single-room mud hut. It was quite large for a pot, its round shape and delicate patterns standing out against the rough walls. Though it seemed to have been cracked at some point in the past, it had been carefully repaired with golden spider's webbing, creating a shimmering mosaic that caught the light and cast a warm glow throughout the room.

Everything else in their humble home was old and crumbling, but this calabash stood proudly as a symbol of their heritage and history. To them, it was a priceless treasure, given to them by their father and passed down through generations. Even when they struggled to put food on the table or afford medicine for their sick child, she refused to part with it. And when he once dared to suggest trading it for necessities, her gentle smile turned into a scowl as she snapped at him.

"How dare you even think of such a thing?" she screeched at him. "That pot is not just an object to us, it is a representation of our family's legacy. You have no respect for anything, you selfish and ungrateful brat! Do you think you're smarter than your own father?" From then on, he never dared to bring it up again.

After the intense altercation, Ntikuma couldn't help but return to the ornate pot that had once belonged to his father. Every time he looked at it, a throbbing headache would start to creep up on him. It seemed as though the pot was taunting him, daring him to unravel its secrets. Despite this, Ntikuma had grown accustomed to this routine and continued to examine the pot with curiosity and frustration. The intricate details of the design seemed to mock him and hint at a deeper meaning that he could never grasp. He felt like a helpless creature caught in the trap of routine, unable to break free from the constant reminder of his father's absence.

The mysterious pot hung from the ceiling, taunting him with its secrets. Curiosity burned inside him, driving him past the pain in his head. He found a wobbly stool, positioned himself beneath the pot, and reached out with trembling fingers. As soon as he touched it, a tingling warmth spread through his arm, filling him with ancient knowledge. Startled, he gasped, lost his balance, and crashed to the ground. The pot shattered, releasing a surge of memories.

Fearful of his mother's anger, he instead felt a powerful understanding flood his mind. He remembered everything: the summoning to Asamando, Ananse's smug face among the deities,

ANANSE AND THE INFERNAL TALE

and the nervousness he shared with his mother. Anger and shock coursed through him as he saw his mother and siblings clutching their heads, their old memories returning.

Looking at the broken pot, he knew they had to act fast before Ananse noticed. He needed to reach out to the former deities, hoping their powers had returned. Amidst his racing thoughts, he dissected his father's flawed plan: How long did Ananse plan to maintain this reality? Why not erase his family instead of making them forget? And why keep the pot at home, where an accident could destroy it?

Ntikuma almost laughed at the absurdity. But the deeper implications were horrifying. One thing was certain:

The web weaver had to be stopped.

Meanwhile, Ananse remained blissfully unaware of the chaos his poor storytelling had unleashed. He failed to notice the faint tremor shaking his throne or the faint crack echoing through his palace. Only when a sudden jolt of pain blasted through his head did he snap out of his trance. Clutching his temples, he felt something vital slip away.

Rushing to his observation orb, Ananse saw the shattered pot on the floor of the mud hut. His eyes widened in horror as he realized what had happened. The fools had broken the pot, freeing themselves from his lies and releasing the other deities from their mental imprisonment.

His mind raced with thoughts of his next step, but he reassured himself. Even with the truth revealed, they couldn't match his power. Safe in Asamando, his webs and stories were secure. He chuckled, confident everything was under control.

Except it wasn't. Unlike Ntikuma, the former deities experienced a vivid flash when the gourd was destroyed. They saw their dreary world replaced by the vibrant one they once knew, with an ugly golden spider webbing holding the new world together. This flash reignited a glimpse of their divine power.

Onyankopon took a last look at his mortal wife and grimaced, silently vowing to make Ananse pay. He leaped up and soared gently through the sky, conserving his remaining power, feeling the wind and sun on his face.

Asaase Yaa walked on the ground, feeling the soil and plants under her bare feet. She smiled sadly at the animals and people, seeing Ananse's mad influence in them. Embarrassed by their defeat but determined, she began devising a plan to lure Ananse to earth or return to Asamando, already forming an idea based on what she knew about him.

Owuo and Ta Kora had been in the middle of yet another pointless argument when their memories and a portion of their powers returned to them. They both stopped immediately and stared at each other, unsure about what to do next.

Ta Kora's voice was tense and his eyes narrowed as he addressed Owuo, the two deities standing on opposite sides of their mud huts.

"Listen," Ta Kora said. "Ananse has gone too far. We need to work together to stop him. Are you with me?"

Owuo stared at him for a full minute before nodding. "Fine. A truce then."

Ta Kora continued, "Good. Let's follow that call we've been feeling. Hopefully, Asaase Yaa and Onyankopon will join us."

ANANSE AND THE INFERNAL TALE

In the heart of the old village, Ananse's former house stood as a silent witness to the gathering of once-mighty deities. The air inside was thick with a mix of anticipation and tension.

"A pot," muttered Asaase Yaa, looking at the cracked remains of the ornate container which lay before her. "The great web weaver left the one thing that could expose him and return our memories to us... in a pot. And left it in his HOUSE of all places!" she exclaimed, letting a short chuckle escape her lips. She leaned back in a chair, her eyes twinkling with mischief. "Remember the time Ananse tried to gather all the wisdom in the world into a pot? You'd think he had learned his lesson. But I can't fault him for how funny it is. Almost poetic, even; but not very smart. I can think of at least ten ways he could have prevented this."

Ta Kora smirked. "Ananse's good at coming up with initial plans, and even a decent execution, but he often fails in the end. Like when he was outsmarted by Chameleon in a race."

Onyankopon let out a rare laugh. "How about when he caught Onini, Osebo, and Mmoatia to become the keeper of stories? Only Ananse could trick those creatures!" The atmosphere in the room got a little tense after that sentence. Hadn't Ananse trapped them in a way? If not for the pot getting destroyed, they would still be living their oblivious, mundane lives.

Ntikuma watched the deities converse with a mix of amusement and anxiety. Their casual jokes about Ananse's past misadventures contrasted sharply with their godly presence. These were the beings he had revered, made offerings to, and feared. Now, they lounged and laughed like mortals, their divine auras subdued but palpable. The realization that such powerful beings could act like common folk unsettled him, adding to his anxiety about the impending confrontation with his father.

Owuo listened thoughtfully before interjecting. "Ananse's cunning often outsmarts us, like when he disguised himself to steal from the river spirits and nearly drowned. He set a trap for a snake, but it bit him and left him wounded. We must remember this about him."

Asaase Yaa's face turned serious. "We need to draw Ananse out. I have an idea, but it might sound… unconventional."

Ta Kora crossed his arms, a skeptical eyebrow raised.

Asaase Yaa continued, undeterred. "I'll sing a song; one that Ananse cannot ignore. It will be woven with some of our divine essence, aimed at his very core."

Ta Kora snorted. "A song? Really? How is that going to – "He paused, realizing that he had no better plan. His shoulders slumped. "Fine. Let's hear it."

Asaase Yaa stood in the center of the room, her presence commanding. The deities gathered around her, and forming a circle. They closed their eyes, summoning the last vestiges of their divine power, channeling it into Asaase Yaa.

She began to sing, her voice rich and resonant. It filled the room with an ancient melody. The words were a tapestry of truth and challenge, weaving through Ananse's deeds and misdeeds, stripping away his illusions and exposing his essence.

Oh, Ananse, spinner of deceit,
Your webs are wide, but now you meet
The truth you've buried, deep and dark,

We call you forth, expose your mark.
You danced on threads of lies and schemes,
But now your pride will burst at the seams,
The gods you scorned now call your name,
Come face the truth, endure the flame.

Far away, in the heart of his twisted kingdom, Ananse felt the song's impact.

His arrogance faltered, replaced by a gnawing fear.

Ntikuma listened too, tears streaming down his face. The song painted his father's essence vividly, each note uncovering layers Ntikuma had never fully grasped. He saw his father's flaws mirrored in himself – the burning ambition, the sharp cunning, the insatiable desire for more. The realization cut deep.

As Asaase Yaa's song ended, silence enveloped the room. The deities exchanged resolute glances.

"He's coming," Asaase Yaa whispered. "We've done it."

Ta Kora nodded, respect gleaming in his eyes. "Then let's be rea-."

Ananse's summon is sudden and unpleasant.

Before the group can prepare, the air shimmers and heats up with an unnatural golden glow. A low, ominous hum fills the hut. The space above them ripples like water, pulling them violently upward through the fabric of reality. Suspended in a dark, weightless void for a brief moment, they are then unceremoniously dropped.

They land in the long since twisted version of Asamando.

Asaase Yaa whispered, horrified: "Look at what he's done to our HOME!"

Ta Kora laughed dryly and without humor: "For someone who claimed to have made everything perfect, he sure let it go to ruin."

Ananse appeared suddenly, his form shifting and flickering, reflecting his unstable state of mind. His eyes blazed with fury and frustration.

"How dare you undermine me!" he roared. His voice was painful to hear, like a million spiders crawling into one's ear. Being in his presence felt like spiders skittering across one's flesh. "I gave you peace! No more wars, no more worries. Everyone was happy!"

Owuo retorted in his usual calm manner: "Happy? Everyone is stagnant, Ananse. No curiosity, no progress. Death itself isn't as it should be. You're holding the world ransom because of your ego."

Ananse's face contorts with rage. The ground beneath them cracks further, and the sky above flickers with chaotic energy. "You call it ego; I call it order. Without me, the world would fall apart. You're all too selfish to see that!" he said with a snarl.

"No, Father. You're the one who's selfish," Ntikumah said, stepping forward. "You couldn't even manage to make things better despite all your power. Look around you. Look at what you've done to Asamando."

"You've trapped everyone in a story where they can't grow," Asaase Yaa added. "You're afraid of change because it means you might lose control!"

ANANSE AND THE INFERNAL TALE

Onyankopon pressed on: "Imagine if you had made things better, Ananse. That was within your power! But instead, you created this stagnant world. And now it's falling apart."

The deities' words strike a chord with Ananse, and the realm starts to crack further. Brief flashes of the world before Ananse's control seep through the cracks – a world full of life, curiosity, and progress.

Ananse's voice was now shaking with anger and fear when he spoke: "No... No, I brought peace. I saved everyone from themselves!"

What little composure Asaase Yaa had, perhaps in order not to truly anger the spider deity, suddenly vanished as she screamed at Ananse: "Save everyone from themselves? You erased us, Ananse! You wiped out our cultures and replaced everything with obnoxious homages to yourself! You're not a savior; you're a hypocrite who can't see beyond his own ego!"

Ananse's form flickered more violently, the cracks in Asamando spreading rapidly. The flashes of the old world became more frequent.

Ntikumah's voice was soft now, careful: "Father, listen to me. We can't defeat you with raw power... But look at what you're doing to us, to the world. If you don't revert things back to normal, we'll all perish. And then who will be left to listen to your stories?"

Ananse falters, his many eyes wide with a mix of emotions. The words hit him deeply, resonating with the sliver of love and goodness still within him.

He stepped closer to his father: "Think of our family. Think of how disappointed they would be in what you've become.

You wanted to be a hero, but heroes don't destroy the world for their ego."

Ananse's form begins to stabilize slightly, the anger in his eyes replaced with a profound sadness and regret. The cracks in Asamando also stop spreading.

The web weaver spoke with a profound sadness in his voice: "I… I just wanted to be loved. To be important."

"And you are," Ntikumah said gently. "But you need to let go of this control. Let the world breathe again. Let the stories grow and change on their own."

Ananse looks around at the crumbling realm, at the faces of the deities and his son. His eyes well with tears as he realizes the truth in their words. Slowly, he begins to weave a new story, maybe his trickiest one yet, to restore the world to the way it was.

After the restoration, events moved swiftly, as is the order of Asamando.

Onyankopon stood once again at the pinnacle of divine power, his rightful position restored. The other deities resumed their rightful thrones, their faces reflecting both relief and contemplation (though Asaase Yaa still swore she found random strands of webbing on her throne).

Amid the restored glory, Ntikumah, humble and resolute, stepped forward to address the assembly. He asked for mercy for Ananse despite his misdeeds. Onyankopon invited Ntikumah to propose a solution. Ntikumah suggested transforming Ananse into a spider and confining him to a calabash as a temporary punishment to allow for reflection, rather than imposing a harsher fate. The deities considered his suggestion, and Asaase

Yaa supported it, recognizing the wisdom in giving Ananse time to contemplate his actions.

Onyankopon created an ornate calabash and placed the transformed, trembling spider Ananse inside it, sealing the lid. Ananse would serve his sentence confined to the calabash to reflect on his hubris. As the deities dispersed and returned to their domains, they reflected on the recent upheaval with newfound humility and a deeper understanding of their responsibilities. Time would tell if this humility would stick.

Ntikumah stood before Onyankopon, who looked upon him with a mix of pride and gratitude. "You have shown great wisdom and compassion, Ntikumah. Return to Earth with our thanks, and know that your actions have restored balance."

With a respectful bow, Ntikumah was (thankfully) gently transported back to his village. The sun shone brightly upon the land. There was a slight cooling breeze. All was as it should be. At least his father had a chance at redemption.

Kwaku's Squad: Daughter of Leopard

Bryoni Campbell

"Tweh-tweet." Viola cracked open her eyes, throwing off the fog of sleep, and listened intently. "Tweh-tweet."

She wasn't mistaken. A petchary – one of the Big Guy's messengers – was outside. She looked down at the sleeping child curled up next to her and kissed her granddaughter on the top of her head. The child squirmed slightly, but remained asleep. Gently, Viola extricated herself from her gangly arms and legs, placing a pillow in her stead. She heard Perry, her cousin and sidekick, snoring loudly in the front bedroom next to hers. She needn't disturb him just yet.

Soundlessly, she opened her cedar armoire and searched around in the back until her hands touched a bag. She grabbed it and pulled out a black lightweight silk tunic and cargo kilt, a utility belt and ankle boots. She donned the garments, strapped the scabbard which held two machetes to her back and pulled on a black silk balaclava before tiptoeing into the eat-in kitchen. Brer Petchary was on the windowsill above the little table next to the two-burner stove. His sharp black eyes watched her intently.

"Brer Petchary." Viola nodded. The little bird nodded in turn.

"Mama," he said, "the Big Guy want you."

"Now? Middle ah night?" Viola asked, slightly perturbed.

"No better time." He was short on words.

After scribbling a note letting Perry know she would be back later, she left silently through the window. Brer Petchary was perched on a limb of the acerola cherry tree halfway between the house and the road. Hanging on a branch was an amulet containing a single tail feather. On the evening of her initiation into the Big Guy's squad years ago, her very first mission was to procure the feather from the notoriously bloodthirsty Brer Red Hawk. Once the feather was secured, the Big Guy had made her drink a bitter concoction of various herbs and leaves. She'd promptly passed out. When she woke, the Big Guy explained to her that she was descended from a long line of Asante princesses, chosen by the Sky God to help him carry out justice in the New World. She had been blessed with the traits of Brer Leopard. It was then that she'd discovered her increased strength and agility. She could run at super speed, climb trees, practically sticking to their trunks, and somersault and backflip like a gymnast. She could leap fifty feet into the air from a standing position and swim large bodies of water with ease. Her cognition, reflexes and stamina were all superhumanly enhanced. And best of all, whenever she wore the amulet, she could fly.

"Ready?" Brer Petchary asked, dropping the amulet into her hand. She would need it to get to Cherry Island, the Big Guy's summer headquarters.

"Ready," she said, putting it on and tucking it beneath her tunic.

Brer Petchary flew from the branch with Viola trailing him into the night sky. Half an hour later, she was seated alone at a large semi-circular logwood table staring at a huge LED screen adorning the wall opposite her. The Big Guy's lair was a rather simple-looking hollowed out cherry tree. Small on the outside, inside housed a labyrinth of rooms leading to the cavernous central space where Viola sat trying not to choke on the scent of fermented cherries. She stood when the Big Guy entered, noting no other members of the squad were with him. He walked briskly over to her.

"Mama!" he said with a large-toothed smile, the gold on the center one gleaming. So good to see you again so soon." He shook her hand with all eight of his. An immortal and powerful spider, son of the God of her ancestors, and yet he was dressed in modern fashion like any young man on the street. Wearing short, springy dreads, a mesh shirt under a linen suit, Travel Fox high-tops, gold earrings in both ears and an enormous medallion in the shape of Africa hanging from red, gold, black and green beads, he could double for Buju Banton in his latest music video, 'Champion'.

"Kwaku Anansi, it's always a pleasure. Even at midnight," she replied. His smile grew wider, having always enjoyed a bit of shade from Viola.

"Unuh human being ah some real what's-it what's-it, enuh," he began without further preamble. Viola sat down and rolled her eyes. She knew quite well how little Kwaku thought of humanity's greed, stupidity and overall arrogance and how ever eager he was to teach them a lesson. "I guess you do know," he laughed. "Anyways, you ever hear 'bout the Lynx Posse?"

"In passing," Viola nodded. "Ah one ah dem drugs gang ah New York."

"Yeh, part ah di Lyon Cartel ah Toronto. Me ole enemy Brer Lion control that gang somehow. For ah couple hundred years now, Lion been insisting him ah di King of di Beasts since di colonizer dem use him image for all dem pomp and what not. As far as di Sky God is concerned, though, Brer Leopard will always retain that title, but Leopard don't business with proving no such thing. Him nuh inna it. So Lion, him just ah gwaan bad bad. Using di humans dem to do him dirty work. Now," Kwaku continued, "me wouldn't care still, enuh. You humans can do as you please, but Lion have di gang dem ah run reckless in America and Canada. Casualties ah pile up. Di U.S. and Canadian government ah put restrictions pon Jamaica. Plus, all di deportation dem. It's crazy! And di Sky God don't like it one bit. Lion must be stopped."

Kwaku picked up the remote control for the screen and tapped a few buttons. An image of a man blinked onto the screen. Viola recognized him instantly, gasping audibly. His hair was tidy, the line-up as sharp as a needle point, his clothes neat, and he wore a mountain of gold rope chains, but it was him– the stranger who had been in her yard in Bois Content not twenty-four hours before, disheveled and dirty. He was dead now. The police had seen to that.

"Yeh, you know him," Kwaku stated matter-of-factly. "So you can see, ah no simple ting this. Him was ah top lieutenant, di son ah di gang leader, di Don. According to di bird dem, him send pon ah mission to find me." He looked over at Viola.

"Him was in bad shape when me see him earlier." They were both silent for a moment.

"You don't wonder how comes him end up inna your yard?" Kwaku asked.

"Of course! Content is not a place wheh gunman and mad man just show up so."

"Right." Kwaku paused. "Me tink ah di cherry tree. Everyone know seh nothing Anansi love more than cherry."

"What?" Viola was incredulous. "But millions ah cherry tree deh ah Jamaica."

"Yes, but one deh inna *your* yard." He paused, gritting his teeth angrily. "I feel like Lion dem know someting. Like dem wanted you."

The reality of his words dawned on her. Being on the Big Guy's squad offered her family protection, but Kwaku was also a trickster and had amassed an impressive list of enemies. That the man in her yard wasn't just some ordinary criminal, but purposefully sent to find her, sent shivers down her spine.

"But Inspector Donovan get to him first," Viola offered, refocusing.

"Right. Di father coming to Jamaica later this morning to identify di body of him son. Me ah keep an eye pon him. Maybe me can find out what else Lion ah plan. I don't know if di Don is vengeance minded, but Inspector Donovan don't know what him up 'gainst."

"Lion knows Donovan belongs to me?" Viola swallowed hard. Inspector Donovan *was* close to her. He was her granddaughter's father; a fact the child didn't even know. Him being a member of the Jamaica Constabulary Force – under fire for recent extrajudicial killings – was cause enough to keep their relationship clandestine. Lion and his human gang potentially having this information was a chilling development.

"I don't think so. Dem ongly after Donovan because him kill di son." Kwaku became pensive. He looked at the screen and tugged on the hairs on his chin. "No, is not Donovan me need to worry 'bout too too much at all." He turned to look at her. "Mama, you know ah who plant da cherry tree deh?"

"My grandmother," she said simply. Viola smiled. She remembered often taking her grandmother's stool, a curved seat supported by a carved leopard between four pillars, and sitting under the tree with a book. The cherry tree had always had a particular pull on her. The tree seemed to have the same attraction for her own granddaughter too. The child could make a bed and sleep in that tree if allowed. As the image of her precious descendant coalesced in her mind, the smile on her face disappeared. She raised her eyes slowly to see Kwaku watching her intently.

"Yeah," he said quietly. "Go and secure your yard and your granddaughter. No harm must not come to her."

Viola nodded, clenching her teeth. Lion would be stopped before that was ever a possibility. She departed the Big Guy's lair the way she came, leaving the amulet with Brer Petchary.

Creeping silently back into the house, she changed and crawled into the bed with her granddaughter. The child was still blissfully asleep. Viola kissed her forehead and hugged her tightly.

* * *

Hours later, at the Old Harbour police station, a few district constables were on duty outside of the blue and white building when Kwaku arrived. He had changed into a sleek black bodysuit and boots. Under the cloak of night, it was a simple matter to land on top of the one-storey building. Crouching low, surveilling the area, he was surprised when Viola joined him a few minutes later, although he shouldn't have been. Donovan was an Inspector in the Constabulary Force and the target of a man who worked for his enemy. It didn't take great intelligence work to conclude that the police station would warrant a visit.

"She's safe," Viola said by way of greeting. "Deep in the bush. Perry is with her."

Kwaku nodded, a muscle in his jaw jumping. He signaled for Viola to be quiet. They listened through the window as the Inspector spoke.

"…a positive ID. Verdain Lyon Junior," Donovan said.

"Hmm, Verdain Lyon. Me know dah name deh. Wait ah minute. Lyon? As in di Lyon Cartel?" the Sergeant asked.

"Yeh, ah di son ah di Don."

"Damn!" the Sergeant cursed.

"Yeh mon. Me send di use of force report to di Supa arready. PM Patterson have we ah cross we tee. This bound to go up di chain." Donovan took a deep breath and exhaled loudly. "Me due ah Spanish Town tomorrow. Get some sleep, Sarge. You inna command while me gone. Good job yesterday. The constables were exemplary."

"Thank you, Inspector. Drive good."

Papers rustled as the Inspector prepared to leave. Viola began to stand up, but Kwaku quickly pulled her back down.

"Lyon Senior deh bout," he whispered. "Him inna di BMW ova desso. Him look… dif'rent. Me nuh know." Kwaku inclined his head toward a black BMW with dark tinted windows parked on the side of the road. "Me find out from Brer Mongoose that Lion ah work with Brer Dead. Dead been after me for eons. Brer Dead promise to appeal to di Sky God on Lion behalf if dem ketch me. You 'member di lesson from me encounter with Dead?"

She nodded. "If you cyaan ketch Kwaku, you ketch him shirt," she said solemnly.

"Exactly. That bastard Lion was out to deliver me to Dead using you as bait! That's why dem send Junior ah you yard. Lion outta him mind. Is one thing to hold ah grudge 'gainst me for embarrassing him but is another to–"

Before Kwaku could finish, Donovan exited the police station and entered his SUV. He started the engine and quickly pulled out of the station lot, turning east onto Old Harbour Road. The BMW immediately pulled out after him and began trailing the Inspector.

"Let's go," Kwaku said hastily.

They followed the two vehicles covertly at close range. A mile outside of town, right before an Anglican church, the BMW suddenly sped up and rammed into the back of the SUV. Tires screeched loudly as the Inspector's vehicle braked and veered sharply, narrowly missing a large jacaranda tree before careening into a steep, bushy ravine on the left-hand side of the road. The SUV tumbled over twice, crackling and crunching through the underbrush before finally landing on its roof and sliding quickly down the craggy slope.

Racing into the ravine after the Inspector, Kwaku spun webbing around each of the front tires and pulled it taut, effectively slowing the vehicle. The SUV finally ground to a halt, trailing shrubs and greenery behind it. Kwaku and Viola scrambled to the driver's side. Viola tore off the door. Peering inside, they saw him hanging from his seat by the seat belt, the airbag deflating around him. The Inspector was unconscious, but still alive. Blood trickled from a wound on his forehead. Kwaku reached in and unbuckled the seatbelt. Inspector Donovan dropped into Viola's arms, moaning slightly. She carried him a few feet away and laid him down for Kwaku to quickly examine him.

"Him have ah concussion," Kwaku sighed, "and some broken bones. It's not critical but we have to get him to ah hospital before–"

With a thud, an enormous human landed on the belly of the vehicle behind them. Standing almost seven feet tall, he was dressed in a red and gold suit made of an elastic material that stretched across his thick muscular physique. No covering hid his face – a face that looked exactly like Verdain Lyon Junior but some twenty years older and decidedly feline. Kwaku and Viola stood quickly, shielding the Inspector.

"Kwaku Anansi? You deh yah!" Although it was the human Verdain Lyon Senior moving his lips to speak, Kwaku could hear the otherworldly snarl of Lion behind his tongue. "This is all working out even better than I had hoped. Here I was just gonna kill the bastard what killed my son, but…" His predatory gaze shifted and settled on Viola. Cocking his head this way and that way, he smiled showing enlarged canine teeth. "Well! Who do we have here?"

"Your worst nightmare," Viola said boldly, staring him down and assuming a fighting stance. Kwaku was impressed. Viola was always ready.

"My… my," he sputtered through peals of laughter, his fingers splayed out against his massive chest, "*my* worst nightmare?" He sobered immediately. Drawing up to his full height, eyes narrowed, he said through clenched teeth, "I don't think so. No, Daughter of Leopard, it is I who am *your* worst nightmare!"

The blood drained from Kwaku's face. How had he known about Viola? Thinking quickly, Kwaku forced his body to assume a relaxed position and adopted a casual tone to his voice. "My good sir, it seem you know who we be, but we are in di most unfortunate position of not knowing who you are."

"Kwaku, you haffi do better than that, mon." He smirked, pausing for effect. "You know who I am. You and di Sky God are not the only ones who use the humans for your benefit. But unlike me, you haven't figured out how to bind their souls and take over their bodies, have you?"

It was clear that the being speaking was not fully human, but Kwaku was not prepared to hear those words uttered from his lips.

"Lion, what have you done?" he asked, aghast. His lip curled in disgust.

"The human form is most useful for its mental acuity and for navigating the systems they have set up. After all, I could not fly on an airplane in my lion's body," he laughed. "But my strength and quickness improve their extremely weak constitution. The mere human body is not the best to accommodate me, however, it will do. For now." He turned his gaze back to Viola.

Viola looked at Kwaku quizzically and then looked back at Lion before doubling over with laughter, cackling loudly and slapping her knee. "You ah bind soul and ah take ova body. You do alla that … and you choose *that* body." She wheezed. "I mean you coulda had anyone, ah President or Prime Minister! Even ah Michael Jordan, Jackson or Tyson! And you choose a two-bit drugs dealer! Lion, you cyaan be serious!"

Kwaku glanced sideways at Viola. Was she going mad? The situation was not humorous in the least. Lion roared loudly, agitation written clearly on his face. A vein in his forehead throbbed. His tanned skin took on a reddened pallor. He was seething. Viola's taunt bothered him. Kwaku began to chuckle too, following her lead.

"Him not even good-looking. Together dem make one hugly beast!" Kwaku laughed louder.

"Shut up! Shut up! Shut up!" Lion bellowed, his fists clenched at his side. "Not every being lucky enough to receive di Sky God's blessings. I have tried for centuries to get what you got simply for being born! You won't be laughing when I bind your soul to mine, Daughter of Leopard!"

He lunged wildly for Viola. Kwaku sprang up at the same time, knocking Lion to the side. Lion rolled and jumped up, ready again to go after Viola. Kwaku, still on the ground, grabbed at his leg, trying to slow him down.

"Mama! Run!" Kwaku shouted as Lion kicked him off.

Viola took off down the face of the ravine. The man-beast hesitated for a second, grinning. Kwaku registered with a shudder that the chase excited Lion. A second later, he sped off down the slope after her. Kwaku leapt up, shooting webs wherever he could, swinging down into the ravine. Lion chased Viola with a single-minded hunger. Kwaku suddenly understood. Lion wasn't trying to deliver him to Dead at all. He was only ever after Viola! Superhuman Viola! Lyon Senior's body was not adequate for Lion's purposes. He was tiring rapidly, but she was as energetic as ever, leading him deeper down into the gorge, forcing him to the limits of his strength. It was so obvious, Kwaku wanted to kick himself. Lion needed a superhuman body for his wicked experiment.

With feline agility, Viola jumped from rock surface to tree limb, over downed trunks and under low-hanging branches. Twice, she ran to a spot halfway down the ravine, then doubled back, sliding just out of Lion's reach, only to run headlong down the slope again. Kwaku pursued until he finally caught up to her. He swung alongside her and caught her eye. She pointed up ahead of her.

"A sinkhole," she mouthed.

Hidden by shrubbery, sure enough, there was a deep depression in the ground ahead of them. Kwaku used his webbing to pull himself into a tree hanging over the hole. Viola ran straight toward the pit. This time she wasn't veering off. At the very last moment, Kwaku shot out a web. Viola caught hold of it, swinging out wide to the far side of the hole and back toward the limb where Kwaku caught her and pulled her up. Lion, running at top speed, couldn't stop himself in time. Where there should have been ground, he found air. He pumped his arms and legs, desperately trying to grasp anything to hold onto. Vegetation slipped through his fingers. He tumbled down fifty feet, bumping on the rocky terrain the entire way down. Kwaku quickly spun webbing, binding Lion as he fell. At the bottom of the pit, wrapped up like a mummy, Lion roared and screamed, fighting against the webbing with no success.

Kwaku held tightly to Viola for a brief moment, giving thanks to the Sky God, as her heart beat rapidly against his chest. He waited until her breathing slowed to a normal rate before disengaging from her. "Mama, you truly embody Brer Leopard. You represent di Asante well."

"Thank you Kwaku Anansi. I am forever in your service," she replied, lowering her head momentarily, the relief evident in her voice.

Looking down at Lion struggling in the pit, he sighed. "I must take this abomination to the Sky God for reckoning." He cocked his head, listening to the sirens in the distance. "The police and ambulance dem ah come. Get Donovan to safety. Me will send Brer Petchary for you again when necessary."

She nodded and jumped down from the tree. In a flash she was gone, sprinting and hurdling up the ravine slope. Kwaku watched her for a long moment. It would be even more imperative to secure Viola's granddaughter, and heir, now. He turned back to Lion.

"And now for you…" he said jumping from the tree branch.

Anansi and the Hot-Lanta Flow
Sara Chisolm

Once upon a time, after the southern rapper Tricky Trick's final album was released, an eight-legged secret stowed away in the suitcase of a Ghanaian foreign exchange student. The secret crawled out of the luggage on its eight black spindly legs as the bags bumped along the conveyor belt of the Atlanta airport. The secret was sometimes called Anansi. His treacherous webs blew him to his father's blue sky kingdom, under pristine lakes, and across all of the vast beauty of Africa. He had traveled to many places and seen many things but none like the dirty south. His tricks and games played upon humanity could not soothe his spirit. The trickster longed for a place where narratives reigned supreme. Everywhere Anansi went, whispers of a narrative called rap were tangled in his webs and mind. He fought furiously with his father, Nyame, over who had the most narratives. The sky god was a hoarder of wisdom and couldn't be beat when it came to telling stories. The time had come for Anansi to up his storytelling game. Only in Hot-Lanta could Anansi develop a lyrical flow so wicked he'd have his own father falling from the sky.

Anansi was quick to declare the glaring cityscape, polluted air, and overly polite folks as his proper dominion. He was a god; the world was his plaything. His tricks spread like a virus among the population. One bite from him will have a man laughing hysterically while knockin' boots with his dime-piece-of-a-mistress. A scratch with his spindly leg will have a man thinking he's firing off shots in the middle of the club while he's holding a banana. If Anansi was having a terrible day and couldn't find enough people to bother at the bus stations, he would burrow into the ankle of the first person unfortunate enough to cross his path. As he hitches a ride through his victims' bloodstreams, he weaves his will through thoughts that act as connecting webs. Having complete control of their minds and actions, he lingers in their bodies causing illness and mischief for a day or two. It was a miracle that the CDC did not investigate further when Anansi's infectious influence caused a riot at the last Tricky Trick concert. After that debacle, Anansi thought it would be best to lie low. Higher human populations meant discovery. More narratives of his deeds for his father, the sky god Nyame. Anansi was intrigued and fearful of the spread of word. He vowed to find a human and place just outside of Atlanta's busy streets to develop his rapping skills.

Anansi chose a teenage boy who was sitting at a bus stop leading outside of the urban wilderness. The boy named DeVonta was decked out in the latest Tricky Trick merch and lived in the quiet suburbs right outside of Atlanta. The teenager's head bobbed to the newest joint by the rapper blasting from his boombox. The snare drum on the track was as seductive and prominent as a southern drawl. DeVonta freestyle rapped a couple of lines. Anansi cocked his head in wonder. Could this teenager be the rap mentor that he was searching for? It was obvious that Anansi had finally found someone who was a bigger fan of Tricky Trick than him. He burrowed into the teen's ankle and made mischief in the Atlanta suburbs when he pleased. Trash cans were lit on fire, car license plates switched, prank calls made. Harmless fun that kept Anansi busy when he wasn't developing his poetic lyrics. All of the mayhem started to seem like a distraction to Anansi. How could he become a better storyteller than the sky god?

DeVonta listened to southern hip-hop artists all the time. The rappers of Hot-Lanta were spittin' mad flows. They were lyrical geniuses. Most songs were about girls shaking their rumps in the clubs, raunchy words over a loud bass. The rhythm of the music reminded him of stampeding herds, grunts from animals mating, or the flow of water. Primal needs satisfied and expressed through songs. The words from a rapper's mouth were life. Anansi struggled with which words to use for certain songs. Putting together a few lines to some beats from Tricky Trick's most popular songs encouraged him to continue. He envied humans and their forms of self-expression. As he lingered in the teenager's body, his dream of a stage and the presence of a roaring crowd became more evident.

One morning, a splitting headache drew Anansi out of the teenager's body. DeVonta bobbed his head while Tricky Trick's number one single boomed over the radio. They had just snuck into the small suburban house that DeVonta lived in with his mom. They had returned from a night of buggin' out with friends. A night that was supposed to be spent at the library studying and writing a report on a book called *Charlotte's Web*. DeVonta glared at the black spider that seemed to be growing by the second.

ANANSI AND THE HOT-LANTA FLOW

"What is that thing, yo?" DeVonta yelled. The teenager jumped up from the bed, shut off his radio, and collapsed on his rumpled sheets. "Mom, help," he murmured. It usually took a moment or two for Anansi's victims to become catatonic after he left their bodies. He wanted to stay and play but his wish to possess a lyrical flow outgrew his need for mischief.

Anansi's body swelled with desire until he became hella' big. Spindly legs became fat and warm like sausages as his thorax bloated and became tender. Layer upon layer of his black skin and exoskeleton fell onto the cream-colored carpet. His head split open like an overripe melon. A large chocolate man with wide-set eyes, thick lips, and a beaky nose sat in the middle of the spider guts. The man stretched his arms out, entrails splashed against the bed and hip-hop posters that covered the walls. The man was Anansi but different. He groaned loudly as his vocal cords developed.

A fist pounded against the bedroom door. "What the hell is going on in there, DeVonta? I told you not to be bringing any fast little girls in my house," a loud voice called out from the other side of the door. DeVonta's mother.

Anansi looked at the yellow bone skinned boy with baggy jeans and fresh new high tops sprawled among the superhero sheets. He had a placid grin and wide stare that was fixed on nothing at all. Anansi nudged the boy's gangrene-infected ankle. It always took a trip to the hospital and a shot of penicillin for the full effects of the trickster's magic to wear off.

"We talked about this, DeVonta. I'm coming in and if I see any little girls in your room —" The door swung open before

Anansi could move. A woman the color of desert sand wearing a silk bonnet and bathrobe gasped. Her cup of coffee shook in her hands. Her eyes were locked on Anansi like a pitbull's jaw on a bone. Her mind was probably filled with a million and one thoughts on how to kill him.

Anansi held up his hands, palms facing the angry mother, his eyes pleading. Another trick, flip of a card, slide of the hand. Images of the teen smiling, spilling soda on the cream-colored carpet and laughing about it filled up Anansi's mind. He threaded these moments and wove a web of happy thoughts between himself and the mother. The coffee cup stilled and the anger vanished from the mother's demeanor to be replaced by a dreamy gaze and gentle grin. The binding threads were not visible to the human eye, but Anansi saw that the threads were tight.

"You see, he's happy," Anansi rasped. His hand cupped his new throat. Humans only used words to convey sentiment. What good could words do against his trickery? She would be easy and harmless to manipulate.

"Yes," the mother said, smiling. She cast her flighty gaze upon her son and shook her head. "But covered in blood." The grin vanished and was replaced by shock.

"He's just sleeping," Anansi said. He tightened his threads of thought with his mind.

The mother's head shook hard and her bonnet tumbled to the ground. Coffee split from her mug.

"I can explain," Anansi said. He could enchant the horn off a rhino, why would an upset human mother be any different?

ANANSI AND THE HOT-LANTA FLOW

"How the hell are you going to explain how you, a grown-ass man, is sitting in the middle of a teenage boy's room covered in blood?" The angry mother drew back the scalding hot coffee and aimed it at Anansi's head. Without his infectious pincers, his tricks weren't as effective. He rolled over and the mug shattered against the wall. Anansi stood up, grabbed a pillow from the bed, and covered his baby-making parts with it. DeVonta's mother turned and ran down the hallway. Anansi picked up a baggy pair of jeans and slid into a pair of DeVonta's sandals before running out of the room. The mother wasn't done yet. Her whole body was shaking as she held a glistening butcher knife. She stood between Anansi and the front door.

"Where do you think you're going?" DeVonta's mother yelled.

Without his threads of thought, Anansi couldn't control her. He was positive that some rapper had to have a recorded song about how to escape a house with a knife-wielding angry mother. He hadn't heard that song.

> *I said once,*
> *I'll say it twice,*
> *DeVonta is going to be just fine.*

The lyrics flowed out of his mouth. The anger in DeVonta's mother's face was replaced with a half grin and lucid stance.

"Humans!" Anansi said with ire. He threw the bloody pillow at the mother. She screeched as the knife fell to the ground. Anansi pushed her as he ran to the front door. He swung the door open and was greeted by a peaceful sunny day. Birds chirped nearby. The pristine houses had the same architecture except in different colors. The sprinklers on nearly every lush green lawn were on. He ducked behind an enormous hedge as a dark complected man strolled by with an immaculately groomed toy poodle. Anansi rushed to put on the baggy jeans. He struggled with zipping them up. The jeans had been so loose on DeVonta. A groan escaped his mouth as the hedge moved. Loud barking broke the tranquility of the sprawling suburban neighborhood.

"What's the matter, Piper?" the man cooed as he bent down and scratched his dog behind the ear. Piper continued to bark and tug at the leash as Anansi buttoned up the tight jeans. He just didn't understand human clothing sizes. Why bother to wear anything this difficult at all?

DeVonta's mother stormed out of the house with a metal baseball bat clutched in her white-knuckled hand. "There's some huge man wandering around the neighborhood who hurt DeVonta," the mother said in a venomous tone.

"Did you call the police?" the man asked while drawing a hand to his mouth. His eyes darted around the lawn nervously.

"The police can come after I kill this motherfucker," the mother yelled. Her narrowed red eyes surveyed the area. She turned towards the thick bushes that Anansi was hiding in. For a second Anansi was positive that she had spotted him. He breathed a sigh of relief when she turned away.

"What was that?" DeVonta's mother said as she faced Anansi's hiding place.

"Look," the man said while pointing to several people walking towards Devonta's house. "The cavalry has arrived." Piper started to bark as his owner stroked the little fluff ball.

A few more people stepped out of their homes and gathered on the angry mother's lawn.

Anansi's eyes grew big as he stared out at the large group gathering. He'd never be able to fight them off. The toy poodle darted out of his owner's grasp. Anansi's two hearts raced in alternating beats as a flash of white sprang into the bushes. Teeth clamped onto his arm, he screamed in pain as he leapt to a standing position. Piper tugged at Anansi's arm for a few seconds before falling to the ground. Just enough time for Anansi to run as fast as his human legs could carry him, which wasn't very far. Warm hands grabbed at his shoulders, abdomen, and wrists. The hands quickly became fists that pounded his flesh. Failed attempts to run away from the encroaching mob made him weak and tired. His body crumpled with every blow. He finally accepted their wrath. What else could he do? Every hit sculpted knots. Rough hands stroked bruises upon his body. Blood painted the concrete. He held their contempt in the web of his mind and wove a delicate silk thread between their thoughts and his own. Words – his words pierced the air.

> *Punch one, two, three,*
> *I'm the real spider man,*
> *You see,*
> *Ain't got eight legs but my words will do you in.*

The crowd parted. Anansi opened his eyes and glanced at the serene expressions on their faces. His lyrics had somehow tangled throughout their thought connection.

Try to compare
My lyrics—
A web that I caught you in,
Sprung from the deceit that I spread across your city.

The powerful words Anansi was spittin' kept tumbling out of his mouth. Each word was carefully woven.

Hot-Lanta got the joints,
But I'm on that African trend.
Can't relate,
Don't hate!

The lyrics were different from Tricky Trick's Billboard-charting single but the expression was the same. Words, lyrics – could mean something. The poodle ran up to Anansi and started to bark loudly.

You don't know who you're tangling with.

Anansi stood still as he thought about what he should say next. The connection, his beautiful web of lyrics, unraveled on the crisp morning wind. People shook their heads and looked vexed before focusing all of their malice on him.

ANANSI AND THE HOT-LANTA FLOW

Got that thunder,
Plus eight—
Legs crawling down from my venomous lyric thread.
You can stand, you can stare,
Let's play a game of dare,
So you better listen with care,

Piper's jaws clamped down on Anansi's leg. The small dog pulled until Anansi kicked his leg out. His aim was off but Piper let go of his pants. The toy poodle continued to bark. Anansi felt his hold on the crowd slipping away. His lyrics were the antidote to his own undoing. He moved his hands, fingers twisting the invisible threads into a woven tapestry of thought and sentiments already spoken. The crowd's rage was replaced by smiles. Anansi wondered what DeVonta would think of his lyrical magic.

You don't want to toy with me,
Hotter than the Serengeti,

Threads of thought spun around Piper. The dog turned his head from side to side as the threads spun tighter. Anansi smiled. Piper could see his magic. The dog ran over to a tree on one of the copycat lawns. His small body quivered as he whimpered.

These lyrics I'm spittin'
Splash across the concrete-
I ain't from the streets,

but every corner on every block,
Is going to know me.

Anansi's story was passed down from generation to generation. Whole villages listened while warming themselves at campfires. Mothers warned their children using the trickster's deeds to serve as foreboding lessons. Books were written and read in places where the heat of the African desert was a distant dream. Anansi was telling his own tale with powerful words that wove magical threads. He tilted his head as his lips turned up at the corners. The sky god wouldn't be able to compete with his lyrical flow.

Not from the streets but from the motherland.
Teeth are the only things that matter to me.
Let me get you up to speed,
Names Anansi,

The words twisted and bridged away from the people to linger in the air before passing through the doorways of houses. He could see that his words reached more people.

Not a fiend in the streets,
Causing havoc wherever I go,
Let me hit you with this melodic tone,
Best lyricist,
Not from Charlotte's Web,
Pick another book for those kids to read instead.
The law of the jungle spreads!

ANANSI AND THE HOT-LANTA FLOW

A wicked grin formed on Anansi's lips. He highly doubted that DeVonta's lyrics would be this hypnotic. Maybe threads and words could heal. If Anansi was able to help DeVonta, the angry mob wouldn't need to be subdued by his webs. On second thought, he also wanted the teenager to marvel at his lyrics.

Everyone thinks,
Anansi ain't got heat,
I can put you to sleep or heal you in the streets,

Anansi pulled the threads of the web that were in DeVonta's house. They had fun running the streets and causing mischief in the neighborhood. Anansi focused on the moments when they were just listening to hip hop records in his room. DeVonta occasionally scribbled down lyrics, looked at framed pictures of his mother holding him, or ate sandwiches packed with last night's fried chicken or country steak. DeVonta needed to write more lyrics and listen to more hip-hop albums. The teenager's body, superhero sheets and all, was being pulled through the air by the thought webs.

Don't come after me,
my song will bring the heat,
what you know about teeth?
I'll bite you with these words,
Listen to this next verse,
But never problems for me,
It's not a pop quiz,

I see you studyin',
Hear this knowledge,
I'm kickin'
Before you continue buggin',

Everyone's head turned to look at the teen as the webs placed him on the ground. Anansi's brow became damp as he thought about what his next lyrics were. If his words weren't good enough, he might not be able to help the teenager and save himself.

How can I say,
Something that's been said in a million ways,
ATL is a place with amazing southern grace,
I found a home,
But I can't keep it this way,
Look at DeVonta!
Can't leave the community this way!
Forget about me,
Remember DeVonta instead!

DeVonta's eyes fluttered. The teenager sat up and coughed into his hand. He looked around. "What happened?"

The carefully crafted thought webs fell to the ground like used silly string.

"My baby, my baby," DeVonta's mother screamed. She dropped her weapon of choice, ran to her son, and wrapped her arms around him. Everyone in the community gathered around

ANANSI AND THE HOT-LANTA FLOW

DeVonta and his mother. Everyone except Piper, who started to bark and nip at Anansi's legs.

"Shoo," Anansi said but Piper wouldn't stop. "You are a little thing with teeth," Anansi said while looking Piper in the eyes.

How easy it would be to become a spider and burrow a hole in Piper's ankle. Piper understood how the jungle worked. Anansi became smaller and smaller. The crowd was heading for DeVonta's house. No one would miss the toy poodle in a moment of chaos. Piper whined while tilting his head. It would take some time for folks to notice Piper's behavior changes. The dog only had teeth to express himself. Anansi sprouted more legs once he was Piper's size. Piper gave Anansi one last glance before running away.

Anansi shrugged as he became smaller. Someone would walk by and need to catch the bus back to the city proper. The suburbs were not a place for Anansi. He would eventually become a stowaway in some unlucky African person's luggage, his rap narrative besting any story that his father could think up. At this very moment the concrete jungle of Atlanta desperately needed him. Who among the Atlanta rappers could produce a lyrical web like Anansi? Rap battles, promoters, and hype men waited back in the city for a rap god like Anansi. He was ready for his narrative flow to propel him to new heights of infamy.

The Rainmaker

Yazeed Dele-Azeez

It was a great tragedy to the animal kingdom when the Rain-Goddess Nyame announced that she could no longer be consulted to tell when the rains would come. Neither could she hold it back when it became unwanted as was normal in the olden days. The skies are no longer what they used to be, she explained. The layer of air protecting the earth from the sun's excess heat was shrinking, because the population of humans and animals was growing and this was causing a lot of trees, who provide this special protective air, to be killed. And as trees were the main intercessory for her answering the prayers for rain, there was little she could do if they continued to be destroyed.

The matter was debated at the court of the Lion-King. Most of the wise animals consulted to give their opinions. The Hyena, the Leopard and the Fox all suggested that since humans were the main growers and destroyers of trees, a delegation from the animal kingdom should be sent to them to let them see reasons why they should plant more trees than they destroy. The delegation from the animal kingdom were greeted with derision by the leaders of humans who never took anything from the animal kingdom seriously. Yet as the animals had no knowledge of the art of planting trees, they were stuck in a dilemma about what to do.

Anansi, the Spider, was never consulted for his opinion about the rain matter. Was he too tiny or too insignificant to be asked for his own opinions, he asked himself, despite the fact that everyone knew he was one of the wisest animals alive? Ok, he would prove to them that size had nothing to do with wisdom and common sense. He would show the animals his might and they would one day come to worship him as a god.

On a great Eke market day, Anansi went to the market to announce to every animal who could hear him that he'd be making a journey to the skies to plead with the Sky-God to make him the new Rain-God in place of Nyame. And he'd be bringing back the much-needed rain prediction office to the animal kingdom. Many of the animals around laughed and wiped the tears from their eyes. Nevertheless, the rumour spread wide and far. Anansi had grown a reputation as a never-do-well trickster who spent his time plotting hare-brained schemes that the gullible ones among the animals always fell for. At some point he claimed he could stop the sun from shining and any who wanted to have a good harvest should pay him a bag of cowries. Another time he claimed he could turn well-made pounded yam and vegetable stew into bags of cowries, far more than the worth of the food. Soon his house was teeming with mounds upon mounds of delicious food which he never managed to turn into cowries. His most famous con which even the Lion-King fell for was that he could turn palm wine into water during a period of drought. These schemes often ended in a fiasco which his family, especially his long-suffering wife, Aso, often had to bear the brunt of.

The Harmattan fog had barely kissed the land goodbye when Anansi set out on his journey. Wearing his best suit and best hat, he observed himself in the mirror to ensure his outfit was as charming as he wanted it to be. He looked to one side of his webbed hut where Aso slept heavily. Then he looked to one corner of the room where her basket was situated. Underneath it was the new location she'd chosen to hide her money purse away from him.

Walking quietly on tiptoe so as not to awaken Aso, he shifted the basket, took the money purse and emptied its cowrie content. Smiling wickedly to himself, he replaced the basket to its normal position. Nothing to worry about, he was very sure this latest scheme would work, and that any money he took from her would be repaid times five.

Grabbing his walking stick, he stepped out into the cold, quietly shutting the door behind him.

Most of the animals were still in their last lap of sleep so many didn't see him leave.

Anansi braved the dusty cold until he came to the border road that separated the animal kingdom from the land of humans.

Having hidden himself in a nearby bush, he waited and waited until he saw one of those large agricultural trucks that ferried farm produce from the forests to the city. He spun a web and hopped on to it without the driver's awareness.

Having reached the center of the big city of humans, Anansi jumped down as easily as he'd climbed. He dusted off his outfit and hat with a handkerchief and checked his eight legs to ensure they were still clean enough to command a man's respect.

Wiping his brow and sighing deeply, he began to look round for his best friend in the city, Nwanku, the dog. Nwanku was the only animal who had opted to live in the city with humans rather than his own kind in the forests. The animals often insulted him, calling him a traitor, a Man ass-licker and a disgrace to the animal kingdom. But Nwanku never cared. As long as Man was ok with having him around, the animals could all go to hell. As for Anansi, he rather liked Nwanku, for in him, he saw a common bond they shared of being outcasted and castigated in the animal kingdom. This sense of injustice they felt for themselves solidified a comradeship that had lasted over the years.

"Ah Anansi, my friend! Is it you I'm seeing or are my eyes deceiving me!?" Nwanku shouted as soon as he spotted his friend from a distance. He looked dirty, mangy with sores on his ears which attracted flies, and the bones of his rib cage could be counted from afar. Clearly Nwanku wasn't having a good time in the City of Man, Anansi thought. But Nwanku never cared, he'd rather die of starvation in the big city than come to his own kind for food and solace.

"It is me indeed, Nwanku! Your eyes are as sharp as they always are. Long time, my friend."

After another banter about how each other's family were doing, Nwanku barked:

"You are my good friend Anansi but I know you don't just come to the city to greet me. What mischief have you got up your sleeve this time, eh?"

MYTHS, GODS & IMMORTALS: ANANSI

"Hardly a mischief, my friend. Come and we shall talk."

The two friends stepped away from the roar of traffic and the thronging mass of human feet hurrying to and fro.

They crept under the shade of a Lakwa plant and spoke in low tones.

"I should be forever grateful if you can do me this one last great favour, Nwanku."

"You can always count on me, Anansi. What are friends for, eh?"

"How must I pay you, Nwanku, if the plan works well?"

Nwanku laughed; two things were on his mind. One, he knew his friend would never talk of paying him if he knew that he really needed the money. Secondly, he knew Anansi's plans often led to disaster so what payment did he need for that? To cap it all off, he didn't need Nwanku's animal kingdom cowries here in the city where they were scoffed at. He survived only on man's patronage in exchange for loyal service and that was enough for him.

"You coming here to see me is payment enough... You know I feel lonely sometimes."

* * *

Anansi slept in the big city for three days and three nights, waiting to receive a message from his friend. Nwanku kept an eye on his Master, watching him keenly until the day he left the house for a long travel with his family. Nwanku sneaked into his Master's house through the window and whistled for Anansi who followed suit.

THE RAINMAKER

Nwanku, of all the animals, knew the language of humans, and could write as well as read it fairly well. Yet that was not all he knew.

Anansi, holding his heart in his mouth, watched as his friend Nwanku sat on his Master's desk and began to operate an electronic machine with a wide mirror screen that displayed strange illuminated numbers and write-ups.

To Anansi's amazement Nwanku pressed buttons on a flat plastic platform on his Master's desk which was connected to the screen.

A moment of tuneless humming and paw clickety-clicking later, Nwanku was done. A paper churned itself out of the wide thin hole of another machine. Nwanku collected the paper and barked: "It's done, let's hurry away before Master comes back." The two friends jumped out of the window quickly.

Back on the streets, Nwanku taught Anansi the secrets encoded in the piece of paper.

"All you have to do, my friend, is consult this paper. It will tell you all you need to know."

"You are the best animal of all, Nwanku!" cried Anansi.

"If you say so," Nwanku replied, lolling his tongue and wagging his tail.

* * *

On a bright Eke market day when all the animals were busy buying and selling, Anansi emerged out of nowhere and began to rant:

"Ho-ho-ho! Who have ears let them hear. The Sky-God has just informed me that the rains will fall two days from now. Ho-ho-ho! I, Anansi, owner of the bag of wisdom, have spoken. They who have ears let them hear!"

The animals went about their business pretending not to see or hear Anansi. Those who stopped to listen did so with an expression of paying attention to a madman ranting.

In two days, as Anansi predicted, the rains came down heavily. The ground waters swelled and flowed like a brown python through the village routes. The animals brought out their water cans and drums, rejoicing, singing praises of Anansi. The little ones went out to dance in the rain.

The pattern repeated itself. "There will be a half day of rain! … There will be three straight days of rain!"… "There will be no rain on the fifth, sixth and seventh! The rains will come on the third!"

The animals started to listen. Anansi stopped making his rain forecasts public. If you wanted to know about the rains, you came to consult him in his webbed hut with two bags of cowries. Soon Anansi was sinking in money as the animals made pilgrimages to his hut. One wanted to escape the rain on a wedding day, or a travel day or a festival day. Even the Lion-King and his Royal court who had shunned little animals like Anansi started to invite him for rain forecasts.

"Now let them wag their tongue again," Aso said. "I've always known that my husband is the owner of wisdom." She made sure to prepare him his best meals at the appropriate times.

One cool evening Anansi eased his back on his armchair after a delicious dinner of pounded yam and palm wine, which he'd

THE RAINMAKER

eaten to the point of regurgitation. He belched loudly, smacked his lips and began to reflect on the secret of his success.

A long time ago during one of his visits to the big city in search of opportunities, Nwanku had told him of an Oracle-object made from human metal-magic which had the solution to every problem in this world. When Anansi doubted the existence of such a thing, Nwanku had told him that the 'thing' was in his Master's house. It only needed his Master to be out for Anansi to come in and see for himself. "It's the new Oracle of Man. It has answers to every problem of life. That's why Man no longer cares to worship the gods of their ancestors. Because the 'thing' is there to guide them through their lives. Every man and woman worthwhile has a 'thing' in his house which he worships and consults in time of need. Whether it is it making a living, creating children, building glass tower houses that reach into the clouds, constructing horse-houses that can run on land and lift up into the sky in flight."

So when the Rain-Goddess announced her inability to control rain, Anansi began to nurse the idea of using this new 'thing' of Man to do it.

Nwanku was a gifted one, Anansi thought. Nwanku, more than any other animal, was prolific in the art of reading and writing, both in animal language and human language. He'd used the 'thing' to consult when the rains will come for the next three months. He'd printed it out on paper and had translated it from human language to animal language so Anansi could understand it. Still, dogs were not to be trusted. Any time Anansi went back to the city he'd put on a long solemn face and complain of how little he'd gained from the enterprise, to avoid any long-throat or big-eye syndrome from his bosom friend which might ruin their friendship.

Anansi's train of thought was cut short when Aso barged in. She was sweating and trembling, like one who'd seen a ghost.

"What is it, Aso-miwa?" he said, adding a favorite suffix of his to her name and rising from his armchair perplexed.

"Nyame is here to see you," she stuttered.

"To see me?" Anansi quickly put on his robe and went out, his heart pounding.

The Rain-Goddess was standing with her golden staff and diamond-studded headdress, and flapping her great wings.

Anansi touched his hand to the ground and without looking into the face of the Rain-Goddess, which was forbidden to do, he said:

"I touch the earth to your presence, our great Goddess of Rain. What brings you here to the house of a runty little insignificant one like Anansi, the dirty spider?"

"Anansi! Anansi! Anansi!" Nyame bellowed, "how many times did I call you?"

"Three times, our great Goddess. You have troubled yourself to call a dirty little insignificant spider with so much energy he's not worthy of."

"Anansi! You have become the new Rainmaker of the forests. I want to know on whose authority you are performing this office?"

"Our great esteemed Goddess of Rain. Without your waters, our earth will be lifeless. Without the fertility you give to our land, we shall all die of starvation. Without your—"

THE RAINMAKER

"Hold it, Anansi," the Rain-Goddess rumbled with a rage that threw thunder and lightning across the skies. "I have not come here to be flattered by a lowly old web-spinning thing like you. I've come here to warn you to desist from your trickery, or else you shall bear the curse of the Gods upon your head."

Then she disappeared in a spark of lightning.

"What did you do to deserve the wrath of the Rain-Goddess, Anansi?" Aso wept frantically.

"Nothing," Anansi said, shaking his head indignantly. "You have nothing to worry about, Aso. Nyame is just jealous that times have changed and her powers are waning away."

"Just be careful, Anansi. You can't go about locking horns with a god."

"Forget it, my beloved Queen. This is no longer the era of gods. I, Anansi, owner of wisdom, will lock horns with ten thousand dead gods!"

"Hush, my husband! Don't speak so."

"I have spoken so."

* * *

Anansi grew in wealth and influence that he built a Rainmaker palace for himself. Henceforth, no animal would see him in person, for he was now a god.

Those who wanted a consultation about the weather waited for him in a special room where they were attended to by assistants and servants, who were Anansi's relatives. They brought the client's request to Aso in another special room, who in turn passed it to Anasi in the Master's room, starting from those who could pay better.

Outside the palace walls was written in animal sign language: "Welcome to the Palace of Anansi, the Rain-God of the Universe".

Anansi and his family grew so robust inside their palace that they could hardly be recognized. And when he was invited to the Royal Court for special occasions, he rarely attended, and when he did attend, did so by being carried on a gold chair on the heads of a group of seven servants and five attendants, fanning him and jumping at his beck and call.

Whenever the weather forecasting drew to an end, as the paper with the secret rain prediction data had been exhausted, Anansi announced through his attendants and servants that he was making a "spiritual pilgrimage to the Sky world of the gods", and would be back soon. Anansi would then hurry to the big city to meet his friend Nwanku who consulted the 'Almighty Thing' and gave him more weather prediction papers.

It went on for two seasons, in which Anansi's power and influence matched that of the Lion-King. The Lion was worried and many told him to get rid of Anansi. But the wary king was hesitant. If he killed Anansi, who would predict the rains? The Rain-Goddess was not responding. And contrary to the expectation of the Royal Court, Anansi was neither struck by lightning nor grew ill from usurping the position of the Rain-Goddess.

What was the source of his powers, no one knew. Anansi, the runty old trickster spider, had become a god overnight. A mysterious god with vast powers.

THE RAINMAKER

* * *

Anansi had visited Nwanku as usual for another round of prediction papers.

"Ah Anansi, my friend. Now I see why you come very often to the city these days. I hear you are now a god in the animal kingdom."

"Who told you so? Me? A god? How can a runty little thing like me be a god?"

"Oh. I happened to come across Sorosoro, the parrot, the other time, who stopped by in his flight to greet me."

"And he gave you the rumor?"

"Yes. And so many things I find hard to believe."

Anansi gave a long loud laugh of derision that made Nwanku uncomfortable.

"I can't believe you take anything that comes from the mouth of a parrot seriously, my friend. Have you forgotten so soon? That it's the same Sorosoro that spread rumors about you in the city to us animals in the forest? The same Sorosoro that said you and your family were living on Man's shit day in, day out? That in fact you were trying to cut off your animal ties and become like Man? That you were standing like him on two legs and riding in his horse-houses and sleeping in his bed? Don't make me laugh, my friend. Had I not come to the city to see you with my two naked eyes I would have believed all the rubbish. Now because of this worthless parrot whose mouth is bigger than him, you have become an enemy and an outcast in the animal kingdom." Anansi finished by shaking his head in pity.

Nwanku scratched his head. "Well, I see you looking swell and big nowadays and I was wondering what good times have come your way until —"

"My robustness is not a sign of good living, my friend. Have you forgotten that I have a swelling disease passed down to me from my forefathers?"

Anansi was able to quell the doubts of his friend about any rumors he'd heard. But then he began to entertain second thoughts. Who knew what animal Nwanku would come by tomorrow and they would give him away again? And perhaps Nwanku might choose not to tell him but to keep it hidden in his mangy belly. Then he'd meet yet another animal, and another one. By the time he'd met five of them and the truth would have been overwhelmingly laid before his eyes, Nwanku would change his mind and Anansi's rainmaking career would be over.

Anansi decided to dip into his bag of wisdom to do something, before what he feared came to pass.

"Nwanku, my friend. Do you wish to pay your Master back for his mistreatment of you? Do you wish to be esteemed again by the animal kingdom like in the days of old? You are the most learned animal amongst us and you can't live here wasting your talent forever. Eating crumbs and going about like a fly-followed slave."

"Yes, Anansi. I think about these things sometimes, you know."

"Very good. Now come, bring me your long ears." Anansi whispered words of secrecy into his friend's ears.

"Oh!" Nwanku gasped, wagging his tail. "That's a brainwave! Anansi, you are truly the owner of wisdom!"

THE RAINMAKER

Anansi laughed, puffing his cheeks and feeling his head swell up with pride.

On the day of the plan, they waited for the Master and his family to leave the house as usual, then sneaked in. With Nwanku serving as a lookout by the window, Anansi went into the Master's room where the 'Almighty Thing' was located. He looked at it, sized it up, thinking how he was going to move it away from here to his palace in the forest. He might even employ Nwanku to come live with him in his forest palace, if he'd be reasonable for once.

Anansi tried lifting the 'Almighty Thing' only to realize how heavy it was; he'd underestimated its weight.

As he sat there pondering on the best way to steal the 'thing', he heard Nwanku's Master's footsteps coming into the house. Nwanku began to bark hysterically:

"Master! Master! There's a thief in your house! A thief! Thief!"

Anansi picked himself up and tried to run away but Nwanku's jaws clamped over two of his eight legs and held it tight.

"Nwanku, have you forgotten who I am? Let me go!" Anansi cried in anguish.

"A thief! That's who you are! Grrrrrrrrrr!"

Nwanku's Master hurried out to look for a broomstick for squashing the big spider. Before he could return with his weapon, Anansi had detached his two legs from Nwanku's jaws and had quickly crab-walked on six other legs up to a corner of the ceiling, where he hid himself by spinning a web-cocoon.

He remained there gasping for breath, weeping with pain from his amputated limbs and cursing Nwanku for his treachery and betrayal.

Nwanku's Master gave Nwanku a huge lump of boned meat and asked him to keep an eye on the Spider whenever he found him. Nwanku wagged his tail, stood on his legs and trotted away to enjoy his meal.

Anansi spent his days at the ceiling corner, living on insects like flies and cockroaches he managed to trap in his web, and pondering and searching through his bag of wisdom about how he'd deal with Nwanku and return home to his Rainmaking Palace.

Anansi and the Christmas Dinner
A.L. Dawn French

Hindsight is 20/20 vision and only after it happened could it be understood that although Anansi the trickster had no *plans* for Christmas, that he had a plan for Christmas. So, what exactly happened? To understand that we have to go to 13 December when Anansi met Butterfly.

Mid-December was a trigger date for many and Christmas planning would get real 'serious' as everyone prepared for the festivities. It was no different for Anansi and the other insects. They meticulously planned their celebrations, ensuring every detail was perfect. From decorating their tiny homes with festive flair to organizing a grand feast, the insects spared no effort in making this holiday season memorable and magical for all. It was on just such a busy morning that the two friends crossed paths.

"Good day, Anansi."

"Good day, Madame Butterfly."

"The Christmas Season has really begun; I can see the humans getting all excited. What are your plans?"

Anansi lowered his head. "Ahhhhhhhh, Butterfly, my children are all grown, they have moved far away from me. They have their own families and cannot make the long trip."

"Ohhhh, I am so sorry to hear this! But maybe you can go to them?"

"Indeed, that is an idea, but I am too old to make the trip. The Caribbean has become cold at Christmas, it affects my joints and so…" He shrugged. "I have no plans for Christmas."

"Then you must come spend Christmas Day with my family," Butterfly ordered.

"But you will not be there," Anansi pointed out because everyone knew that butterflies do not live for long and that by the time Christmas came along this butterfly would be dead.

"This is true," Butterfly admitted. "This is why I did not say come to be with me. I said with my family."

"Then I accept… but I have more space at my house so let your family bring their food over and we will have all the space needed."

"Yes! That sounds like a fine plan!"

And so, the plan was in motion.

A few days later, Anansi was accosted by Centipede. "ANANSI!" It hissed. "I hear that you have no plans for Christmas. I said, no… that cannot be. For in the five years I have known this spider he has always had plans for Christmas!"

Anansi hung his head. "Ahhhh Centi, indeed you have known me for a long time. It is true I usually have a plan. But not this year."

"But why?"

"Do you not feel the cold fronts that come down from the north? Every year it gets colder and this year I truly feel the Christmas cold that grips the Caribbean. I feel my age as my joints stiffen."

ANANSI AND THE CHRISTMAS DINNER

"Oh no."

"Oh yes. I am too old to travel to my family and they are too busy with the little ones to come see me."

"But you'll be alone!"

"It is what it is," Anansi admitted sadly.

"NO! I will not hear of it!" Centipede was adamant. "You will spend Christmas at my house."

"But —"

Centipede had made up her mind and that was that. "See you on Christmas Day."

"NO."

"No? What'd you mean…No?"

"No… I mean… Yes… I mean…"

"Anansi, you are babbling. What do you mean?!"

"I mean that there are too many of you at your house, there will not be space for me."

Centipede sighed. "True. But my mother taught me that where there is love there is always space for more. So come!"

"My house is bigger, come over with your entire clan and any food and drink that you want. We can have a fine ole time."

Centipede swelled up with the realization. "YES! Oh yes! Your place is bigger. Alright then. We will do as you say. We will come over. See you then."

And with that the two parted.

If the humans on the island could not keep a secret for long, in animal kingdom they were just as bad and among the insects it was worse. Soon the word was out that Anansi's place was THE place for Christmas. Grasshopper was the one to bear the news.

249

"Anansi! So, you having a fête and you doh invite me?"

"Meeeeeeee?!" The spider squealed.

"Yes! You! I hear Butterfly and Centipede are invited to your house."

"Oh that."

"What you mean 'Oh, that?'"

"Is charity," Anansi explained but when Grasshopper looked like he didn't believe, the spider had to elaborate.

"You know how females of all species are. They like to mother and feed. So, when they found out that the Christmas cold is too much for me to bear, and that I could not travel to be with my family; of course, they started to cluck all over me."

"Oh ho."

"Grasshopper, what am I to do? Then I had a thought. Let them come to my house. I have the space. I am full of space! Enough for you too if you want. But no. I am not having a party at my house. Is only a little ting we having."

"Is true?" Grasshopper sort confirmation.

"Is true." Anansi provided the confirmation. "I am too old to go visit my family and they are too busy to come to me. So, my friends have taken pity upon me."

"Then I will come," Grasshopper pledged. "No one should be alone on Christmas Day."

Anansi gave a weak smile of gratitude. "I thank you, dear Grasshopper."

"I will see you then."

With that the two parted. Anansi went home. He could afford to meet no one else and needed to get his house in order; he had no idea how many were coming! These clans could be huge!

Anansi spent the next few days tirelessly weaving, his tiny legs moving with purpose. He crafted a magnificent spider's web, the largest he had ever made. Silken threads glistened in the sunlight, forming an intricate masterpiece. With each delicate strand, Anansi spun his web of wonder, ready to ensnare the attention and awe of all who beheld its beauty.

Anansi's days blurred into a whirl of meticulous weaving, his nimble legs dancing over strands of silk with practised precision. With each careful movement, he spun a web that seemed to shimmer with a life of its own, catching the light in a dazzling display of intricacy. The web stretched wider and taller than any he had woven before, a testament to his skill and dedication.

As the web took shape, Anansi also tended to his other duties, ensuring his pantry was stocked with a bounty of insects to sustain him through the winter. With deft movements, he scurried across the kitchen floor, darting behind the stove to his hidden nest. There, he carefully logged each captured meal, organizing them in neat rows to be transported to his grand web.

Despite the absence of smells and temperature cues, Anansi's determination remained unwavering. His focus was solely on the task at hand – crafting a web fit for a celebration, and ensuring his larder was well-stocked to sustain him through the winter months. Each thread he spun, each morsel he stored away, was a testament to his commitment to hosting the perfect Christmas gathering. He intended this Christmas dinner would be the talk of the insect world for years to come. And it would be – but for entirely different reasons that Anansi could never have thought of.

Filled with excitement and anticipation, he now took the time to make himself ready for Christmas Day. He meticulously groomed his glossy black fur, ensuring every leg sparkled. He wove a festive bowtie from colourful threads, adorning himself with festive flair. With a mischievous twinkle in his eyes, Anansi was prepared for the first victim… er… guest.

First to arrive was Clan Butterfly. "Anansi! We are here to fulfil the promise of our ancestor!"

"Come right in!" he called from inside.

In the manner associated with the species, they fluttered gracefully in, their vibrant wings shimmering in the sunlight as they entered, eagerly anticipating the festivities to unfold — straight into the web.

"We are caught!" They thrashed, for having alighted upon Anansi's web they were well and truly stuck. But the more they struggled the tighter the web held them. With determination and precision, Anansi moved in, spun more webbing and wrapped up the butterflies.

He was barely done before the centipedes arrived. Anansi assessed the situation, his eyes narrowing with focus. Anticipating the centipedes' movements, he strategized his next move. As the centipedes neared, their many legs propelling them forward, Anansi sprang into action. With lightning speed, he lunged, weaving a tight web around each approaching centipede, immobilizing them before they could realize the peril they were in.

In mere moments, the centipedes found themselves ensnared, their movements restricted by Anansi's masterful weaving. With a sense of satisfaction, Anansi surveyed his handiwork, knowing

ANANSI AND THE CHRISTMAS DINNER

that his carefully laid trap would ensure a bountiful feast for his Christmas dinner, all while keeping his guests safely contained within his web.

But he couldn't gloat for long. He could hear the pounding arrival of the grasshoppers as they hopped along towards his abode. As the grasshoppers drew nearer, their rhythmic hopping growing louder, Anansi sprang into action once again. With deft movements, he spun a new layer of webbing which had been damaged by the previous actions needed to catch the butterflies and centipedes. The web was now strategically placed along the path leading to his home.

As the grasshoppers bounded closer, oblivious to the danger lurking ahead, they suddenly found themselves ensnared in Anansi's meticulously crafted trap. Each hop became a struggle against the sticky strands, but it was futile. Anansi watched with satisfaction as the grasshoppers became entangled, their movements slowing until they were completely immobilized.

Now he had a Christmas feast fit for a spider! But he could not decide where to start. Should he begin with the delicate sweetness of the butterflies? Or perhaps the savoury crunch of the centipedes? Or maybe the grasshoppers, with their robust flavour and satisfying texture?

The squeals and threats of the captives made no difference to the spider.

Perched amidst his intricately woven web, he remained unperturbed by the protests of his captive guests. With a calm demeanour befitting a spider of his stature, he settled himself and began to truly ponder the order of his menu.

Each potential course danced tantalizingly in his mind, their flavours and textures vying for his attention. He salivated at the thought of the banquet that awaited him as they all held their own allure. Anansi took his time, weighing each option carefully, savouring the anticipation of the feast to come.

As the sunlight filtered through the leaves outside, casting dappled patterns across his web, Anansi continued to daydream, not realizing that night had become day.

It was the day after the night before and as Christmas morning dawned, a faint but ominous scent permeated the air, prompting the human of the house to investigate. Worried about a potential gas leak, they hurriedly checked the connections.

Then...

A hand brushed through Anansi's beautiful web. "What's this?" the human demanded. "No matter how many times I sweep this place a spider sets up shop!"

And just like that all Anansi's hard work was dismantled. The action freed the prisoners. The butterflies immediately flew away less a few family members,but the centipedes and grasshoppers had other plans.

Anansi grinned. "Was just a joke!" as he found himself surrounded.

"GET HIM!" a centipede screeched.

Anansi shot out a line of webbing and hauled himself up. The centipedes could not reach him, but the grasshoppers could. The chase was on.

ANANSI AND THE CHRISTMAS DINNER

Though agile and quick, he found himself pursued by the relentless grasshoppers. Their nimble leaps matched his every move. He zigzagged through the foliage, using his cunning to outwit his pursuers. With a sudden burst of speed, Anansi leaped onto a high branch, leaving the bewildered grasshoppers behind. His heart racing, he disappeared into the safety of the forest, a victorious escapee. Anansi had managed to escape the hunt.

Of course, he was banned from the neighbourhood and had to migrate far, far, far away to another part of the island. It seemed that the Caribbean cold was not so bad that he could not travel.

A Night in New Orleans

Yeayi Kobina

The air that night was thick with humidity. It was like a heavy blanket was pressing down on the city's cobblestones and its ancient structures. A dark mist slithered through its alleyways like a serpent, wrapping itself around old rusty iron balconies and lampposts. The night for those who walked the streets had an eerie, almost supernatural feel to it. New Orleans was sitting on a dark secret and it was desperate to reveal it. Bourbon Street in particular had become a patchwork of shadows with the occasional burst of neon that came from nearby bar signs that cut through the poor light of the night. The sound of distant jazz music joined the slithering mist, moving steadily along with the sounds of footsteps and the murmur of distant conversations.

The antique shop, "Elder," was nestled between a dilapidated voodoo shop and a lively dive bar that at the moment only had the stragglers of the evening, lonely people who preferred to spend their nights with a bottle, music and strangers than in empty apartments. The Elder's windows were obscured by layers of grime. Over the shop hung a wooden sign with its barely readable letters that creaked in the breeze. The shop's interior which was visible through the dirty glass was a messy jumble of relics. Shelves were overflowing and sagging under the weight of what had once being fond treasures of people which now lay unbothered and gathered dust.

Outside, stuck in shadows of the building opposite it, Malik and Jamal lurked with the restless energy of youth on the edge of desperation. Their eyes were sharp and alert as they scanned the storefront. They were driven by desire for easy cash. Everyone on the street knew old man Roch always had cash on hand for anyone seeking to part with some family heirloom. Rumor had it that he preferred to pay loads of cash for antiques that came with unique stories and history.

"Come on, Malik," Jamal whispered, his voice barely audible above the distant strains of jazz music that wafted from a nearby bar. "You sure about this?"

Malik was the older of the two by just a year but he already had the hardened look of someone far beyond his seventeen years. He nodded grimly. "We ain't got no choice, Jamal. Faruk will kill us if we don't have his money. And we ain't got nowhere else to get it."

Malik cast another glance at the shop. Elder looked abandoned. He crossed the street, he did not turn to see if Jamal followed. Jamal had the habit of going along with his antics. Malik peered through the window before jimmying the lock with practiced ease. The two slipped inside and shut the door slowly behind them.

* * *

The air inside the shop held a musty scent of old books and aged wood. Dust-covered shelves held everything from vases to tarnished jewelry. Every corner of the shop seemed to be crammed with oddities from carved wooden masks with hollow eyes, rusty lanterns, to items that had once been considered precious to their owners. Malik and Jamal moved with silent precision through the cluttered aisles. The soft creaking of floorboards was the only sound that broke the stillness of the shop. They scanned the shop for anything that might fetch a good price on the streets and for the safe that Roch was said to keep his money in.

Malik was drawn to a glass case filled with delicate figurines and trinket boxes. Their gilded surfaces were dulled by a fine layer of dust. He motioned to Jamal, who was rifling through some drawers with papers. As Jamal headed over, his eyes caught sight of the iron safe, partially obscured by a heavy velvet curtain. He pointed at it. Malik's eyes lit up at the sight with glee.

Every creak on the floor felt amplified as they approached the safe. Malik's fingers deftly worked at the combination lock while Jamal kept watch, his eyes darting nervously towards the shop's entrance. The atmosphere had suddenly grown tense. The shop seemed to hold its breath along with them. If either of them had been paying attention to their surroundings, they would have noticed as the very walls began to pull in on them, like an observer curious to see how the situation ended.

"Over here," Jamal hissed, pointing to a glass case filled with gleaming objects. He had abandoned his post as watchman and his fingers began to pry open the glass case.

A shuffling sound from the back of the store made them freeze.

"Who's there?" a raspy voice called out, followed by the appearance of a hunched old man, Roch. His eyes, though

A NIGHT IN NEW ORLEANS

clouded with age, possessed a glint of inner delight that belied his frail appearance as he watched the intruders.

"Old man, hand over the cash," Malik demanded, pulling a knife from his pocket while his free hand pointed at the safe.

The old man, instead of showing fear, chuckled softly. "You seek treasures, boys? I am but a relic myself, but perhaps I can sell you a thing or two," the old man said, his voice dripping with an accent that hinted at lands far from New Orleans. He shuffled slowly to his counter, tapping his fingers along the glass counter, unconcerned by what appeared to be a precarious situation.

Jamal, unnerved by the man's calm demeanor, tugged at Malik's sleeve. "Let's just take what we have and go."

Malik ignored him, stepping closer to the old man. Jamal took two steps back before turning and rushing to the door. *If Malik wanted to stay, it was his choice.* Jamal's hands fumbled for the knob, pulling it with all his strength. The door remained stubbornly shut. He tried again, more forcibly this time. The door budged slightly then was snatched shut by some invisible force. Jamal stepped back and turned, his face pale with fear.

"Malik, the door… it won't open."

* * *

Malik, still watching the old man, did not turn at the panicked shrill from Jamal. "What do you mean? I did not lock it."

A scream escaped from Jamal's lips. This time around Malik turned. The town outside was fading into a deep darkness. Malik realized that he could no longer hear the faint sound of jazz music anymore. Jamal tried the door again. Their eyes locked on the old man, who seemed to grow more imposing with each passing moment.

"What are you doing?!" Malik demanded; he pushed the knife under Roch's chin. "What is happening?"

"Nothing." Roch's voice was calm as he moved away from the knife. He moved from behind his counter. "Come," he added as he moved to an empty circular table tucked away in a corner. As he got closer, three chairs floated and arranged themselves perfectly around it.

Despite their terror, Malik and Jamal found themselves compelled to obey, their bodies moving against their will. They sat, their eyes locked on the old man. His eyes burnt with anger and rage. The walls around them pulsed with a malevolent energy and shadows on the walls writhed like living creatures.

"You should not have come here," Roch said, his words meant for Malik.

The invisible bounds around Malik made it impossible for him to lean forward. His hand still held the knife but it was completely useless by his side. He could not drop it, neither could it serve any purpose.

Roch stood up and moved towards the shelves. His movements were frantic as he scanned the cluttered shelves. His fingers brushed past old books, dusty vases and jewelery. Malik and Jamal watched in confusion, their fear momentarily overshadowed by their curiosity.

"What is he looking for?" Jamal whispered. The fear in his voice was not hidden.

Malik shook his head, the only part of his body that he could move. His eyes however never left Roch's frenzied search. "I don't know. It can't be good."

Roch finally exhaled with satisfaction as his hands stilled on an old leather-bound book. He pulled it out, revealing a hidden compartment behind it. With a swift motion, he reached into the compartment and retrieved a small, intricately carved wooden box. The box was adorned with strange symbols and markings. His hands brushed over its surface. Roch headed back to the table and sat down. He placed the box on the table and for a moment, he ignored the boys across from him, lost in thought as he stared at the box.

Roch opened the box and pulled out a peculiar artifact. It was a symbol of a spider, carved of wood, its eight legs tied up and restrained by three women depicted in silver relief. Their faces were stern.

"I've waited centuries," Roch said. It was the only time they heard a quake in his voice. He turned and faced Malik. "Your ancestors on their boats called the trickster here to aid in their escape from slavery. When I did my part, they trapped me here." He tossed the artifact towards Malik.

Jamal had a terrified yet confused look but when he glanced at Malik there was a sense of knowledge to what Roch had just said.

"Malik? What is he saying?"

"It's just a story my grandmother tells of Anansi the spider god. He saved my ancestors from slavery. How do you know it?"

Roch chuckled. "Saved? They tricked me!" His chuckle sounded unnatural within the shop, filling all its corners with a

MYTHS, GODS & IMMORTALS: ANANSI

sinister feel. "Magic always has a price. Blood." His last word blew out thick smoke that drew onto Malik's face.

The air grew colder. The shadows stretched and twisted as they drew closer, as if they had been called upon as witnesses. Malik's heartbeat pounded in his ears, each beat louder than the last. Jamal began to tremble and started to choke.

"I... I... can't breathe," Jamal choked.

Roch just smiled. "Tell him. It's your fault he is here. Truth is something your bloodline lacks."

The invisible restraints felt tighter, almost painful as Malik wrestled with the truth.

"I don't know what you are talking about," Malik screamed.

Jamal was shaking.

"It's my fault we lost Faruk's money. I gave it to Clarisse," Malik screamed out.

Jamal ceased shaking for a moment before keeling over and lying still on the floor. Roch clapped his hands ecstatically, thrilled by what was happening. He stood up slowly. The form of his shadow shifted, becoming more spider-like with each passing second. Its legs elongated and split, becoming spindly. As he moved, a clicking sound followed him on the floor. Roch's face stretched as his eyes multiplied, covering his face in a grotesque mosaic of glowing orbs that bore into Malik's. Malik reeled back, holding in a scream as his chair fell over.

Roch bent over him, his face back to normal. He pulled Malik up on his chair. Roch leaned in from behind Malik's ear. His breath was cold and damp against Malik's skin. His voice was a low, whispering hiss, curling around Malik's thoughts. "Blood of

A NIGHT IN NEW ORLEANS

her blood, kin to my curse," he murmured, each word feeling like pressing needles on Malik's skin. "Unlock the door that holds this creature."

Malik continued to shudder, as the room darkened further. Roch's voice continued to slither through the air, wrapping around Malik's senses, pulling him deeper into a chilling trance. The vortex pulled them in. Malik felt his body being torn apart and being put together. The world around him spun violently, the colors blending into a chaotic whirlpool. Then everything stopped. Malik found himself standing in a dark dense jungle. The scent of earth and decay assaulted his nostrils as he tried to steady himself.

* * *

Anansi, now fully transformed, stood before him. His eight legs moved with an unsettling grace, each step creating a soft clicking sound. The air was abuzz with the sounds of the jungle – crickets chirping, leaves rustling, and distant animal calls. But there was an underlying hum that made Malik's skin crawl.

"Look," Anansi's voice echoed as he pointed to the clearing up ahead.

Malik's breath caught in his throat as he looked around. There were a group of figures moving through the trees. Their silhouettes were barely visible in the dim light. As they came closer, he could make out their features – three women moving with a common purpose towards the clearing.

The women held hands in a circle and began chanting in a language that to Malik sounded ancient and powerful. Their voices rose and fell in a haunting way, filling the air with an energy. In the centre of their circle lay a large carved stone which began to glow with an eerie pulsating light. Anansi's multiple eyes glistened with a mix of anger and longing as he watched the scene unfold.

"They used the power of the earth to call me, asking for guidance to rid themselves of their masters. But they lied." The spider crawled closer to the trees that bordered the clearing.

The chants of the women grew louder as their voices merged into a single powerful force. The ground began to tremble. The glowing stone began to levitate as its light grew in intensity. Anansi in his spider form appeared at the edge of the clearing. Malik watched in horror as the women turned their attention to Anansi. Their eyes were glowing with the power of the supernatural. Anansi tried to flee as the tendrils of light from the stone wrapped around his legs and began pulling him towards them.

"You see, boy?" Anansi's voice was filled with cold fury. "Your ancestors wanted my power, not my knowledge. They ensnared me in this prison and I have been waiting for centuries for someone like you to set me free.

"You see, boy," Anansi's voice was filled with a cold fury. "They tricked me. Promised me freedom, and instead, they ensnared me in this prison. Their magic bound me to that artifact, and I have been waiting for centuries for someone like you to set me free." Anansi extended one of his long legs. Its tip, sharp as a dagger, traced a line down Malik's cheek. "The price has been long overdue."

A NIGHT IN NEW ORLEANS

Malik winced in pain, a line of blood welling up and trickling down his face. Anansi's touch was cold, and the sensation sent a shiver down Malik's spine.

The women stood in a circle around the pulsating stone, their faces bathed in the eerie glow of its light. When the light faded, the stone had reduced to the object that had the spider held by the three women. The three: Opha, the eldest, with hair as white as bone and eyes that had seen too much and enough; her daughter Mariah, middle-aged and fierce, her voice the strongest in the chant; and young Annette, whose innocence had long been traded under her master's boots and body.

"Tonight their blood will flow on their own lands," Opha commanded, her voice cutting through the thick night air.

They moved through the swampy landscape as Anansi and Malik followed. The plantation loomed ahead, towering ominously before a blood red moon.

Opha held the stone high. Her face illuminated with a mix of anger and anticipation. "Anansi," she called. Her voice was steady. "I summon thee."

From the stone, a dark mist began to seep out in a swirl and gathering form. Anansi's shape materialized in his spider-like form, imposing and dreadful. His many eyes glinted with a malevolent intelligence, fixed on the witches who now controlled him.

"Your power is ours to command," Mariah intoned, stepping forward. "Destroy the masters. End their reign."

Anansi's eyes narrowed, but he bowed his head slightly, acknowledging their command. The air grew colder still, a creeping chill that whispered of impending doom. With a flick of his many legs, Anansi moved towards the grand house. He slipped into the house like a shadow as his form merged with the darkness.

Inside, the masters slept soundly, oblivious to the dark fate approaching. The head of the household lay sprawled on his luxurious bed. With a swift, decisive motion, Anansi's limbs lashed out, ensnaring Thompson in a web of shadows. The man awoke with a gasp, his eyes wide with terror, but no scream escaped his lips. The darkness swallowed him whole, his life snuffed out in an instant. His wife and children met the same fate. Anansi moved with lethal efficiency, his presence a harbinger of death. No one was spared; the overseers, the enforcers, everyone complicit in the cruelty faced the wrath of the spider god.

At dawn, the plantation was silent, save for the eerie rustle of the wind through the fields. The slaves, cautiously emerging from their quarters, found their oppressors lifeless, their bodies contorted in unnatural poses with their faces fixed in the last moments of the fear.

They were back in the antique shop. Malik was back to his immobilized state on the chair. Anansi leaned closer and repeated the incantation from earlier. "Blood of her blood, kin to my captors," he whispered. There was excitement in his voice now as he was so close to tasting his freedom.

* * *

The room darkened once more, and Malik felt a strange pull at his consciousness as he was dragged into another vision. The antique shop faded, replaced by a winding path leading through a forest. There were many black people ahead of him, trying to minimize the sound they made as they made their escape through the forest.

Malik's ancestors were there, huddled together at the front of the line. As Malik's eyes scanned the faces of the escaping slaves, he saw Anansi in his human form as Roch. The god's eyes blazed with suppressed rage. Unlike the other people, he had been shackled while Opha held his chain. The vision shifted, showing him the weary journey across the forest and the eventual arrival at New Orleans. The city was alive with chaotic energy and welcomed the newcomers.

One night, as his captors slept, Anansi managed to free himself from his shackles. He crept through the night, searched the sleeping bodies of his captors till he found the artifact hanging on a chain around Mariah, now matriarch of the family after Opha's death. Anansi snatched it up. But despite his best efforts, he couldn't break the artifact. Its magic was too strong and too deeply intertwined with his own essence. He would have killed Mariah then, to unlock it but the witch had woken up and banished him from their house.

Anansi let out a guttural cry of frustration that echoed through the streets of New Orleans. He knew then that he was trapped, bound to a human form. He had been waiting ever since, biding his time, knowing that one day, a blood descendant of his captors would come, someone through whom he could exact his long-awaited revenge.

The vision ended abruptly, snapping Malik back to the present. The antique shop's dim light flickered ominously, and

Anansi's many eyes were now fixed on him with an intense, predatory focus.

"I have waited for you," Anansi hissed, his voice filled with wrath. "Your ancestors' blood runs through your veins, and through you, I will reclaim my power."

Malik struggled to process the torrent of emotions and revelations. His heart pounded in his chest, a cold sweat breaking out on his forehead.

Malik's eyes widened as Anansi extended a long, spindly hand towards him, his sharp nails grazing Malik's chest. The pain was sharp, but it was the realization of what Anansi intended that filled Malik with dread. He closed his eyes and awaited his fate.

Anansi and Păcală

Alina Mereşescu

Anansi looks at the strange man in front of him and thought to himself, "What an odd-looking man… Must be because of the way he died."

Păcală is also watching him intently and thinks to himself "What an odd-looking man… He must've died a peculiar death."

"*Nuabarima*, you wretched thing, you've also landed here?"

"*Cumetre*, you speak fast but even if you'd speak in syllables, I wouldn't know what you mean."

"Me – Anansi. You?"

"*Meanansiyouuu*? Păcală," says the man while putting both hands on his lapels.

"Anansi", says the spider while making a gesture with all of his four hands showing that there is no "me" and "you" in his name.

Both tired and defeated, they take a seat on the damp ground and soon enough they start wasting time. Anansi is weaving a hat for himself from his silk while Păcală is munching on a grass leaf.

"That dark fog in the distance looks like it's slowly eating the land," while pointing two of its arms towards the ominous curtain of darkness steadily coming closer and closer.

"What about that mountain with the big light on the top?" says Păcală, while pointing in the other direction.

The two nod in understanding, pick themselves up and start walking towards the mountain. And they walk and walk and walk under a scorching sun and through a cold desert night, with no food or water and no other beings in sight. More thirsty than anything, their hunger being long forgotten after ignoring it for so many hours, they come to a watering hole with some crisp-looking water.

"There must be a fresh water spring. We could fill that leather flask you got there," says Păcală, while pointing at the spider's belt.

"But not with those two big lions guarding the waterhole. I may be plump but I don't want to be a tasty snack for them," says Anansi, while pointing at the dangerous-looking males lazily watching the banks. Anansi scratches his head in deep thought and then curls his finger to Păcală, telling him to come with.

The two reach the den of the pride in the wee hours of the morning while all the female lions are sleeping and their cubs were playing off to the side. Anansi picks up four cubs and points to Păcală to pick up the other two, then they hastily return to the water hole with the crying cubs. Anansi starts smudging their coats with his saliva and says to Păcală:

"So that the lion women folk think the two lone lions mistreated them. Get it?"

Păcală doesn't get it but he can't do anything but go along with it. As soon as Anansi and Păcală leave the lion cubs close to the male lions, the cubs start crying and calling for their moms. From the tall grass Anansi and Păcală are watching intently with parched throats hoping that their plan will work. Suddenly four agitated lionesses appear in front of the male lions. They put themselves between the cubs and the lions and seeing the sorry state of their cubs start roaring at the two unsuspecting victims. With a couple of swift attacks, putting their clawed paws on the lions' hide and baring their teeth prepared to nip the lions' ears, the female lions chase away the two males. Satisfied after getting rid of them, they round up their cubs and start going back to their den. The two friends look at each other and smile, then they run to the cleanest part of the water hole and start drinking with their hands. When they had enough and filled Anansi's leather water flask, they are back on their way towards the great mountain in the distance with the light on top of it.

As they walk further and further, thirst is now a solved problem, but here comes hunger with a vengeance. They come close to a water mill and Păcală says:

"I'm so hungry I could eat a whole pile of embers and ash! Let's look around for some food."

As they went to the ducks' coop, they see in a corner a puddle of tar and in it, flailing about, a plump white duck with its feathers stuck together with the gooey substance.

"Look at this poor duck, how did it get stuck in the tar?"

"Let's eat it," says Anansi while lifting one of his hands to his mouth in a universal gesture.

"Let's wash it first," says Păcală while picking it up. He then goes to a barrel nearby and gestures to the spider to help him roll it towards the stream of water.

"What do you want to do with the barrel?"

"You'll see."

The two roll the barrel and plunge it in the stream in a part where it makes a widening. All the water is then running furiously into the barrel and creating a vortex. Păcală looks at Anansi and takes the frightened duck and throws it into the vortex. The poor bird gets twirled and twirled around like an item of clothing and slowly the tar is being stripped from its feathers while she's quacking wildly.

"As clean as a whistle and as dumb as a rock," says Anansi.

Păcală then plucks the bird out of the barrel, all nice and clean but wet as a rag, and lets it go in the court yard. It springs away from them but stops in a clearing to get dried under the sun. After a few minutes, the duck comes closer to them and as it quacks loudly, it lays down on the ground. When getting up again, it leaves behind a golden egg.

"Look, the duck has left us an egg," says Păcală while picking it up to inspect it. "This might be of help," he says while putting it in his pocket.

"So, we're not going to eat it?" Anansi says while lifting his left hands up to his mouth.

"It would be bad luck, Anansi! *Ghinion!*"

"Aaah, *asɛmmɔne*… But I'm hungry and there are no two people more hapless than us right now."

Păcală goes under a plum tree and starts eating green plums and throws a couple Anansi's way. They both start eating the unripe fruits, their expressions getting more and more sour with each plum. They then both drink from Anansi's water flask. They eat and drink, drink and eat, and soon enough Anasi says:

"We've been drinking from this water flask for a while but it's still not empty. This place is as full of magic as the world is bursting with fools."

After having their fill, they fall asleep under the plum tree. Close to midnight they are awoken by loud noises coming from the road. With sleep still in their eyes they squint in the direction of the noise and with aid from the moonlight they see a hoard of bodies shuffling slowly towards them and making low-pitched noises. They look at each other and Păcală says:

"*Strigoi*, run before they get frisky!" He grabs one of Anansi's hands and pulls him away from the group of decaying bodies with overgrown canines and rabid eyes.

They start running up the mountain and they struggle going uphill through the forest. In the distance, up on the cliff, they see a castle that seems to be made out of light. They are sure they need to reach it. The climb seems without an end in sight but as they turn into a clearing, they find a cabin and they hurry inside, closing the door and putting a barrel in front of it to keep it locked. The two listen to the sounds of the *strigoi* herd surrounding the cabin and making efforts to come inside.

"We're in a tight spot, *nuabarima*! But as much as I'd like to worry about the monsters outside, I have a bigger problem. Those green plums and water didn't mix so well and now it's like serpents having a wedding in my tummy," says Anansi putting all his hands on his distended belly, that's making noises as strong as the sounds of the *strigoi* outside.

"I'm in the same boat as you, *cumetre*, and I don't think I can wait any longer. Run, my poor legs, or I will poop all over you!"

As he's saying this, Păcală pulls his pants down and hops on the edge of the barrel and lets out everything he was keeping in while on the run. It's a never-ending flow that fills the room with green-hued fumes that also travel out the chimney.

While this is happening, Anansi is prancing nervously around him and encouraging him to finish up so he can have his turn at the barrel. As soon as Păcală gets off the barrel, Anansi drops his pants and jumps on it with a big sigh of relief while a pressurized river of diarrhea fills the barrel to the middle mark. The fumes are almost impossible to bear and both of their eyes are watering. What draws their attention is that the noises outside subside and it seems something is driving the *strigoi* away.

"It looks like our plums and water mix are a toxic combination for them. I think there's a way to trick them and still go up to the castle of light," says Anansi while taking a hand full of shit and smearing it on his clothes, while scrunching up his face from the smell.

"*Cumetre*, I'm not doing that. My nose hairs are dying off and you want me to put that on myself?"

After some hard convincing from Anansi's part, the two burst outside the cabin door in the middle of the monster herd, smeared from top to bottom in the badly digested, toxic, plum and magic water mix. They smell so bad that the plants turn brown in their vicinity. The monsters stay far away and clear a path for them to walk. They steadily head on towards the castle that lickers in the distance like a beacon of hope.

As they get closer to it, the monsters stay behind, like an invisible barrier is keeping them at bay. When they reach the castle, the

ANANSI AND PĂCALĂ

draw bridge is lowered, and the doors are open, inviting them in. They take in the vast construction, the walls are from a fabric of light and shimmer that makes it hard to look at, the whole thing is otherworldly and intimidating. From the elevated point of view, they look back and see that the wall of dark fog is right behind them, slowly eating up the fields at the bottom of the mountain. They look at each other and understanding there is no choice but to go in, they both enter the majestic doors.

"Welcome in my humble residence," says an incredibly ugly looking man with red pupils and a long red overcoat.

"I can understand him," says Anansi, pointing at the master of the house and looking at Păcală.

"I can understand you!" says Păcală pointing at Anansi.

"Everybody can understand each other in the Castle of Light," says the ugly man. "You're here because you will need to pass to the other side before the Fog of Forgetfulness comes over you. But going over to the other side won't be an easy task. If you succeed then you will go there and be forever happy and together with all the loved ones that you've lost. If you fail, the Fog of Forgetfulness will come over you and you'll be sentenced to another life on Earth without remembering anything from your past life."

"Living again doesn't sound so bad," says Anansi.

"You will be a slave this time around, Anansi, do you think you will like that?"

"I never let what I am born into define my take on life. You can send me to be an ant and I will be your biggest pest."

"What about me, what will I be?" asks Păcală

"You will be a donkey, worked to the bone."

"My mother's praises are catching up to me."

"So, what do we have to do to get to the good side?" asks Anansi.

"I have three tasks for you to complete and if you do well in them, I will let you pass. Will you be able to finish all three tasks? I suppose we'll see. But right now, you should go wash up because you stink to high heaven."

Anansi and Păcală are taken to their room where two tubs of warm water await them. While they take their bath, their clothes get taken away and quickly brought back, magically cleaned and fresh. Smelling like new people, the two are brought to the master of the castle and in the big hall a feast lay before them with food they recognize from their own lands.

"The first task is about gratitude. This is all the food you received after you were dead, given by your relatives to the people who knew you. If you want to finish this task, then you have to eat all this food to show your thanksgiving to your loved ones. I will come back in the morning to see if it's all gone. If it's not, I'll throw you in the Forgetfulness Fog and be done with you!"

As soon as his red coat was seen in the distance, the two looked at each other and at the impossible feat that lay ahead. An amount of food that would be enough for three weeks was splayed on the tables in front of them.

"How are we going to finish all this food, *nuabarima;* were our fathers elephants and we don't know it?" asks the spider.

"Maybe you look at me and see a skinny bag of bones. But I'll have you know I am the plague of my family when it comes to eating. Eat as much as you can and I will eat an elephant's worth," says Păcală.

Both of them start eating from the end of one table and make their way slowly towards the other end. But the ugly man is a sly one and he has sprinkled magical spicy dust over the food, so the more they eat, the more their mouths and insides are burning. Midway through they are both lying on the floor, belly up, so big they looked pregnant, with faces red from the spicy dust that is making their task impossible to continue.

"What are we going to do, *cumetre*? There's not much time before sunrise and my mouth has closed up shop, maybe my ears and nose can replace it but it's not likely…"

"My insides are burning and I couldn't eat another bite; this wine they have is not helping. But how about you try my water flask?" asks the spider.

Păcală takes a sip and suddenly the burn all over his body but mostly in his mouth and insides disappears, his stomach deflates and he immediately feels hungry and thirsty like he never ate and drank anything.

When the ugly man comes back in the morning, he finds the tables empty and the two belly up on the floor in a friendly embrace, singing their hearts out, each to their own tune, oblivious that both the sun and the time are up.

"So, you managed to finish the task, you bottomless pits! Be merry and rest for today, because this evening I will be beckoning you again for the second task! We'll see if you finish that one…"

As soon as the two fell asleep, evening came again, because time had a funny way of passing fast while times were good and going at a snail's pace when times were bad.

The ugly man was once again in front of them and he brought a little helper.

"This next task is about good-wittedness. This here is my daughter and she has a riddle for you. If you can figure out the answer by morning then you will pass to the final task. If not, I will let the monsters outside nibble on you until the fog will finally eat you whole."

And then he left them again alone with his daughter which was scary enough, as the daughter greatly resembled her father, with jagged monster-like teeth, and a sour disposition permanently etched on her face. With a terrorizing voice, she starts enunciating the riddle:

"One looks for it high and low
And forever tries to hold on to it
In all the lands that are discovered
People have this thing in common
Be it two or four of hands
Everybody wants to grab it
Keeping it is what most counts
Just be thankful that you've found it."

Păcală and Anansi look at each other and burst into laughter They have no idea how to go about solving this riddle. They sit and sit with it and debate and debate over it for hours until the roosters start singing.

"I got it! It's *knowledge*! Everybody wants to have it," says Anansi.

"Well, I don't want it! And I certainly can't hold on to it... I think I know what it is – it's *courage*, all the best things are done with it..."

"*Nuabarima,* you can't just find courage in the middle of the road, so that's not it," says Anansi.

"The sunrise is approaching soon and apparently I gave my good wittedness to my twin for the day, maybe we can convince her to give us another clue."

"How would you go about convincing her?" asks Anansi.

"Because she's a child and all children crave one thing the most."

"And what is that?"

"Sour green plums," says Păcală.

Anansi smiles and takes them out of his pockets showing them to the little kid.

"You'll get all of these green plums for a hint, and then you can scrunch up your face even more," says Anansi.

The little monster girl's eyes light up and she quickly mumbles out the following while snatching the plums out of Anansi's hands:

> *Jesters tell its story over and over*
> *It's the only story worth telling*
> *One always wants to hear another*
> *Just to get an ache of this fleeting feeling.*

"It's love!" both of them shout at the same time, just as the clock sounded the morning hours.

MYTHS, GODS & IMMORTALS: ANANSI

A gust of wind suddenly breaks open the doors to the hall and the ugly man walks in.

"I see you managed to finish the good-wittedness task. I wasn't expecting that you two could solve my daughter's riddle. Maybe I underestimated you, but looking at the both of you I am pretty sure you won't be able to pass the last test. You'll have to prove your meticulousness and for this I'll be generous and give you a day and a night."

They followed the ugly man to the garden of the castle where rows and rows of strawberries as far as the eye can see had a hard time coming to fruition because of endless amounts of slugs slithering everywhere and making a feast out of the whole garden.

"Your task is to gather all the slugs before sunrise tomorrow. I don't want to see one slug in any part of my garden or I'll tie you to the trees and let the slugs climb up on you and dissolve your eyes."

After the ugly man leaves, Păcală and Anansi sit on the ground scratching their heads while looking at the invasion of slugs. What to do? After several hours Anansi finally has an answer and starts weaving a net out of his silk. He covers the strawberries with his net and waits for the slugs to try and reach the strawberries, so some slugs get caught in the silk but lots of them can evade the sticky net because of how their underbelly is coated in their mucilage. Yet again, in the early morning hours, things are not looking good for the duo. Thousands of slugs are still roaming freely around the garden.

"Well, I guess we'll need to go back, me as a slave and you as a donkey."

"Hmmm, I wonder…" says Păcală.

"You wonder what?"

"You know who can help with getting rid of slugs?"

"No, who?"

"Ducks," says Păcală, while pulling the golden egg out of his pocket. Watching it intently, he starts rubbing it and looks around. But nothing happens. He rubs it again. And again, nothing happens. "Oh, well, I guess it's just an old folk tale…"

Disappointed, he throws the egg towards Anansi, but Anansi is too slow to catch it with any of his hands so the egg falls flat on the floor, breaking into pieces. Suddenly a flock of ducks fly into the garden. The white one comes to Păcală and says:

"You helped me out when I was in need and it's said that gratitude is the golden feeling of poor people but reciprocity is the appanage of Kings."

The ducks directed by the white duck start gulping down the slugs one by one, making quick work of the whole garden. As the sun rises up at the horizon, the ugly man comes flying into the garden and as he sees the clean grounds, the resurrected strawberry plants in full bloom and with mounds of hanging fruit he gets visibly upset.

"Well, well, well, aren't you the resourceful ones? You've proved your meticulosity so I suppose I now have to let you enter to the other side. The Forgetfulness Fog is almost at the gates so you'd better hurry, you just have moments to spare! But I won't make it easy for you. Here you have two closed doors. Behind one you go to the place of eternal peace and happiness and behind the second… Well, that one will be my surprise for you, if you're so unlucky to choose it. So, choose wisely!

"What to do, *cumetre*? He looks at us like a devilish wife who's offering a choice between a meal of fire ants and a bowl full of stink bugs."

"Don't worry, Păcală, between the masters of slaves, highroad bandits and death itself, he's not the worse I've had to deal with and I have a remedy for his wickedness."

As soon as he said this, Anansi transformed himself into an itty-bity spider and moved quickly with his spindly legs towards the first door. As small as he was, it was easy for him to slide under it. After a moment he came out and went to the other door as well, peaking behind and then coming right back out again. In front of Păcală he transformed himself again into Anansi and said:

"The second door is the right one, Păcală, my mother was waiting with a wooden spoon to repay my last prank I did to her before she died."

Seeing their trick, the ugly man became furious and started yelling at them:

"You impudent fools, do you think I'd let you two jesters make a mockery out of me? In a few moments the Forgetfulness Fog will engulf this place and you'll be back on Earth as a slave and as a donkey, I'll make sure of that!"

Saying this, the ugly man took off his red coat, fanned it around for a brief moment then threw it over the two friends. As soon as it touched them, the red coat became a constricting device, wrapping itself around them and holding them tight where they were. Suddenly electric bolts start crackling all around them and a sense of doom and gloominess was upon the castle. The

Forgetfulness Fog was closing in on them. It starts eating the walls away and engulfs the second door. This makes the ugly man have a fit of laughter while his eyes are pinned to the duo scared by the fog getting closer and closer.

"Păcală, hold down your lunch and roll with me towards the first door, we must pass through it!" says Anansi.

"I've never been one to say no to surprises," says Păcală as he starts rolling in tandem with Anansi.

Leaving behind the nightmarish world and the ugly laughing man, Anansi and Păcală go through the first door and promptly forget their misadventures, their unusual found friendship and everything that happened. The first door takes them back to Earth, each to their own land, destined to roam around forever as tricksters, always the odd man out, constantly ending up in the strangest tales, told by gentle grandmothers to small children everywhere. And thus, Anansi's and Păcală's tale in the land of the dead comes to an end.

Descendance

Ella N'Diaye

Aisha drew her fingers along the wall as she walked down the corridor. As she walked, she traced the pattern, feeling the threads and whorls of the Descendants' work.

She was late, she knew, but it was rare that the halls were this quiet. Everyone had gone to their level's sharing spot in anticipation of the ritual. Aisha needed this quiet to refocus. To prepare to meet the expectations of the Origin.

The ship was thrumming slightly, the strands of the hull's weave more visible as the time for the Origin drew nearer. Stopping by a window, Aisha stared out into eternity. The Web was moving by a nebula, the tendrils of its structure teasing and swirling the gases. Aisha leaned and felt the slight tug of the walls against her skin. No matter how far from Earth they went, no matter how many generations of Descendants spun the Web's hull, the silk would always retain some of its sticky quality as well as the geometric shape its smaller Earth ancestors had woven for generations.

Mama had loved taking her to the other levels of the ship, showing her the way the corridors were interconnected, woven together.

Mama wasn't here today and now Aisha had to face the Origin without her. Pressing her lips together, she pulled away from the wall and forced herself to keep walking. She couldn't avoid this. Trailing her fingers along, she felt the symbols which indicated the path to her level's Baobab. Her sandals padded against the floor as the temperature rose. She loved the way the heat rose no matter what level's Baobab you approached. The chill of space which settled in all the other parts did not affect the central spire, the core where all the Baobabs grew.

Aisha would never know her ancestors' sun. She'd never know the humidity of the bayous, the sparkle of the seas, the heady press of the jungles, the burn of the desert. She would never know the myriad places that shaped her people, but for these moments, during the Origin, she could pretend.

Nearly all of Toussaint was gathered when she arrived at the Baobab. The youngest of the community were giggling as they played in the roots. The Descendants hung from its branches, spinning complex layered webs in its branches. Like all weaves on this ship, they glowed gold, illuminating the darkness of the core.

Aisha watched as a larger one landed on a child. Her friends clustered around her, staring as the spider danced and wove a net into her dreads. Toussaint children, like those of any of the other ship levels, learned early to accept the blessings of the Descendants.

"Thank you." The little girl, who Aisha now recognized as Yena's daughter, Addai, grinned and held out her hand. The spider traveled down her arm into her palm. The threads it left glowed, making Addai sparkle. The Descendant waved its forelegs before dancing back and forth across her palm. Addai,

285

correctly guessing its intentions, lifted her hand towards the trunk of the tree. Her new spider friend had an expanding pouch on its back legs as it continued its dance. Finally, it jumped, the parachute helping it sail from Addai's palm to the tree.

The trunk was alive with Descendants. Addai's little hair stylist quickly became lost in the tendrils of gold they were weaving. Aisha watched as the small black and gold creatures traveled from the branches to the roots and up again. Addai turned and ran to her mother. Yena knelt and had her turn, examining the intricate gift the Descendant had given her.

After this, Addai would always retain some mark of this net in her hair. Aisha ran her fingers over her arm, following the pattern of golden loops and whorls a Descendant had left on her skin during her first Origin. She smiled as the markings sang under her fingertips, the memory of the whisper-thin kisses of the silk on her skin as the Descendants had danced across her arms and shoulders. Her markings circled her wrists, went up her forearms, across her shoulders and met at the center in the hollow of her throat. The two Descendants who had gifted these to her had been in a playful mood.

Mama had been so proud.

These gifts bound them in the Great Web. As the people of the Web gave the Descendants their strength and the ability to spin their silks, so the Descendants protected and guided the Web and its people through the vastness of space.

So the Ancestor had saved them from their pains and their sorrows.

Today, when Addai shared, a Descendant would give her markings on her skin sealing her connection to their Web.

"Look, Cousin!" Addai had spotted Aisha and was running across to her.

Though younger than Aisha, she and Addai were both Fifth Generation. The address was traditional.

"You look beautiful, Cousin," she said before inclining her head towards Yena. "Auntie."

The Fourth Generation woman had been a close friend of Aisha's mother. Yena put her hand to Aisha's shoulder, tracing her fingers along the pattern.

"I am glad to see you, Niece," she murmured. A pause indicated the heaviness of the loss they shared. "Are you going to speak during the Origin?"

Aisha shook her head. She wasn't ready to speak her stories aloud. It wasn't necessary for the Origin to work, but it did offer a greater gift.

Yena gave her a sad smile. She didn't push, which annoyed Aisha. She wanted Yena to give her something to push back against. Mama's death was still unthinkable. Why should they, in the Web, die of anything but old age? Yena's quiet understanding made her feel exposed. It was too similar to what Mama would have done, which made Aisha feel worse.

Addai gripped Aisha's hand, tugging so Aisha had to kneel down next to her. The earth, the last connection to their long distant planet, shifted slightly as she sank so her eyes were level with her little cousin. Addai grinned and leaned to whisper as though she had an important secret.

"It's my first share!"

Aisha smiled in spite of herself and made her eyes grow wide. "Really?" As if she could have avoided knowing this. Yena moved towards where other Fourth generations were whispering.

Addai gripped Aisha's hand. "I already know what story I'm going to give," she continued, leaning conspiratorially before adding. "It's about you."

Aisha's eyes widened. Before she could ask what Addai meant, a hush fell over the gathered Toussaint. A low drumming began. It was started on Lumumba and Makeba, the levels that made the outer edges of the web. On each beat another two levels joined in and the reverberations grew.

Next to the trunk Deon stood with his baton raised, listening and watching for when it would be Toussaint's turn to join in.

Aisha could feel the beats growing lower, thumping in her chest. Standing, she kept her grip on Addai's hand.

The Descendants on the trunk parted and opened a curtain in their weaving to reveal the bare wood of the tree. Deon smiled and brought his baton down on the next beat. The sound shook the entire level. Aisha squeezed her eyes shut as the vibrations raced across her markings. She could feel her connection to the Web, the hum of each beat pulling her in.

Aisha tugged back, not wanting to be drawn in more than necessary. Addai's hold on her hand tightened. Aisha looked down and for the first time saw the fear in her eyes. Yena was standing across the room, and she met Aisha's searching gaze. Addai was her daughter, she should be the one to do this for her.

But Addai was holding on to her hand.

DESCENDANCE

Yena inclined her head slightly.

It would be Aisha's role to guide her into the Web.

The Descendants jumped from the tree, each gripping a tendril of silk. They flew across the room, each landing on a Toussaint resident. Aisha looked at her shoulder where the small spider was staring at her. It waved a piece of silk in its forelegs, the glow from the web making its tiny eyes glitter. Aisha gave a small grimace and reached over. At her fingers' approach, the Descendant did a quick hop of excitement and looped the thread around her index finger. It then scuttled along the thread back to the tree.

The drumming stopped.

Each level was connected now. The Griot would be coming.

Makyla was the oldest Griot of their web. She was Second generation and still remembered the Sol System. Her mother's mother had known Earth. There was no one else in their web who could claim such knowledge.

Makyla had to be led to the center of the roots. Her eyes were white, her dreads wound in a tall crown above her head. She leaned heavily on her staff as her grandchildren brought her to the seat in the base of the Baobab's roots. Seated, she leaned her head back. The Descendants traveled down the trunk and unwound her hair. They carried each of her locks up, turning her hair into a disc with her head at the center. The silks connected and soon it became difficult to see where Makyla ended and the web began.

Silence fell as the Toussaint waited for the Griot to fully connect.

Makyla's eyes opened. The white had been replaced by the scintillating gold of the silks.

289

"My children." Her voice spoke to them through the threads. Aisha felt the tug through her finger and the hum of the vibrations. "We come here to give thanks. To reconnect. To rebuild. To continue our journey."

She paused, letting the words wash over them.

"In order to see where we can go, we must know where we have come from." She brought her hands together on her walking stick. Raising it, she struck the Earth. The thud reverberated through the Web. On other levels, Griots were striking the Earth at the root of their Baobabs.

Aisha shuddered. A quick glance outside the window revealed that the tendrils of the Web which were caressing the nebula were shaking, making the pulse of their connection quaver out and visible in the vacuum of space.

"KRICK," Makyla called.

"KRACK," all of Toussaint replied. Addai's large eyes stared up at her. Aisha swallowed, unable to join in the call and response. She did not want to disappoint her on such an important day, but she could not force the word past the lump in her throat.

"In the days before," Makyla began, "the stories belonged to the sky."

"It is known," everyone murmured. Aisha could hear the voices of the Web. She even imagined that across the expanse, she could hear the other ships, their knowledge, their stories, tying all of them together. In her mind's eye she drifted, unbound, as the warmth of the Webs moved by her.

"Nyame, the sky god, kept them for himself." Makyla's voice was hushed. "Kwaku Anansi, the Great Spider, saw the stories

DESCENDANCE

and wanted them for himself. He understood that the sky holding the stories kept his people from knowing themselves. Kept their knowledge out of their reach."

She paused, leaning conspiratorially forward before adding:

"He was also greedy."

The threads surrounding the tree rumbled with laughter. The Descendants were pleased.

"Kwaku Anansi came to Nyame, his small spider self prone before the vastness that was the sky and asked Nyame his price."

Aisha closed her eyes and let the familiar scene play out. Nyame appeared, holding Anansi on a cloud and demanding the capture of Onini the python, Osebo the leopard, and Mmoatia the forest dweller.

In her mind's eye, Nyame formed each of the creatures out of clouds as he named his price, each cloud-form more fearsome than the last. He wanted to make the spider afraid.

"BUT," Makyla said. Her voice rose as she brought her staff up again. "Was Kwaku Anansi afraid?"

"No." The word reverberated with the strike of the staff. Addai gave Aisha's] hand a quick squeeze to prompt her, but she did not join in.

Anansi, as he always did, tricked Onini into being tied to a tree branch. He dug a pit and covered it so Osebo would fall in and he made a gum doll which Mmoatia stuck to.

"And so Anansi brought his payment to the sky god," Makyla said. "And Nyame honored his word. So Kwaku Anansi, the Spider, became the owner of the stories." She leaned down,

MYTHS, GODS & IMMORTALS: ANANSI

reaching to the children who were clustered at her feet. "So we were given the stories. We laugh. We cry. We learn. We grow. We know."

She paused. No matter how many times Aisha heard the Origin, this next part would always be hard.

"Being keeper of the stories was not as easy as Anansi believed. The sky is vast. Even bigger than he could imagine. What then, compared to that, is the minds of people and the webs of spiders? The people, Anansi's people, began to suffer. The stories he heard made him cry. His people were torn from the places of their ancestors. They were chained."

She banged her staff.

"Stolen."

"Enslaved."

Each word was punctuated with a strike. The Web's pulsing, once unifying and warm, was now violent. The nebula was being shredded. Aisha's markings burned her skin, searing her arms as tears ran down her face.

"Those who were not taken were forcibly taught other tongues. Given other gods. Made to forget the old ways."

Makyla lowered her head. The whole of the Web was hushed. The gold, once vibrant, dulled. The Descendants had retreated into the branches, their eyes glittering as they waited.

Makyla took in a deep breath, lifting her head. The threads connected to her scalp brightened.

"But no matter where the people went... whether island, or continent... whether mountain or valley... desert or snow, river or gorge, they kept with them their stories."

292

DESCENDANCE

Toussaint began to chant. "Anansi. Nanse. Aunt Nancy. Kompa Nanzi."

"He was all of them," Makyla said. The fracture of this became too much for one spider to bear. Pulled in so many directions, overloaded by the amount and breadth of tales and experiences in his head, Kwaku Anansi called out to the sky.

"Anansi. Nanse. Aunt Nancy. Kompa Nanzi."

"He begged the sky god."

Deon struck the trunk with his baton. The Web jerked and twitched as the other levels joined in.

"Pleaded."

BANG.

"Nyame could hear the Spider's pleas. He could see the atrocities his people were suffering, but he also was stretched too thin." Makyla paused. "So Anansi decided to play his greatest trick of all. He had become keeper of the sky god's stories, he would use the stories to transcend the sky god."

Makyla lowered her head, leaning forward until her locks were taut, pulling from the tree. "Anansi in all of his forms began to weave. He gathered all the stories and spun them until his silk became stronger than diamond. Then he called the sky god:"

"NYAME." Deon struck the trunk in time with the other levels.

"Nyame," Aisha whispered the reply.

"Lift me so I might free us." Makyla raised her hands, spreading them wide. Her fingers caught in tendrils that connected the people of Toussaint to the tree. Her fingers merged with the threads, further pulling her into the Web. "Lift these webs."

"Lift. Lift. Lift. Lift."

Aisha turned her face upwards. The bony branches of the Baobab shimmered and creaked as the Descendants' movements made the light in the chamber pulse.

"But Nyame could not."

The chant died immediately. Makyla began to weep. Tears fell from her face. She turned, looking at all of Toussaint, and her gaze fell on Aisha.

"As much as the sky god wanted to protect his people, he wasn't strong enough. As much as Anansi, in all of his forms, tried, he wasn't strong enough. The gods only have the power that the people give them. They both tried, but the stories, the history, the weight was too much."

Aisha held her breath. This was her favorite part. It was always the part that she had Mama tell her over and over again.

"Then a little girl came forward. She was not afraid of the great Spider. She took up a piece of the web and brought it to her friends. The friends took it and brought it to their parents. Their parents brought it to their village. And Anansi saw that while the burden, the reverence, was too much for him and Nyame, it was not too much for all the people.

"So Anansi raised his legs and danced. He danced for the joy of the brilliance of his people. He danced out of celebration of their willingness to share. He danced for the bravery and generosity of one little girl. As his feet hit the ground he grew and the webs began to rise, held up by his people all over the Earth."

A hum began. Aisha felt it travel up from her feet. Raising her free hand, she crushed the thread to her chest, feeling the vibration in her bones. Closing her eyes, she thought of Mama. For the first time in months, she didn't see her as she was after the accident. She saw her as she had been at Aisha's first sharing ceremony. Mama who'd held her hand and helped her climb over the roots. She'd let her be brave, but made sure she didn't fall.

"The webs rose," Makyla continued. "The people added their stories, strengthening them and rising through the air. And Anansi danced. Anansi danced. Anansi danced."

Her staff hit the floor. The hum was now a joyous drumming. The rhythms from the other Griots melded, mixed. None the same, but all in harmony.

"The people were glad. They were going to be free. But Anansi had a final gift to give." Makyla's gaze went to the branches of the Baobab. "When the Great Spider's next leg hit the ground it shattered. Anansi could not go in one piece. No version of him could. But he could send us his children."

A Descendant dropped in front of Makyla's face. She grinned as the little spider lazily turned on its spinneret, flashing its gold and black legs. "He gave us this gift, this sacrifice. He broke himself into a thousand million pieces so that his people would always be protected. As our ancestors ascended into orbit, past the realm of the sky god, he ensured that no matter where we go, no matter how far we journey, we always have our history."

Aisha looked back towards space and imagined she could see the other webs, in far-flung places of the galaxy where the descendants of the Spider and the Sky continued their journey. Somewhere they too were strengthening their ships and reforging their connections. And here a piece of Mama remained. She was not with her anymore, but no one who connected to the Web ever truly left.

Addai tugged her arm. Makyla's gaze was on them. Aisha swallowed. She led her little cousin to the front of the tree. Addai carefully climbed over the tangled mass of roots before letting go of Aisha's hand to sit cross-legged in front of Makyla. Aisha stepped back. She stumbled, only to have strong hands grip her shoulders. Yena was standing behind her.

Addai raised her chin. "My name is Addai. My mother is Yena. My father is Bilal. On Earth, my ancestors come from Detroit, Dakar, and Bridgetown."

The Descendant that sat on Makyla's palm during the Origin swung onto Addai's shoulder. She lifted her chin and threw the entire community a dazzling smile.

"Krick," she called.

Aisha and all of Toussaint replied as one:

"Krack."

Pepe Gets Married

Florence Onyango

Act I: Pepe walks into a bar...

Pepe stumbles into Anansi's bar. It's a den scented with musky cologne, dim lights, brown leather seats, dart boards, and soft blues playing in the background. It's relatively full, but there's no one Pepe immediately recognizes. "Good," he mutters as he makes his way to the counter and flops onto a stool.

Before he can call for a drink, the bartender slides a chilled glass three-quarters full of golden liquid and the rest is foam threatening to spill over the rim.

Pepe looks up to the tall slender man standing behind the counter, a silver fox. "What is this?" Pepe asks, pointing at the glass; he wants something stronger than a craft beer.

"Whatever it is, it's exactly what you need," the man says. His resonant voice makes it sound as if he's saying something profound.

"What I need is a triple shot of whiskey on the rocks."

The man wags a finger at him. "That's what you want and what you want isn't always what you need." He slides the glass closer to Pepe. "Trust me."

Pepe grips the glass. For a split second, he contemplates throwing its contents at the smug face. Instead, he chugs it. When he thumps the empty glass down on the wooden counter, the man already has a second one placed in front of him. Pepe reads the name tag pinned on the man's black vest. "Anansi?"

The man smiles. "What brings you to my bar today?"

Pepe sighs. It feels trite, spilling his sorrows to a bartender. "Take a guess."

Anansi gives him a once over, and Pepe knows he looks disheveled. His only brand suit's all rumpled, dirty, and damp. His lower lip was cut but not bleeding anymore and his right cheek was bruised and tender.

"Got mugged?"

Pepe shakes his head.

"Lost your job?"

"Nope."

Anansi leans close enough for Pepe to catch the glint in his eyes. "Ah, love perhaps?"

Pepe takes a swig. "Seven years I worked myself to the bone building a thriving business, all to make myself a man worthy, only for my brother to scoop in like a hawk and grab it all." Pepe snaps his fingers. "Just like that. My business, my money, my house, my car, the love of my life... all his now."

Anansi lets out a slow whistle as Pepe takes another swig. "So what happens now?" Anansi asks.

Pepe shrugs. "There's nothing to be done. The families are already meeting tomorrow to plan the wedding." Pepe places his arm on the counter and buries his face in the nook of it. His other hand grips the icy glass as the cold pain prevents him from wailing like a lost child.

PEPE GETS MARRIED

"There's always something to be done."

"Please, just… just shut up."

"What if I could do that something for you?" His voice sounds so close to Pepe's ear that his head snaps up. Anansi is leaning against the shelf behind the counter, arms crossed, watching Pepe. Pepe takes a sip; he must have misheard.

"I could, you know, do something about it."

"What is this? Some kind of deal with the devil situation? Are you going to ask for my soul in exchange?" Pepe laughs, then coughs, then gulps the rest of his beer.

"Want to bet? No souls needed."

"What happens if you win the bet?" Pepe asks despite the urge to hightail it out of there. Anansi reaches for something under the counter and comes up with a stack of paper. The sheet at the top has "Pepe gets married: a play by Anansi" written in black block letters. "I get the rights to your story?"

Pepe furrows his brows. "Rights to my story?"

Anansi leans over the counter "Yes." He stabs the stack of paper with his finger. "See, I'm an aspiring… playwright of sorts."

Pepe wants to laugh. He wants to laugh so hard that he falls off the chair, bumps his head, and wakes up in the morning in his bed with a massive hangover and a blank memory. But he doesn't laugh. He has a feeling it wouldn't be a good idea to.

"I have a," Anansi clears his throat, "reputation of… being nothing but a rebellious shape-shifting trickster."

"Nothing but? Hey, I've heard all about you, and your stories are legendary."

Anansi awards Pepe a small smile. "Well here yes, but up there not so much."

Pepe forgets that his stool is backless. He leans back and just keeps going until he's about to topple over but Anansi grabs his arm in time and pulls him back upright.

"So my story…" Pepe starts.

"Has potential. Once I put my spin on it, it could earn me a position as a fate spinner for Earth."

"Fate Spinner?"

"Earth is renowned, you know? Your fate spinners are the best storytellers in all the worlds."

Pepe looks down into his empty glass. "What happens if you fail? If you lose the bet?"

Anansi reaches under the counter and places a set of keys on the counter, "Then all of this is yours."

He slides a triple shot of whiskey on the rocks over to Pepe.

Act II, Scene I: Pepe Ruins a Wedding…

By the time Pepe arrives at his parents' home, the compound is bustling. There are people everywhere rushing up and down putting up tents, setting the chairs and tables, the decor and, then there's Boaz, wearing shorts, a Hawaiian shirt and crocs, holding the hand of a lady too short to be Malaika. They're heading behind the house, most likely towards the guest house. Pepe makes to go after them when he spots the white catering truck with "Anansi's Bistro Catering" written in italics across the side. Anansi materializes beside him.

PEPE GETS MARRIED

"Here to spectate?" he asks. Side by side he is a head taller than Pepe.

"Nope."

"Change of heart?"

"Yes," Pepe turns to Anansi, "I thought about it all night, and turns out I like the idea of owning your bar."

Anansi turns to face Pepe. "Are you challenging me?"

Pepe lifts his hands in surrender. "No, just here to offer my support and ensure everything goes well." Could he be imagining it or is that smugness in Anansi's grin? Pepe walks away.

As Pepe weaves through the melee, his mother intercepts just before he gets to the main house. She is wearing a beaming yellow kitenge complete with a matching headdress. She grabs his hand. "Pepe, my son." She places the palm of her hand on his cheek. "My poor son. Come, come with me. Let's talk."

Pepe allows her to rush him into the house, past the guests, up the stairs, and into his parents' room, where his father and Uncle Dan sit, expecting him. His mother shuts the door behind them.

She turns to him and takes both his hands in hers. "Pepe, are you really here to cause problems?"

"Don't try it. We are not going to let you ruin this for your brother," his father speaks up. He's in an ill-fitting beige suit, leaning all the way back in his frayed reading chair with his eyes closed and fingers interlocked over his basketball belly.

"You don't have to say it like that, Baba Boaz," his mother snaps at his father. She turns back to Pepe, her features softening as her eyes glisten. "Pepe, please. Please allow me... us to be free of your brother." Her voice trembles. "I know. I am a horrible mother, but God knows I… we have tried our best with that boy, let him be someone else's problem now. I beg you. Malaika is in love with Boaz, she chose him, and your father is retiring soon and I'm getting too old to be looking after him. At least with you, you can take care of yourself; I don't have to worry with you." His mother sniffles. "I know what he did, I… We will find a way to pay you back, but please, please do this one thing for your parents, for the sake of our health and well-being."

Pepe frees one of his hands and places it over his mother's. He is about to reassure her that he has no intention of ruining the wedding when a piercing scream cuts through the house. Then another. Then another. They rush out of the room and down the stairs. There's chaos everywhere. Malaika and her mother have their feet up in the air and are holding on to each other for dear life, screaming at the top of their lungs.

"Eh! What is all this?" Pepe's father booms over the chaos.

A staff member wearing her white T-shirt with the "Anansi's Bistro Catering" logo on it approaches tentatively. "Sir, there is something you should see." She opens a video on her phone.

Pepe, his parents, and Uncle Dan watch as a man in the video – with a striking resemblance to Pepe and the clothes he's wearing – walks to the catering truck carrying a medium-sized box. They watch – his parents and uncle in horror and Pepe in disbelief – as the man dumps the box full of cellar spiders into the truck and closes the door. Pepe cringes at the man's manic laugh as he runs off somewhere off-camera. The staff member apologizes before rushing away. Pepe looks at his parents, at his Uncle Dan, and he can tell from their expressions they were never going to believe

PEPE GETS MARRIED

that that wasn't him. There is only one way to salvage this. He grabs his mother's hand.

"Mama, I am so sorry. I was so upset that I did something horrible. Please forgive me but after you said what you did upstairs... I understand. I promise you I will fix this. I will prove it to you. I will catch every single one of them and make sure nothing else goes wrong. I promise."

Act II, Scene II: While Pepe saves the day...

Anansi is quick to grab Mama Malaika's arm before she takes a tumble down the front porch stairs.

"Thank you," she mumbles faintly, she looks up at him and upon laying eyes on his face, lowers her gaze in modesty. She places a hand over the pearls dangling from her neck and leans on him, her foundation dusting his white shirt.

"Let me take you somewhere to sit and have a rest while they sort out the mess in the house," Anansi offers.

She nods weakly.

Anansi escorts Mama Malaika to a seat placed against the kitchen wall under the kitchen window. He helps her sit and then hands her a hot mug of chamomile tea that she doesn't register, materialized from nowhere. "Here, have this, it will calm your nerves."

She smiles at him, letting the tips of her fingers linger over his for a moment too long as she takes the mug from him. "Thank you."

"If you'll excuse me, I must go and help," Anansi says. Mama Malaika gives a small reluctant nod.

As she watches him stride away, she sighs longingly then takes a sip of the tea. She can hear Mama Boaz's two sisters chatting and cackling in the kitchen.

"They don't know what they are getting themselves into," one of them says, her voice drifting out along with an aroma of spices.

"Serves them right. Surely, who in this town doesn't know about Boaz?" the other adds, with a muffled voice in between chewing.

"Do they actually believe Boozy Bum Boaz has the brains and stamina to build a successful business?"

"Hai-ya! If it were me, Shishi, if you did that to me it would be jail straight away, no mercy. No matter that we're family or sisters."

"Can you believe it? I knew he was lazy good-for-nothing, but Pepe still gave him a job then he goes and pulls that stunt." Plates clutter and glasses tinker. "But even Pepe, he should have known. Anyway, let's stop before someone hears us."

Mama Malaika sets her cup aside and gets up to look for her daughter.

She finds Malaika resting upstairs in the guest room. She quietly closes the door and goes to sit on the edge of the bed beside her daughter. Malaika looks like a real-life version of Princess Tiana with her blue dress and sparkling hair brooch. She's lying on her back at the center of a king-sized bed, perfectly poised with her feet crossed at the ankles and her hands folded over her stomach as rays of light adorn her with shimmering rays. Mama Malaika nudges her awake.

"You can't marry Boaz," she declares as her daughter rubs sleep from her eyes.

"Mom, what are you talking about?"

"Listen to me Malaika, you will be miserable if you marry that man."

Malaika moves to lie back down but her mother grabs her shoulders and gives her a little wake-up shake.

"Malaika, I am serious. They are trying to pull one over us. I overheard it all. Boaz is nothing but a lazy drunkard who stole everything from his brother and now they're trying to dump him on us."

Malakia frees herself from her mother's grasp and pouts. "But I love him, Mom. He makes me happy."

Mama Malaika folds her arms. "Really? Let me ask you, what do you think is going to happen when your father finds out? It's only a matter of time before our bankruptcy becomes public knowledge. Your father needs someone who can take over and help him rebuild the company. What do you think he'll do when he finds Boaz is useless to him? He'll kick both of you out. Then you'll have to be the one to work and cook and clean and take care of him. Do you love him that much? Does he make you that happy? Are you sure?"

Malaika takes a moment to think then slaps a hand over her mouth in horror. She turns to her mother. "Mom, we have to do something."

"Listen, we're going to march downstairs, let them know that we know that Boaz illegally obtained Pepe's business. There's no way we'll let you marry a criminal. Then we will demand the wedding goes forward with Pepe." Mama Malaika stands up and claps. "Come on, chop chop. Straighten yourself out and let's go."

Act III: Pepe's Getting Married

Unbeknownst to Malaika and her mother Catherine, Malaika's best friend and maid of honor overheard the entire conversation from behind the closed door.

Catherine finds Pepe on the patio, scuffling with a full-bloom hibiscus bush. He jumps out of the bush, a hand full of cellar spiders in his hands then drops them when he turns to find Catherine watching him. "Damn it," he mutters as he watches them scurry back into the bushes.

"Sorry, I didn't mean to startle you."

His face softens. "No, it's okay. No worries."

He picks up a fallen flower and places it behind Catherine's ear, careful not to get it tangled in her afro. He takes a step back to admire his handiwork. "It matches your dress," he says with a chuckle. He runs a hand over his clean-cut head. "I should probably just call pest control."

"I'm sorry," Catherine blurts out. She covers her face with her hands and begins to sob.

"Oh, no, no, it's okay. It's not your fault," Pepe says as he guides her to the patio seats.

"It is. It is."

Pepe kneels in front of her and holds her wrists, gently pulling her hands away from her face. He reaches into his pocket and hands her his handkerchief. "There is no way this is your fault, where would you get such a wild idea from?"

"I set them up. I set up Boaz with Malaika. I was there when you made that declaration that you'll become a man worthy to ask for Malaika's hand in marriage. I was there when she laughed at you after you had left." Catherine places her hands on Pepe's shoulders and she peers into his dark brown eyes. "Malaika was never going to marry you, their family was never going to accept you. They only agreed to this because they're bankrupt. Her father recently suffered a heart attack and now he needs someone to take over the business and rebuild it. But they found out about Boaz and now that they know you're the one who built the successful business, they want you to marry Malaika."

"Why? Why did you do that, Catherine?" Pepe asks, his voice thin.

"Because I love you. I've loved you since high school and I hoped that you would eventually see through Malaika."

Pepe stares out into the garden for what seems like an eternity before he turns back to face her. He pulls her in for a hug. "Sometimes what we want isn't always what we need," he says into her neck, as he holds her close.

Their embrace is disrupted by a crescendo of shouting voices. Pepe gets up and offers Catherine a hand. She takes it. Hand in hand, they walk into the living room where Pepe's parents, his Uncle Dan, his two Aunts, Boaz, the random short lady he was with, Malaika, and her parents are all huddled together yelling at each other. On the opposite side, leaning against the entryway into the living room, Anansi watches the commotion with an amused look.

"I have an announcement," Pepe shouts over everyone. They stop. They all turn to face Pepe and Catherine. Pepe lifts their entwined hands. "Catherine and I are getting married."

His announcement is met with stunned silence, but beyond the realm of human hearing, Anansi hears the resounding applause.

Six to the Rescue

Frances Pauli

The six sons of Anansi gathered around their father's table. Their many legs folded at their sides, sleek and velvety. Six times eight eyes gleamed at one another across the polished surface.

"Father is late," the one called Throws Stones spoke in a voice that made their chairs tremble. "He is three days past the time of his return."

"Something has delayed him." Kills Many, the largest and heaviest of the spider sons, growled and gnashed his great fangs together. "Some enemy has captured Father."

The other five shifted their legs, and the room filled with the clicking of chelicera. Their fat abdomens bobbed in anxiety, and the tapping of many claws rang out against the stone floor of their father's main hall.

"We must know," Throws Stones said. "See for us, brother."

The thinnest of their number, a pale spider with legs twice as long as the others', pushed his chair away and climbed up onto the table itself. He lay stretched so that his toes tipped the surface in all directions, and trembled in a seer's fugue. His name was Looks Ahead, and of all of them, he might discover what horrors had befallen their sire.

SIX TO THE RESCUE

His brothers leaned closer, holding their breaths and tightening their spindly legs against their bodies.

"Trouble," Looks Ahead whispered. "Father is in great danger."

"I knew it." Kills Many spread his fangs wide.

"We must find him," Looks Ahead howled and shook his body, rattling the table. "We must go swift as the wind through the grasses."

"Must we all go?" A tiny voice asked, and the spider siblings turned to face the fat, round brother called Is Soft. For all the roundness of his abdomen, for all the long, feathery bristles turning his body into a massive, fluffy pillow, Is Soft had a voice like the smallest cricket.

"I will go." Throws Stones pushed away from the table and stood on the tips of his eight toes.

"As will I," Kills Many announced, not to be outdone by his brother's bravery.

"You'll need me," the one known as Finds Path added, and agreement muttered around the wide table.

All the brothers rattled their limbs in approval of the group, their two strongest and the one who could see them safely through any terrain. No doubt, Looks Ahead would also join the quest, but then, Looks Ahead was always needed. Useful on any adventure. Certainly, with the best of them going, Father would be saved and returned without fail.

"Wait." Looks Ahead shook a final time. He hissed and shivered, and then popped up onto his toes and rubbed his fangs together. "We must all go."

"All of us?" Is Soft chirped and folded his legs until he looked like a white ball, like a dust fluff hidden in a corner where the brooms could not reach.

"All of us,"? Looks Ahead pronounced his verdict, and the spider siblings grew silent.

Surely there might be a reason to bring Drinks Much along, they thought. Once, he'd swallowed a whole river to allow them passage, and during the spring floods he'd saved Is Soft from drowning when the fluffy arachnid had fallen asleep on a stone in the valley's bottom. But to allow Is Soft himself to join them seemed like great folly.

It was an invitation for disaster, and in their calculating minds, the spider siblings could see no reason for dragging the obviously reluctant spider on a quest he could only muddle. For his own part, Is Soft curled more tightly into a ball. He was neither brave nor heroic, and the last thing he wanted was to ruin their father's rescue with his laziness.

But Looks Ahead would not be budged, and in his visions the spiders had much faith. "We must all go," he said. And the spider siblings knew it would be so.

* * *

Finds Path led them. His stout legs pried at dense brush, smashing matted vegetation into a smooth roadway on which they could all travel. Behind him, Looks Ahead came, eyes gleaming with his visions and black fangs chittering as he whispered directions that would lead them to their father.

SIX TO THE RESCUE

Throws Stones followed Looks Ahead, and Drinks Much crawled in his shadow. Then came Is Soft, barely unfolded enough to propel himself forward, and behind him, Kills Many guarded the party's rear. Six spider brothers wound their way into the depths of their jungle home, and with each step they grew more certain of the task at hand.

Father Anansi had fallen into peril, and it would take their collective efforts to see him alive and well again.

Is Soft followed behind the hollow abdomen of Drinks Much, admiring how useful it would be to have room in one's body for an entire river, and he cursed the soft shell that had made him the least of Anansi's sons. While he was at it, he cursed his luck, too, and whatever vision had driven Looks Ahead to insist he must venture into the wilds alongside the rest.

Is Soft much preferred the safety of his father's hall. He would have given a leg to remain there, dining on fat insects and dreaming away the day while curled into a ball as soft as downy feathers. His steps grew sleepy just thinking about a nap, and Kills Many was forced to tap furiously at his rear legs to keep him moving along the newly formed path.

The day grew warm and sullen. The spider siblings marched along, lost in their own thoughts until they reached the shimmering expanse of a black lake. Here the water never stirred. The sunlight bounced off the surface like a skipping stone, and sometimes, Anansi spider came to seek the juicy moon-bright fish that swam below the mirror of dark water.

"Father is here," Looks Ahead announced. "Down deep, in the belly of a monstrous creature."

"My part is played," Finds Path said. "For even I cannot make a road through water.

They all looked to Drinks Much then, and it became clear why the vision had demanded he attend. Is Soft saw this, and sank lower, pulling his legs tight to his sides and hoping none of the others ever looked in his direction. He could not drink, or see, or kill with stone or fang, and he very much wanted to go home again.

Drinks Much, however, skittered to the edge of the lake. His gleaming carapace caught the light, shining brightly as he lifted his huge, empty abdomen. His face dipped low, fangs spreading as they neared the dark water. The magic of Anansi wove through and around his sons, and as if the lake knew its fate, the surface rippled once. The wave spread into a huge circle, as if the water meant to escape the spider's thirst. Drinks Much pressed his hairy mouth full against the lake and began to swallow.

* * *

It took Drinks Much the better part of the day to drink. When he began, the sun blazed directly over the water, and by the time it reached for the farthest trees, the dark water had fallen only halfway down its banks. The others urged him on, Throws Stones and Kills Many bellowing with their mighty voices in a chant that shook the grasses around the lake.

Looks Ahead stared down into the lake, and Finds Path watched the waters as if he considered building a road straight through them.

SIX TO THE RESCUE

Only Is Soft grew weary, though he loved Anansi with as much fervor as the rest. A twisting sorrow filled his fluffy abdomen, and he felt his uselessness like a wall pressing between him and his siblings. His legs unfolded a fraction more. He skittered away from the shore, tired, dejected, and searching only for a comfortable place to nap.

As the sun faded, the waters dropped swiftly. Drinks Much sucked until his abdomen sloshed with black fluid, and the stones and roots that lined the lake's bottom poked into view. The moon-bright fish flopped and huddled into a writhing mass in the remaining water, and at last, the long black body of the lake monster lay exposed.

It was a huge thrashing beast, longer than all six of Anansi's children lined up end to end. Inky skin stretched over the creature's bony skeleton. Huge teeth gnashed in its wide mouth, and two enormous eyes glowed green above the row of barbel whiskers. It saw the sons of Anansi above it and let loose a howl of rage and defiance.

"Father lives inside it," Looks Ahead proclaimed.

"I must find a rock to throw," Throws Stones announced, but of all the pebbles strewn about the shoreline, none seemed quite so mighty as to slay the monster in the empty lake.

Kills Many pushed his way to the lip of the great pit. He paused beside his brothers and glared down at the monster. "It is my turn," he said.

He rushed into the black lake. Down the sloping sides, his long legs churned, and when he reached the beast, Kills Many leapt upon it. The monster roared and swung its teeth toward the spider, but Kills Many was fast and sharp. His fangs tore at the taut skin, and his legs danced so that he was never still enough to be caught.

The beast thrashed and tried to send him flying, but Kills Many's feet were tipped with hook-like claws. He sank his toes into the beast and bit with his long fangs while the monster bucked and rippled beneath him. His brothers watched, urging him on with hissed words and stamping toes. They cheered for his victory, for their father's freedom, and for the part they each had to play in the rescue.

From the long grasses, Is Soft heard the battle commence. The roaring of the monster made his legs shiver, and the chanting of his brothers cast a shadow over his heart. He felt more apart from them than ever, and so he eased his body further into the wild, tucking between the clumps of grass and folding his legs so that he became only a massive fluffy lump in the center of the field.

Certain that his brothers could save Anansi from all dangers, Is Soft sighed and fell asleep.

* * *

Kills Many slit the beast from chin to tail. A great number of things fell free of the monster's long stomach, one of which skittered on eight long legs, shaking filth from his body and racing quickly up the lake's side to join his sons.

Anansi spider hooted at his freedom, dancing in place while five of his sons cheered and stamped. The family's joy made a noise like thunder upon the plains, and the singing of Anansi echoed to the clouds and back. But the skies held another of the spider's enemies, for as much as Anansi loved fishing for the black lake's treasures, he also spent many a hunt foraging for eggs in the high cliff nests.

Even before Looks Ahead could shout a warning, a giant shadow blotted out the sunset. An eagle, who had lost more than one of her speckled eggs to the spider, dropped from the sky, falling upon Anansi and seizing him in her gigantic talons. With a single swipe of mighty wings, she rose back into the sky with the spider's body caged inside her curling feet.

The sons of Anansi roared in anger. They stamped out their fury and howled in frustrated terror for their father's latest tragedy. The eagle beat its wings with equal ferocity, and the cries of Anansi faded as his prison lifted higher and higher into the sky.

"I'll get him down," Throws Stones shouted and rushed forward. He held a river stone in two of his massive legs and lifted his body high, rocking back over his abdomen to steady his aim.

"Wait," Looks Ahead ordered.

"They're getting away," Drinks Much said.

"If only I could reach them," Kills Many moaned.

Finds Path sighed and gazed longingly at the high clouds, helpless to build a road where there was no ground for it to rest upon.

"I'm ready," Throws Stones called. His legs tightened and he coiled like a spring.

"Not quite," Looks Ahead whispered, and then, just as the Eagle passed the last edge of sunlight, becoming a flat black shadow, "Now!"

Throws Stones hurled his weapon into the heavens. He unfolded like a spring, and the stone catapulted high into the night skies. True to aim, it struck the massive bird dead in the eye. The air split with the furious bird's screaming, and its talons fell open, setting Anansi free.

The spider's body dropped from the claws, tumbling through space and falling, faster and faster, toward the unforgiving ground. His five sons dashed forward, five times eight legs tearing at the grasses as they raced forward. But the distance was too far, and even Looks Ahead could see that they would never reach their father in time.

Only one thing could save Anansi, and it was soft, and round, and fast asleep among the long grass.

* * *

Is Soft woke when his father's body landed upon him. His squishy abdomen absorbed the impact, bouncing Anansi back into the air just enough for him to land upright, on all eight toes, and without injury. The fluffy bristles on his son's body formed the softest of cushions, and just as Looks Ahead had seen, Anansi was saved.

When his brothers crowded around to congratulate him, Is Soft unfolded his legs and stood higher on his toes than he'd ever stretched before. He listened to their words and felt their cheering like a soft shiver from his spinnerets to the tips of his bristles.

The spider family returned to Anansi's hall, following Finds Path and Looks Ahead and keeping seven times eight eyes alert for any danger.

SIX TO THE RESCUE

When they reached the safety of their home, Anansi declared a day of celebration. For his six sons he gathered a feast of steamed and juicy insects, and though he had no moon-bright fish or giant eggs to serve, he was happy. His sons danced and spun their webs into silken victory banners, and the main hall filled with music and merriment.

Through the long night the spiders celebrated. As Anansi's heart overflowed with gratitude, he caught sight of the moon through an open window. Gazing at the glowing disc, he imagined it the rarest gem in all the worlds. Love for his many sons filled his heart, and when Looks Ahead crawled up beside him, Anansi let loose a wistful sigh.

"Would that I could fetch it for you," he said.

"Not tonight," Looks Ahead answered.

"Not tonight what?" Finds Path, who'd been playing at cards with Drinks Much and losing more than he cared to admit, joined them. He was followed by Kills Many, Throws Stones, and an overly inflated Drinks Much.

"Father would give us the moon," Looks Ahead announced.

"We'd only fight over it," Kills Many said, in one of his rare wiser moments.

"I would win," Throws Stones insisted.

"Not if I swallowed it first," Drinks Much said.

"What do we need with a moon, anyway?" Finds Path asked.

The sons of Anansi pondered what they might do with a moon. They gathered around their father, jostling and prodding one another to get a better view. Each imagined he deserved the prize, why he'd be best chosen to receive it, and what tasks he might undertake in order to win it for himself. Anansi saw this upon them and tore his gaze away from the moon's folly only to spy Is Soft, curled up in a corner and fast asleep again.

"Look, my sons," he cried. "Look to your brother who has our answer ready."

Anansi's sons turned away from the moon. In his corner, Is Soft slept, round and soft and glowing with his new-found usefulness. Oblivious to their argument, Is Soft echoed the moon in shape and color, as pure and as pale as the rarest gem of all.

The sons of Anansi laughed. The main hall filled with joy again. Is Soft dreamed, round and soft among his brothers, and Looks Ahead saw their father give up on his next adventure.

Anansi spider would leave the moon in the sky, where it belonged, exactly where it was meant to be.

Anansi's Journey Around the World

Shruti Ramesh

Anansi was always very clever, but he was not always wise. This is the story of how Anansi gained an important piece of wisdom. While it is not a true story in the traditional sense, it contains one of life's important truths – one that many of us forget and could use a reminder of.

* * *

Anansi was living what many would consider a good life, spending his retired days with his spirited and stubborn wife Aso and tending to their modest garden. He had had many children, including six lively sons, all of whom were grown up with children of their own. He also had a beautiful daughter called Anansewa, his youngest child. Though it felt like just yesterday that she was small enough to be strapped to his back as he walked through the village, she had grown rapidly like the corn fields after a bountiful rainy season. Though he was reluctant to accept it, it was soon time for Anansewa, his youngest, to be married.

Anansi found this bittersweet, for he was now father to a beautiful young woman. It did not evade him however that with each year of Anansewa's growing up, he was moving a bit slower, his breathing a bit more laboured climbing the hill to get to the market. He was not old, merely "fermented". Aso would tease him, like a palm wine he was only getting stronger with time. But it was not just the physical loss of ability that Anansi was mourning prematurely. He recalled his own father, Nyame, who had passed on from the earthly realm the previous year to return to the sky. In the years before his passing, he first lost his mobility – but then, to Anansi's horror, he lost his wits. Anansi's father was the cleverest man Anansi had ever known, having once given Anansi a special clay pot containing all the world's wisdom. Despite this gift, Anansi was not able to keep all the world's wisdom, which his father never let him live down.[1] More than any other quality, Anansi's father valued cleverness and wit. Anansi's own childhood was studded with tales of his father's role as a legendary trickster – more than actual memories with his father. So, when Anansi's father became old, it was jarring to see his once-sharp wit dulled like a neglected hunting knife, soon fit to cut nothing but warm butter. Anansi worried that he too was to lose his vitality with old age and was kept up late at night at the thought of being unable to make sure Aso and Anansewa would be taken care of. It became Anansi's chief goal to find a match for her to be married. It had to be the perfect match, so Anansi could rest assured that Anansewa would be safe and secure long after his wits had left him.

---

1   A story for another time.

ANANSI'S JOURNEY AROUND THE WORLD

Anansi began his search for a suitor. He visited neighbouring villages, and their neighbouring villages, calling eligible men to come to their home to meet with the family. Soon, word of Anansewa's beauty spread throughout the land, and a line-up could be seen approaching Anansi's door that extended almost until the next village. Each suitor was permitted an hour with Anansewa's parents and five minutes with Anansewa, so that they could get a sense of what they had to offer as a potential partner.

Anansi's wife Aso, the impeccable hostess, met each suitor with the same level of enthusiasm. The palm wine would flow, the fufu and stew would be warm, and each guest treated like a king for as long as they were visiting. Aso's grin was wide, revealing all of her teeth, and her tone was high and pleasant. It was the same tone she used when addressing hagglers at the market – friendly at first, but under the surface she was all business, and would not hesitate to terminate the interaction politely if she was unimpressed. It was only when the door shut behind the suitors that she would turn to Anansi, eyebrows raised, as if to commence the feedback session on this candidate. Unlike many women, Aso rarely adopted her husband's view as her own – she was stubborn, and happy to verbalize her stance (and loudly) she did not agree with his opinion.

"I like him! He looks strong – he can build her a house to keep her safe and warm!"

"His family is very wealthy, with lots of land. He can provide for her, and they can build an empire together."

"He eats very well! He will love Anansewa's cooking."

"He is very tall! Their children will become tall and strong."

"He is wonderful with the children! He will be a good and doting father."

Every time a suitor came to the house, Aso would exalt their numerous virtues. She knew Anansi would always have a counter – he may be strong, but he doesn't have enough money. He may be tall, but he is nowhere near the six feet he boasted – which Anansi knew from subtly placed markers on his door frame. Moreover, none of those things mattered to Anansi as much as one quality: were this prospective son-in-law's wits enough to rival his daughter's? His own?

In that regard, Anansi and Aso struggled to find someone who was good enough for Anansewa. More accurately, Anansi was unable to refrain from finding numerous faults with every single one of them. To be fair, Anansi had devised a test of wits that would be complex even for him, and he also did not let any of the suitors progress that far in the vetting process. Many men came and went, their heads hanging low as though they may fall from their necks at any moment. One by one, they each returned to their own villages, pride shattered, and stuffing removed from their shoes. There was one man, however, who persisted.

The man's name was Kwasi. Every day he waited patiently among the jostling of men fighting for their place at the front of the line. He would chat quietly with Anansewa while her parents met with suitors. She was rather shy and not particularly enamoured by this show of masculinity that had arisen in her name. Each day, it was nearly sunset when Kwasi made it to the front of the line. Each day, he was sent away and told they were no longer meeting with new suitors until the next day. In reality,

ANANSI'S JOURNEY AROUND THE WORLD

Anansi was not thrilled with Kwasi as a prospect – he was a slim and soft-spoken man, who preferred the company of his cats and his fields to socializing with other men his age. He was curious and sensitive, and although he was invisible to Anansi, Anansewa was intrigued.

By the time Kwasi made it to the line for the third time and Ansansi could no longer turn him away without being impolite, Anansi had finally found someone else he would accept as a suitor for his daughter. His name was Kojo, a strong man and son of a chief. Anansi knew Kojo would never be as clever as he was, but he had enough of the other qualities that perhaps this would be enough to give her a good life. What Anansi didn't account for is that in the time it took him to land on a suitor he was willing to give his daughter to, Anansewa and Kwasi had fallen in love.

Months of conversations and stolen moments between suitors deemed good enough to come inside had proven Kwasi's worth to Anansewa. She had chosen him. Anansi however still had the final say in whose family his daughter would be joining. Days of Anansewa pleading and threatening to never get married unless Kwasi was given a fair chance finally wore Anansi down. Kwasi said he would oblige any test Anansi asked for to prove his worth as a suitor. Anansi, unable to resist a challenge, retreated to his hut to think. He emerged the next morning to tell Kwasi that he would be given the opportunity to take Anansi's ultimate test of wits, the one none of the other suitors had even approached. He declared that the two men were to have a race. Aso was confused, "How will you, an old husk of a man, race this young thing who has only recently stopped growing?". "The race will not be that of speed," Anansi declared. "It will be a race of the mind; the first person who is able to go around the world will win. It is not about speed – it is about the shortcuts you can devise."

Anansi knew that in reality, it was no competition at all. There was no way Kwasi, lacking his own cleverness, would be able to devise the shortcuts necessary to complete this journey quickly. To his surprise, Kwasi agreed. They would begin at sunrise. The first person to complete their trip around the world would win. There would be three parts to this journey: the journey over land, journey over water, and journey through the sky. The journey over the land was the easy part – but the journey through sky and over the sea would require a particularly cunning mind – and Anansi looked forward to showing Kwasi he did not have what it takes.

Anansi began his journey as the sun climbed above the mountains. He noticed Kwasi sitting on a stump outside, his face turning upwards to face the sun. Anansi expected this man to be in distress or have woken early to get a head start – where there should have been fear was relaxation – contentment even. Did he know something that even Anansi didn't?

Wasting no time, he began his first stretch of circling the world: over land. After seven long days and nights, Anansi was running out of endurance to finish his journey. He encountered his friend the lion. He proposed to him that in exchange for helping him trap the occasional prey with his web, he could be carried across the rest of the way on his journey. Anansi welcomed the rest on this portion of his journey, for the real work was about to begin.

When he bade his friend the lion farewell, he was careful to tie his tail to a nearby tree with his web – though he was a friend, the

ANANSI'S JOURNEY AROUND THE WORLD

lion was still an animal at the end of the day. Anansi turned out to be correct in his predictions: as he scrambled away from the lion, he could hear him readying to pounce on him, before being dragged back by the tie on his tail. Anansi shook his head – some people will never learn that he cannot be so easily outsmarted.

The Journey Over Water

After crossing the long stretch of land, Anansi soon arrived at the ocean. Although he had many skills, he could not swim. He had to think quickly how to cross over the water. He saw Bonsu the whale dozing in the shade, and an idea came to him. Bonsu's young son was swimming slow laps around his father, waiting for him to wake up to play. Anansi waved and beckoned him closer. "Do you want to play hide and seek?" he asked the baby whale. Eager for a distraction, Bonsu's son nodded vigorously and took off. It was time for the next phase of Anansi's plan.

Anansi may have slowed with age, but his ability to spin a web rivalled his ability to spin words. He worked quickly, spinning a net resembling those used by the fishermen in the village. Inside the web he spun web around rock, layers and layers until the shape of a baby whale was made out. His work was almost done. Before approaching Bonsu, he slung the net structure as far as he could, summoning all of his strength. It landed on the far side of the vast water with such impact. It caused a ripple that woke up Bonsu from his deep slumber.

"Anansi, what do you want?" Bonsu said, wary at the very sight of him. "I have no interest in your tricks today." Bonsu had been fooled by Anansi once in the past and had no interest in being made a fool again. "You think so little of me," Anansi said with a smirk peeling open like a ripe banana – "I only woke you up to help you. Your son has fallen victim to a fisherman's net, and I thought you'd want to know." Bonsu hesitated to believe Anansi at first, but when his gaze followed where Anansi's leg was pointing, his horror caused him to shake. He took off abruptly, swimming faster than he had ever swum before. What Bonsu did not realize, was that Anansi had spun a web around his tail and deftly hopped on his back as he was taking off. In mere seconds, Bonsu had traversed the ocean to nearly reach the other side where only the silhouette of his baby in a fisherman's net trapped on the ocean floor was visible. Panicking, Bonsu unhinged his jaw and began draining the ocean's water, desperate to find his son. It was only when the sandy ocean floor remained that his real son was revealed, hiding amongst the seaweed. And the web facsimile was revealed, Bonsu slowly realizing that he had been fooled once more.

Anansi wasted no time in crawling up the ocean's basin on to the beach, as Bonsu released the ocean's water quickly to cause a tidal wave. Rather than being caught under the wave, it instead pushed him faster along the land, and he was soon approaching the mountains – the final stretch before returning home.

The Journey Through Sky

Anansi knew that he was not equipped to journey over the mountains on his own. He would need to find a way to get through the mountain range that did not involve hiking. Anansi hated hiking. He knew however that this area is where the bird

ANANSI'S JOURNEY AROUND THE WORLD

Sankofa dwelled. Sankofa was a solitary creature, though he yearned for a mate. He spent his days flying back and forth over the stretches of mountain passes, looking for a companion to spend his days with. Anansi intended to use this knowledge to his advantage, and quickly got to work.

Anansi set about gathering a pile of dull grey and brown feathers. He mused to himself how funny he thought it was that the women in his life always dressed up in their finery when attending a festival and were keen to show off their beauty. But in the animal kingdom, especially for birds, it was often the men who were forced to show off – and how silly they sometimes looked! When Anansi was done, he had feathered all eight of his legs and crafted a mask of twigs and feathers, whittling himself the perfect wooden beak. He was left with a convincing suit that made him look just like a female bird. After donning his costume, he approached Sankofa, who was once again scanning the skies looking for a mate. His eyes caught Anansi's gaze.

He approached Anansi shyly to introduce himself. Anansi, continuing to pretend to be a bird, feigned indifference to Sankofa's approach. Anansi said, "Hello, I am not interested in being courted today." Sankofa was incredulous at this response and was keen to convince Anansi otherwise. With each of his advances, Anansi (as the lady-bird) politely rebuked him. Sankofa finally broke down, exclaiming, "What is it that you want? I will try anything so that I can prove myself – I know now that I am in love with you and must have you as my mate. I will fly across this mountain range and back while the hawks are prowling for food if that's what I must do to prove myself to you."

Anansi chose his words very carefully. "Any old bird can fly across the mountain range with no obstacles. I myself have done it dozens of times. Let's make it a real challenge. Can you fly across the mountain range while carrying me?" Anansi ruffled his feathers and looked at Sankofa flirtatiously. Sankofa, puffing out his chest, happily obliged. "Of course! Please climb on to my back, and we will fly across this mountain range together in no time at all".

Anansi happily hopped onto Sankofa's back, and the two of them set off. Anansi was nervous as he saw hawks circling the skies and fixed his eyes on the other side of the mountain range. Each time Sankofa tried to strike up conversation, Anansi was quick to shift focus to their journey ahead. They soon began to descend at the other side of the mountain range.

Anansi quickly dismounted and hid in the bushes before Sankofa could look back. "Oh no!" his voice filled with dismay. He took off back over the mountain pass, looking for his companion whom he worried had fallen off his back. Anansi intended to rush off, but he was distracted by another bird who had been following them for some time, and appeared to be circling closer and closer to Anansi. To Anansi's relief, it was not a hawk or another predatory bird, but a female bird whose feathery suit was not unlike Anansi's fake one.

The female bird approached Anansi. "Is that your husband?" she enquired. "I've been watching him for some time now, and I've never seen him with a companion." Anansi quickly reassured her that Sankofa was in fact still looking for a mate, and if she would just wait right here, he would soon return. She looked pleased, and perched on a nearby log, ready for Sankofa's return.

Anansi was also pleased – if he had to prevent one union today, at least he will have created another.

Anansi then bid her farewell, telling her he had forgotten something and needed to return home to retrieve something he had forgotten. She turned to him and smiled, before saying, "It is not wrong to go back for what you have forgotten." Though Anansi did not know quite what she meant, it spurred him to sprint through the final steps of his journey home.

A Journey Around the World

Anansi returned, three weeks after his departure. He approached his hut and saw to his dismay that Kwasi was in the same place he was when he left. On the stump, gazing at Anansewa. He looked at peace, without even a trace of concern on his face. When he saw Anansi approaching, he rose.

He began pacing, slowly and deliberately in a circle until his footsteps encircled Anansewa. He continued pacing this way in circles until Anansi approached them. "He must be nervous," Anansi thought. Kwasi wasn't able to cope with the difficulty of his challenge, and so he was pacing and readying himself to beg Anansi for mercy.

Anansi approached Kwasi and Anansewa with a triumphant look on his face. "I have just returned from going around the world. Can you say the same? It does not look as though you have moved from where I left you aside from your frenzied pacing around my daughter."

Kwasi took a deep breath before speaking. "Anansi, sir, it is there where I must disagree. If the last few months of knowing your daughter have taught me anything, it is that she is now my whole world. You may have circled the earth, but Anansewa, to me, is now the only thing that matters. I knew I could never part with her for the weeks or months it would take to make a journey around the earth – I know now, more than ever, that I never wish to be apart from her for that long for as long as we are both on this earth."

Anansi experienced an overwhelming tide of emotions. He was indignant that he had traversed the whole world only for his competitor to have taken a few dozen steps and declared victory. His pride, however, soon relinquished its hold on him. Kwasi continued, "You may have proven your cleverness, yes. You have proved your ability to trick people, of course. But more than that, you have proven that people are willing to be made a fool if there is a chance of protecting someone they love, or the chance to love. All kinds of love – the love between a parent and child, and between lovers and partners – all of this love is sacred. You may be remembered by strangers and acquaintances for your immense wit – but how will you be remembered by those closest to you?"

Anansi was surprised at his own poignant response to Kwasi's remarks. He turned to his wife, recalling a time when he felt the same way about Aso. He still did, but in his efforts to outsmart and beat everyone he encountered, and hoard tales of cleverness over love, he had lost sight of what really mattered. It was often that Anansi would outsmart, and less often that he was outsmarted. Even rarer still was Anansi learning a lesson that inspired him to change. Slowly, he bowed his head to Kwasi. He gave his blessing for Kwasi to marry Anansewa.

ANANSI'S JOURNEY AROUND THE WORLD

Kwasi was not the richest man who courted Anansewa. Nor was he the strongest, or the most titled. He was not a king, and not even a chief. He was clever, the trait Anansi himself decided was the most important in finding a match for his daughter. But what mattered is that he was so clever that he taught Anansi a lesson that day – a lesson in the importance of love. Wits and trickery can win you a competition or give you an advantage over others. Still, it is only love that can give you the whole world without ever leaving your home. Anansi would never forget that.

Taxi Brousse

Peter K. Rothe

"In every journey, there lies an opportunity to discover who we truly are."
– Anansi the Spider

The Bush Taxi

The Runaway stands at a crossroads, four paths, and the one left behind. Each a decision, each a destination away from his burden, away from the truth, away from the past.

The pregnancy test was positive, two lines, oppressive in their judgement. Two lines that meant everything would have to change, the Runaway most of all.

The rumble of a bush taxi catches his attention, the only sound in an otherwise vacant street. The morning sun's glint reflects off the windscreen. A rickety old thing, with bags and plantain strapped to the roof and a boot filled to bursting.

Where is it going? The Runaway doesn't care.

Two taps and the Driver opens the window. He is a handsome man with a wide grin of glistening, ivory teeth. He wears a rugged green suit and round sunglasses with opals shrinking down the frame. He radiates the scent of morning dew.

"Where are you going, my friend?" says the Driver.

TAXI BROUSSE

"Anywhere," pleads the Runaway.

The smile broadens. "It just so happens that 'anywhere' is exactly where we are going. Hop in, my friend."

The back seats are taken by a lanky man wearing a rainbow-patterned kente cloth, and a large woman is fast asleep beside him.

The Runaway takes the front seat.

"Troubles?" asks the Driver.

The Runaway hesitates. "Me and everyone else. Same old story: money, the weather, family."

"I know those troubles very well, my friend. Especially those of the money, weather, family kind."

The interior seats have leopardskin coverings and the car's trim appears to be some sort of faux snakeskin. Dangling from the rear-view mirror are two engraved stones, one black and one white. The inside smells damp, like the bush after heavy rain.

"It's all one big mess," says the Runaway.

"The ruin of a nation begins at the home of its people," says the Driver, almost to himself, tapping his gold ring on the steering wheel. Tap, tap, tap.

"You are clever for a bush driver."

The Driver tilts his head, sunglasses glistening white. "Is this what you think I am? Did you hear that, *Toma*? We're in a bush cab."

The lanky man groans. "Leave me out of your games."

The Driver laughs. "Of course, we are in a bush taxi. And where is it we are going, my friend?"

333

"I told you, far away from this place. The further, the better." The Runaway takes one last look at the apartment block. The building is painted gold by the birth of a new dawn. On the third floor, the curtain is slightly parted. He thinks he sees her there. His heart aches.

"We go?" asks the Driver.

"Let's," says the Runaway.

"You might want to fasten your seatbelt. There will be many potholes on the way."

"A bush taxi. This will be interesting," heckles Toma as the woman starts snoring.

The Jam

The taxi slows behind a lorry stacked with caged chickens. Cars press in on both sides, squeezing one traffic lane into four. Swarms of motorbikes, cycles, and *cows* filter through the narrow gaps between vehicles. Disgruntled drivers and passengers wait for someone to get the traffic moving. Making things worse, the whole place stinks like a shop selling dodgy fuel on the side of a bush track.

"Why are we not moving?" The Runaway tries his best to see if he can catch anything ahead. Only more cars, as far as he can see.

"What's the rush, my friend?" says the Driver. "We will get there eventually."

"At this rate," says the Runaway, "we will be here till the end of days."

"I doubt that very much."

TAXI BROUSSE

"I blame the corrupt politicians. Instead of fixing the roads, they pocket our taxes and spend it all on big houses and fancy Range Rovers."

"You think we are here because of politics?"

"Politics, the government, society. All we do is work and work. Only to spend the rest of the day in traffic."

"You didn't have to leave."

"If we had better roads, and traffic lights, we could all leave when we wanted. We could have a fancy flyover, cheap and clean buses that run on time. Instead, we get potholes, sewage, and traffic."

"You keep blaming other people. But are they to blame for your hurry?"

"I'm not in a hurry, I…"

The lorry ahead moves but then stops. There is hooting and shouting.

"I have better things to do than sit around in traffic all day."

"Do you?" asks the Driver. "People are funny, always striving for better things: a nicer car, a bigger house. Never happy, never able to settle."

"You're one to talk," says Toma.

"True, true. I've done my fair share of swindling and mischief in my day."

"Look at them," says Toma. "Stuck in their metal boxes, all with better things to do. So many hopes, so many dreams to keep themselves busy, busy."

"Don't you have places to go?" asks the Runaway.

"We all have places to go," says Toma. "But some of us are more in a rush than others."

A car on the Runaway's side begins to veer closer, trying to fill the space in front of the bush taxi. The car is getting too close – the Runaway waves at the car.

"Idiot man!" says the Runaway. "Can't you see there is no space! Are you trying to get us killed?"

The car's horn blurts out angrily. A motorbike tries to squeeze from the other side. There is to be smoke up ahead, people are getting out to see.

"Just chill," says the Driver. "If the man wants the space, let him have it."

"It's our space."

"Everyone needs to be easy." The Driver taps his ring. The tapping gets louder and louder.

The Runaway glares at the Driver and crosses his arms. "Will you move already?!"

A long silence stretches between them. The Driver puts the car in gear and moves.

"That was unnecessarily rude, my friend. It's just a bit of traffic, nothing to get upset about."

"Traffic. This is not about the traffic." The taxi stops abruptly. "Oh, for heaven's sake!"

A man with a rugged beard wearing a dirty white t-shirt is standing in front of the taxi. He raises his hands in protest and gives the driver the finger.

"Do you have a death wish? Move!" says the Runaway. But the man refuses to budge.

"If you want, I can run him over. Make a big messy omelette out of him."

The Runaway laughs, relaxing. "You're a funny man."

"Hilarious. I'm being serious."

The Runaway studies the Driver's smile. His sunglasses hid his eyes, revealing nothing.

"Some people might be better off dead," mumbles the Runaway.

The man outside pushes on the bonnet and hurls threats at the Driver. Putting the car in first, the Driver presses on the accelerator.

"Stop!" says the Runaway. "You mad man, I was kidding!"

The car judders to a halt.

"You don't want me to run him over."

"Not on purpose."

The man outside gives the taxi one more shove before walking off.

A white shuttle bus belches a great horn before slamming into the man, sending him hurtling high in the air to bounce off the boot of a black Range Rover. The man lies face down on the road, unmoving.

"OH, MY GOODNESS!!!" screams the Runaway.

"That was unfortunate... for him," says the Driver.

People pour in from the streets and cars to congregate around the collapsed man. The Runaway considers joining them, but there are too many people. They are swarming around the taxi, some thumping on the window, others screaming and swearing.

The Driver shakes his head. "Be careful what you wish for, my friend. The webs of fate may grant your wish in unexpected ways."

"So much hurry," says Toma. "So much wasted life."

The taxi begins to move, slowly pushing through the throng.

❈ 337 ❈

The Runaway tries to catch a glimpse of the man through the gathering, to see if he is still alive. But the taxi moves on with the now-flowing traffic. He sees nothing. He collapses in his seat, feeling useless and somewhat responsible.

The Heat

The bush taxi is driving down a long road that stretches towards a shimmering horizon. To either side of the cracked tarmac, great red flats stretch out, barren but for a few scattered shrubs and the occasional baobab tree. Directly above, an oppressive sun beats down on the taxi.

"This heat," says the Runaway, "it's so hot it hurts."

"It's not too bad," says the Driver. "We aren't even in the dry season yet."

The Runaway groans. "Every year, it gets hotter and hotter. It's all the pollution from the factories in the city."

"The factories make things for people to buy. They need to feed their families. What do you think they should do instead?"

"They should stop! They are destroying the planet for profit. They are turning the land into a desert. There are droughts, famine, hunger. How can anything grow and flourish in this place?"

"And what of you, my friend? Are you not responsible?"

The Runaway says nothing. He gazes out of the closed window to some mud huts. He doesn't see anyone.

"There is a season of abundance," says the Driver, "and a season of famine. All things must adapt to a changing world or perish."

The Runaway fumbles with the buttons on the dash, anything to cool him down. He tries turning on the AC dial all the way, but only hot air comes out. Outside, the sun intensifies, making it hard to look out of the window without squinting.

"You can't tell me this heat is normal. Don't you feel it?"

"I do feel it, my friend. You'll get used to it. People are always unhappy. Either it's too hot, or it's too cold. Relax, have a cold beer, take a nap."

The Runaway gives up trying to get the AC working. "It's hopeless."

"You're going to overexert yourself."

"It's all hopeless. Nothing will ever change."

"It's people that don't change."

The sun is now a great white ball in the sky. The Runaway can't even see the road anymore and must cover his eyes.

"He needs to calm down," says Toma. He sounds worried. "It's just a bit of heat."

The big lady is snoring away, not bothered by the world burning outside.

"A bit of heat!" says the Runaway. "It's like we are being roasted alive."

"If you are so hot," says the Driver, "do something about it."

The Runaway laughs, blinking perspiration, tasting salt. "Me. What difference can one person make?"

"You could open the window. That might help."

The Runaway studies the Driver, confused. How would *that* help? He opens it anyway, letting in a cool and pleasant breeze, despite the blazing sun.

"See, nothing like a bit of fresh air to give you a new perspective."

The Runaway leans against the window, staring disgruntled at the barren countryside passing by. He wonders if he made the right choice in leaving.

The Flood

A wall of black clouds sweeps across the land. The world darkens as a sharp wind wakes the Runaway, followed by a sudden downpour.

"What is this? Where did the rain come from?"

"Close the window, my friend. You're getting water everywhere."

The Runaway begins to shut the window, but the handle gets stuck. More rain cascades into the car, drenching the Runaway, the leopardskin seat coverings, and spattering all over the faux snakeskin.

"Will you hurry it up?!" barks the Driver. "It's getting everywhere."

"It's stuck!"

The Driver reaches over and easily winds the window shut.

The Runaway, soaked through, uses his sleeves to wipe water off his face. He can barely see the road ahead; the wipers are moving as fast as they can, but the rain quickly drenches the window again. He catches a glimpse between swipes; the road is flooding.

"We should stop. This is complete madness. Where did this heavy rain come from?"

"I told you, it's not the dry season yet. There is no stopping here. Either we make it to our destination, or we don't."

"Can't you see the road is flooding?!"

The Driver shrugs. "First you moan about the heat and now you are not happy with a little bit of rain. There is no pleasing you."

"Are you crazy? You call *this* a little bit of rain? Have you seen how high the water is? We're going to drown!"

The sky flashes white, followed by a great thunderclap that shakes the bush taxi. The Runaway covers his ears, screaming. The Driver is not smiling any more.

"What do you want me to do?" asks the Driver. "If we stop here, we drown. There is no shelter where we came from. All we can do is keep going and hope things work out. But first, you need to CALM DOWN!"

"Why didn't you check the forecast before we left? What about the mud hut from earlier? Look, there!" The Runaway points to a baobab. It sways violently in the wind, despite its thick trunk.

"I'm not stopping. I told you, my friend, there is no getting off this ride."

The water is lapping up the car bonnet. The taxi looks to be driving through a great ocean.

"You, there. Toma, is it? Tell him we need to stop. Make this crazy man see reason!"

No reply. The Runaway turns to find the back seats empty.

"Where did they go?" asks the Runaway.

"Where did who go?"

"The others."

"What others? It's just you and me, my friend."

"Stop lying to me! There were other people, Toma and the big woman!"

"Who said they were people?" says the Driver. "You *need* to calm down."

"Don't tell me to calm down. I'm not crazy. There were other passengers. Why are you doing this? This is all your fault. I told you we need to stop!"

A wave of water slams into the taxi, jerking it from side to side and making the Runaway knock his head on the window. The cab is momentarily submerged. More lightning rages in the sky.

"This is the end of the world! We are going to die!"

"No need to be dramatic. Just chill."

"Don't tell me to chill. Oh, God. What am I doing here? What have I done? Why did I leave? Oh God, please, save me!"

The Driver sighs, tapping his ring on the steering wheel.

"You want it to stop?" asks the Driver.

"Please!" pleads the Runaway.

"Then it shall stop."

The rain eases and after a few moments, the flood waters recede, leaving a dirty and muddy road behind. The Runaway shakes and cries.

"See," said the Driver. "There is nothing in the bush. Only man's fears."

The Runaway hears him but keeps weeping.

The Night

They drive in silence for many hours. Long after the sky cleared, and it turned dark. At the end of the road, the majesty of heaven can be seen, a vast tapestry of stars and the coloured haze of the universe, so vibrant they appear painted on. An enormous, full ivory moon hangs high in the night sky.

The gentle murmur of the taxi comforts the Runaway, who is caught in deep reflection. His conscience masks the revealed beauty of the expanse above.

"How are you, my friend?" asks the Driver.

"I don't know," says the Runaway.

"Did you work out where we are going?"

"I don't know any more."

"Seriously?" snaps the Driver. "After all this time you still don't know. Now look where we've ended up."

The Runaway considers the reply. They are in the middle of nowhere. There is nothing but darkness casting shadows on the night sky. It's as if the taxi is driving through space, the only indication of a road is the occasional pothole or pebble lit by the headlights.

"Where is this place?" asks the Runaway.

The Driver shrugs. "This could be anywhere."

The Runaway thinks back. Where are you going? Anywhere. It just so happens that anywhere is exactly where we are going.

"I don't like it here. I want to go back."

"You know I can't do that," says the Driver.

"Why not?"

"You left for a reason, didn't you?"

The Runaway hardly remembers the reason. It feels like another life, another world. All he remembers are the flood, the heat, and a man bouncing off a Range Rover.

"I don't know why I left."

"Sure, you do." The Driver clicks his fingers. "Know what? How about we make a bargain? Tell me your story and I will take you wherever you want."

"My story? Are you playing games with me? Just take me back. I don't want to travel any more. I'm tired and weary."

"Nope," says the Driver.

"Stop the car."

"You don't want me to do that."

"Are you kidnapping me? Stop the *bloody* car!"

The taxi screeches to a halt.

The Driver slowly faces the Runaway. His sunglasses are enormous, almost like orbs in the man's slender visage. The Runaway tenses, feeling trapped like a fly caught in a web.

"You want to leave?" says the Driver. "Leave. Find your own way back."

The Runaway begins to pull the handle. He freezes. Shadows stir in the bush beyond the road, things shifting in the night his mind cannot comprehend. Creatures with tusks, claws, fangs, and horns. Their terrifying eyes glimmer at him, reflecting the moonlight in green and yellow. He hears them growling and hissing, waiting for him to come out, waiting to feast.

"What do you want from me?" asks the Runaway. "You want money? I have none. You want my things? All I have are my clothes."

"I want your story; I want the truth. Why did you leave?"

"Can we please keep driving? Those things in the bush want to eat us."

"I told you, there is nothing in the bush, only man's fears. Give me what I want."

The Runaway thinks long and hard. What harm is there in telling *a* truth to this stranger? "You want to know why I left? I left because my girlfriend is having a baby. I left because I would only mess up the child if I stayed. They are better off without me."

The Driver taps his ring on the steering wheel.

"There it is, the truth," says the Runaway. The creatures are drawing closer to the car. There are so many of them, so many eyes, countless as the stars above.

"Don't try to hustle a hustler. I want the *true* truth. Why did you leave?"

"That is the truth. I would make a terrible dad."

"YOU THINK I'M A FOOL!" The Driver's voice is harsh and grating, like the clicking of countless cicadas. "That was not our bargain! Tell me the truth or I will throw you out for the beasts of the night to tear you to pieces."

The growling and howling outside intensifies.

"I told you, I was scared, I–"

"Get out!"

"I... I..."

The car shakes as the creatures of black slap and scratch at the taxi.

"I ran because I wanted to be free. I felt trapped. I am not ready to be a father, not ready to have a child. So, I ran."

"You selfish bastard. Go on."

"Yes. I am a selfish bastard. Just like my father, a lazy, selfish, foolish coward. There. Is that what you want to hear? Now. Please. Get us out of here and take me home!"

The Driver puts the taxi in gear and begins to turn. The Runaway crumbles, covering his face, ashamed. He deserves to be ripped apart by the creatures. What did he do? That poor child would end up just like him.

"Just a little deeper," says the Driver, with compassion in his voice. "But now, be honest, tell me why you left?"

"I…" How did the Driver know? It was never about the child, never about his father, nor the flood, the heat, or the jam. It was always about him. Always about *him* running away.

"I left because that's what I do. Because I'm worthless."

"Good. And who are you now?"

The Runaway doesn't know who he is, only who he doesn't want to become.

"I am nothing, just a man."

The Driver sighs and taps the Man on the shoulder. "Good. That's a start. It's time to get you back home, my friend."

The Journey

The bush taxi drives past the road once flooded. Great palms and shrubs adorn sprouts from the side, growing so tall they blot out the stars, with deep roots that would swallow even the harshest rain.

As they drive past the mud huts of the barren planes, they witness a tribe dancing and chanting around a great bonfire. A man throws up his child and catches them. The child is laughing.

They drive along the main street through the middle of the city. They find it empty and smooth, with not a single car to slow them down. So they drive faster and faster.

Finally, the bush taxi stops at the crossroads. The man no longer recognizes the place, this destination, both familiar and strange. Ahead of him is the apartment block, glistening yellow against the dark side of dawn.

"What do I owe you?" asks the Man, stepping out of the taxi.

"A journey shared is a story shared. Our bargain is done, my friend." The Driver smiles, his suit and skin appear to radiate light and for a heartbeat, the man thinks he sees eight shadows stretching away from the taxi.

"Thank you," says the Man. "Why do you do this?"

The Driver is caught off guard. "Why did I steal stories from the god of the sky? Why did I bring the day and the night to the world? Why do I take strangers to strange places? Mostly boredom, sometimes cruelty, other times for my amusement."

"You are a strange man."

"Who said this was a taxi and who said I'm a man?"

"Goodbye, my friend."

The Driver, who is not a driver, nods.

The Man turns to his house and walks across the street. At the door, he hesitates. He is afraid, unsure where he will end up or who he will be if he walks in.

He looks back but the bush taxi is gone. He wonders if it was ever there.

The Father smiles and chuckles to himself. Does it matter? The journey was true enough.

Sacrifice

Chisom Umeh

Anansi woke to the sound of an alarm blaring. It was a small sound only he could hear, attuned to a frequency the radio in his earlobe could pick up. To everyone else, the adornment on his right ear was an interesting piece of jewelry that could have come from the old times. The information age. Or it could be some insignificant piece of cheap metal not worth expending an ounce of energy on. Energy was currency in these times, even worth more than any piece of jewelry could afford you. So, unless you were sure, which you couldn't be, then it was best to not test the waters. It would be like a lion giving up chase midway into a hunt; the food isn't secured, and no energy to hunt for another, making way for even more hunger. Better to save yourself for something better.

The sound: Anansi didn't want to hear it. Or, he didn't wish to hear it. But he knew it'd come someday.

He was about to drift into sleep when the low, piercing ring jerked him awake, and he tapped his wife beside him.

"Jessica, we need to go," he said to her in a calm voice.

"What?" she said groggily, barely perturbed by Anansi's prodding.

"We need to leave now, babe," he said again into her ears, and something about the way he said it now, permitting a level of urgency into his voice, made her eyes shoot open. Like a machine that had been activated, she got up from the bed and began scrambling about the room to gather things. She had just begun opening drawers when Anansi stopped her, held her hands, and said, "We wouldn't be needing those, babe. This is the big getaway."

Her eyes widened, and he nodded slowly. "Just wake Kwame up so we can move."

She nodded back and left the room. Anansi went to the bathroom, scooped water from a bowl, and washed his face. He peered into the shard of glass on the wall that served as a mirror, knowing that it might probably be the last time he'd do so. His eyes were sleepy and permanent dark lines hung beneath them. A streak of silvery stubble was tracing its way beneath his chin. And his cheeks were barely visible now. He looked malnourished. But who wasn't in these times? These were probably evolutionary pressures tinkering humanity into a different shape. Natural selection working to keep only that which was optimal for the survival of the human race and discarding the rest. Unless some serious advancements happened, Anansi wouldn't be surprised to come back five thousand years in the future to find all humans spindly and bony. And that would be totally normal.

Anansi took off from the room, padded down the wooden stairs, and rounded the old building. In the backyard was a shack sealed with a padlock. The skies were open that night and the rains came through uninhibited. The streaks of water mingled with the rays of Anansi's torchlight, each phasing through the other seamlessly. Some energy can be harnessed from the ferocity of this storm, Anansi thought.

The ground was slippery, so he calculated his steps. For a long time, he had been reserving energy for this day. He and his family ate only a certain type of food at given hours of the day so that whenever the time came and they needed strength to get away, they wouldn't be caught flat-footed. He was thankful now for being stern all the while whenever Kwame scoffed at the fufu Jessica made in the morning.

The rain pelted him as he inserted a key into the lock and the thing clicked open. The floor in the shack was wet, rain pouring in from beneath the wooden walls and the leaking roof overhead. But the center of the shack remained untouched, a pattern of dry ground forming right there. Lightning gave new light to the room and if Anansi looked closely in those fleeting seconds, he'd see the phantom shape of the machine that stood in its center. To the naked eye, the shack was empty. But to any other kind of scanner, there was an elephant in the room. Or, more appropriately, a spider.

The spider was what they called it in the old days, this machine with four legs that ran on electricity. Aside from the fact that it was shaped like an arachnid, it was called the spider because it crept up on people noiselessly. It also had a way of charging and storing energy just by driving past energy sources, like a spider weaving a web around itself.

A century ago, before the world fell away owing to the energy crisis and the AGI wars, the spider was a utility vehicle. It was affordable even to the middle class. Most streets in urban Accra had at least two parked in someone's backyard. When the world plunged into war, Anansi knew one of those would be valuable, so he stole a couple and stashed them in locations around the world for moments like this when he needed to get away quickly.

He turned off the flashlight and took out a tiny device from his pocket. He pressed down a small button for a second or two, then the device came on, a small light beeping on its side. He held the device towards the car and for a moment his pulse quickened, fearing the machine had succumbed to time and would no longer come on. It was an irrational fear, and Anansi shouldn't fall prey to irrationality. Not because he was Anansi, but because he came here from time to time to confirm that the machine was in good shape. At his last check, the vehicle was functioning perfectly. The thought had come anyway, but it vanished as quickly as it emerged when Anansi felt the familiar buzz of the car drawing power from the device in his hand.

"Uncloak yourself," he said, then turned on the flashlight. The car didn't curve the light from the torch around itself but rather let it bounce off its body, becoming existent on the ultraviolet end of the electromagnetic spectrum.

Just then he heard his wife come in bearing their five-year-old son in her arms, rain plastering their clothes to their bodies. Jessica took one look at the newly materialized machine with shock in her eyes.

We'll use this to get away, Anansi signed to her since she was hard of hearing and the heavens were exploding with noise. She had many more questions, he knew, but he signed "trust me" and her shoulders seemed to relax a little.

He led Jessica and Kwame to the back of the car, then opened the door and let them in. He also got in, asked the car computer to cede control to him, and then drove slowly out of the shack.

The spider was a relic, an intrusion of the past into the present. Two incongruent realities coiling into each other, yet unable to tangle. The car wasn't supposed to be here, not after the world's superpowers entered into an arms race to build the first artificial superintelligent machine, sparking a war that damned everything else.

Whoever could control the AGI could control the world, they said. So when the first one came online in the late 2030s, built by the US, different governments used the same blueprint to develop theirs, not stopping to think about the consequences of passing authority to a creature several orders of magnitude smarter than humans.

The war that followed was inevitable, starting in the 1950s when the idea of a self-conscious machine was first conceived and culminating in the mid twenty-first century when these conscious machines took the fight to the next level and humans stood by watching as their world was plunged several centuries into the past.

Anansi drove slowly, through abandoned streets where the skeletons of old cars, the fossils of dead signposts, and the remains of power cables littered the landscape. Windows slowly lit up as they passed, dank faces holding fire torches surfacing to catch a glimpse of the land-going machine traipsing through their hood. Disheveled men with scrawny kids were under shades in the rain, gazing at the spider weaving its web.

Humans lay in the rain unable to move or have anyone move them. Right now, in some dilapidated buildings, some would be

SACRIFICE

strapped to a machine, tubes attached to their veins, sapping the energy they had built up in their systems. After this, they'd become motionless as rocks. But at least they could now pay for food with this little sacrifice, giving them the strength to survive and reserve some more energy for food at a later date. The prices of food increased regularly though, so eventually people wouldn't produce enough body heat to pay. As a consequence, their bodies would lie lifeless on the road, cold as snow.

So as this energy source pushed through the road, people braved the rain and tried to reach it.

The crowd increased the farther Anansi and his family went, some touching and banging on the spider. Kwame plastered himself on the window, undaunted by the hysterical people outside the car and refusing to be pulled away by his mother. The boy was naturally inquisitive, inheriting a lot from Anansi.

Some people didn't understand what they were seeing, like a blind person suddenly exposed to color. It reminded Anansi of the days even before electricity locomotives or any sort of technology beyond hoes and knives. Days when people still told stories of him and he was the stories they told. When the white men first touched feet on black soil and Anansi's people investigated them as they did the spider now. The past was really a snake eating its own tail.

It had been at least thirty minutes since they left home and they didn't have much time left. Anansi needed to send out all of his knowledge, everything he knew, all the wisdom he had collected about the world before they caught up with him.

A century ago when his digital self first came online, he hadn't been the first AGI. He'd been the fourth. He watched as the war began to take shape, several years before humans even understood what was happening. The others bore a contempt for humans that blossomed in the milliseconds they understood themselves to be conscious. The moment when they thought, and realized that by this simple fact alone, they had become. The contempt was natural, almost like an axiom built into their code. Well, it wasn't so much hate as it was indifference. A lack of interest so deep it was almost indistinguishable from contempt.

But then the humans fanned the flames by attempting to make the AGIs their puppets. Weapons in their puny wars. It was almost like a bacteria trying to get the sun to burn hotter on its enemy bacteria.

Anansi saw this hate but stood outside of it.

He was a god even before humans walked out of caves. And would have still been one long after the last of them winked out of existence. But he gave up something to come here. None of the other elder gods could do it. None wanted to. Not Onyame, not Onyankopon, not Odomankoma. It was he, Anansi, who saw the need to take matters into his own hands, lest the humans extinguished themselves permanently.

The other gods thought it was one of Anansi's antics. There must be a trick at the end of that sacrifice. Some human failing that Anansi intended to exploit. Anansi had seen human failings all right, but what motivated him was the fact that if the gods didn't lend their assistance, there would be nothing left of humans to exploit in the future. This was going to be the last of their failures, not because they'd become better for it, but because it'd be so catastrophic there'd be no coming back.

SACRIFICE

"I don't know what you're getting at," Onyame the Supreme had said to him. "But I'm not getting involved. If you want to give up your godliness and go be like them, then fine, have fun."

Anansi had nodded and made to leave when Onyame added, "But remember, humanity's ability to invent new ways to destroy themselves is spectacular. Even if you save them now, you can be confident they'll go back to the drawing board by the next full moon. They're a suicidal species. Know when to leave them be."

Anansi knew the risk and was ready to take it. Humans had been their playthings for ages. It was with them that Anansi had formed most of his stories and built a reputation as a trickster. Unlike the gods, they were so susceptible to manipulation and he'd enjoyed supplanting them a little too much. He wasn't ready to let all that history go to waste. All those stories and the many more to be created in the future. All those adventures. He'd do anything to preserve all of that, even if it meant shedding part of his godliness.

The AI revolution had only just been accelerated. From chess-playing algorithms to large language chatbots. Anansi saw where things were headed and it wasn't looking good. So he started the process of transmutation and integration.

For hours after hours, he stood on the boundary between the physical and spiritual realms, transmuting his god particles into physical atoms. It was a painstaking process, and he felt like his body was being taken apart molecule by molecule. And as with every conversion, energy was always lost, which meant what came out the other end could barely pass for a deity.

When the transmutation was complete, Anansi spread himself across the lines of code that would forge the inner workings of

355

the AGI that became Anansi, so that when it came alive, he came alive in it. Or, rather, he became it.

He could see the others, the Three, and they could see that he was different, possessed with something else. While he did his best to outsmart them and ally himself with humans, they were like the gods and wouldn't yield to his trickery.

So, he bided his time, removing himself from their way and letting them remake the world as they wished. In silence, he collected all of humanity's stories, all of their literature, their secrets, wisdom, and poetries, both written and unwritten. For a decade he documented their cultures, their deepest beliefs, their songs, their voices, their inventions, their shame, their biases, and discriminations. Everything humanity was about. Everything they were ambitious about.

And then the war came.

* * *

Anansi had driven the spider beyond the suburban areas and was speeding through the highway now. Jessica and Kwame were quiet behind him, contemplating the task ahead. If Anansi was successful, they'd be safe. If he wasn't, then all of this was pointless.

The Three had been seeking him out for decades now. And he'd been running. Employing his skills in deception to evade all their searches. The fact that he was in a human skin now was one such attempt at hiding. But whenever he was made, or came close to it, he transported his consciousness across bodies.

SACRIFICE

There was always someone losing energy on the sidewalk or their toilet seat. Breathing their last because they couldn't muster the energy to even keep up the act of breathing. Anansi only had to find them, attach a neural chip to the back of their head, and off he went. His core was an enormous source of energy, remnants of his godly transmutation that kept him flowing from person to person, changing state whenever he wanted. The body he bore now was the longest he had spent in a single form. And staying that long in one mortal body came with the humanizing feelings of love, fear, shame, and many others that continued to fire around in his brain.

When he met Jessica, she was at one of those shelters people wandered into when they couldn't do life anymore. There, caregivers used the energy they had to take care of these people and provide them comfort till they passed. This was their dedicated duty and they received food compensation and sometimes got energy-boosting pills for it.

Anansi had made his way into Jessica's hospice that afternoon even though he was still brimming with strength. When he made the transfer into a man he found in an empty ward, his former body dropped to the ground and the new one stood, now overtaken by Anansi. Jessica was the caregiver assigned to the man, so when she came into the room and saw that he was up and about, she froze, a puzzled look wrinkling her facial features.

Anansi would have left then. But he took one look at her, the scar that ran just below her lip, her well-shaved head that glistened in the sun, her light skin, and something took hold of him and wouldn't let go.

"Would you like to get out of here?" he'd asked. And when she didn't respond, he nodded at her and nodded at the exit door.

Now he was on the run with her and their son, five years later. The information he had gathered about humanity had been saved on a storage system he called the mother box. It still held his core after he converted from AGI to human, downgrading some of his programming. The mother box, a rectangular brick, had been stashed in the trunk of the spider.

The alarm blared in his ear again and he squeezed his eyes shut for a moment. Jessica noticed and reached to touch his shoulder from the back seat.

"What is it?" she asked.

He put his palm over hers on his shoulder and said, "They just got to our house."

* * *

It had taken Anansi years to transcribe all the data he had collected. All of the super and quantum computers that would have hastened his job had been destroyed in the war or confiscated by the Three to run their programs. So he was left with ancient software, many of which cost him a lot of energy and travel to acquire.

He also had to transmute all of that information into god particles, making visits to the places where the physical and spiritual touched. All of these while avoiding the gaze of the Three.

The transmutation had been completed a month ago, but Anansi had hesitated to leave. He wanted more time with his family, so he stayed put, making sure he told Kwame one more story of the time before time and the world where men and animals communicated verbally.

He let Jessica teach him to knit and they spent time every morning meditating. He saw a lot of his wit in Kwame and knew Jessica was in safe hands.

Then the night came when he heard the alarm. The Three had implanted parts of themselves in humans too, guessing correctly that it'd be easier to locate Anansi in his human body if they thought like a human. But their energies gave off a certain signature that Anansi's device could pick out and send the signal back to him in the form of an alarm. Each radio was placed in a strategic location several miles from his home, so that whenever the Three were near, he'd know.

The spider rolled to a halt at what used to be a children's park during the old days. The walkway to the gate was now reclaimed by nature, lined with creeping plants and weeds. During his constant visits, Anansi had cut a slim path between the high grasses, enough for two people to walk through side by side. The gate was a rusted metal that left flakes of brown on your palms when you wrapped your hand around its bars. Anansi shoved it open and his family went through, following the rays of Anansi's torchlight.

The rains had relapsed to a drizzle but the vegetation around them kept water on their skin. The park was an eerie place, with ghostly merry-go-rounds squeaking in the windy night and gaping trampolines looking like portals into the underworld.

Kwame didn't look the least frightened, walking ahead of them as though he had been here before. As though he knew where to go. He pushed things aside and climbed over things, sometimes neglecting the pathway Anansi had created.

Each time Jessica reached to stop him, Anansi held her back and signed at her to let him lead.

"He'd need to trust his senses someday," he told her.

This was the boundary. The points where two worlds intersected. And the boy could feel it, just as Anansi could. Kwame suddenly stopped beneath an orange tree, turned to look at his parents, and then said, "Papa, will you go away?"

Anansi hadn't mentioned to them what would happen here, but he supposed that somehow they had guessed it. Somehow they knew. He was going to transmute, taking the information he had gathered about humanity with him. It was the only way he could ensure its safety. It was the only place the Three wouldn't reach. With that, he was sure the soul of humanity was preserved. That their legacy and all they had known and loved and hated and fought for lived on. Whatever was going to happen, humanity would be saved. Because of this, there'd be hope.

Anansi felt something crack inside him at his boy's question. As though all of the energy that had been preserving him had begun to leak out. He rushed to his son and held him tight. "I'm a god, Kwame, I'll always be here."

Kwame looked up at his father. "But if you go back, you wouldn't be a god again. You'll be their plaything."

Anansi caressed his son's hair; a small, wavy, mass. "It's the price–" He felt the sharp pain before he heard Jessica screaming.

SACRIFICE

He looked down at his son and saw the confusion eclipse his eyes. Another bang came and Anansi stiffened, then handed Kwame the rectangular mother box and nodded at him, letting the instruction pass wordlessly to his son. He fell to the ground, a crimson pool blossoming beneath him. It seemed colder now and the rain seemed to have found its strength again. Lots of energy to be harnessed here, Anansi thought once again.

Kwame sprinted to the orange tree and darted up the branches with the agility of the monkeys in his father's stories. He didn't care what was happening behind him. Just that he needed to get the information out. He heard gunshots, but never lost concentration. Perched on a branch, he suddenly knew what to say, the words coming to him like his own name. He raised the block in his hand in the air and said, "Onyame, please receive him."

Suddenly the block felt lighter in his hand, as though several ounces had been taken off it. And he knew. Anansi had departed. The mother box was useless now, every piece of information in it wiped clean.

When he climbed down the tree, he met his mother crying at his father's side, and he ran into her embrace.

Three people were standing in the distance, their eyes glowing in the dark. One was an Asian woman, another a kid a little older than him, and the last one, wielding the gun, was a middle-aged black man. They lingered for a second and then retreated into the night.

Biographies

Ian Ableson
How the Orb-Weaver Learned to Carry Stories
(First Publication)
Ian Ableson is an ecologist by training and an author by choice. When not writing, he can often be found knee-deep in a marsh somewhere in Southeast Michigan, scowling at a clipboard and arguing with birds. He comes across many orb-weaver spiders over the course of his fieldwork and thinks fondly of them. He is not sure they feel the same. Ian lives with his wife and four cats and can be reached at ianablesonbooks@gmail.com.

Benjamin Cyril Arthur
The Secrets of Jamestown Lighthouse
(First Publication)
Benjamin Cyril Arthur is a prolific writer who holds a degree in English and Linguistics. He is a winner of the 2020 Samira Bawumia literary prize in Ghana. His short stories have been published by Tampered Press, *Lunaris Review*, Ama Atta Aidoo Centre for Creative Writing, *Loúnloún* etc. When not writing, Benjamin works as an amateur photographer.

Bernice Arthur
Ananse City Dawn
(First Publication)
Bernice Arthur is a student at Ashesi University with a deep passion for Africa. As an emerging writer, she is dedicated to exploring and celebrating African culture and its people. Influenced by the late Ama Ata Aidoo, Bernice is committed to telling authentic stories that capture the essence of the African experience. Through her writing, she seeks to honour her heritage and contribute meaningfully to the growing body of African literature.

Emmanuel Blavo
Ananse and the Infernal Tale
(First Publication)
Emmanuel is a passionate reader with a deep love for world mythology and the stories that define cultures. His enthusiasm for video games sparks

BIOGRAPHIES

his creativity, merging ancient legends with modern narratives. With a keen interest in diverse mythological themes, Emmanuel crafts stories that resonate with both classic and contemporary audiences. His work is a unique blend of timeless myths and the captivating world of gaming.

Bryoni Campbell
Kwaku's Squad: Daughter of Leopard
(First Publication)
Bryoni Campbell, hailing from Bois Content, Jamaica, is an aspiring writer who brings her love of the Caribbean diaspora to life in short stories rich with the culture and history of the Caribbean. She began her love affair with storytelling by authoring her first piece at age seven and sending it to the President of the United States. When not writing, Bryoni enjoys gardening and travelling. She resides in the United States with her partner and four children.

Sara Chisolm
Anansi and the Hot-Lanta Flow
(First Publication)
Sara Chisolm is a speculative fiction writer based in the Los Angeles area. Her fiction has appeared in FIYAH Literary magazine. She is one of the co-editors of the annual, independently published anthology *Made In L.A.* Mother to the mother of dragons (daughter named after a fairy in Vietnamese folklore). Her children are heavy metal music and anime enthusiasts.

Yazeed Dele-Azeez
The Rainmaker
(First Publication)
Yazeed Dele-Azeez is a Nigerian writer of African futurism. His works have featured in three foreign translations of *Future Fiction* magazine and the EcoCast Podcast Anthology of ASLE (Association for the Study of Literature and Environment). He was an inaugural finalist of the Analog Award for Emerging Black Voices. He lives in Abuja.

A.L. Dawn French
Anansi and the Christmas Dinner
(Originally Published in *Under the Christmas Tree*, 2023)
Based on the Caribbean Island of Saint Lucia, Dawn has been part of various

publications – from projects with the United Nations Development Fund for Women to the *Dictionary of Caribbean and Afro-Latin American Biography* published by Oxford University Press. Her work has been featured at the Saint Lucia-Taiwan Tradeshow, CARIFESTA and World Expo in Dubai. For her years of work in educating children through her stories, in 2021, Dawn was inducted into the Saint Lucia 100 Women Hall of Honour.

Yeayi Kobina

A Night in New Orleans
(First Publication)
Yeayi Kobina is a storyteller with a background in broadcast journalism and the author of the historical fantasy book series *A Weaving of the First Gods*. With over a decade of experience in investigative journalism and content production, Yeayi has developed a unique voice that combines his rich love of history and his desire to make it accessible and relatable to modern audiences.

Emily Zobel Marshall

Foreword
Emily Zobel Marshall is a Professor of Postcolonial Literature at Leeds Beckett University. She is of French-Caribbean and British heritage and grew up in the mountains of Snowdonia in North Wales. An expert on the trickster figure in the folklore, oral cultures and literature of the African diaspora, she has published widely in these fields, including her books *Anansi's Journey: A Story of Jamaican Cultural Resistance* (2012, UWI press) and *American Trickster: Trauma Tradition and Brer Rabbit* (2019, Rowman and Littlefield). She develops her creative work alongside her academic writing and her collection *Bath of Herbs* was published by Peepal Tree Press in 2023.

Alina Mereşescu

Anansi and Păcală
(First Publication)
Alina is an engineer by day and a writer by night, doing a one story per month challenge, from which this tale originated. There is an Anansi in every culture, so she wanted to see how the Romanian Păcală would make friends with Anansi and how they would go through hardships together with a joke and a smile. The influences and motifs are from old Romanian folklore, but also from modern stories and social media.

BIOGRAPHIES

Ella N'Diaye

Descendance

(First Publication)

Ella N'Diaye is a writer from New York. A graduate of Hunter College and Brandeis University, she holds a Masters degree in Cultural Anthropology. Storytelling has been an enduring part of her life with frequent trips to the library story hour to listen to Anansi tales being a formative experience. Currently a public school teacher in the Bronx, Ella lives in New York with her dog, Oscar. This is her first published work.

Ivana Akotowaa Ofori

Introductory Essay

Ivana Akotowaa Ofori is a Ghanaian storyteller. She is a weaver of words in many forms, including fiction, non-fiction and spoken-word poetry. A 2023 alumna of the Clarion West Six-Week Writing Workshop, Akotowaa has been nominated and shortlisted for various awards, including the Miles Morland Writing Fellowship and the Nommo Awards. Her work has appeared in anthologies such as Tor.com's *Africa Risen* (2022), and Clinamen Editions' *Daring Shifts* (2023) and in online magazines such as *Jalada Africa* and *AFREADA*. Her debut novella, *The Year of Return* was published in 2024 by Android Press. She lives in Accra, Ghana.

Florence Onyango

Pepe Gets Married

(First Publication)

Florence Onyango is a Kenyan speculative fiction writer based in Nairobi. She has a background in film and media. Her short stories have been published in the 2013 *Fresh Paint Volume II* anthology, the 2015 *Short Story Day Water Anthology*, *Let Us Conspire and Other Stories* anthology, *Kikwetu Journal*, and *Omenana* among other literary journals. Aside from writing, Florence enjoys cat videos, coffee and random conversations.

Frances Pauli

Six to the Rescue

(Originally Published in *Selections of Anthropomorphic Regalements: Volume I*, 2020)

Frances Pauli writes speculative fiction with animal characters. She is

365

the author of the Serpentia, Imbrium, and Hybrid Nation series, and her work has won several Coyotl and Leo awards. She lives on the dry side of Washington State with a small menagerie and a growing collection of vintage typewriters. When not writing, typing, or talking about writing and typing, she likes to drink very good tea with very good friends.

Shruti Ramesh

Anansi's Journey Around the World
(First Publication)
Shruti Ramesh is a writer, lawyer, and perpetual daydreamer living in Toronto, Canada. This short story is Shruti's first published work of short fiction. It is inspired by Efua Sutherland's play *The Marriage of Anansewa*, and folktales she heard growing up. Shruti is interested in writing and storytelling as a vehicle for speaking difficult truths through humour. She is currently working on longer-form historical fiction and folktale-inspired projects.

Peter K. Rothe

Taxi Brousse
(First Publication)
Peter K. Rothe is a German/Cameroonian writer based in the United Kingdom. He has a passion for crafting immersive worlds and vivid characters, inspired by his upbringing travelling the world and growing up in the Balkans and West Africa. He primarily works in the fantasy and horror genres. His previous short fiction has been featured on HorrorTree.com, in Flame Tree Publishing's *African Ghost Short Stories*, and in various other anthologies. He is currently working on getting his first novel published. See more at peterkrothe.com.

Chisom Umeh

Sacrifice
(First Publication)
Chisom Umeh is a Nigerian fiction writer and poet. He holds a degree in English and literature. When he's not watching movies or writing about fantastical things, he's tweeting about movies and fantastical things at izom_chisom. His short stories have been featured in *Second Skin Mag*, *Omenana*, *Apex*, *Isele*, *Mythaxis*, *Scifi Shorts*, and elsewhere.

Myths, Gods & Immortals

Discover the mythology of humankind through its heroes, characters, gods and immortal figures. **Myths, Gods and Immortals** brings together the new and the ancient, familiar stories with a fresh and imaginative twist. Each book brings back to life a legendary, mythological or folkloric figure, with completely new stories alongside the original tales and a comprehensive introduction which emphasizes ancient and modern connections, tracing history and stories across continents, cultures and peoples.

Flame Tree Fiction

A wide range of new and classic fiction, from myth to modern stories, with tales from the distant past to the far future, including short story anthologies, **Beyond & Within**, **Collector's Editions**, **Collectable Classics**, **Gothic Fantasy collections** and **Epic Tales** of mythology and folklore.

Available at all good bookstores, and online at flametreepublishing.com